Books by Mariah Stewart

Published by Pocket Books

MARIAH STEWART

MOON DANCE

POCKET BOOKS
New York London Toronto Sydney

This book is a work of fiction. Names, characters, places and
incidents are products of the author's imagination or are used
fictitiously. Any resemblance to actual events or locales or persons,
living or dead, is entirely coincidental.

An *Original* Publication of POCKET BOOKS

POCKET BOOKS, a division of Simon & Schuster, Inc.
1230 Avenue of the Americas, New York, NY 10020

ISBN-13: 978-0-671-02624-0
ISBN-10:   0-671-02624-0

First Pocket Books printing January 1999

10 9 8

POCKET BOOKS and colophon are registered
trademarks of Simon & Schuster, Inc.

Cover art by Tony Greco.

Manufactured in the United States of America

For information regarding special discounts for bulk purchases,
please contact Simon & Schuster Special Sales at 1-800-456-6798 or
business@simonandschuster.com.

Dedicated with love to Debbie Apalucci,
who put wings on our daughters'
feet, and a song in their hearts.
She taught them to dance.

MOON DANCE

prologue

The hospital's hallway was quiet and well lighted, the doors all closed more than three quarters of the way to ensure the privacy of the occupants of the rooms on this most private of floors. The young woman stepped off the elevator and looked both ways, trying to determine which way the room numbers might run. Seeing the nurses' station off to the left of the narrow lobby between the bank of elevators, she made her way toward it on quiet feet, as befitted the solemn surroundings.

"I'm looking for Mallory Edwards's room," she said to the gray-haired woman who stood behind the desk.

"Are you family?" the woman asked without looking up.

"Just a friend."

The nurse raised her head then. Mallory Edwards had been a patient in this small private hospital outside Baltimore, Maryland, for more than a week. No family had come to visit, although someone had made arrangements for the best of rooms and the best of care. The Edwards girl was young; barely twenty-seven. The nurse bit her bottom lip. Would it hurt if she bent the rules just this once?

"Room three twenty-one, to the right," she told the visitor, "and if anyone asks, you're her sister."

"Thank you," the young woman nodded, and headed off past the silent rooms in the indicated direction.

The young woman paused in the doorway of Room 321, listening for a sound from within, but there was none. Cautiously she pushed aside the door and peered inside. The room was dim, the curtains drawn to keep out the light of a particularly bright and sunny February morning. The lone bed stood against the middle of the left wall, and the visitor's first impression was that of having walked into a nightmare. The patient lay on the bed, her head and shoulders slightly elevated, tubes seemingly everywhere. Drawn into the room by a combination of concern and morbid fascination, the young woman took several steps forward.

"Who's there?" a faint voice from the bed rasped.

"Georgia Enright," the visitor replied.

The figure on the bed paused, then repeated softly, "Georgia Enright." A few seconds later, she asked bluntly, "Why?"

"I . . . I just wanted to . . . to . . ."

"To see if what they said was true?" The voice dropped to a whisper. "That death's door was closing on Mallory Edwards? Are you here to start picking at the bones already?" The figure made a harsh sound, as if trying to laugh, but it rang hollow. "No pun intended . . ."

"No, I . . . I just . . ." the young visitor, obviously disconcerted, shrank back slightly toward the door. Then, as if to justify her presence and give herself courage, she said, "I brought you some flowers."

"Flowers?" the patient asked. "You brought me flowers? Why would you do that? I don't recall ever having been particularly nice to you."

"You haven't been."

"Then why . . ."

"Because I felt bad for you." She stepped forward to hand the bouquet to the figure on the bed and tried not to show repulsion at the overly thin arms that reached out to accept the gift.

"*You* felt bad for *me*?" Even in this sorry state, it was obvious that Mallory Edwards was still the diva.

The principal ballerina in Baltimore's famed Harbor Troupe, Mallory Edwards had been a legend by the time she was nineteen years old. That Georgia Enright—a mere member of the corps—felt sorry for *her*, would have made Mallory Edwards laugh under any other circumstances. As it was, however, the discovery that someone—even a member of the troupe's corps of dancers—was genuinely concerned for her came as a big surprise. Mallory knew she had never done anything to earn that kind of consideration from anyone she'd ever worked with; witness the fact that she'd had no other visitors, and the only flowers she'd received were from her brother, who was too busy to pay a personal visit. She was touched in spite of herself.

"Well, then, Georgia Enright, I suppose I should probably thank you." Mallory pushed the button to elevate the head of the bed a little. "As you can see, I haven't been exactly inundated with cards and letters to wish me a speedy recovery."

Thin, thin fingers traced the lacy leaves of the dark-green fern and the white petals of the daisies in the bouquet. Mallory raised the flowers to her face, seeking the scent of something sweet; something that did not smell like a hospital room or any of the accoutrements of having been confined there for better than a week.

She glanced at the young blond woman who stood so still at the side of the bed watching her. Of course, Mallory had known who she was when she entered the room. Georgia Enright had been with the Harbor Troupe for as long as had Mallory herself. The difference between them was that Mallory had quickly moved beyond the confines of the corps of dancers that formed the backdrop of every performance—the "chorus" of the dance. Georgia Enright never would. Though she worked hard, and it was evident that she always gave everything she had to every performance, Georgia Enright was not the stuff prima ballerinas were made of. Physically, Georgia fell just short of the mark for a dancer; just a tad rounder in the hips, breasts just a smidge fuller, and legs just a bit shorter than the ideal. And while Georgia's movements were studied, if not inspired, and certainly not without grace, she lacked that singularity that set apart a good dancer from one who could mesmerize an audience and hold it in the palm of her hand.

Mallory had been a dancer who dazzled. Georgia Enright, at her best, was very, very good.

Was the Enright girl aware of her deficiencies, or did she still believe, as all young dancers believed, that someday she would be the principal dancer in a prestigious troupe? Mallory wondered if perhaps she couldn't best repay Georgia's kindness by telling her the truth.

"The flowers are lovely." Mallory softened. "It was very thoughtful of you."

"You're welcome," Georgia replied.

"What are they saying about me? About my illness?" Mallory had to ask.

"That you're being treated for—" Georgia stopped suddenly, thinking perhaps she should have been prepared with a quick off-the-cuff response to the question.

"Now, I wonder, are they saying 'fatigue'? 'Exhaustion'?" Mallory looked almost amused.

"They're not really saying anything publicly." Georgia shrugged.

"No, of course they're not. Ivan is not one to let dirty little secrets out, now, is he. And 'eating disorders' sounds so tawdry, don't you think?" Mallory leaned back slightly into the pillow. "How is the little son of a bitch, anyway? Still as tyrannical as ever?"

"Yes. Of course. Ivan never changes."

"Ivan the Terrible. He's earned the name a hundred times over." Mallory smiled at Georgia and motioned for her to sit down. The girl's kindness aside, there was news to ferret out. Mallory knew there would be a long line of would-be successors waiting for her demise or, at the very least, her retirement. She wondered who the strongest challengers would be.

"Now, tell me what's going on at the studio. Who is replacing me?"

"Ivan's been working with Elena Howard this week . . ."

Mallory's eyes narrowed and she bit the inside of one hollow cheek. "Well, I hope she enjoys the limelight, for the short bit of time she'll have it. She's not the stuff that prima ballerinas are made of. Besides, I'll be back in six weeks . . ."

"Six weeks?" Georgia looked at the frail figure in the bed. Did she really believe she would be fit to dance in six weeks?

"Oh, yes," Mallory Edwards's chin leveled. "Six weeks from Monday I will walk into the studio and I will be ready to resume my role as principal dancer. Tell Ivan the Terrible that when you go into the studio tomorrow, Georgia. Tell him I will be back, good as new, in six weeks."

chapter one

Georgia nimbly leaned over to tie first her left, then her right running shoe before standing and stretching from side to side to limber up. Though in top athletic form after nine years of dancing professionally, she still performed an exacting ritual before setting out on her daily run. Side-to-side stretches, forward lunges, jumping jacks, leg lifts. Twenty of each. Her warm-up completed, she left her sixth-floor condo, locked the door securely behind her, tucked the key into the pocket of her dark green hooded sweatshirt, and set off for the ground floor. On foot.

Taking the stairs only prolonged her prerun warmup, she rationalized. It was good exercise, good for her heart, good for her lungs. Why ride when you can walk? And besides, elevators made her claustrophobic.

Georgia skipped through the lobby, but once outside the imposing front door of the building she had called home for the past five years, she broke into a measured trot and took to the pavement. At the corner, she turned onto Pratt Street and set a pace that would carry her to her destination within her allotted twenty minutes. Despite the day's valiant attempt to cultivate a sunny disposition, a late winter chill hung about Baltimore's Inner Harbor. Filling her lungs with air heavy with the faint, tangy scent of the sea, Georgia jogged briskly past lingering piles of dirty snow that huddled in the shaded areas around the Convention Center. Off to her far right beckoned Harborplace—two glass-enclosed shopping malls that provided tourists and residents alike a shopping fix on a grand scale—and the first of the piers that jutted smartly into the harbor. A little farther ahead would be the World Trade Center, and beyond, on Pier Three, the National Aquarium, field-trip mecca for elementary schools up and down the East Coast.

At the corner of Gay and Pratt, Georgia stopped for traffic, then crossed the street and proceeded straight up Gay as she began her cool-down pace, slowing slightly until she reached the small restaurant with the faded red-and-green awning. Several small, round tables for two had been set up out front with plaid tablecloths and some healthy optimism that the day would, in fact, warm up.

It was still early enough that the last of the breakfast crowd remained inside. Georgia pushed open the curtained door and stepped inside to the warmth of clean brick walls and the smell of fresh bread. She winked at the young man who stood chatting with a customer at the cash register as she strolled to the back of the restaurant.

"Ah, there she is," a male voice called out from behind immaculate stainless-steel counters. "Maria, didn't I tell you that Georgia would be here before nine this morning?"

"Why, yes, you did," the young waitress nodded. "Maybe you really are psychic, Lee."

"Well, there have been times we've suspected he might be, but not this time," Georgia laughed, "since I called him at eight to let him know I'd be stopping by."

"Fake." Maria flashed dark eyes good-naturedly at the tall man with the clipped, graying beard and the mildly amused expression.

"Spoilsport," he stage-whispered to Georgia, who laughed again. "So, what can I get you?"

"Water is fine," Georgia told him, "and I can get it."

"Help yourself." Lee Banyon gestured toward the refrigerator. "I have one last omelet to fix, then we can sit down and chat. Can I make something for you? I have some lovely ham," he added, a tease in his voice, knowing full well that Georgia was what she termed semivegetarian—eggs, dairy, on rare occasions perhaps fish, but never meat.

"I'll think about an omelet." She lifted a glass from the counter and filled it with chilled spring water. "And you know what you can do with your ham."

Lee laughed and juggled three dark green peppers before lining them up along the counter.

Leaning back against the cool steel, Georgia watched as Lee effortlessly chopped one of the peppers and several mushrooms and slid them into a pan, all the while moving with the grace of a dancer, which he had been until his self-imposed retirement eighteen months earlier. The death of Lee's longtime companion, David, had brought home the fragility of life, and Lee had quit his position as the principal male with the Inner Harbor Dance Troupe and had taken over running the restaurant David had opened six years earlier.

Tall, lanky, dark-haired, and handsome, Lee Banyon had been Georgia's best and closest friend from her earliest days with the troupe. Georgia's support and compassion during David's illness had won her a place in Lee's heart for all time. There was no question that Lee would walk through fire for her, would slay her dragons, if need be. Right now, Lee judged from the look in her eyes, a dragon lurked somewhere nearby, and as soon as he finished this last order, he would make it his business to find out where.

"Ready for a nibble, Georgey-girl?" he called to her. "You can't jog and dance and who knows what else without the proper fuel."

"Actually, I've been dreaming about one of your veggie concoctions for days. You know," she grinned, "the one with the broccoli, zucchini, onions, roasted red peppers . . ."

"You're on." He poked in the refrigerator for the last of the zucchini he had shredded earlier that morning, and set about making breakfast for his friend.

"So, Miss Georgia," he said as he garnished the plate with thin slices of orange and wedges of cantaloupe, "what's on your mind this morning?"

"What makes you think that anything—"

He held up one hand to stop her.

"Please, we've known each other far too well for

much too long to start playing games now. I can see it in your face, *cara*." He guided her through the kitchen door into the now-emptied dining room and to a table near the window, pulled a chair out for her with one hand, and placed her plate before her with the other.

"*Ummm*." She bit into a piece of broccoli and sighed. "Heaven. No one makes a veggie omelet like you do, Lee."

"Right. It's my secret combination of herbs and spices," Lee said dryly as he sniffed at a pot of coffee. Convinced of its freshness, he poured two cups and brought them to the table. "Don't try to change the subject. Tell Uncle Lee what's bothering you."

"Did you know that Mallory Edwards is in the hospital?" she asked.

"Yes, I had heard."

"I went to visit her a few days ago." She was avoiding eye contact and he knew it.

"I don't recall that you and Mallory were friends." A frown creased his brow. "Now that I think about it, I don't recall that Mallory had any friends at all within the troupe."

"We're really not, and I don't think she does."

"Then why the act of mercy?"

"I felt sorry for her, Lee. I was there when she collapsed. It was a terrible thing to see. One minute she was dancing, the next minute she sank to the floor like a marionette whose strings had all been cut at exactly the same time." Georgia shivered at the memory of it.

"Surely you've seen people faint before."

"I have, but this was different. This was . . ."—she

struggled for a word, then shook her head and repeated—"different. Everyone saw her fall, and no one helped her. Ivan stood over her yelling at her to get up. . . ."

"Ah, yes, Ivan would be the very soul of compassion," Lee, who had known the temperamental artistic director for years, murmured sarcastically.

"Finally one of the girls checked her pulse, and had a real hard time finding one. At first Ivan didn't want to call an ambulance, he kept insisting that she just wanted attention, that she would get up on her own. Of course, she did not, so we called nine-one-one."

"Over Ivan's objections, I would suspect."

Georgia scowled. "He didn't want paramedics coming into the studio, can you believe that? He actually wanted us to carry her into the lobby."

"I've always said that Ivan was a prince among men."

"Here's the scary part." Georgia sighed and put her fork down quietly. "Everyone knows that Mallory collapsed from malnutrition. We all know that she suffers from eating disorders. I'm not certain which one, but we all know there's something seriously wrong. She is a very ill young woman. In the hospital, she was hooked up to skatey-illion tubes and IVs, and yet she was talking about coming back in six weeks and taking over her old spot."

"And she probably will." Lee shrugged. "Surely you know that she's not the only member of your troupe who thinks she's found an easy means of weight control?"

"Easy?" Georgia's eyes widened, recalling Mallory's hollow cheekbones, pencil-thin fingers, large eyes set in a gaunt face. "If that's the easy way, I'd sure as hell hate to see the hard way."

"Well, I do not have to tell you, of all people, how unreasonable Ivan can be where his dancers' weights are concerned."

Georgia met his eyes across the table, but did not answer. She herself had been the victim of Ivan's tyrannical rages when she had weighed in a pound or two above the director's limits. For each of his dancers, Ivan kept a notebook in which he recorded their weights on a daily basis. Those whose weight fluctuated by a pound or two might be ridiculed in front of the other dancers, but those whose weight gain might exceed that would be subjected to humiliation of the cruelest form. Ivan could indeed be terrible.

"No," she told him. "I know that a lot of the dancers do dreadful things to themselves to keep their weight down. Not just in our company, but in just about every one that I know of."

"Eating disorders are as old as the dance, Georgia. Consider yourself fortunate that you never were afflicted."

"I do. But Lee, there's more." She averted her eyes again.

"Isn't there always?" Lee sighed and gestured for her to continue.

"Yesterday Ivan announced his choice to fill Mallory's spot. He made a big deal out of it in front of everyone."

"Let me guess." Lee narrowed his eyes and pretended to think. "His choice was . . . Georgia Enright."

"How did you know that?"

"Ivan is a petty, wicked little man and is as transparent as a beam of light. Somehow he must have found out that you had visited Mallory in the hospital. Ivan being Ivan, he will want to punish Mallory for disrupting his routine. How best to punish her? By replacing her with the only person who has shown her any kindness."

"I didn't realize that you knew him that well," she said softly.

"I have known Ivan for more years than I like to recall. We were in the same company in Boston, and then again in Houston. It was only coincidence that we both ended up in Baltimore together. Oh, yes, we go back a very long way. But that's old news." He leaned back in his seat and crossed his arms over his chest. "Did he give the other dancers the opportunity to challenge you for the role?"

"You do know him well, don't you?" She nodded glumly.

"He's done this before—set several dancers against each other. Offer one a part, then ask if any of the others would like a chance to win the role away. Divide and conquer, so to speak. It's a means of maintaining control, you know. And it never fails to create a little drama, a little tension. Ivan, as we know, thrives on both."

"Well, so far, only one dancer has asked to audition. Sharyn Heffern. She was new last year. She's a wonderful dancer, Lee. She deserves the role much more than I do."

"What is the role, by the way?" he asked.

"Giselle."

Lee rolled his eyes to the heavens. "A very important ballet. A challenging one. And definitely not a role for novices. What in glory's name could the man be thinking? *Giselle* is demanding, it's difficult. It's dramatic ballet at its best, and it's—" He paused. "Did you accept Ivan's offer?"

"I didn't accept or not accept. I was stunned. I couldn't respond. And he did his usual, you know, drop the bombshell, then turn heel and leave the room."

"Well, how do you feel about it?"

"I feel like . . . like I'm being used. It's just like you said. Like he's trying to hurt Mallory. And at the same time, he's humiliating me. He knows I don't deserve the position, he knows I'm not good enough. Sharyn can dance circles around me."

"I wouldn't be surprised if he had suggested to Sharyn that she audition—it would be just his style. So, what are you going to do?"

"I don't know." Her voice dropped to a whisper and she looked into her friend's eyes, hoping for guidance. Georgia knew no one who could better understand her predicament. "On the one hand, it's the chance I always dreamed of. On the other, I know I will make a complete fool out of myself because I know that I don't deserve the role."

"And of course, to decline, you would have to publicly admit that you don't feel you're good enough, which will give Ivan sufficient cause never to offer you another shot at moving out of the corps."

"Which I probably would not ever get anyway." Georgia's shoulders sank a little farther. "If I accept, my limitations will be glaringly evident. It's a lose-

lose situation for me. He's set me up, Lee. He knows that there's no way I could ever best Sharyn. She's young—eighteen—but she is exceptional. She's the one who deserves the big break."

She frowned, then added, "And there's one other thing that's bothering me on a somewhat different level."

He gestured for her to go on.

"If I accept this offer, I will knowingly be assisting him in hurting Mallory."

"Of course. That would be Ivan's intent." Lee rubbed his chin thoughtfully. "Quite a dilemma for you, Georgey-girl."

"What would you do if you were in this situation, Lee?"

"Me?" He nodded thoughtfully, tapping his fingers lightly on the polished wood tabletop. "Well, actually, I was in a similar situation once."

"And?" She waited for him to continue.

"And I think that whatever I say will influence your choice, and I do not want that responsibility, Georgia. Whatever you decide to do, this is your call, *cara*." He paused and watched her face, suspecting that, for Georgia, this was both a moral as well as a career decision. "Maybe it would help if you took a look at your goals at this stage of your career."

With a slightly rounded fingernail, she traced the delicate embossed motif on the white paper napkin that lay on the table. "You know that all I ever wanted to do was to dance. From the time I was a little girl, I never dreamed of doing anything else."

Her eyes drifted toward the front window and the clouds that were gathering in a lazy gray sky.

"It never mattered to me that I had to work hard at it. I even loved that part. Working toward the goal was very important to me. I was very proud of myself when I met that goal, Lee. But I always knew that I would have to work harder than some of the other girls, and my dream of becoming a prima ballerina died when I was twenty-three. It took me a long time to accept that some dancers are just gifted—that if you don't have that gift, you will be limited in how far you can rise as a dancer." She smiled a lopsided smile. "I have known for several years that I did not have the gift, Lee."

"You are a lovely dancer, Georgia," he told her honestly, wishing that he could, in all good conscience, assure her that she could one day be a star. But caring much too much for her to lie about something so important, he simply took her hands between his and gave them a squeeze.

"But I will never rise to that next level, and we both know it."

"So, then. This is leading somewhere. . . ."

"I think I need to decide where I want to go from here. If I want to stay in dance, or move on."

"That's pretty drastic, Georgia."

"I'm twenty-six years old, Lee. I have no education to speak of. I started dancing professionally when I was sixteen. I had a tutor for my junior and senior years in high school and have a GED. I never gave a second's thought to college. I have never known anything but dancing. I never wanted to."

"And now?"

"Now I'm wondering if there isn't something more for me somewhere."

"All this because of Ivan?"

"Yes. And no." She shook her head. "Let's just say he's given me cause to evaluate my situation."

"And what have you found?"

"That I am a good dancer in a world of very good dancers. That I am as good as anyone else in the corps. But I will never be great and I will never go beyond where I am. And I will never be Giselle, Lee. As much as I wish I could be, I can't lie to myself." Her green eyes began to glisten with tears. "At best, I have maybe five or six more years when I can realistically expect to make my living as a dancer. And the question I have to ask myself is, What then? Where do I go from there? And will it be easier to get there if I start now, instead of when I'm in my thirties?"

"I don't know what to say to you, *cara*." Lee reached across the table and wiped her tears away with his thumb. "Did you ever see one of those movies where the earnest young understudy finally gets her chance to prove her stuff when the star breaks a leg or gets pneumonia or something equally dramatic?"

"Yes, but in the movies the understudy always knocks 'em dead. I'm afraid that won't happen in my case, Lee, but it will for Sharyn." Georgia sniffed and forced a smile. "Ironic, isn't it? *Giselle* is my favorite ballet—the role I waited a lifetime to perform."

"Perhaps if I worked with you at night . . ."

"You are a sweetheart and my best friend, Lee, but no amount of rehearsal will give me what I don't have."

"Another dance troupe, then," he suggested. "I

know several directors who would surely be pleased to give you an audition."

"I don't know that things would be different anywhere else."

"You wouldn't have Ivan to contend with."

"True, but Ivan isn't really the issue. I'll never be better than I am—regardless of where I go—and I'll always have the same questions in my mind." She spun her spoon around on the table in slow circles. "Maybe it's just time for me to move on, Lee."

"Move on to what, *cara?*"

"I have no idea. Do you realize that, outside of my family, I hardly even know anyone that I haven't met through dance? I exercise. I cook. I read. I dance. I lead a mostly solitary life, Lee." She shook her head. "Scary, isn't it? That I've lived for twenty-six years and I've never seen much of anything beyond the edge of the stage. Even my first love was a dancer."

"Mine, too," he deadpanned, and she laughed in spite of herself.

"I think you should perhaps discuss this with your family. Your mother. Your sister," Lee said. "This is a very big decision, Georgia, one you should not make in haste."

"Actually, I've been thinking about it for a long time now."

"What's a long time?"

"Since last summer."

Lee took one of her hands in his and rubbed the top of her wrist thoughtfully. He had suspected that something had been bothering her for the past few months, but hadn't realized it had been anything this serious. "Tell me."

"I feel restless. Besides the fact that I feel more and more that it's time to move on, I also know I'm missing so much in life. It didn't used to bother me. Now it does." She swallowed hard. "My brother Nicky got married last summer."

"I remember. He got married at a lighthouse."

"Yes. Devlin's Light. His wife's family owns it. After the wedding, I walked up to the top of the lighthouse. You can see all the way across the bay from New Jersey to Delaware from the top of Devlin's Light, and way out toward the ocean. It made me realize just how narrow my own boundaries are— how limited my own little world is. It's bothered me ever since, Lee. That's when I began thinking that maybe it's time to push the boundaries back a bit."

"And how might you go about doing that?"

"I'm not sure, but I'm thinking a good place to start might be to take some time off to think things over."

"An excellent idea. When was the last time you had a vacation?"

"I haven't had one since I started dancing professionally. Not a real one, anyway."

"Then I would say you're long overdue." He clapped his palms together. "Didn't you tell me that your 'new' sister owns an inn near the beach somewhere?"

Georgia smiled at his use of the word "new" to differentiate between Laura Bishop, the half sister whom Georgia had met for the first time only the previous year—the child Georgia's mother had been forced to give up for adoption many years before— and Zoey Enright, the sister with whom Georgia had grown up.

"Yes. Laura owns the Bishop's Inn."

"This might be the perfect time to pay her a visit. Take a few weeks off. Talk to her. See what she thinks. Walk on the beach—it's wonderful this time of year. It'll help clear your head. Things always look so much clearer when you take a step back."

"Ivan isn't likely to give me any time off." She frowned.

"Just how unhappy are you, *cara?*"

She looked up at him and allowed her normally cheery facade to fall away. Lee saw a beautiful young woman with hollow cheeks and circles under her eyes.

"Then take an indefinite leave," he said softly. "No one, especially Ivan, is worth your health or your happiness." Lee watched her face as his words sank in, and waited for her reaction.

"These other directors that you talked about . . ." She drew the words out slowly, as if weighing each one of them. "Where might their dance companies be?"

"I have friends in Boston, Princeton, Savannah, and New Haven."

"Supposing I asked for time off and Ivan refused and I left the company . . . Supposing that after some time off—a few weeks or months or whatever—I decided that what I really wanted was to stay in dance for however many more years. Is there any reason to think that any of these other directors might be willing to give me an audition after—"

"After having walked out on Ivan?" He dismissed her fears with a wave of his hand. "I am certain that I can arrange that for you. Ivan is brilliant, but he is

21

known to be difficult. He has the well-earned reputation of being a son of a bitch. You would not be the only dancer to have left a troupe because of him." Then he winked, adding, "And besides, the director of the Princeton company is an old and dear friend of mine. No, *cara*, you need not fear that leaving Ivan the Terrible behind will close the door on your career—should you decide you still want one. If you need the security of knowing that you can go back, I give my word that a door will be open for you."

Georgia played with her flatware, stacking spoon onto fork onto knife, contemplating Lee's words. It had not occurred to her that there might be other real choices, not just abstract possibilities. The thought that there might be many other options both warmed and confused her.

"You know, I'll think about it. I will." She leaned across the table and kissed Lee on the cheek. "Maybe I'll give Laura a call later and see if she has time for me to visit."

"It may turn out to be the best thing you've ever done for yourself." Lee's chair scraped against the wooden floor as he pushed it back from the table and stood up. "Give me a hug, Georgey-girl."

Georgia hugged Lee and thanked him for breakfast, then zipped up the front of her sweatshirt, promising to let him know what she decided to do as she left the friendly warmth of Tuscany for the crisp cold streets of Baltimore.

She walked, rather than ran, back toward her condo, hesitating as she passed the walkway leading to the aquarium. On an impulse, she took the path to her left and made her way down to the harbor. Maybe

Lee was right. Maybe a leave of absence was just what she needed. Time to think and time to search her heart. Time to step back and take a good look at the big picture—something she had never done—and put things into perspective.

Georgia stood at the far end of the pier, huddled inside her sweatshirt, and watched a yacht as it began to make its way through the passage that led to the Patapsco River and the wide Chesapeake beyond. The blue-gray water was dense and choppy, and swirled with small glossy rainbows left behind by drops of fuel from the last boat to cruise across the harbor. A stern wind snapped at the small yellow flags atop the mast of the yacht, sending them flapping like the busy mouths of gossiping crones.

Even from this distance she could see the colors moving about in a rapid, erratic motion. Fat drops of water began to fall from a gunmetal sky, and soon cold, sharp spears of freezing rain began to strike her cheeks. A little colder and there might be snow. Georgia pulled her hood up and turned her back on the harbor and the great bay beyond. She picked her way around a small gathering of hardy tourists who had ventured out of the aquarium, and headed back toward Pratt Street.

She tried to imagine what it would be like to go a whole week without dancing. Two weeks—three. Unprecedented. What on earth would she do with her time?

Georgia passed through the lobby of her building mechanically, her mind clearly someplace else. She twirled her door key around on its chain in a wide arc somewhat absently as she climbed the six flights to her floor, then unlocked the door and entered into her own white world.

The carpets, the furniture, the walls of Georgia's apartment—all were white and cool and soothing. She sat on a large square ottoman in the living room and took off her running shoes, then her socks, still replaying her conversation with Lee. She tried to envision herself going through a day that did not find her at the barre with the other dancers. Oh, she had had a few of those—holidays and such—but not so very many since she had committed herself to dance. Even summer vacations were spent attending special workshops. The hours at the studio not spent in rehearsal were spent in class. Her whole life had revolved around dance for so long that she wasn't sure she could fill even a week's worth of time if she was not dancing.

And yet, the last time she had visited Laura, there had been a pull toward the beach, where she had sat in the sun and just watched the rhythmic roll of ocean onto sand. Later there had been pleasant hours spent curled up in one of the little sitting rooms, where she had read a book, cover to cover. It had been a delightful day. Laura, an avid reader, always had lots of books available for her guests. Georgia pictured herself lounging in one of those oversized chairs pulled up close to the fireplace . . . or maybe snuggled amid the plump cushions on the window seat that overlooked Laura's gardens. Not that she would expect there to be anything in bloom this time of year, but it would still be a pretty view. Laura had bird feeders outside just about every window of the inn, and there would be nuthatches and titmice at the feeders, cardinals and blue jays on the ground below, pecking at the spillage.

Georgia glanced at her watch. Her mother would be working in her spacious office on the first floor of the carriage house on her "gentleman's farm" tucked amidst the hills of Chester County, Pennsylvania. A mystery writer, Delia Enright kept a meticulous schedule, particularly when she was just starting a new book. Georgia recalled that her mother's latest project was now a healthy three weeks old, and she would be allowing herself a leisurely lunch hour around one, the best time of day to reach Delia by phone. Georgia knew that Delia would support all her children in absolutely any endeavor that made them happy. If Georgia felt she needed a break from dance, Delia would encourage her to take one. If dance was no longer fulfilling, Delia would be the first to urge her to move her life along. Georgia needed to hear her mother tell her exactly that before she spoke with Ivan.

Georgia knew, of course, exactly how Ivan would react. He would get that malicious little gleam in his eye, and it would all go downhill from there. Very publicly—and very loudly.

First he would compliment her on her public acknowledgment that Sharyn was, of course, the better dancer, and one so much more deserving of the coveted role. How mature of you, Madame Enright, he would coo as he walked around her slowly. How very *gracious*.

Then he would begin to belittle her for running from the challenge, then segue into all the reasons why she would not have been selected for the role.

Before long he would have dredged up every error—every misstep, every wrong turn—she had made over the past six years, all of which would be openly discussed and demonstrated for the rest of the dancers.

Her face burned at the thought of the ordeal, of the humiliation Ivan would heap upon her right before dismissing her. There was, however, no way around it, other than to just never show up again. As much as she dreaded the very thought of the certain confrontation, she could never be that much of a coward. She would tell Ivan face-to-face of her plans to take a leave of absence from the troupe. And she would take the consequences—however harsh they might prove to be, she vowed as she dialed her mother's number—praying that it would, in the end, prove to be worth it.

Disappointed when the answering machine picked up instead of Delia, Georgia left a brief message, then gathered up her discarded shoes and socks, depositing them on the bedroom floor before heading into the shower, where she would rehearse her lines before taking on Ivan the Terrible.

Matthew Bishop stood at the passenger side of his battered black pickup truck and waited until Artie, his dog, had climbed in before slamming the door with a vengeance. His sister, Laura, was making him crazy with worry. Ever since she had found her birth mother, she'd become more and more involved with her newly discovered family. He just couldn't understand it, why Laura would feel this need to immediately open her heart to this stranger, who had, after all, given her away as a newborn and hadn't bothered to look for her until thirty-five years had passed.

"Take it easy," he'd tried to tell her. "Go one step at a time with these people. You don't know them, you don't know what their motives are—"

'What motive could there be, Matt?'' Laura had snapped. "Delia just wants to get to know me. I have two half sisters and a half brother, I've gone a lifetime without even knowing of their existence—they want to know me, too. And I want to know them. What is it that you're afraid of, Matt?''

"The truth?'' He'd asked, not wanting to have to say it.

"Of course, the truth.'' Laura had insisted.

"I'm afraid that she'll abandon you again.'' It had hurt him just to utter the words, but she had asked for the truth and he would give it to her. "That one day the novelty will wear off for her, and that she'll just slip back into the life she had before she found you.''

"That will never, ever happen, Matt.'' A shadow had passed over Laura's beautiful face, in spite of her words. Perhaps she had secretly feared the same thing?

"You don't know that, Laur.''

"Well, I guess only time will prove that I am right, and you are wrong,'' Laura had said. "Delia gave me life, Matt. I need to know her. I know that you don't understand, but you have to trust me.''

No, Matt didn't understand. He had memories enough of his birth mother—hazy though they might be—to know that he never wanted to so much as hear her name spoken aloud. In his mind and in his heart, Charity Evans Bishop, who had taken him in as a terrible-tempered toddler and had loved him fiercely, *was* his real mother. It had been Charity who had loved him before he had been lovable, had rocked him when he screamed with rage and frustration, and had held him while he sobbed out his fears.

Having been mostly neglected and ignored since birth, Matt had come to the Bishops' home as a four-year-old who, having rarely been spoken to, could not speak beyond a very limited vocabulary. The social workers who had found him living in squalor when his drug-addicted mother had overdosed that last time had immediately declared the boy to be retarded, but the police officer who had been called to the scene had sensed something else—something fierce and alive. The officer had called his cousin from the hospital to ask if Tom Bishop and his wife still wanted that son they had talked about adopting. From the minute she had laid eyes on Matthew, Charity had declared that there was nothing wrong with the boy that a loving family could not cure.

For the most part, she had been right.

And so Matt had gone from the hell of abandoned houses to the luxury of a historic inn; from near-complete solitude to a loving family that had included the daughter the Bishops had adopted twelve years earlier. Laura had adored Matt from the day he had been brought home. She had played with him and read to him, taught him the things that a child living with the bay on one side and the ocean on the other needed to know. She had become his big sister in every true way, and together they had been the children that Tom and Charity had prayed for.

And hadn't Tom Bishop been the sort of dad that

every boy deserved? One who taught him to fish and played ball with him; went to all of his ball games and cheered him on, from Little League through high school? It had been Matt's darkest day when they lost Tom, who, with his last breath, had reminded his son that *he* was the man of the family, now.

"Take care of your mother and your sister, Matt. . . ." Tom had whispered.

"I will, Dad. I promise," a teary Matt had vowed.

Oh, and just look at how well you kept that promise, Matt's conscience poked at him. *You couldn't protect your mother from getting sick, but you could have done a better job watching out for Laura. If you had been on the ball, maybe she'd never have married . . .*

Exasperated with himself, Matt marched to his truck, haunted by promises not kept.

Well, this time he wouldn't let his father down.

Tom and Charity had given Matt a home and a family, a name and a sense of self-worth, and—most important—they had given him unconditional love. He owed it to them—and to Laura—to make sure that she wasn't hurt.

He wished that Laura had just told that Enright woman to take a hike when she first showed up. But she hadn't, and she had opened her heart immediately and welcomed all the Enright clan like—well, like long-lost family. Laura had always been one to lay all her cards on the table. Her open, loving nature had caused her to be badly burned once before.

If she wasn't wise enough to be a little more cautious, a little less trusting on her own account, then Matt would have to be vigilant for her.

"Damn stubborn woman," Matt mumbled as he

shot into the driver's side of the cab and caught a glimpse of his sister in his side-view mirror as she approached the truck.

"Matt, I just wish you would be a little more rational about this. I can't understand why you are so closed-minded . . ."

"Closed-minded?" He rolled the window down and stared into Laura's face. "Because I'm trying to protect you, that makes me closed-minded?"

"Matt, I don't need anyone to protect me. Delia is my *mother*."

"Laura, your *mother* is wasting away over in Riverview."

"Matt, that was unkind. Are you implying that because I'm establishing a relationship with Delia, I'm somehow neglecting Mom?"

"Does the shoe fit?"

"No, it doesn't fit. I still drive out to see Mom three times a week, just as I have since the day we took her there, Matt, and for two cents right now, I'd drag you out of that truck and drop-kick your ass from here to the Atlantic. I really resent—"

"Yeah, well, I really *resent*, too . . ." he muttered as he shifted the truck into gear and prepared to pull out of the driveway.

"Matt," she called after him. "If you would only spend just a little time with Delia—talk to her, get to know her—you'd see that she doesn't have any ulterior motives, that she's—"

"I don't have the time or the inclination to get to know *Delia*, or anyone else named Enright." He hung one arm out the window and waved. "You do what you want, Laura. You will anyway. Just remember that you have a family that loves you, one that has always loved you. We were here before she came back into the picture, and we'll be here for you after she leaves."

"Matt, she isn't leaving!" he heard her insist as he pulled away.

In his rearview mirror, Matt could see Laura standing where he'd left her, her hands folded across her chest. That one foot tapping on the asphalt surface of the parking area behind the inn left no doubt in his mind that his sister was *really* angry. Well, he was none too happy with her at that moment, either.

Laura turned heel and stomped up the back steps leading to the inn.

Forced by oncoming vehicles to stop abruptly about ten feet from the exit of the narrow lot, Matt backed up, then waited as both a light blue Jeep and an oil delivery truck prepared to pull in. The Jeep drove past him briskly and swept into a spot to his left, but the driver of the oil truck had cut too wide an arc, and Matt had to back up yet again to permit the truck to enter the parking lot. Mumbling oaths under his breath, he sat and watched the truck slowly maneuver through the entry.

He heard the slam of a car door, and turned his head to the left in time to see a young woman round the back of the Jeep and open the cargo door. She was a tiny thing, and looked as delicate as spun glass.

A trim little bottom wrapped in denim leaned into the back of the Jeep to retrieve several bags and a box from the cargo area. While shifting items from one arm to the other, a canvas bag dropped to her feet. As she bent to retrieve it, unbelievably long hair—pale as corn silk and reaching near to her waist—slid over her shoulders in a thick wave. She turned, and in one motion, awkwardly slammed the cargo door with her foot. From ten feet away, Matt could see big, wide-set eyes, a pert little nose, and full lips that bore no trace of lipstick. It was a face a man wasn't likely to forget.

"Nice." He nodded objectively. "Very, very nice."

The blonde hoisted the canvas bags over her shoulder, holding a box upon which balanced another bag, and walked toward the inn.

She moves like music slipped unbidden through his mind, and he wondered where the thought had come from.

"Looks like we left one day too soon, Artie." Matt said aloud.

The dog panted noncommittally.

"Probably a tourist, making her way up the coast. *Ummm,* maybe Florida to New York, what do you think?" Matt said, playing with his dog the game he had, as a child, played with his sister; trying to guess who the inn's patrons might be, where they were from, and where they might be going.

Artie thumped his tail loudly on the black leather.

"Yeah, that's what I thought, too."

The blonde dropped the bag she'd been balancing, and struggled to do a deep knee bend to pick it up.

"Aw, there are some opportunities that a man just can't pass up," Matt said. He opened the cab door and hopped out. "You wait here, Artie. This is strictly a one-man job."

"You look like you could use a little help," Matt called to her.

Matt's long legs had carried him halfway across the parking lot before the blonde was able to grab the errant bag. He picked it up with one hand, and with the other, reached for the box that was wobbling perilously on her knees.

"I'm afraid I'm one hand short," she said, her smile pure sunshine, her voice carrying the traces of an unheard symphony.

She was even prettier up close, he discovered, with eyes a sultry green, skin clear and fresh as a new-born's. She even smelled wonderful.

"You're in luck. I have two to spare." He reached down and offered her one. She held one small hand up to him, and he took it, helping her to pull herself up to a standing position.

She was even smaller than she had looked from across the parking lot—shorter in height; her bone structure fine and almost fragile.

"Thank you. I'm usually not this clumsy. I should have made two trips and saved myself from this futile balancing act," she said wryly.

"But then I wouldn't have met you, would I?" He grinned.

They reached the back of the inn, and he was just about to add that he hadn't actually met her, since he didn't know her name, when Jody, the inn's young cook, pulled into the parking lot and came to a screeching halt in her vintage Buick.

In customary shorts and T-shirt, Jody always appeared younger than her late twenties. She had a pretty face, a saucy manner, and a one-track mind: the culinary needs of the Bishop's Inn.

"Oh, Matt, I'm glad you're here," she called from the open window even before she turned off the ignition. "I need a hand carrying this meat order into the kitchen. Mr. Haley couldn't make the delivery today because his son broke his foot over the weekend and he's shorthanded. . . ."

Alighting from the car, she glanced over her shoulder to where Matt stood close by the pretty little blond woman.

"If Laura sees you hitting on the guests, she'll have your head," Jody teased. "Now, if you wouldn't mind . . ."

The little blonde laughed and set her large canvas bags onto the ground, then reached for the belongings that he had carried for her.

"I can manage," she told him. "I'll come back for the bags."

"Oh, but—" Matt protested.

"I'm fine, really. I think your hands are needed more elsewhere." She looked up into his face, and he thought he'd never seen a sweeter smile in all his life.

If only he'd canceled his office hours for this afternoon, he could stay awhile, and bask in the glow that seemed to surround her. Right at that moment, nothing else seemed nearly as important.

Grumbling, he turned his attention to assisting Jody in removing several heavy boxes from the back of the car. When he turned back around, seeking one last glimpse of long blond hair and faded blue denim, the woman was out of view.

He shrugged reluctantly. Not that it mattered; their paths weren't likely to cross again.

Matt hoisted the box over his shoulder and headed for the back door that led into the kitchen. By the time he came back out, even her canvas bags had disappeared.

chapter two

Georgia had always been somewhat of an early riser, but *this,* she thought as she trudged behind Laura across a hard packed stretch of beach, *this is the middle of the night.* The stars were still out, a cloud-shrouded moon hung low over a barely visible ocean, and it was cold as hell.

"Let's get up early tomorrow and watch the sun come up over the ocean," Laura had suggested the night before.

It had seemed like a good idea at the time, but now, in this predawn hour, Laura's words rang through Georgia's mind in singsong fashion.

Georgia grumbled aloud. "Whatever was I thinking?"

"Did you say something?" Laura called back over her shoulder.

"Nothing important." Georgia sighed, stopping where Laura had stopped, down closer to the water,

36

where the sand was a little softer and the sound and smell of the sea were more acute.

The wind whipping fiercely off the ocean threatened to knock Georgia from her feet, and she swayed slightly in resistance.

"You'll thank me later," Laura assured Georgia as she unrolled the down sleeping bag she had brought for warmth. Without waiting for a comment, she tossed one end of the sleeping bag to Georgia and said, "Here, wrap up in your end and I'll wrap up from the other, then we'll sit down at the same time."

"Okay," Georgia said without enthusiasm.

Laughing at the younger woman's attempt to be a good sport, Laura wrapped the thick layer of down around her body and motioned to her sister to sit.

"Tell me again what the point of this little igloo-type thing might be?"

"To keep us from freezing while we wait for the sun to appear." Laura cozied back into her half of the shelter they had created. "It may not be particularly pretty, but it will keep your butt from turning blue."

"You're too late. My butt is *already* blue," Georgia muttered. "It's been blue since we left the inn. Laura, it's *cold* out here!"

"*Ummm*, it is, isn't it?" Laura tilted her head to the heavens and drew in a piercing breath of frigid air. "It's lovely."

"You're crazy."

"Quit whining and snuggle yourself back into the down. It'll keep you warm, I promise."

Georgia did as she was told and waited for the warming process to begin.

Laura coaxed her hands out of heavy fleece gloves and poured a cup of steaming coffee from a thermos into one of the plastic cups she had tucked into her backpack. "Here, this always helps, too." She passed the cup to Georgia, who took it gratefully and wrapped her fingers around it.

"You sound as if you do this often."

"As often as I need to."

"Why would anyone *need* to get up in the middle of the night, trek across the frozen tundra, and sit on a cold, deserted stretch of beach in frigid weather in the dark?"

"Ask me that again later."

Georgia shivered and sank back a little farther into the plump nylon cocoon that surrounded her. She did feel a little warmer.

Together they stared out across the unseen ocean, eyes searching for that first thin slice of light that would signal the impending dawn, that faint whisper of gold in an endless blackened sky that would soon be alive with color.

There. There, smack in the middle of the horizon. Gold and yellow, then yes, just a hint of orange followed. Inch by regal inch the day unfolded and spread its gentle majesty around the two women sitting on the sand. Lifted by an unseen hand, the ball of fire rose dramatically, bright and alive, and the glow fanned out from its center to push toward the edges of a near-purple sky. Streaks of light flashed across the surface of the water, a golden carpet being unrolled across the distance to the shore as the very sky seemed to raise itself up from the ends of the sea.

The two women sat wordlessly sharing the morning, watching the show unfold.

The ocean began to shimmer with the reflected light, and Georgia leaned against her older sister and sighed gratefully. "Thank you."

"You're welcome."

"I'd forgotten just how spectacular a sunrise could be."

"Most of us do need reminding from time to time." Laura nodded.

A line of birds in crisp V formation crossed the skyline.

"Geese?" Georgia whispered.

"Double-crested cormorants," Laura replied.

Georgia frowned. "How can you tell the difference?"

Laura laughed and sipped at her coffee. "By their crooked necks. Geese hold their necks straight out when they fly, as do most of the cormorants. The double-crested, however, fly with their necks sort of bent."

"You bird-people are all alike. You're almost as bad as Zoey. She thinks she's an expert on birds because she went on a bird count at Devlin's Light with Nick and India," Georgia grumbled, referring to their brother and sister-in-law, who lived on the Delaware Bay. "Zoey has gone twice now, and thinks she's an authority on seabirds."

"Don't you go with them?" Laura asked.

"No."

"Why not?"

"If I tell you, you'll laugh at me."

"No, I won't."

"Promise?"

"Yes."

"I get seasick."

"You do?"

"Yup." She shook her head. "Remember when we had to take the boat out to the lighthouse for Nick and India's wedding? I thought I'd die. Literally. It was all I could do to keep from getting sick over the side of the boat."

"I remember. If I'd known ahead of time, I'd have gotten you some medication to keep you from getting sick." Laura pulled her hand out from the down wrapping and patted Georgia on her shrouded knee. "Remind me, next time."

"Next time?" Georgia raised an eyebrow.

"Sure. If you think watching the sun come up over the ocean is a thrill from the beach, wait till you've watched from the prow of a boat afloat in a dark sea."

Georgia blanched at the thought. "I think this is as much early-morning drama as I can handle."

"When we were little, our dad used to take Matt and me out on this old Boston Whaler he had. We would sit right up front on the prow and watch the little shards of light come alive on the water." Laura smiled at the memory. "It's like nothing else you'll ever see. It's always surprised me that Matt didn't go into a field that would have kept him near the water; he's always loved it so much."

"What does he do?" Georgia asked, curious about the boy who had been adopted by Laura's adoptive parents.

"Matt finished veterinary school last year and is doing a sort of extended internship at a vet hospital up toward Cambridge. Eventually he'll be opening his own clinic."

Georgia was about to ask where Matt wanted to go into practice when Laura shrugged out of her wrappings and stood up.

"I really should get back to the inn and help Jody with breakfast. We were shorthanded yesterday— flu season, you know—and I don't know who will be showing up to work this morning." She leaned down and stuck the thermos bottle in the sand next to Georgia's foot. "You might want a little more of this."

"Wait. I'll come with you and give you a hand."

"No." Laura said firmly. "You are on a well-earned vacation and you are going to relax. You just sit and watch the ocean; it's beautiful this time of the day."

"But I could wait on a few tables. . . ."

Laura had already turned toward the dunes. "No, you can't," she called over her shoulder.

Georgia peered out from the dark-blue hood of the sleeping bag that was draped over her head. The beach was deserted for as far as she could see. She wondered what time it was, but there was no way to tell. Sliding her hands out of her gloves, she poured a half cup of coffee and watched the steam rise from it before taking a tentative sip.

If I were back in Baltimore, I'd probably just be getting up now. Maybe go for a run. Back to the apartment for a shower and a light breakfast. Probably wouldn't have seen a soul I knew or spoken a word aloud until I got to the studio.

She contemplated the difference between waking in Baltimore and following her usual routine, and waking in Bishop's Cove to watch the sun rise over the ocean with Laura. There was, she concluded, no real comparison to be made. Nothing—but nothing—could have been more wonderful than sharing this cold, early morning with her older sister. It had filled her somehow in a spiritual way, and she felt better for it.

Of course, she reminded herself, now that the sun had risen and the day had begun, there were hours to fill with . . . what? Back in Baltimore, a typical morning would find her at the studio no later than nine-thirty. By ten she would be at the barre for an hour or so, practicing endless pliés in all five of the classic ballet positions before moving to the center of the room, where another hour would be spent working on jumps and pirouettes. Then, if there was a performance to prepare for, rehearsal would begin immediately after the exercise session had concluded. If Ivan was feeling generous that day, they might have a lunch break that lasted more than thirty minutes. However, because the breaks were generally so brief, allowing for little time for their food to digest, few of the dancers ate more than yogurt or fruit.

A tide of panic began to rise inside Georgia. She should be there, at the studio, changing into well-worn pointe shoes and pinning up her hair; not here, on a quiet stretch of beach, fighting back the feeling of playing hooky. But of course, she sighed, she had pretty much burned that bridge when she told Ivan that she would like to take a leave of absence.

She had tried to make a private appointment with Ivan to discuss her wish to take some time off. She began the conversation in the doorway to his office, fully intending to close the door behind her to ensure that whatever transpired would be kept private. But Ivan had walked past her, forcing her to follow him into the studio as he walked away and gestured for her to follow behind and continue talking, as Georgia had feared he might do.

Ivan's eyes had smoldered as the full meaning of her words sank in.

"A *leave*, Miss Enright?" he had crowed archly. "A *leave?*"

He stood in the middle of the studio floor, hands on his hips, his head tilted to one side with a slight exaggeration of motion.

"Quiet, ladies," he waved at the chattering dancers, a breezy command made with one hand. "Miss Enright, I don't recall that anyone has ever taken a *leave* from this dance troupe."

He had glared at her, his eyes narrowed, his mouth a tiny pucker. Whatever she said from this point on would be met with scorn. Georgia had seen him punish so many others for any number of sins or omissions over the years. Today would be her turn, and she braced for it.

"It's out of the question," he told her before she could respond. "Simply impossible. This is a dance company, Miss Enright, not a social club." He half turned toward her, his brows arched.

"Ivan, I had every intention of discussing this with you in private—" Georgia began in a low voice, exuding a carefully rehearsed calm she most certainly did not feel.

He waved away her response as insignificant. "I demand an explanation. What could possibly be so enormously important that you would even consider disrupting not only my schedule but that of your fellow dancers, as well?"

"I want to take some personal time off."

"*Personal* time?" He thundered. "There is no *personal time* in a dance troupe, Miss Enright. And why now, Miss Enright? Did I not make myself clear enough when I offered you the opportunity to dance a principal role . . . ?"

A sly, malicious smile spread slowly across his narrow face. "*Ahhhh*, but perhaps Miss Enright is afraid to take such a giant step away from the security of the corps. Perhaps she fears that she will discover that she was meant always to be a sparrow, but never a swan?"

"Ivan, I would be more than happy to discuss this with you in your office, but I really don't think that this is the—"

"Well, that's it, of course," he interrupted caustically. "You know that you are not now, and never will be, the stuff prima ballerinas are made of, don't you? That you are good, but not good enough? That this chance that I offered you will be as close as you will ever get to dancing so much as a solo?" His voice became harsher with every word, his eyes widening and taking on a barbarous glow. Georgia knew the signs all too well. And Ivan was just warming up.

"This is ridiculous." Recognizing the futility of attempting a serious discussion with such an individual, Georgia shrugged her shoulders and turned toward the dressing room, wondering if she would be able to escape with a scrap of dignity intact.

"What?" He bellowed at her back, grabbing a white towel from the barre and throwing it at her head. He missed, but didn't seem to notice.

"There is no point in continuing this discussion." She spun around, willing her back to stay straight and her voice to remain strong.

"So you are simply going to go into the dressing room, prepare for your exercises, and take your place at the barre calmly, as if you had not disrupted my morning?" His back arched at the very thought of something so incredible.

"No," she replied. "I am going to empty out my locker, pack my bags, and leave."

It took a long moment for her intent to sink in, but when it did, his demeanor turned murderous.

"No one has ever walked out on my troupe, Miss Enright, and I can guarantee that if you do so, you will never dance with a reputable troupe again. Never!" His voice rose another few octaves.

The other dancers stared in disbelief. Had Georgia Enright just *quit*?

Forcing herself to look him squarely in the eyes and refusing to blink, she said in a level voice, "I'm sorry we were not able to resolve this in—"

"Oh, we have resolved this, Miss Enright!" He

moved toward her stealthily, the other dancers taking furtive steps back as he advanced. "You may consider yourself dismissed. Dismissed! Whatever made me think that I could make anything of you but what you are? Why, if not for the fact that your mother is so generous with her endowments, I would never have even taken you on. . . . ooh, it appears we may have struck a nerve, doesn't it?"

She had turned back slowly to face him, his words ringing in her ears.

"Surely you know that your mother heavily supports the arts?" Ivan sneered, leaving no doubt in Georgia's mind—nor in the minds of her fellow dancers—of his implication. "Why, what better way to attract some of that lovely money than to invite Delia Enright's daughter to join your troupe?"

Georgia's face flushed scarlet and her eyes widened. She blinked back tears she refused to let him see and slipped into the dressing room, where she grabbed the backpack she had not even opened that morning. With Ivan's insinuations ringing in her ears, she fled down the steps without another backward glance, leaving Ivan to fume and fuss. As she closed the door behind her, she silently begged forgiveness from the other dancers for having unleashed the beast that was Ivan, and leaving them to deal with his wicked wrath.

Fleeing to her apartment, she sat in quiet rooms with shades closed against the sun, where she could contemplate the enormity of what she had just done. Fear filled her and she began to cry, wondering what had ever possessed her to even consider such a thing.

Maybe Lee was wrong and Ivan was right. Maybe he *could* keep other directors from hiring her. He was certainly not above telling terrible stories, the truth of which might or might not be questioned. Maybe she should have thought this through a little more thoroughly.

Fear gave way to panic, and she began to pace the length of her living room. What would she do if she could never dance again?

And had her mother, as Ivan implied, paid for her position with the Inner Harbor?

Georgia's hands began to shake as she contemplated this last insult of his. Ivan was not above lying, but the troupe had gone through a period when money had been terribly tight. And then there had been talk of an anonymous benefactor who had gifted the company with money for the costumes, the travel expenses, the new stage equipment. . . .

Had that anonymous person been Delia Enright? There was only one way to find out. Georgia reached for the phone and dialed her mother's number.

"Sweetie, you've done what?" Delia had asked with no small amount of disbelief when Georgia called to relate what she had done just an hour earlier.

"I quit the dance troupe," Georgia repeated in a whisper.

"I'm sure you had a very good reason," Delia said levelly. "And I feel certain that any moment now you're going to tell me what that reason is."

"Oh, Mom—" Georgia sighed—"It all seemed to make sense at the time."

"And I'm sure it still does." Delia bit her bottom

lip. It had been clear to her that her youngest child had been less than happy for the past several months. Though Georgia had never complained about anything in particular, her mother had not failed to notice that her eyes now lacked some of their usual sparkle and, too often, her smiles had appeared somewhat forced. "Why don't you start from the beginning and tell me what exactly brought you to this point."

Georgia tried to explain the growing malaise, the feeling that she had gone as far as she could go. The feeling that there might perhaps be something more to life than blistered, bleeding feet and ceaseless hours of practicing the same steps and the same exercises to the same music. The feeling that she could do more, be more. . . .

"Oh, Mom, are you terribly disappointed in me?" Georgia lamented when she had finished.

"Darling girl, why ever would you think that?"

"Well, I always thought that you liked the idea of having a ballerina for a daughter."

"I always liked having *you* for a daughter. Yes, of course I was proud of you; what mother would not be proud to call so wonderful a girl—so beautiful and graceful and talented a girl—her own? But whether you chose to continue with dance or pursue another path, why, Georgia, that's entirely up to you. It's your life, sweetie. It's your heart that you have to answer to, and all I've ever asked of any of my children is that they follow their own hearts." Delia tried to speak evenly, tried not to let concern creep into her voice. "Now, do you have any thoughts on where you might like to go from here?"

"Actually, I thought I would take some time off to think about it. I thought maybe I'd see if I could visit Laura for a few days."

"A wonderful idea," Delia enthused. "I'm sure that Laura will be delighted to have your company. I doubt the inn sees quite as much business this time of year as it does in the warmer months. And besides, some time away from Baltimore will do you a world of good. Broaden your horizons, sweetie."

"That's sort of what I was thinking." Georgia paused and bit her lip in the same manner in which her mother, on the other end of the telephone line, had done. There was something she had to know.

"Did you . . . I mean, have you . . ." Georgia hated to ask, but needed to know the truth. "Did you give money to the troupe to hire me?"

"What?" Delia exploded. *"What?"*

"Did you give money to the troupe—"

"What a preposterous suggestion," Delia exclaimed. "What on earth would make you ask such a ridiculous question? As if I had to—" She cursed under her breath and asked, "Where would you get such a thought?"

"When I tried to tell Ivan that I wanted to take a leave—and that's all I really wanted, Mom, just some time off to think things over—he went totally off the wall. Not unexpectedly—and I was pretty much prepared for his reaction—but then he . . ." Georgia paused. The entire idea was odious, and suddenly she wished she hadn't bothered to bring it up at all.

"He suggested that I had perhaps *purchased* a place for you?"

"Well, he intimated that you had made large contributions."

"I made the same contributions that other parents made during your pledge season, those fundraisers he was always having." Delia's jaw tightened. "I always thought Ivan was a little twit. What a perfectly nasty little man he is. And I suppose that he told you he'd have you blackballed or some such nonsense if you left?"

"How did you know?" Georgia fought back hot tears.

"Because bullies always say things like that. I wouldn't give Ivan Markovich a second thought, darling. You're good enough to dance in any troupe you set your sights on—"

"In the corps," Georgia said pointedly.

"What's that, sweetie?"

"I said I'm good enough to dance in just about anyone's *corps*. But I'll never go beyond that."

"Oh, sweetheart, I remember a time when that was all you dreamed of." Delia sighed. "When the dance itself was enough to feed your soul. Is it no longer enough, Georgia?"

"I don't know, Mom. That's one of the things I was hoping to learn."

"Well, then, I say to hell with Ivan the Terrible. You cannot live your life hoping to please the likes of him. Casting pearls before swine, as my father, the very Right Reverend William Hanesford Hampton used to say. You're far better off without having to deal with such negative influences in your life."

"That's what Lee said."

"*Ahhh,* and Lee would know." Delia smiled. She

had liked Lee Banyon from the very first time she had met him, and it had been obvious that he had taken Georgia under his wing. He had been a steady factor in her daughter's life, and had become a dear and trusted friend. "Lee truly cares about you, Georgia; he would give you only his very best advice. And I would imagine he is not without influence in the world of dance. . . ."

"He said he'd help me to find another company when I'm ready to go back."

"There you are, then," Delia said. "Have your cake, sweetie, and take all the time in the world to eat it."

"Mom, you always know just what to say."

"That's because I'm the mom. Actually, I had been hesitant to pry, but I had thought there was something not quite right for some time now. I was hoping it wasn't anything serious. I hadn't expected it to be anything quite like this, although . . ." Delia stopped, wondering just how much liberty a mother should take.

"Although . . . ," Georgia encouraged her to continue.

"I can't say I'm sorry to hear that you're taking a break, sweetie. You've never really seen much of life beyond the barre."

"That's pretty much what I was thinking, Mom. Maybe after some time off I'll find that there really is nothing else that I want to do. And that would be fine. But I can't help but feel that maybe there's something else, somewhere. . . ."

"Well, then, Georgey-girl, I'd say it's time to find out. And I think that the Bishop's Inn is a fine place to start. Now, I want you to hang up this minute and give Laura a call to let her know that you're on your way. Pack a few casual things and set off for the beach. I was there for a week last month, before I started this latest book, and I can tell you that there's nothing in the world that will clear away the cobwebs like a cold breeze off the ocean."

Frigid wind is more like it. Georgia recalled her mother's words with amusement as she shivered inside the down sleeping bag. But Delia had been exactly right about the restorative powers of a cold and windswept beach. Georgia did feel renewed, filled once more with the same sense of resolve she had experienced when she had first discussed the matter of her future with Lee.

Georgia felt hopeful and almost whole, and, coming on the heels of Ivan's humiliating tirade, *hopeful* and *almost whole* were nothing to sneeze at.

She took a deep breath of cool sea air and leaned her face up to catch the light. The sun was well up now, and the first of the scavenger seabirds had joined her on the beach. Tiny birds chased the tide and pecked frenetically at the sand, searching for breakfast that hid just below the surface, while the larger birds—gulls, Georgia assumed—fought over larger prizes plucked from the surf. Just as Georgia pitched the remains of her coffee onto the sand, a voice from behind called, "Wait! Don't!"

Startled, she turned to face a silver-haired gentleman who wore a dark green corduroy jacket and a horrified expression.

"Was that coffee you just tossed away so casually?" he asked.

Georgia laughed. "It was. But it was cold. . . ."

"Even cold coffee has its place on a day like this. I was about to offer to buy it from you." He shoved his hands in his pockets and grinned. "You wouldn't know where I could purchase some of my own, would you?"

"The Bishop's Inn serves breakfast." She smiled back, then hesitated. "At least, they do for guests. I don't know for sure if the dining room is open to the public, though."

Georgia shook the sand from the sleeping bag, struggling to hold on to to it as the wind whipped up underneath the fabric, causing it to flap loudly.

"Here, let me help you." The gentleman reached for the escaping end of the bag and returned it to Georgia to fold into a puffy rectangle.

"Thank you."

"You're welcome." He stood several feet from her, and nodded out toward the ocean. "I trust you enjoyed the sunrise."

"Yes."

"Spectacular, wasn't it?"

"It was. I didn't see you on the beach, though."

He turned and pointed down the beach to their left. "I was watching from the dune. I try never to miss a sunrise over the ocean—when I'm in the neighborhood, that is."

"I didn't know that anyone else was as crazy as Laura."

"Laura?"

"My sister. She talked me into coming down to watch the sun come up."

"But you're glad that she did."

"Eternally grateful. I won't soon forget it."

"Well, I'll let you in on a little secret." He lowered his voice: "If you come back tomorrow, you'll get to see it again."

"I just might do that."

Georgia bundled the sleeping bag to her chest and leaned over to lift the thermos from the sand, then shook it to see if it was empty. "I thought I might have a little coffee left to offer you, but it appears I've polished it off." She shrugged apologetically.

"That's very thoughtful of you, all the same. Perhaps when I've finished my walk I'll stop at the . . . what did you say the name of the inn was?"

"The Bishop's Inn. It's on the corner of Sea View and Bay Boulevard."

"A big, rambling old Victorian place with a mile or so of porch wrapped around it?"

Georgia nodded. "That's it."

"Well, then, perhaps I'll see you there before too long. It's been my pleasure, miss." He touched his fingers to the brim of his hat and nodded before walking off toward the far end of the beach, where the stone jetty reached into the Atlantic.

He walked close to the shoreline, carrying himself straight as a soldier across the sand. *A pleasant-enough fellow,* she mused. *Must be close to Mother's age, maybe a bit older, but only by a few years, I'd guess.*

Georgia trudged through the soft sand to the wooden steps that led up to the sidewalk beyond. Pausing at the top, she looked back. Her mystery man had climbed onto the rocks and stood at the end of the jetty, his hands shielding his eyes from the reflection of the sun off the ocean, as if searching for something. *Dolphins, maybe, unless it's too cold for them, too*, she thought as she turned back toward the path that would take her to the inn. It occurred to her then that if she hurried, she might make it back to the inn in time to have breakfast with her niece, Ally—Laura's daughter—a lively and wonderful five-going-on-six. She quickened her pace, leaving the beach and the stranger behind.

chapter three

"*U*mmm . . . something smells wonderful."

Georgia stood in the kitchen doorway and sniffed appreciatively. Felled by a cold two days after her early morning visit to the beach, she had been living on chicken soup and herb tea for three days thereafter.

"I thought you might be ready for something a little more substantial now that you're finally venturing beyond your sickbed." Laura lifted the pot of steaming pasta from the stove and turned to the sink, where she dumped the contents into a waiting colander. "Jody made a fabulous pasta primavera for the inn's guests tonight, and there appears to be just enough left over for Ally, you, and me."

"Sounds wonderful. And I think my cold has pretty much run its course. How annoying to get sick on the first vacation I've had in years. I've done nothing but sleep and read and sleep and drink tea and sleep since my second day here."

"Must have been all that cold beach air the other morning."

"I think it's more likely the result of stress; lowers your defenses. I'm in great shape physically, you know. I get tons of exercise, I eat only very healthy food—don't drink, except for an occasional glass of wine, never smoked—but stress will bring me down every time." Georgia paused to ask, "Where are we eating tonight?"

"I think the sunroom." Laura's dark hair slid forward onto her forehead as she nodded to the doorway on her left.

"Good choice." Georgia stepped into the small cheerful room off the kitchen and turned on the light. "Would you like me to start a fire in the fireplace after I set the table?"

"If you like." Laura moved aside a potted plant that sat in the middle of the small round table and replaced it with the bowl of pasta. "Think you'll feel well enough to take a drive tomorrow?"

"Sure." Georgia took her place at the table between Ally and Laura. "Where are we going?"

"I need to drive up to Pumpkin Hill to—" Laura began, and was interrupted by a cheery "Yay!" from her young daughter.

"Pumpkin Hill!" Ally jumped excitedly out of her chair. "Pumpkin Hill! I want to go to Pumpkin Hill!"

"Sweetie, you'll be in school," Laura reminded her, and the child's face eased into a frown.

"But Mommy . . ."

"Next time. I promise I will take you next time." Laura leaned over and kissed her daughter on the forehead.

"But I love Pumpkin Hill. It's my favorite place in the whole entire world. Next to the beach." Ally had not yet run the gamut of her protests.

"What's Pumpkin Hill?" asked Georgia.

"It's an old farm that's been in my mother's family forever—since well before the Civil War. My mother was born there. Her sister, Hope, lived there until she passed away last year. The farm passed to Mother when Aunt Hope died, and I try to get up there every few weeks or so to make sure that the local kids haven't turned the old chicken coop into a clubhouse, or burned down one of the barns."

"Mommy, why would somebody want to burn down the barn?" Ally frowned at the thought of one of her favorite haunts catching fire.

"I don't know that anyone would want to, not on purpose, anyway. But sometimes people get careless."

"Like throwing away cigarettes? We saw a film on careless smoking in school. A lady in a car threw a cigarette out of her car window and it started a forest fire," Ally related. "The trees burned, and so did some of the animals. You must be very careful with fire,"—she pointed a finger at Georgia—"or very bad things can happen."

"You're absolutely right." Georgia bit her lip to keep from smiling. Ally had an earnest streak a mile wide.

"And it's best not to smoke at all." The child finished her lecture and focused her attention on her dinner plate, where she moved a piece of broccoli out of the way in search of a carrot.

"Right again," Georgia replied, nodding. "And a

ride sounds great. I'm afraid I have a touch of cabin fever. A change of scenery would be nice—not that I don't love the inn," she hastened to add. "But I am beginning to feel like a bit of a slug. I've barely left my room since Tuesday."

"Ugh!" Ally groaned. "Slugs are so yucky."

"And that's why I don't like feeling like one. I'm used to a higher level of physical activity than I've had over the past few days. It makes me feel a little restless to be so sedentary." Georgia speared a wedge of zucchini. "What time would you like to leave?"

"After we get Ally off to school."

"Would I have time for an early morning run?"

"I'm sure you would, if you think that's wise after having been sick for three days."

"I promise I'll make it a short run, and I'll only go if the weather is decent." Georgia smiled, touched by Laura's concern.

"I heard the weather report: sunny skies and temperatures in the fifties."

"That sounds like a heat wave after the cold we've had. A short, early morning run and a trip to Pumpkin Hill sounds great."

"Aunt Georgia, I bet I can beat you at Candyland." Ally tugged on the sleeve of Georgia's dark blue sweater.

"Oh, you think so, do you?" Georgia narrowed her eyes and tried to appear to be seriously sizing up the competition.

"Yup, I do. I can beat anyone at Candyland." Ally popped out of her chair and hopped to the built-in shelves that ran under the windows. She hunted for the white box that held her favorite game, then brought it back to the table and announced proudly, "I even beat Corri Devlin."

"Well, then, you must surely be a force to be reckoned with," Georgia told her, recalling that Corri—her brother Nick's stepdaughter, almost seven—took her games very seriously. "Let's just clean up these dinner dishes, and then we'll see who the Candyland champ of this family really is."

Ally giggled as she set about the task of beating both her aunt and her mother three times out of four, before an untimely roll of the dice sent her back to the swamp and allowed Laura to reach the castle first, winning one game and costing Ally a "sweep."

"One more game?" Ally had begged, causing both Laura and Georgia to collapse, groaning, across the game board.

"It's almost your bedtime," Laura reminded Ally.

"And I have to get up early," Georgia told her.

"You guys are afraid I'll beat you again, that's all." Ally grinned. "I beat Mr. Chandler *seven* times today after school."

"Seven times? You made poor Mr. Chandler play seven games of Candyland?" Laura chuckled. "My, he is a good sport, isn't he?"

"Mr. Chandler is neat." Ally turned to Georgia and asked, "Do you know what Mr. Chandler does?" Without waiting for her aunt's reply, Ally said, "He finds old ships that are under the ocean and goes down in the water to bring up all the neat stuff that is still on the ship."

"This Mr. Chandler sounds like an interesting man, Ally." Georgia tossed the game pieces into the box.

"Oh, he is." Ally nodded enthusiastically.

Laura slid the lid onto the box and handed it to her daughter. "You can put this back on the shelf on your way out of the room to get ready for bed."

"Who will tell me a story tonight?" Ally solemnly studied the two women, her hands resting on her hips.

"I believe it would be my turn tonight." Georgia nodded. "You pick out a book and I'll come read it to you when you're ready for bed."

"Okay."

"Who is this Mr. Chandler, whose interests run from Candyland to sunken ships?" Georgia asked after Ally had skipped from the room.

"He's a guest here, checked in on Tuesday afternoon. And oh, is he ever charming. Late fifties, well built, muscular, handsome, laughing eyes . . ." Laura grinned.

"Does he have silver hair?" Georgia asked.

"Yup."

"Slightly long, pulled back in a bit of a pony tail?"

"That's the one." Laura nodded. "You may have seen him around the inn."

"No, I've hardly moved from my bed these past two days. But I did see him on the beach, the morning we went down to watch the sun rise."

"Ah, then you must have been the 'lovely young woman who so highly recommended the inn' to him."

"I believe I did suggest he stop by for the coffee. . . ."

"Well, I thank you for doing so. It's an honor to have someone like Gordon Chandler as a guest."

"Gordon Chandler?" Georgia frowned. "Why is that name familiar?"

"He's been in the news on and off over the past few years. He's a salvager; finds sunken ships, just as Ally said, then recovers the cargo. He's written a book about a Spanish galleon he found off the coast of Florida about three years ago. He's been on CNN a lot recently."

"Wait—he's the one who's challenging the laws governing ownership of recovered loot, or whatever you call it."

"Right."

"Well, how about that?" Georgia mused. "Wonder what he's doing in Bishop's Cove?"

"Oh, he's looking for the *True Wind*," Laura told her.

"What's the *True Wind*?"

"A pirate ship that sank off the coast here in the late seventeen hundreds. It had traditionally been thought that the ship sank farther down the coast, closer to Assateague Island. But Mr. Chandler thinks it went down closer to Bishop's Cove."

"Really? How exciting." Georgia's eyes gleamed. "A real live pirate-seeker. I'll bet Mom would love to talk to him. She has always been fascinated by the whole pirate mystique, and I'll bet your Mr. Chandler knows lots of good stories. She might be interested in meeting him."

Laura guided Georgia by the arm out of the room and to the foot of the steps. "I'll give her a call in the morning. Why don't you go on up and get Ally into bed, then turn in early yourself. You want to feel well enough to make that trip to Pumpkin Hill with me in the morning."

"I do," Georgia agreed, "and maybe I'll run into the intriguing Mr. Chandler on the way up."

"I doubt that you will tonight. He mentioned this afternoon that he was going to be having dinner with Derrick Hubble."

"Who's that?"

"Captain Hubble is a local fisherman—an old seafarer from way back. Mr. Chandler wanted to pick his brain about local lore as well as water depths, currents—that sort of thing."

"You don't think he's planning on diving in the ocean in this frigid water, do you?" Georgia shivered at the mere thought of it.

"No. He said it takes him a while to gather his data and decide whether or not to pursue a certain vessel."

"Well, I'll be pleased to see him again." Georgia turned toward the steps. "Are you sure there's nothing else I can help you with before I go up to read to Ally?"

"That's more than enough. Thank you."

"Don't thank me—" Georgia grinned—"I'm getting the opportunity to read books I haven't even thought about since I was a child. And I'm loving every minute of getting to know my niece."

Georgia gave Laura a casual peck on the cheek and headed up the back stairs to the family quarters on the second floor.

The inn fell quiet as Georgia's footsteps trailed off down the hallway above, and Laura smiled. What a wonderful gift she had been given that day when

Delia Enright had arrived at the local historical society to speak to the members. Long a fan of the popular mystery writer, Laura had been thrilled at the prospect of meeting her favorite author, and hearing how she often used organizations just like the Bishop's Cove group when she researched her books. Never in her wildest dreams could Laura have expected that that day would change her life forever. Had she not attended that meeting, she might never have discovered that Delia Enright—internationally acclaimed best-selling author—and Cordelia Hampton—the faceless name on Laura's birth certificate—were one and the same person. The truth had come as both shock and salvation.

At first Laura had been certain she had not heard the speaker correctly. But as the words passed from the authors lips—"My maiden name is Hampton. Cordelia Hampton."—Laura's head had popped up in surprise to meet Delia's eyes across the crowd, and in that moment Laura knew that Delia not only *knew*, but had planned this meeting to seek out the daughter she had relinquished thirty-five years earlier. It had been all Laura could do to keep from passing out. At the end of the program, Laura had approached the speaker's podium nervously and introduced herself.

"My name is Laura Bishop," she had said.

"Yes," Delia had answered very softly, "I know."

The two women had stood for an achingly long time before Laura broke the silence by saying, "Would you like to stop at the Bishop's Inn for tea before you leave this afternoon?"

"I would very much like that." Delia's eyes had

visibly misted and her hands were shaking as she touched Laura's arm hesitantly.

Delia had stopped at the inn that day, and had ended up staying for the rest of the week. There had been so much to talk about, so much to learn about each other, so many feelings to explore, tears to shed, so much of their past lives to share. While life with the Bishops had been wonderful, finding the woman who had given birth to her—finally understanding why she had been placed for adoption, that it had been Delia's parents who had arranged for the baby to be turned over to adoptive parents immediately after her birth, that the seventeen-year-old Delia had been whisked away to college as if the child had never been born—had only served to add another dimension to Laura's life. Learning that she had two half sisters and a half brother had been an added bonus. She had found much common ground with each of the Enright girls—Zoey, whom she so resembled, and Georgia—and had found staunch allies in her half brother, Nick, and his wife, India. With the exception of one episode, life for Laura had been mostly sweet. Discovering this whole new family had made it only sweeter.

If only Matt weren't such a stubborn cuss where the Enrights are concerned. Laura sighed as she rinsed out the pasta pot.

In all fairness, she thought she understood—even though he obviously did not—that he felt threatened by the growing presence of this other, new, family in Laura's life. As a young boy whose nights had been haunted by ugly dreams—the sad aftermath of years of neglect and pain—Matt had found a redemption in the Bishop home that perhaps even Laura could not fully fathom. Laura had been but days old when Tom and Charity Bishop had brought her home. She had never known other parents; another life. Matt's early years had left scars that even now, Laura acknowledged, might not be fully healed. That Tom Bishop had died, and that one never knew for certain what or whom Charity remembered from one day to the next, were an endless source of grief for both their children, but maybe, in some ways, just slightly more so for Matt, who had so fiercely loved the couple who had taken him in and saved his life—and his soul—in so many ways.

Laura, too, had loved her parents, but it seemed that now, when she most needed their counsel—when it seemed that dark forces gathered to frighten her, to hint that unspeakable things could happen to her child—that guidance was being denied her. Laura could not bring herself to tell Delia about the threat that hung over her—to show her the frightening letters, to draw her birth mother into the ever-tightening web in which she found herself entangled—because then she'd have to explain about Gary. Oh, someday, she knew, she would need to tell her, *but please, Lord, not yet*—not while the Enrights were still getting to know her, still forming their opinion of her. Later, when they had come to know her, maybe, *but please, not now. . . .*

Mom always said to deal with one thing at a time. To focus on the here and now.

Laura rubbed her temples, trying to push it from her mind; to refuse to acknowledge that just that morning, another white envelope had arrived. For a moment she wished that she hadn't thrown it away—wished that she had left it where Matt could have found it. But Matt blamed himself for not having seen through his brother-in-law, for not recognizing Gary for what he was, as if, somehow, *he* should have seen what she herself had not.

Don't dwell on the other. It's what he wants. If I let him frighten me, I am giving him control over me. . . .

Laura leaned against the wall, inhaling sharply, exhaling slowly, as if to expel any last unpleasant thoughts, forcing her fears from her mind. There were other, more immediate issues to consider tonight. There was Matt, and there was Delia—and there had to be a way to join these two pieces of her life.

Laura switched off the kitchen light, then paused to look out the kitchen window at the dark, late winter sky that hung over Bishop's Cove. Through the bare draping branches of the wisteria a star winked at her, and she stepped outside into the cool night air to take a better look. It was a bright and bold star—a wishing star—and so she wrapped her arms across her chest against the cold night air and closed her eyes to make a wish.

chapter four

"Okay, sweetheart, just take it easy," Matt crooned quietly to the German shepherd that lay uneasily on the examining table. "Just another minute and you can get down."

The dog watched Matt through wary brown eyes, but she had stopped struggling.

"Do you think it's something more than hip dysplasia?" The dog's concerned owner, a middle-aged man in khakis and a worn Johns Hopkins sweatshirt, petted the dog affectionately.

"Well, judging by the symptoms—the difficulty in rising from a prone position, a reluctance to run, her age, and the fact that shepherds are prone to the condition—I'm pretty certain that's her problem. The X rays will tell us definitively, but she's a candidate for bad hips, Barry. I see on her chart that her mother had it, as well as her grandmother. We know it's an inherited condition. Just a few weeks ago I read a study that placed the incidence of hip dysplasia in German shepherds at close to eighty percent." Matt sat on the edge of the table and rubbed the side of the dog's face. She was a sweet-tempered old girl, and he was fond of her. "We'll know as soon as they bring the X rays back . . . there's Chery now with the films."

Matt hopped off the table and went to the door, took the large square films from the technician, and held them up to the light. It was clear that the hip's ball and socket were poorly formed, and the signs of an arthritic condition were unmistakable in the dog's hip joints.

"Here, right here, see?" With his index finger, Matt traced the areas of arthritis on the X rays.

Barry nodded anxiously. "What can we do for her?"

"If she were a few years younger, I'd recommend surgery, but she's thirteen now, and surgery can be very traumatic for an older dog. I'd like to try a new type of drug that Dr. Espey has had some promising results with. It's called PSGAG—polysulfated glycos-aminoglycan. It helps stimulate repair of the damaged cartilage. There's actually a form of glycosamine available to human arthritis sufferers." Matt stroked the dog's hindquarters, and she turned her head to watch but did not otherwise react. "I think it's worth a try."

"Thanks, Dr. Matt," Barry said as he and the young intern helped the dog down from the table. "We really appreciate that you have stayed on to help Dr. Espey out. We all know it's hard for him right now. . . ."

Matt stuck his hands into the pockets of his white jacket. "I owe a lot to Dr. Espey. I'll stay as long as he wants me to." Matt patted the dog on the head and her owner on the back as they walked to the reception area. "Liz," he said to the receptionist, "give Barry two weeks' supply of PSGAG. And Barry, you'll call me at the end of the week if you see any change at all in her condition. And you'll call me if you don't. Either way, we want to monitor this carefully."

"Thanks again, Doc."

"You're welcome." Matt nodded, then turned to receptionist and asked, "Who's next?"

The back door, not having been properly closed, blew open with a sharp gust of wind, drawing Matt's attention to the parking lot. A dark green Mustang took a spot at the farthest end of the lot. As Matt prepared to close the door, a short blond woman got out of the car. Matt stood, mesmerized, holding his breath, every nerve in his body on standby. When she turned toward the building, the air fled from his lungs in one gush.

It wasn't her.

But, of course, he'd known that it wouldn't be—

"Matt . . ."

"Oh. What?"

"I said, is something wrong?" Liz looked concerned.

"No. Nothing. You were saying . . . ?"

She handed him a stack of charts. "Let's see, in room one, you have Mrs. Myers and her diabetic cat, and out back you have two dogs waiting to be spayed. Out front you have an epileptic parrot, a ferret with hairballs, and a cocker spaniel with cataracts. Oh, and the McKays brought in their latest litter of basset hounds to be inoculated."

"Ferrets with hairballs," he muttered as he opened Room 1, and greeted Mrs. Myers and Fluffy, the diabetic Javanese who meowed loudly at the very sight of the vet. It had the makings of a very long day.

By five forty-five that afternoon, Fluffy's diabetes had been brought under control, the ferret's hairball had been removed, the cocker had been referred to a vet outside of Baltimore who specialized in eye surgery, both dogs—a Pekinese and a mutt—had been spayed, the parrot was sent home with a week's supply of an experimental drug for his epilepsy, and all the basset pups had been inoculated. Matt rubbed the back of his neck as he walked to the front desk and opened the door into the waiting room to double-check that no last patient had strolled in unannounced. Satisfied that the workday was, in fact, over, he locked the front door.

"Liz, looks like we're done for today." Matt leaned around the corner of the small office area to where the receptionist ruled. "Why don't you just leave that pile of paperwork until the morning?"

Liz hesitated, debating with herself, then frowned, picked up the stack of bills, and stuffed them into a battered brown leather case. "I'll take them home. It's close to the end of the month, and I want to make sure the bills are taken care of. Besides, I'm off tomorrow, so it will give me something to do between the talk shows and the soaps."

Matt laughed, knowing that Liz would no more spend a day watching television than she would robbing banks. At sixty, Liz was lively and energetic, and would most likely spend part of the morning at her aerobic class and a good part of the afternoon volunteering at the local hospital.

"Will you be stopping to see him?" Liz asked as she slipped her arms into a green down jacket.

"Yes, I thought I might." Matt nodded, knowing who "him" was.

Liz smiled and patted Matt on the arm affectionately. "You're a good boy, Matt Bishop. I know that Tim appreciates the fact that you're keeping his practice going. We all do. Tim Espey has run this clinic for almost fifty years. He's treated just about every animal—farm and domestic—in the county. If you hadn't stayed on after he had that first stroke last year, I don't know what we'd be doing."

"Everyone would be driving over to Dr. Peterson in the next county." Matt shrugged, knowing full well that Dr. Espey's patients might well end up there, eventually, once Matt left.

And they wouldn't be happy about it, Matt reflected as he drove his pickup down the lane leading to Dr. Espey's house, but there it was. As long as Tim Espey owned the clinic, Matt Bishop would be there to keep it open. Doc Espey's first stroke had felled him, and the last stroke had left him unable to walk and with a weakness in both arms. Matt didn't know how much longer the old vet would hold on to the clinic, but Matt would be there with him to the end.

It had been Dr. Espey, a respected professor of animal husbandry as well as a practicing vet, who had taken Matt under his wing when Matt had first started his veterinary studies, and Dr. Espey who had urged him on every step of the way. Having recognized Matt's innate gentleness and uncanny diagnostic abilities, Tim Espey had personally funded Matt's tuition the year Tom Bishop had died and the family finances were in an uproar. He had never bothered to tell Matt that the "scholarship" he had been awarded at the last minute had not come from the school's financial aid committee, but from his own checkbook. He hadn't wanted the boy to be beholden to him, and it was a source of pride to him that it had been Matt who had asked to intern at the Espey Clinic, and Matt who had offered to stay on and keep the clinic open even after his internship had been completed. Matt Bishop was the son Tim Espey had never had, and the old vet loved him dearly.

Matt parked his truck near the side door of the old house, right next to the blue Buick that belonged to Eva, the old doctor's lady-friend. Liz, who had lived all her life in the area and knew everyone's secrets, had confided to Matt that Eva and the vet had been sweethearts long ago, but he had enlisted in the early forties and sent to Europe. In his absence, she had fallen head over heels with the new pharmacist and had married him. The good doctor had retaliated by bringing home the British nurse who had tended his wounds after he'd been injured during the last few months of the war. Both Eva's pharmacist and Tim Espey's nurse having passed on within three years of each other, the vet and the love of his childhood had started seeing each other again. The old man's strokes had not diminished her affection for him, and she cared for him with great tenderness.

"He was wondering if you'd be stopping by." Eva

73

greeted Matt at the door before he'd even knocked on it.

"I told him I'd be here to bring him up to date on some of his favorite patients."

"He's in the sunroom." Eva reached for Matt's jacket and he shook his head, telling her, "I won't be staying too long tonight. I left early this morning, and I'll need to get my dog out. He's been cooped up all day."

"Well, then, why not run on back and get the dog and bring him back, and then you can both have dinner here?" the voice from the sunroom called to him. "I've got a new dog-food recipe I want to try out."

"Another one?" Matt laughed from the doorway.

"Yup." The old man in the wheelchair chuckled. Long a proponent of natural foods for both man and beast, Tim Espey had been experimenting with home-prepared pet foods and holistic forms of treatment for the last twelve or fifteen years. And for the past three of those years, Matt's rottweiler, Artie, had been his favorite guinea pig.

"What's in this one?" Matt sat down on the large square ottoman in front of the wheelchair.

"Oatmeal, ground turkey, and some raw vegetables," Dr. Espey replied. "A little bonemeal for calcium, some vitamin supplements, and some tamari sauce for flavor."

"Put enough raw carrots in, and Artie will eat just about anything." Matt grinned. "His breeder says he's giving rottweilers a bad name. Artie would rather have broccoli than beef any day. And a bowl of salad is his idea of heaven."

"I think if people knew just how much dogs like vegetables, they'd give them more. Which reminds me—you mentioned that Barry Enders was bringing his shepherd in today. How's she doing?"

Matt leaned forward, his forearms resting on his thighs. "Well, she's developed a pretty serious arthritic condition. She doesn't get around so well anymore."

Doc Espey nodded. "I whelped that bitch . . . and her mother, and *her* mother, back about six generations. Every one of them developed hip dysplasia after they hit about ten or so. What did you give her?"

"I gave her two weeks' worth of PSGAG and told Barry to give me a call at the end of the week and let me know how's she's doing."

Doc Espey nodded in agreement. "Good choice. But I'd like to see her on fifteen hundred milligrams of vitamin C a day, as well."

"I'll give Barry a call first thing in the morning."

"Tell him to divide the dosage in half and give it twice a day. If she's no better at the end of two weeks, maybe we should send her to see Linc Milner."

Matt smiled. "How do you think Barry would feel about taking his dog to a chiropractor?"

"If he thought it would help his dog, he'd do it. Did wonders for that collie we sent down to Milner last year."

"I'll mention it to him."

"Dinner's almost ready, Matt." Eva poked her head into the doorway. "Are you staying?"

"He's staying." Tim turned to her. "He needs a good meal and a few hours out. The boy has no social life to speak of, and can't make a decent meal for himself unless it comes frozen, out of a box, and fits into the microwave. Of course he's staying. Go home and get Artie, Matt, and we'll let him try Dr. Tim's new doggie formula. And after dinner I'll let you read the letter I got today from my old student Hank Stevens. He's developed a very interesting homeopathic approach to treating behavioral problems in dogs using flower essences. . . ."

It was well after nine P.M. when Matt returned to his small rented bungalow just off the main street of Shawsburg, Maryland. He checked the messages on his answering machine—a call from his sister, one from a woman, Beth, he'd met at a party a few weeks earlier and thought he might be interested in seeing again, and a call from one of his old fraternity brothers, wondering where he'd been hiding. He played the messages a second time, debating on whether or not it was too late to call Laura and whether or not he wanted to call Beth at all. He dialed the number of the inn and listened as the recorded greeting began.

"Thank you for calling the Bishop's Inn. For general information, please press—"

"Hello?" Laura had picked up.

"Your dutiful brother promptly returning your call."

"Oh, hi, Matt."

"Is everything all right? Mom? Ally? Laura?"

"We're all fine, Matt. Mom is the same—"

"Which is not fine," he interjected.

"No. That's not fine, but at least she's still relatively healthy and has some lucid moments and she can still carry on a conversation," Laura reminded him. "That's about as good as it gets at this stage of her disease, Matt."

"I know that. I just hate it," Matt told her bluntly.

"I hate it, too. But I can't change it." Laura sighed wearily. "I just wanted you to know that I'll be going up to the farm tomorrow, and I was wondering if there was anything in particular I should be looking at."

"Check the attic ceiling to make sure that the new roof is holding." He thought for a minute, then added, "And check the basement to make sure there's no water down there. We've had a lot of rain these past few weeks."

"Anything else?"

"Nothing else I can think of. How's Ally?"

"She's fine."

"Well, tell her that her favorite guy is on the phone and wants to talk to her." The thought of his little niece brought a smile to Matt's face. He loved Ally dearly and spoiled her every chance he got.

"Well, right now Georgia is reading her a story—"

"Georgia?"

"Georgia Enright," Laura told him.

"Oh."

"Oh, Matt—meet her, would you please, before you form a judgment?" Laura sighed with exasperation. "You would love Georgia, Matt, she's just the sweetest person."

"I'm sure she is," he replied dryly.

"Matt, for someone as smart and clever and kind as you are, this blind spot you have—"

"I've heard this one before, Laura. Look, it's been a

very, very long day. Have a nice visit with your sister. Give Ally a kiss for me. And keep in touch." He lowered the phone to its base and exhaled loudly. More annoyed with himself than he wanted to admit, he went into the kitchen and poured a glass of water, trying to understand just why he saw red every time he heard the name *Enright.* It wasn't fair, and it wasn't rational, he admitted, but it was fact. He swished the water around in the glass, then blew another long stream of air from his lungs.

He knew that Laura was disappointed by his reaction to her finding her birth mother. He knew that she wanted him to get to know her new family. He also knew that something unexplainable came over him every time he thought about it—something that caused him to break into a sweat and brought the slightest tremor to his hands.

Maybe, Matt thought, he should get Dr. Espey's former student to prescribe some of those flower essences—the ones that were said to improve one's mental state and emotional well-being—for *him.*

He poured the rest of the water from his glass into the sink and opened the back door. Stepping outside, he scanned the night landscape for something moving across the yard. Artie, black as the very night, could be seen only as a streak of horizontal movement across the vertical background of trees. Matt whistled, then listened to the crunch of dried branches as Artie fled through a nearby thicket from the neighbor's yard.

"What have you been up to?" Matt asked as Artie tried to slink past his master into the kitchen. "Not so fast, Arthur. Sit."

Torn between escape and obedience, Artie sat.

"What is this stuff all over your face?" Matt frowned, hoping that the red liquid was something other than blood.

The phone rang.

"Yes, Mrs. Dobson? Oh, he did, did he?" Matt turned a stern face to the dog, who chose that moment to casually turn his back. "I'm so sorry. I'll be right over to clean it up. No, it won't happen again. I'll see you in a minute."

Matt hung up the phone and stood with his hands on his hips.

"So, Mrs. Dobson tells me you stopped by for a late-night snack."

The dog licked at his front paws, as if pretending not to hear.

"And that you raided her trash can to get it. Leftover lasagna, was it?" Matt pulled several sheets of paper towels from the roll on the counter, wet them from the faucet, and knelt down to wash the dog's face and paws. "Artie, you've got to stop knocking over people's trash cans and helping yourself. It's 'no, no, bad dog' stuff, understand?"

Matt looked down into the big, warm brown eyes of the rottweiler. The dog looked up. A large pink tongue—now devoid of tomato sauce—slurped across Matt's face contritely.

"Yeah, yeah, I know. We've had this discussion before." Matt stood up and tossed the paper towels into the trash. "And don't even think about going after *them*; I'm taking the trash bag out with me. You can just wait right here till I get back. Stay, Artie. . . ."

Artie sat, his tail thumping tentatively on the kitchen floor.

"You just sit right there and think about what you've done," Matt muttered as he closed the door behind him and set off to clean up the scattered remains of Mrs. Dobson's garbage, three doors down.

Later, the apologies made once again and the cleanup completed, Matt settled into his favorite chair with a favorite book, *The Sign of Four*, by Sir Arthur Conan Doyle. As he opened to the first page, he recalled the phone calls he had not returned that night. He would call his fraternity brother over the weekend. The woman—Beth, from someplace around Havre de Grace, he recalled—he probably would not call at all. Between taking care of Doc Espey's clinic and worrying about both the good doctor and his own mother, Matt had little energy left for anything else.

He leaned over to switch on the lamp and in doing so, knocked a photograph from the small table onto the floor. He picked it up, and as he replaced it his eyes dropped to the picture within the brass frame. Laura and their mother stood on the back porch of the Bishop's Inn amid hanging waves of wisteria, smiling generously for Matt, who had taken the picture with a camera he'd received for his seventeenth birthday.

Their faces were both so dear to him. Charity Bishop had been a beautiful woman, right up until the time her illness had started to drain the life from her eyes. Matt could barely stand it that, more often than not, she did not know him when he visited. Every week he made the trip from Shawsburg to the convalescent home, midway between Bishop's Cove and Pumpkin Hill, hoping that *that* day would be a good day; that she would remember who he was, maybe even greet him with a smile and a cheery "Hi, Matty." Those days were coming less and less frequently now as her disease progressed, and it broke his heart. He knew that the day would soon come that he would have to accept that there would be no more recognition of anyone who had once been so dear to her.

Anger welled up in him once again as he studied the features of the woman who had been mother and savior to him, then those of his sister. Laura had been his champion and his best friend. She had allowed him to sleep on the end of her bed when, as a four-year-old frightened by the newness of the Bishop home and all the mysterious things it held, he would awaken in the night and cry out all the fears he lacked the verbal skills to express. It had been Laura who had patiently taken him by the hand and taught him the words he did not know. She had read to him, played with him, taught him songs and stories, and walked with him on the beach. While the social workers had held little hope that the neglected toddler rescued from a drug house would ever develop normally, Matt had astounded all of them when he started school a mere one year later, his verbal skills almost on grade level. Charity had been determined that her boy would learn and excel, and he had. Much of his success, Matt knew, he owed to Laura's diligence.

And I need to be as diligent for her sake as she has been for mine, he told himself.

"No one is going to hurt Laura," he whispered, and Artie looked up at the sound. Matt dropped a hand down and scratched behind the dog's ears. Satisfied that he had identified the reason behind his Enright-phobia, he reopened his book and began to read the careful exchange between Sherlock Holmes and Dr. Watson regarding the great detective's use of cocaine, his defense of his habit, and the good doctor's earnest protests thereof.

chapter five

"Is this it?" Georgia eased her right foot onto the brake and tilted her head to look out the front window, asking, "Is this where I turn?"

"Yes," Laura pointed ahead to the gravel driveway that ran past an old farmhouse the color of faded sunshine. "Turn in here and just pull straight on back."

Straight on back led past the house to a wide expanse of farmyard, with an old weathered barn on the left, a somewhat smaller barn—the clapboard of which had lost much of its white paint to the elements—almost straight ahead, and another structure, smaller still and surrounded by a wire fence, stood off to her right.

"Welcome to Pumpkin Hill." Laura smiled and jumped out of the passenger door and began to look through her pocketbook for the thick ring that held all the keys she would need here.

Georgia leaned across the steering wheel and briefly surveyed her surroundings. The old farmhouse stood on the right side of the drive opposite the barn. Behind the house was a fenced-in area. Some gnarled apple trees in desperate need of pruning ran between the back of the fence and the smallest of the three outbuildings, and, behind all, deep fields stretched back to a wooded area far behind. Georgia turned off the ignition and hopped out.

"Ah, I love the smell of this place, even in the throes of winter." Laura inhaled deeply.

Georgia thought to remind her sister that March was hardly the throes of winter, but decided to let it go. The air did smell wonderful; pine mixed with something else that was earthy and elemental.

"We used to spend a lot of time here in the summer when we were kids," Laura told her. "Mom and Dad were always so busy at the inn during the summer months that we never got to go away on vacations as a family, so they used to send us out here for a few weeks at a time. We always had such fun, Georgia. Aunt Hope was such a character." Laura shook her head, remembering. "Funny and tough. She was the farmer in the family. She kept up the house and plowed the fields and planted crops and gardened and canned and preserved. Poor Jody can't bear the thought that she'll have to rely on other sources for her tomatoes and zucchini and herbs this year. Aunt Hope supplied us—and several other local restaurants—with all of our fresh produce in the summer."

"I'm impressed."

"You should be. She kept up with all this until she died last September at the ripe old age of seventy-seven. Still worked the fields, though she had cut back on the number of acres she planted over the past few years. But she still cared for the property by herself. Oh, once in a while one of the neighbors would stop by to check on her, and Matt came back every few weeks and would stay for a few days." Laura turned and pointed to the big red barn. "For years, Matt has kept an apartment there, in half of the second floor of the barn—he still comes back on a pretty regular basis. But for the most part, Aunt Hope was on her own. She always said she liked it that way."

"She never married?"

"Oh, yes. She married her high school sweetheart, but he left for World War Two about three months after they were married. He died on the beach at Normandy."

"So she never had children?"

"Just Matt and me." Laura grinned. "She always said we were all the kids she'd ever needed." Laura's voice softened. "I miss her very much."

"It must have been hard for you, losing your father a few years ago, then your aunt last year, and, in a way, your mother, all in so short a time."

"It has been. I think maybe I don't always appreciate just how difficult it's been, but if I stop and give it too much thought, it all but overwhelms me. On the other hand, while I've lost a lot over the past few years, I've gained a lot, too. I'm only sorry that Matt—" she stopped, reflecting back to one of the wishes she had made the night before. "—well, that Matt still seems to have so many empty places in his heart."

An ill-tempered crow dropped to the ground in front of the Jeep and began to scold them for trespassing. Soon several others joined in.

"Ah, they didn't happen to film a movie out here, did they?" Georgia frowned. "One with lots of birds . . ."

Laura laughed and searched through the keys on the brass ring. "They're just being ornery and territorial. Come on, let me show you around. We'll start with the big barn."

With practiced efficiency, Laura quickly worked off the padlock and swung aside the barn door, flooding the open space beyond with light. Something scurried noisily off to their left, and Georgia jumped back.

"Probably just a wild cat," Laura shrugged, unconcerned.

The air was cold and dusty and heavy with a sweet lingering trace of hay.

"Aunt Hope used to keep goats." Laura pointed to a row of empty stalls. "We had to send them off to a neighbor after she died. Matt and I couldn't take care of them, but we couldn't bring ourselves to sell them, either. Mrs. McCoy down the road is tending to them for a while, until . . . well, until there's someone here who can look after them."

Laura's boots scuffed along the concrete floor in the direction of a row of old farm equipment that stood along one wall. She walked from one machine to the next, her fingers tracing lines in the dust that covered old fenders and massive black rubber tires, the treads of which were deep and noticeably free of mud and dirt. With one hand Laura swung herself up into the seat of a small tractor the color of new spring grass.

"Nineteen thirty-nine John Deere Model L," she said softly. "Two cylinder engine. Nine horsepower. Your basic all-purpose tractor."

Georgia watched as Laura touched this knob and that before hopping down and walking around the next piece of equipment.

"Now, this one"—she patted one of the back tires—"this is a nineteen fifty-six Model sixty—another Deere machine, of course; my grandfather never bought anything but. You might notice that this one boasts a number of modern features for the modern farmer." She climbed up into the seat and pointed to what Georgia assumed was the engine. "This baby has a two-barrel carburetor, a hot and cold intake manifold for faster warm-ups, and a water pump in the cooling system."

Georgia wandered over and pretended to know what she was looking at.

"Did your aunt use this?"

"Damn near every working day of her life." Laura nodded.

"It has directions on it?" Georgia leaned forward to peer closely at the decal on the body of the tractor.

"Sure does." Laura laughed. "Remember that these tractors were intended to replace farm animals. Now, men who had relied on the use of horses or mules to plow their fields knew how to care for their animals. You cooled them down, you gave them food and water and rest when they came in from the fields at night, and the next morning you just hitched them back up and headed on back to the fields again. Machines need a little more maintenance. John Deere placed these little decals everywhere to remind the farmers when and how to do just about everything, from changing the oil in the crank case and tightening the clutch to how much air pressure to maintain in the tires."

Laura turned the steering wheel almost unconsciously as if lost in thought somewhere.

"Wonder if it still has gas?" Laura asked idly as she pushed a button on the side of the engine. The resultant roar almost threw Georgia backward.

"Wow!" Georgia yelled up to Laura, who sat grinning atop the old plow seat. "You could have warned me!"

"Sorry," Laura mouthed the word, then turned the engine off. "Sorry," she repeated. "I forgot how loud she is."

For a moment Laura stroked the side of the tractor much as one might stroke the flanks of a well-loved horse.

"Want to see upstairs?" she asked suddenly as she climbed back down off the old tractor.

"Sure."

Georgia followed Laura to one end of the room, where a wide wooden stairway led to a second floor.

"They used to store hay here." Laura paused to push open a window at the top of the steps. "Let's bring a little fresh air in. All the dust from the hay is going to give me a headache."

Georgia walked the length of the barn to gaze out the big windows at one end. With a tissue she rubbed the dirt from the glass, and peered through the clean spot to the fields beyond.

"I want to take just a quick check into Matt's apartment." Laura studied her keys. "I think this is the one."

She walked back to the stairwell and slipped the key into a door that was set into the wall on the right side of the landing. With a twist of the knob and a gentle push, the door swung open.

"Come on," Laura called over her shoulder as she passed through the door.

Georgia followed tentatively, overwhelmed by the feeling that she was trespassing into a very private place. The door in the barn wall led into a galley-style kitchen that had a very fifties look, from the speckled linoleum—red and white—to the white wooden cabinets that hung above the short counters on either side of the enamel sink. The narrow refrigerator and stove were white, as were the walls and the curtains that hung over the one small window. The counters were bare except for the ceramic canisters in the shape of apples, all painted shiny red with stems for handles, that lined up close to the wall in descending size. Georgia had half expected to see a few dishes stacked in the sink of this bachelor apartment, but there was not so much as a cup or spoon to be seen. There was nothing to identify who might live in this place other than a large white dish that sat on the floor near the sink and bore the name *Artie* in red block letters.

Laura's footsteps moved away somewhere beyond the kitchen. Georgia followed, stealing an inquisitive peek through the doors that led to a study, its walls lined with books, on the left off the hall, and a large square living room, furnished in nondescript fashion, to the right. Three steps at the end of the hall led down to the bedroom that was, she discovered, as neat as the rest of the apartment. A worn quilt of faded green-and-white squares covered the old maple double bed, and the bedside table held a brass lamp, a small alarm clock, and a small stack of books. Several framed photographs stood atop the wooden dresser, and the closet door was snugly closed. A mirror covered the wall behind the dresser, and the other walls held framed black-and-white photos and several ink prints. An old movie poster—John Barrymore as Sherlock Holmes—hung nearby a newer one—Basil Rathbone, dressed in the close-fitting ear-flapped cap known as the deerslayer, and a long gray traveling cape, a magnifying glass held up before his face. Georgia stepped closer to study the series of small pen-and-ink drawings, and stopped before the first. Two men forcibly led a woman in a Victorian-era gown. Precise letters across the bottom of the print identified the scene as "The abduction of Miss Nurnet in *Wisteria Lodge*." The second print—a tall, gaunt man with deep-set eyes, wearing a dark overcoat, his hands holding a top hat behind his back—bore the legend "The Napoleon of Crime, Professor Moriarty, from *The Final Problem*."

Laura watched from the doorway as Georgia went from one print to the next.

"Matt's a sucker for Sherlock Holmes," Laura told her.

"So I see." Georgia pointed to another of the prints

and read the neat print across the bottom aloud: "'The body of John Openshaw is fished out of the Thames in *The Five Orange Pips;* by an unknown French artist, circa nineteen twenty.'"

"My brother has tons of Holmesian collectibles. He even named his dog after Sir Arthur Conan Doyle."

"Ah." Georgia nodded. "The 'Artie' of the water dish."

"Exactly." Laura nodded and walked to the windows, where she straightened the shades that really had not appeared to Georgia to be in need of adjustment. "Let's go on out and I'll show you the rest of the farm."

They left the apartment not as they had come in, but through a door that opened off the tidy living room onto an outside landing and steps that led down the side of the barn. Once at the bottom, Georgia tried to shake off the feeling that she'd just taken far too close a look into the life of a man she had met only briefly, but who had found his way into her subconscious and refused to leave.

"This used to be an old workshop," Laura said as they walked past a clapboard outbuilding that seemed to grow like an appendage from the old barn. "And that over there"—she pointed to a smaller building to their right—"was the chicken coop. That fenced-in area behind the house was Aunt Hope's kitchen garden."

"Sounds like Aunt Hope was a busy lady," Georgia noted.

"That she was. Idle hands, and all that . . ." Laura paused in the driveway, then said, "Let me just check the mailbox before we go inside."

Georgia followed Laura down the drive toward the mailbox.

"Matt sometimes gets mail here, and sometimes people stuff circulars in and such." Laura opened the old metal mailbox from the front and stuck her hand inside. She pulled out a mass of paper. "See what I mean? Advertisements for everything from water beds to pizza."

She folded the small stack of papers and placed it under her arm.

"Let's go inside and check to see that all is well." She pointed to the walkway of wide, flat gray stones that led to the front door. "And don't let me forget to bring back some of Aunt Hope's preserves. Jody will hang me if I don't. She swears that those homemade jams are one of the reasons that people come back to the inn."

Georgia followed her up the walk and waited on the narrow porch while Laura unlocked the front door, then pushed it gently aside.

They were greeted by the faint smell of must and camphor and old dust. The door opened directly into a squared-off living room with long, wide windows running from floor to ceiling along the front and one side. A fireplace with a simply carved oak mantel stood in the wall nearest the door. Straight ahead, steps led unceremoniously to the second floor. To the right, one passed through a darkened dining room into a large square kitchen that overlooked the fields beyond the house.

"It's so still and close in here," Laura remarked. "Help me open a window or two. Let's get a little fresh air circulating."

Laura walked from the dining room through the living room, pushing back curtains and opening windows throughout the downstairs. The temperature inside the house was already cold, the thermostat having been lowered to provide just enough heat to keep the pipes from freezing, but bringing in the cool morning breeze did a lot to dispel the empty feeling of the old house.

Not entirely empty, Georgia thought as she wandered from room to room. The living room held a collection of upholstered furniture of indeterminate style and age, all of which were covered by white sheets intended to protect the old fabrics from dust. A porcelain bowl of waxed fruit still served as a centerpiece on the old pine dining room table, and along the window ledge several painted pots of dried plants sat where they had died of neglect. Little particles of dust danced in the hazy sunlight that spilled through the panes of old glass.

Georgia wandered through the first floor, then followed Laura up the old stairwell that bisected the front foyer.

The steps were a little steeper than they appeared, and led straight up to a dark landing. Laura turned on a lamp that sat on a small dresser, then, one by one, opened all of the four bedroom doors.

"This was my room when I was little," she told Georgia, pointing to the room off to their left. "I loved it here." She entered the room and sat on the end of a narrow bed covered by a white bedspread with small yellow flowers. "I could fall asleep listening to the crickets, and wake to the song of the wrens. It was wonderful. Matt slept right here"—she pounded on the wall behind the wooden headboard—"and at night we used to tap messages to each other."

She tapped lightly on the wall, as if sending a remembered greeting in code to her brother.

"We used to chase fireflies long past dark, and we'd put them in old jars with a piece of screen over the top and use the jars like lanterns. Of course, we'd always let the bugs out of the jars before we went in to go to bed, then we'd go back out the next night and catch more." She leaned on the window ledge and looked out, as if seeking something in the fields beyond the house and the old barns. "Some nights there'd be so many fireflies that the entire field would be lit up. Aunt Hope used to say they were the ghosts of all the soldiers heading home after the war." Her voice dropped into a modified drawl as she explained, "Now, of course, that would be the War of Northern Aggression."

"Ah, your family had southern sympathies, then."

"Some did, but not all. My great great uncle Peter fought for the Union. His cousin Ted fought for the South—ran off to join Magruder's rebels when he was just seventeen. Maryland was really divided during the war." Laura pulled aside the curtain and pointed to the woods. "Back behind those trees is a small tributary of the Nanticoke River, which leads eventually to the Chesapeake, which was, as one might imagine, a real hotbed of activity during the war. The farm two over,"—she pointed out the window toward the left—"was owned by Quakers who were suspected of running a stop on the Underground Railroad, so there was a lot of nocturnal activity over there. But over this way, closer to town, stood the home of a major in the Confederate army."

"I imagine that the residents of O'Hearn must have had some lively discussions over the years," Georgia mused.

"You can bet they have." Laura gestured for Georgia to follow her to the window on the other side of the room, where she pushed aside the curtain and pointed to the lone tree that stood in the flat expanse of unplowed field behind the barn, its enormous canopy spreading out in all directions. "That's the wishing tree."

"The wishing tree?" Georgia's eyebrows raised slightly.

"It's an elm," Laura told her, "but the locals always refer to it as the wishing tree. The story is that whatever you wish for while sitting under the tree's canopy will come true. Legend has it that during the Civil War all the young brides and brides-to-be would gather here and wish for their loved ones' safe return."

"What if you had no loved one?"

"Ah, there's legend for that too." Laura grinned. "It's said that he who falls asleep under the tree will see the face of his true love, upon awakening."

"Do you think it works?"

"Nah. I've fallen asleep under the tree many times and it didn't stop me from—" Laura paused in midsentence.

"Stop you from what, Laur?" Georgia asked.

"Maybe I just didn't wish hard enough." She turned away from the window with a shrug.

The *tick tick tick* of the wall clock suddenly seemed

very loud. Georgia waited, thinking that Laura was about to confide in her, perhaps finally share something of her mysterious relationship with the man who had fathered her child. But when Laura opened her mouth to resume speaking, it was as if that tiny window into her past had never been opened.

"Anyway," Laura said briskly, "Matt and I used to have picnics out there. We'd eat, then read for a while, then maybe go for a swim in the pond. Life was very simple in those days. There was always something to do, something to see. Aunt Hope put us to work, but we never complained. We were always happy here. I still always feel safe here."

"Safe from what, Laura?" Georgia asked gently.

"From . . . from . . ." Laura seemed flustered, unable to get the words out.

"Laura, is there something you want to tell me about?"

For a moment Laura seemed to hesitate, as if inwardly debating, before saying, "I don't. At least not today. And not here. Please, Georgia," she seemed to plead, "not today. Maybe another time, I might be able to. But not here. And not now."

Georgia nodded slowly, not having expected such a response. It had not been a pouring out of the heart between sisters, but neither had it been a denial that something was bothering her. It would do, for now.

"Okay. We'll let it go for now," Georgia agreed, grateful to see the window open back up again, even if only by an inch or two. It was a start. "You were talking about growing up in the country. We grew up in the country, too, but we didn't farm."

"Somehow, I just can't seem to conjure up a picture of Delia Enright seated atop one of those John Deeres." Laura forced a smile, and the unwanted topic slid into a place where it could not—for now anyway—touch her.

"Neither can I. Mom dearly loves her country life, and is very fond of her horses, but she likes someone else cleaning out the stalls and feeding them. And I don't know how she'd feel about goats."

"The goats were adorable," Laura told her. "Followed my aunt around like puppies."

Laura dropped the curtain back into place and took one last look around the room. "I love that it never changes here. Matt's room is still the same, Aunt Hope's room is still the same."

"Are you going to keep the farm, now that your aunt has passed away?"

"Oh, absolutely. It's such a big part of our family, I couldn't imagine parting with it, not ever. I hope it's still here for Ally when she grows up. And besides, Matt is planning on opening a veterinary clinic here, eventually. This land has been in my mother's family for over two hundred years. It will pass to Matt and me when my mother dies, and someday to Ally—and any children Matt might have, if he ever finds a woman fool enough to marry him."

"Why do you say that?"

"Matt is a troll. He's stubborn as a mule and just about as thick-headed. On the other hand, he's the most gentle man you'd ever want to meet."

Laura wandered into the hallway and poked into each of the open doors to ensure that nothing was amiss. Satisfied that all was well on the second floor, she motioned to Georgia to follow her back downstairs.

"I want to check the basement and make sure that water from the last storm didn't find its way inside." She shivered as she hit the bottom step. "I feel chilly. I'll put some water on for tea when I come back up."

"I'll do it," Georgia offered.

"Tea is in the small canister there," Laura pointed to the row of tin containers lined up across the counter.

Laura unlocked the basement door and bounded down the steps. Georgia walked to the stove and picked up the old blue spatterware tea kettle, rinsing it out in the sink before filling it with cold water. She set it back on the stove, turned on the burner, and searched the cabinets for two cups and saucers. She poked into the tin and found loose tea leaves, and in a drawer that was crowded with old silverware of several mixed patterns, she found several silver tea balls.

"Wonder of wonders, the basement is perfectly dry, even after all the rain we've had," Laura announced from the doorway. "Ah, I see you found Aunt Hope's tea balls. She never used tea bags; thought they made an inferior cup of tea."

"I don't know how much to put in." Georgia frowned.

"Aunt Hope used to just fill one half of the ball."

Georgia opened one tea ball and dipped half into the loose tea, then repeated the process with the second.

"You know, I meant to check the attic while we

were upstairs. Matt asked me to make sure that there are no leaks," Laura said. "I'll just run up and check that all the windows are closed tightly. I'll be right back."

"Take your time," Georgia told her, and took the opportunity to look around the big, square room.

The walls were pale yellow, and the floor, worn linoleum squares of black and white. A round oak table sat snugly in a rounded bay window that was adorned with café-style curtains of sun-faded yellow-and-white gingham. Salt and pepper shakers of heavy green glass stood in the middle of the table next to a wooden napkin holder that still sported the same yellow paper napkins that Hope herself had probably placed there. The crisp white enamel stove and refrigerator looked surprisingly new. All in all, the room was tidy and cozy, and looked like exactly what it was: a working kitchen on a working farm. The kettle whistled, and Georgia poured the boiling water over the tea ball in first one cup, then the next.

There was something calming and satisfying about the small act of making tea the old-fashioned way in a centuries-old kitchen, and Georgia smiled to herself as she set the cups on the table and pulled out a chair to await Laura's return from the attic. It was a cozy place, and Georgia could easily imagine sitting just so, lingering over a second cup on a cold winter morning, watching billows of snow drift past, or perhaps on a summer evening, when the scent of roses might catch a ride on a passing breeze and drift lazily through the open windows. The very thought of it relaxed her, and she sank into the chair with a smile on her face.

A row of small photographs set atop the window ledge caught her eye, and she lifted the first small brass frame. Beautiful Laura, blue eyes shining in a tanned face alive with laughter, as she held a tiny Ally to the camera's adoring eye. Georgia replaced the photo on the ledge and picked up the one next to it. A ruggedly handsome man in his twenties, his dark hair tumbling onto his forehead, embraced a sturdy-looking woman wearing a straw hat, sunglasses, and a gray cardigan sweater the same color as her hair. Matt, and the woman, their Aunt Hope.

Georgia studied Matt's face—his laughing eyes and broad smile—thinking that the camera didn't do him justice, hadn't quite caught the twinkle in his eye or the way sunlight bounced off that dark hair. . . .

Hearing Laura's footsteps coming back down the stairs, Georgia replaced the photo on the sill and pushed aside the curtain to look out onto the backyard. A tubular bird feeder—its seed long gone—stood a few feet from the glass.

"Aunt Hope loved her songbirds," Laura said from across the room. "She used to keep that feeder filled with thistle for the finches. There's another, bigger feeder." Laura leaned over Georgia to point toward a low-hanging branch of a nearby apple tree. "She used to put a different kind of seed in that one. A lot would spill onto the ground for the cardinals. I meant to stop and get some wild bird seed to fill those feeders. I wish I'd remembered."

Laura lifted her cup and sipped at it. "*Ummm*. This is so good. Aunt Hope would be proud of you. I never could get it quite right, you know. I always need a bag to make a decent cup of tea. This is just like Aunt Hope used to make."

She leaned back against the counter and said, "All's well in the attic. A few years ago we had some shingles blow off in a bad storm, and we had a lot of water come in. I'm always afraid it will happen again. I hate the house being vacant." Laura finished her tea in two more sips, then peered into her cup before rinsing it out in the sink, and said, "If Aunt Hope were here, she'd read our tea leaves."

"I never met anyone who could do that."

"It's supposed to be a gift"—Laura grinned—"a type of second sight that I don't have. Aunt Hope was uncannily good, however, and many a time, spooked me with just how good she was."

"You really do miss her a lot," Georgia observed.

"Yes." Laura nodded. "You would have loved her, Georgia, and I think she would have loved you, too."

"Did she know about . . . about Mother . . . ?"

"Yes. I told her after I met Delia. I had to talk to someone and, unfortunately, it couldn't have been Mom."

"How did your aunt feel about it?"

"She thought it was nothing short of a miracle. She was very happy for me, actually. I think she understood completely how I felt about Mom and Dad, how much I loved them. But I think she knew, too, that Delia was a blank page in my life, and that it was a wonderful thing that she had gone to such great pains to find me—to help me to complete the story, as it were. Aunt Hope understood long before I did that I had little missing pieces that I needed to find.

Delia just found me first, before I had felt compelled to look for her." Laura looked around the room as if checking to make sure they hadn't forgotten anything, then said, "If you're finished, I guess we can head back home."

Georgia went to the sink and washed out her cup and placed it next to Laura's, then went back to the table and slid her chair slowly back into place. For reasons she could not explain, Georgia felt reluctant to leave the warmth of the old house.

Following Laura from the room, she turned back to snap off the overhead light and paused to look around. The photograph she had earlier inspected caught her eye, and the face of the dark-haired man held her gaze for a long moment.

Troll or not, Georgia smiled to herself, *Matthew Bishop was one hell of a good-looking man.*

chapter six

"Damn!" Laura grumbled between clenched teeth. "I knew I'd forget something."

"What's that?" Georgia pulled into the parking lot behind the inn and turned off the ignition.

"The preserves for Jody. She's really going to be disappointed. And she made a point of reminding me three or four times not to forget several jars of peaches because she had a cobbler planned for dessert this week for a party that is checking in tomorrow."

"Can't she substitute something else? Canned peaches or something?"

Laura smiled grimly. "Jody does not substitute ingredients. She will substitute a different recipe, and she won't be happy about it. She prides herself on the high quality of her cooking. I'm really very fortunate to have her, Georgia; for so young a woman she's amazingly accomplished. I do everything I have to do to accommodate her, which is why she has her own room at the inn and she's treated like family. She *is* like a member of the family—the one who controls the kitchen. I hate to disappoint her."

"Why don't you just bring all of the jars back to the inn?"

"What, and empty Aunt Hope's cupboard?" Laura shook her head. "I never even considered doing that. For one thing, Matt raids the cupboard of plum jam— that's his favorite—every chance he gets, and, for another, Ally and I do still spend an occasional weekend there, and we like being able to go downstairs and select a jam for our breakfast toast. But mostly, I guess, I sort of feel that as long as some of Aunt Hope's put-up fruit and preserves are down there, it's just a little more of her that we still have with us. I know the day will come when there's nothing left, but for now . . . does that sound silly?"

"No, not really. Maybe a bit inconvenient, at times like this, but I understand the sentiment. We'll just drive back tomorrow and get whatever it is that Jody needs." Georgia brightened at the thought of returning to Pumpkin Hill. There had been something peaceful and welcoming about the place, and she was hoping there'd be reason to go back at least one more time before she returned to Baltimore.

"I can't." Laura hopped out of the Jeep. "I have a conference with Mother's doctor at eleven, and that party of eight is checking in tomorrow afternoon for a writers' retreat."

"I'll drive back first thing in the morning," Georgia told her as they walked toward the inn. "It's an easy drive, and, besides, I have nothing better to do."

That much was certainly true. Georgia had tried helping out in the kitchen, but had clearly been in

Jody's way. The chambermaids each had their assigned rooms, so helping there wasn't an option, either. While Georgia was grateful for the time she was having with Ally when school let out in the afternoon, there were long, idle hours between breakfast and the end of the school day; hours that had, back in Baltimore, always been filled. Here in Bishop's Cove, she could run in the mornings and take long walks after lunch, but she was becoming a bit restless with the decrease in the level of physical activity, and being brought down with a cold for three days hadn't helped.

Accustomed to long hours of aerobic exercise day after day for years, Georgia's body seemed to be experiencing a form of withdrawal brought on by her sudden sedentary behavior. She missed the routine, the strenuous exertion, as much as she missed having something to focus on. For most of Georgia's life, ballet had been her focus. She had never—not since the age of five—gone an entire week without dancing. She felt edgy, agitated. Mentally and physically uneasy, she keenly felt the loss of her routine, of that which had served as her very center, and wondered if perhaps she hadn't acted hastily. Her edginess only served to cause her to question the wisdom of her recent decision.

Had she been impulsive? Should she have given more thought to the consequences of her actions? And maybe she shouldn't have pushed Ivan. . . .

And what, she tried to recall as she took the back steps to her room on the inn's second floor, had been so important that she had felt compelled to take time off from dancing, anyway?

Sitting on the edge of her bed, Georgia stripped off her sneakers and socks and padded in bare feet to the suitcase that sat open on a chair in the corner of the tidy room she had occupied since arriving a week earlier. She pushed aside the sweatshirt and dug beneath the clothes, her hands seeking smooth leather. There—there they were, right under a nightshirt. She pulled her worn pink ballet shoes from under the pile and sat down on the floor to put them on. The simple act of slipping them onto her feet calmed her the way a glass of wine might calm some, a long drag from a cigarette might soothe another. As familiar to her as her name, the slippers hugged her feet and seemed somehow to remind her of who she was.

In one fluid motion she rose to her feet, heels together, legs stretched straight, her toes turned outward to form a straight line, in perfect First Position. She straightened her back, raised her chin, and curved her arms, raising them to the level of her chest. Exhaling, she slid into Second Position, opening her arms to the sides to form a gentle O. Then into Third, the heel of her right foot snug against the middle of her left, her right arm raised in a graceful arc. To Fourth, her right foot forward, parallel to her left, right arm over her head, left arm dropped back into First Position, and so into Fifth, her right foot close up to her left, the toes of each foot touching the heels of the other, her arms softly overhead. She pushed back the small table that stood inside the door and began the series of floor exercises she had practiced daily over the years; exercises to make her back limber, to stretch her legs, to develop her stomach muscles.

Thirty minutes later, having finished what she considered to be a short round of stretches, Georgia sat in the middle of the floor and cried.

She was still sitting there, feeling glum and purposeless, when Ally flew in after school. Seeing Georgia on the floor, her legs straight out in front of her, Ally saw all that a five-year-old *would* see.

"Hey! You're wearing your pink ballet slippers! I have pink ballet slippers, too! I'll put them on"—the little girl flew back out through the door, her voice trailing excitedly down the hallway—"and we can dance!"

Georgia smiled in spite of herself. How can one remain gloomy when a happy five-year-old wants to dance?

"Do you take dancing lessons, Ally?" Georgia asked when her niece returned proudly sporting her prized pink ballet shoes.

"No, not anymore." She shook her head. "Mrs. Carlson had a baby and stopped teaching."

"Do you remember anything she taught you?"

Ally sucked on the side of her top lip, trying to recall. She stared down at her feet, the toes of which were pointed in opposite directions, and said, "No."

Georgia stood up and corrected Ally's feet, bringing the heels together gently. "This is First Position, Ally. Now, raise your arms like this . . . good, but a little more of a curve. Your hands should be leveled between your waist and your chest."

Georgia took a step back and studied Ally's pose. "Very good. Now, do you remember Second Position?"

"No." Ally shook her head.

"Like this." Georgia showed her, mentally adding a few feet of length to that barre she had wished for earlier. "And this is Third . . ."

"Aunt Georgia, you're a good teacher," Ally told her. "See, I remember First, Second, and Third." She slid from one position into the others with motions unskilled but determined, the light of pride in her eyes.

How long ago that same light was first lit within me, Georgia reflected. *When had it started to dim?*

The afternoon's earlier fear and uncertainty began to melt away, and a calm assurance began to return and spread through her. Having lost the total joy she had once found in ballet, stepping back now *was* the right thing to do. Georgia sorely missed her routine, missed her classes, missed the exercise, but she had not been wrong to leave the troupe. She would, temporarily, seek another direction. If it led her back onto the stage, fine. If it led her someplace else, well, that would be fine, too.

For right now, she would dance with Ally. Later tonight she would seek out Gordon Chandler and ask him about his exploits. Tomorrow morning she would rise early and walk down to the beach to watch the sun rise over the ocean. Then she'd go for a long run. She'd run until her legs ached and sweated, and then she'd take her time walking back to the inn. She'd shower, have breakfast with her sister, and then she'd go back to Pumpkin Hill. All in all, tomorrow had all the makings of a very good day.

The alarm buzzed rudely in her ear the next morning, and Georgia fought the initial impulse of slapping it into silence. Knowing she had a goal that day, however, coerced her body from under the warm flannel sheets and cozy quilt and propelled her into her running clothes. The stillness of the small coastal town in this predawn hour wrapped around her, and she welcomed the sound of the surf hitting the beach as she walked across the sand. Wrapping the blanket around her as Laura had taught her to do, she sat down and soaked up the early morning sights and sounds. The majesty of the sunrise was shared with a stray gray-and-white cat that strolled down from the dunes with grand nonchalance, and an elderly fisherman who stood at the edge of the sea and tossed his line into the barely visible waves. Georgia sat back and just enjoyed.

When the first thin fingers of sunlight had finished their upward stretch into the morning sky, Georgia stood and shook the sand from the blanket. She'd drop the old quilt off on the front porch of the inn, then run for thirty minutes, all according to plan. Glancing back at the horizon as she climbed the old wooden steps at the edge of the beach, she congratulated herself on having had the good sense to give herself these moments of wonder. She had begun to feel pretty bleak, and it had perked up her spirits tremendously.

Georgia returned to the inn from her early morning run to find Laura pacing around the kitchen, the phone to her ear and a panicked look on her face.

"Was anything damaged?" Laura asked of her caller, oblivious to Georgia's return. "Was any of the equipment stolen?"

Georgia poured herself a glass of water, watching Laura with curious eyes.

"There were two vintage John Deeres and a few attachments; a plow and cultivator. Not much else. Oh, thank goodness. I'm glad they're still there." Laura caught Georgia staring and placed her hand over the receiver to explain. "Some kids broke in to the barn at Pumpkin Hill—yes, yes, Chief Monroe. I'm here. Well, if the door was still locked, how did they get in?"

Laura rolled her eyes to the ceiling and said, "I did that. I was there yesterday and I opened a window on the second floor. I forgot to close it before we left. How 'bout Matt's place? Did they get into the apartment? Oh, good. There's a blessing. . . ."

Appearing to calm slightly, Laura reached for the cup of coffee she'd left on the counter and lifted it to her lips to take a sip.

"Yes, I know . . . I suppose you're right, Chief. It has been vacant for too long. I'd hoped that Matt would be back by now, but as you know he's still living in Shawsburg. No, I have no idea when he'll be able to move back." Laura sighed a long, low sigh of resignation. "You're right, of course. I'll write up an ad and call it in to the local paper there. Yes, I'll start looking right away. Thanks, Chief."

Laura hung the phone back onto its base and turned to Georgia, saying, "One of the neighbors, on his way home from the night shift at the chicken processing plant on the other side of town, saw some lights on the second floor of the barn and called the police. They found a bunch of teenagers with a Ouija board and a few six-packs having a séance."

"I guess you're lucky that's all they found."

"Yes. We are. And as the chief just reminded me, we may not be as lucky the next time. If anyone had wondered about the status of that farm, now everyone will know for certain it's vacant—which is not a good thing."

"Did he have any suggestions?"

"Yes—that we find a tenant as soon as possible. He said with the place being vacant for so long, it's a prime target for vandalism which, sometimes, he tells me, takes the form of arson. I don't know what we'd do if anything happened to Pumpkin Hill, Georgia. It's such a big part of my family. . . ."

Laura stood and stared out the window for a long minute, then reached for the phone. "I guess I better call Matt and see if he can drive out to the farm today to meet with the Chief to see if anything has been disturbed in the house. And I want to let him know that I'll be putting an ad in the paper for someone who's looking for a short-term lease."

"What do you consider short term?" Georgia asked thoughtfully.

"Six months to a year. Hi, Matt? I'm glad I caught you before you left for the clinic. Listen, I just got a call from Chief Monroe . . ."

Georgia poured her coffee and went out through the back door. She inspected the wisteria for the first signs of green and, finding none, strolled down the path to the wide porch that wound around the front and sides of the inn. A handsome gray-haired man in an Irish knit sweater and a pair of tan corduroy slacks stood on the top steps looking in the direction of the beach.

"Good morning," he called to her as she rounded the corner of the open porch.

"Well, good morning to you, sir." Georgia smiled and climbed the steps, happy to greet the very gentleman who had been the object of her unsuccessful search the night before. "Now, would you happen to be Mr. Chandler, the same Mr. Chandler who holds the record for Most Games of Candyland Lost to a Five-year-old in One Week?"

"Ah, news travels quickly in a small town, doesn't it?" He laughed good-naturedly. "And might you be the Aunt Georgia who managed somehow to beat this same five-year-old twice in one night?"

"By luck, not by skill." Georgia grinned and took the outstretched hand he offered to her. "I'm Georgia Enright."

"Gordon Chandler," he told her, "and I am in your debt."

"How is that?"

"If not for you, I might not have found this wonderful inn."

"Well, it's pretty hard to miss. It's the only inn in Bishop's Cove."

"True. But if I hadn't stopped for coffee the morning I met you on the beach, I might not have decided to move from Ocean City, where I'd been staying in a motel, to this much more amenable, infinitely more convenient lodging, with its nightly entertainment of board games and tales told by the locals. And, I might add, the food is superb."

"Well, then, I'm glad we ran into each other on the beach. Have you been back to watch the sunrise?"

"On several mornings," he replied, nodding.

"Though I have to admit that I enjoy it a great deal more without that arctic blast that was blowing for a few days last week."

"I couldn't agree more." Georgia shivered, recalling her first morning seated on the beach in the dark, so stark a comparison to the peace of that morning's more gentle dawn. "By the way, I saw you on CNN a few months ago. The debate with the archaeologist and the congressmen . . ."

"Ah, yes. And a lively debate it was." Gordon Chandler's eyes began to twinkle.

"I'm afraid I missed much of it, so I didn't fully understand the issues."

"Oh, it's a complicated mess, that's for certain." He leaned back against the nearest porch column. "There's been a battle brewing for years between the salvagers—commercial treasure hunters—and the marine archaeologists."

"I'm not sure I understand the difference." Georgia frowned.

"As a general rule, a salvager seeks to recover sunken ships to sell off the artifacts he or she recovers for profit, whereas a marine archaeologist might want to recover that same vessel and its cargo intact to preserve it."

"And you are which?"

"Actually, I am a salvager, but I do like to think that I am a bit of a preservationist, as well. I have, in the past, sold off a limited amount of the artifacts I've found, but I've also donated a goodly portion of the bounty to interested historical groups."

"It must be hard to recover your expenses if you're giving away your loot."

Chandler laughed. "This isn't a business one enters solely to make money. Maybe at one time there might have been fortunes to be made. My grandfather and father both are perfect examples of that. But in nineteen eighty-seven the government enacted the Abandoned Shipwreck Act, which gives the coastal states the right to claim title to any ship found up to three miles offshore. These days, if you are lucky enough to locate a wreck with cargo worth pursuing, you can spend as much time negotiating to keep a portion of the artifacts as you do trying to bring it up."

"Then why do it?"

"Why breathe?" He grinned boyishly. "Why eat? Why sleep?"

Smiling, she caught his drift.

"I see," she said.

"Besides, it isn't totally without financial benefit," he explained. "I negotiated the rights to the ship I'm searching for now when I helped the state of Maryland recover several Civil War cannons from the Chesapeake a few years back. So whatever I find out there"—he nodded toward the beach—"I get to keep. Plus, I get the movie and book rights."

"My mother would be fascinated by this," Georgia told him. "She's a writer, and is always looking for interesting things to slip into her latest novel."

"Oh? Would I know her books?"

"Delia Enright."

"Of course. You did say your name was Enright. I know your mother's work well. As a matter of fact, I met her all too briefly, a few years ago, at a booksellers convention in Boston. A lovely, lovely woman, I recall," he said thoughtfully.

"She is, yes." Georgia drained the last bit of coffee from her cup. "If you're around in two weeks, you'll probably run into her. She's coming down to see Ally's school play."

"Ally?" He seemed puzzled by the connection. "Oh, of course. Laura's daughter would be—"

"Mother's granddaughter." Georgia nodded. "We're all planning on attending. The Bishop's Cove Kindergarten Spring Production is quite the thing, they tell me."

"Well, then, I'll just have to see if I can beg a ticket."

"We'd be delighted to have you join us. And I'm sure Mother will be delighted to see you again." Georgia smiled. *And if she isn't, we'll take her somewhere and have her head examined.* "Well, I think I'll go in and see if there's anything I can help Laura with this morning. It was fun talking with you. I'm sure we'll run into each other again."

"We will if you're planning on staying at the inn for a while. Or do you live here with Ally and Laura?"

"Oh, no. No. I'm just here for a visit."

"I hope it's been a pleasant one."

"It has been. Thank you," Georgia said as she opened the big front door and slipped through it.

She strolled across the oriental rug in the lobby and poked her head into the kitchen. Laura was biting her lip and tapping her fingers on the counter.

"Oh, Georgia," her face brightened. "You were going out to Pumpkin Hill today anyway for preserves. Would you mind going through the house to make certain that there was no break-in there as well? I really don't want to postpone the meeting with my mother's doctor. Matt said he'd try to reschedule some appointments if he could, but he couldn't make any promises, and Chief Monroe wanted us to check out the house as soon as possible to see if anything's been disturbed. You were there just yesterday, so you'd know right away if anyone's been in there."

"I don't mind at all." Georgia leaned on the wide wooden molding that framed the kitchen door. "As a matter of fact, I'm on my way up to shower. I'll leave as soon as I'm dressed."

"Wonderful. I'll tell the Chief that you'll meet him out there. Thank you."

"I'm happy to help." Georgia took the steps two at a time, grateful to be able to do this small thing for Laura, who had so much on her own plate: the running of the inn, an ill mother, and the full-time job of being a single parent.

Georgia wondered, not for the first time, what had happened to Laura's husband. Whenever she had inquired, Laura changed the subject without acknowledgment. As Georgia climbed the steps she reflected on the fact that there were no photos of the man anywhere, as far as she had seen, nor had Ally ever mentioned her father. *I don't even know what his name is,* she pondered as she closed her bedroom door behind her and stripped off her running clothes. Not his first name anyway. *Harmon* is his last name. Georgia had seen Ally's kindergarten report with the name Allison Hope Bishop-Harmon across the top.

Maybe this Harmon fellow had abandoned them;

slipped away and disappeared so that he wouldn't have to pay alimony and child support. *Or maybe,* Georgia thought more charitably, *he had died.* An accident, perhaps, or an illness. Curious though she was, Georgia could not bring herself to press for information concerning a subject that her sister obviously did not care to discuss. She'd asked Zoey, who had no more information but as much curiosity as Georgia herself had. She'd asked Delia, who'd been quite vague on the subject, making a comment to the effect that if and when Laura wanted to talk about it, she would, but for the life of her, Georgia couldn't understand Laura's reluctance. It appeared that Laura's husband—Ally's father—would just have to remain a mystery until such time as Laura felt inclined to enlighten her.

At the very least, it would have to wait until Georgia returned from her trip to Pumpkin Hill.

It was a relatively short, and definitely easy drive to the small country town of O'Hearn, really just two turns once you left Bishop's Cove, Georgia realized. It was less than thirty minutes from the inn to the farmhouse that sat just outside the town limits, and she turned slowly into the drive and parked alongside the house, near the fenced-in garden. Chief Monroe must not have arrived, she surmised, there being no patrol car in sight. Jiggling the keys, she swung out of the Jeep and headed for the back door, then turned back to the garden fence. Something looked different this morning. What was it?

The latchless gate, which Laura had closed the day before, had been pushed open, probably, Georgia thought, by the wind. She began to pull the gate closed, then stopped and stared at the garden that lay within the old fence. Someone had obviously paid a visit between yesterday afternoon and this morning. Here and there plants were half pushed from the ground, and the tall stalks that had stood dried and tall just the day before, now lay broken on the dirt. Fresh grooves cut into the earth at random angles, and the remains of last summer's root crop, half-eaten, were strewn messily about. The whole effect was that of hungry vandals having come through the night before to plunder. Georgia stood with her hands on her hips, wondering why someone would do such a thing.

She pulled the gate shut as tightly as she could, then turned to look at the house, wondering if perhaps the same intruders who had created such chaos in the garden and had broken into the barn had managed to get into the house, as well. Surely the police would have checked, but she decided that a cautious look around before going in was always a wise move.

The tall grass that grew around the foundation of the old farmhouse stood as upright this morning as it had the day before, showing no sign that it had been trampled flat by invading feet. Georgia strolled around the outside of the house, checking to see if all the windows and doors were intact. It appeared that the kids who had stopped by in the night had confined their pillage to the garden and a visit to the barn. Satisfied that there were no unwelcome guests lingering about, Georgia went to the back door and unlocked it with the key Laura had given her. She stepped into the kitchen, paused, then locked the door behind her. Just in case.

The early morning sun flooded through the windows to welcome her, and Georgia smiled without realizing she was doing so. The room was warm and pleasant and homey. She left her purse on the kitchen table and walked through the house to make certain that all was well. She passed through the dining room into the living room, then into the small sitting room beyond. Nothing was out of place, and she headed up the steps to check the bedrooms. The house was quiet but, oddly, did not feel vacant, as if the life that had filled this place lingered long after its occupants had departed. It was not, Georgia realized, at all disconcerting, but rather a pleasant suggestion of welcome. The feeling of ease followed her back down the steps to the kitchen, where she unlocked the basement door and turned on the light. Laura had given her a list of things to bring from the jelly cupboard downstairs, and she pulled the small piece of paper out of her pocket as she descended into the basement.

Georgia found the ancient pine cupboard just as Laura had described it, and opened the double doors. Rows of jars were aligned precisely across each of the shelves. Stacking her arms with dusty jars of the requested peach, plum, and strawberry jam, she carried them carefully up the stairs to the kitchen, where she placed them on the counter. On the second trip down she moved several jars around, searching in the dim light for the peaches Jody had asked for, and found herself marveling at the contents of the cupboard, of the jewel-like colors and the shapes that shone through the clear sides of the glass containers. There were small canning jars of deep amethyst-purple grape preserves, strawberry jam as dark and rich as garnets, and emerald green piccalilli. Larger jars of tomatoes gleamed as bright a ruby red as they had when Hope Carter had placed them there the year before. Jars of deep brown apple butter and golden peaches stood side by side on the top shelf. There was a beauty to the colors, an artistry to the arrangement, that Georgia could not define. She knew only that for some reason, it brought a smile to her face to look into those shelves and see the preserved bounty of Pumpkin Hill spread out before her. She found herself wishing that she had known the woman whose hands had created such a pattern of perfection from the fruits of the earth, and in that moment understood Laura's reluctance to empty the cupboard of its contents.

Georgia took down three large jars of peaches, two small jars of apple butter, and slipped in one of pumpkin butter as well. It would be a shame when the day finally came that these shelves stood empty, she found herself thinking as she closed the doors to the old cupboard. She went back up the steps and lined the jars up with the jams, then searched in the space under the sink for a dishcloth she could use to wipe dust from the jars. Once they were cleaned up and the cloth rinsed off, her small task complete, she was free to leave the house and could wait outside for Chief Monroe to arrive, but found herself not yet ready to lock the door behind her. What would it hurt if she sat at that old round table and had a cup of tea while she waited for the police chief to arrive?

She put water on to boil and filled the silver tea ball with loose tea. The same slightly chipped white cup she had used the day before seemed to be waiting for her on the counter where she had left it. Something about being able to do that—to use the same cup two days in a row—gave her a sense of history here, brief though it might be, and it pleased her. When the tea kettle began to scream, she turned off the burner and poured her tea, swirling the tea ball around in the bottom of the cup until the color was just right. She removed the silver ball, now hot and dripping with amber liquid, and placed it on a saucer she'd left on the counter, then sat in the chair closest to the window to sip her tea and study her surroundings.

At ten o'clock on an early spring morning, Pumpkin Hill stretched out impatiently around the farmhouse. The fields beyond the barn were ready to be plowed for spring planting, and the trees were eager for their buds. There was silence where the whine of a tractor should have filled the air, stillness where the bustle of farm life should have brought the landscape to life.

How sad, Georgia thought, *that a farm should be idle*.

Absentmindedly she picked up a photo from the windowsill and studied the face of the old woman who had brought such vitality to this place, whose passing was mourned even by the land she had left behind. There was a strength in the woman's eyes, a sureness in her smile, and Georgia quietly saluted her. She replaced the photograph on the sill, and picked up the one next to it, the one of Hope with Laura's brother, Matt. There was a third, smaller picture behind the two larger ones, and Georgia lifted it out of the sun's glare. A laughing Ally, at maybe one year old, riding atop Matt's shoulders. The same photo stood on Ally's bedside table, and when she had first seen it, Georgia had mistakenly assumed the man in the picture was Ally's father, the man and the child had seemed so in sync. She had been surprised to learn that the man was Ally's uncle. Georgia had thought at the time it was odd that Matt's picture would hold a place of honor and that Ally had no photos of her father on display.

Georgia drained the last of the tea from her cup, then rose to rinse it, pausing to gaze at the amber remains in the bottom. What had Laura said about Hope reading tea leaves? *Was there a book one could read to learn about such things?* she mused. What might that little clump of leaves near the handle signify? Or that tracing along the one side? She washed out the cup and dried it before reaching to return it to the cupboard.

The sound of tires crunching on the pebbled drive drew her attention, and she pulled aside the curtain just in time to see the local law emerge from a dark blue police car. She left the warmth of the kitchen and went out the back door.

"Hello!" she called. "Chief Monroe?"

"Yes." The short, middle-aged officer with a slight paunch removed his police cap as he walked across the yard toward Georgia. "You must be Georgia. Laura called and said you'd be waiting. Have you had a chance to look around?"

"Yes. The house is fine. No sign of anyone even going near it. There is something I think you should see over here, though." Georgia pointed to the garden. "It looks like someone went on a tear in here."

Chief Monroe went to the fence and peered over it. "*Hmmph.* Would you look at that?"

He pushed open the gate and walked up and down the disheveled rows. "*Hmmph,*" he said again.

"Why do you suppose they did that?" Georgia asked, pointing to the uprooted plants.

Chief Monroe shook his head. "Doesn't look like kids did this. For one thing, they swore they didn't do anything but sneak into the barn. Said they never came near the house, and from what you're telling me, they didn't. I'll ask them about the garden, but to tell you the truth, it doesn't look like something kids would do in the dark, you know what I mean?"

"Well, it's curious, Chief. Laura and I were here yesterday, and the garden was just as neat as . . . as if it had been tended last week."

"I'll ask the kids again." He nodded slowly. "In the meantime, we'll keep an eye on the place as best we can. But as I reminded Laura, we're a very small, rural department and don't have a lot of man-hours to spare. She and Matt should make some sort of arrangements to secure the property. Last night's group wanted nothing more than a place to drink a few beers. Who's to say that the next time someone won't get careless with a cigarette? It would be a terrible shame if something were to happen to the barn or to the old farmhouse. The Evans place has been part of this community for two hundred years. I'll do my best to look after it, but I sure wish Laura would rent the place out. At least there'd be someone on the premises, know what I mean?"

Georgia knew what he meant.

She thanked him as he got back into his car and waved good-bye as if to an old friend when he turned the car around and headed down the drive to the narrow country road that would lead him back into town.

Georgia loaded the glass jars of preserves carefully into the Jeep in two trips, then returned to the house to lock up, making one last round through the first floor, reluctant to leave. This was a house that had been filled with purpose, with peace, and she felt the comfort of both. Having no real reason to stay on, and knowing that Jody was awaiting the bounty from Hope's cupboard, Georgia left through the back door, locked it behind her, and climbed back into the Jeep. She pulled out of the driveway and headed toward Bishop's Cove, hardly noticing the battered black pickup that sped past her in the opposite direction just as she entered the first curve in the road.

"Why do you suppose someone would do that?" Laura frowned after Georgia told her about the mayhem she'd found in the garden. "I really hate it that there's no one there. I wish Matt could come back and take over."

"Why can't he?" Georgia asked.

"Matt trained under a truly wonderful vet when he was in school. Dr. Espey was very, very good to him, helped him out in many ways. Matt did his internship with him, and planned to open his own clinic at Pumpkin Hill. Dr. Espey had a stroke last fall, and

Matt stayed on to keep his clinic running. He'll stay there as long as Dr. Espey wants him to. As much as I hate having the farm vacant, I couldn't ask Matt to come back while he's still needed there. Dr. Espey loves Matt like a son, and Matt loves him like a second father." Laura tapped her fingers on the counter. "I wrote out an ad for the local paper. I think I'll run it in the *Baltimore Sun,* as well. Here. Read it over. How does this sound?"

Tenant wanted! 97 acres with fully furnished farmhouse, barn, chicken house. Available immediately. Please call . . .

"Does that sound too desperate?" Laura frowned.

"It sounds to the point."

"You know, I hate the thought of strangers moving in to Aunt Hope's house. Sleeping in her bed. Using the things she used, things that have been in our family for so many years. I guess we'll have to take a weekend and pack up the things of sentimental value so that her dishes and her collection of old cut-glass vases don't get broken or stolen. I really do hate this, Georgia. I just don't have much choice."

"Actually, you do." Georgia said softly.

"How do you figure?"

"Why not rent the farm to me?" The words were out of Georgia's mouth before she could give herself a chance to change her mind about the idea that had been blossoming inside her since she had poured that cup of tea in the old kitchen just a few hours earlier. "I'll be your tenant. I'll stay at Pumpkin Hill."

"But why would you want to do that? It's miles from everything, it's in the middle of nowhere . . ."

"The middle of nowhere is fine for now. I've been

wanting to get away from the city, have some time to myself. Why not Pumpkin Hill?"

"Are you sure?"

"I'm positive." Georgia nodded. "I thought about it on the way back today. I like it there. I like the way I feel when I'm there. It's exactly the feeling I left Baltimore to find."

"But your condo . . ."

"I'll call my friend Lee. He always seems to know someone coming in from out of town—dancers, actors—looking for a furnished place to lease for a few months."

"Georgia, I'd be delighted to have you at the farm. Thrilled, to tell you the truth."

"Good. Then we're both delighted. You have your tenant and I have a lovely old farm all to myself. We both win. Call Chief Monroe and call your brother and tell them that neither of them has to worry. I'll drive back to Baltimore tomorrow to get my things together, then I'll move in over the weekend, if that's all right with you."

"That would be wonderful. Great." Laura nodded as Georgia hugged her and happily skipped from the room.

"Great," Laura repeated to herself as she reached for the phone to place a call to the police to let them know the farm would be inhabited by the weekend.

Then she'd have to call Matt. Laura grimaced at the thought of it.

Telling Matt that she'd found a tenant was one thing. Telling him that she'd agreed to lease Pumpkin Hill to Georgia Enright was something else.

chapter seven

Georgia's move from her Baltimore condo to Pumpkin Hill was relatively painless and without complication. With the help of her sister Zoey, who had a rare weekend off from her job as a sales host for the nationally televised Home MarketPlace home shopping network, it took but two days to pack clothes, books, music, and some personal items. As she had hoped, Lee did in fact know of a stage actor who would be in Baltimore for six months in an off-Broadway production and was eager to find a place to hang his hat while he was in the city. As she locked the condo door behind her, Georgia had handed the key to Lee so that he could show the apartment to the actor on the following Tuesday.

By mobilizing her family and packing each of their cars with boxes, suitcases and garment bags, Georgia was able to make the move in one trip. Mrs. Colson, her mother's housekeeper, had piled hampers of food for the moving crew into the back of Delia's car. Once the move was completed, a wonderful midafternoon feast awaited, reheated and served by Nick's wife, India, and her aunt, August Devlin, on the old pine table in the dining room at Pumpkin Hill.

"Just look at the view you have from these windows!" Delia had exclaimed as she had gone from room to room. "Why, in a month or so, the trees will be all leafed out and there will be buds on those apple trees. And those lilacs will be in bloom before too long . . . do make sure you cut bunches of them and bring them inside." Delia sniffed at the imaginary scent and sighed. "Heaven!"

"Not bad, Georgia," her brother had remarked, nodding his approval after making the obligatory inspection of the farmhouse's mechanics and locks. "It's secure and well maintained. Of course, we'd all feel better if you weren't living here alone. . . ."

"Or at the very least, get a dog," Zoey suggested.

"We'll loan you one of ours," Ben Pierce, Zoey's fiancé, volunteered. "I'll bring Dozer to visit for a while. By the time you're ready to send him back, maybe you'll have him housebroken."

"Ah, thanks, guys," Georgia laughed, "but I don't think I want to take on the responsibility of a dog right now. Besides, I don't know how long I'll be here."

"I thought you didn't really have an official lease." Six months pregnant, the diminutive India sagged against the doorway for support.

"We don't." Georgia nodded somewhat absently as she sorted through the boxes. "We're basically taking it month to month, but who knows where I'll go from here? Nick," she turned to her brother, "would you carry these boxes of clothes upstairs for me?"

"Sure." He hoisted a carton onto his shoulder. "Which bedroom are you using?"

Georgia paused to ponder this. The rooms she had seen on the second floor—Laura's old room and those of Matt and the departed Aunt Hope—had all seemed to still belong to someone else. She wouldn't feel comfortable moving in to any one of them. The guest room would have to do.

"You could leave everything in that front bedroom," she told Nick. "The one to the right of the steps."

"How 'bout these boxes of books?" Zoey asked.

"Just leave them in the living room."

"Your stereo?"

"Living room." Georgia nodded.

"Are you sure you have enough juice for all that electronic equipment?" Nick stood in the doorway with his hands on his hips, mentally trying to calculate the power requirements of the stereo with its CD, tape, and recording components, the television and VCR combination, and the microwave oven that Laura and Ben were carrying into the kitchen. "Sometimes old places like this have low wattage electrical service."

"Oh, it shouldn't be a problem." Laura poked her head through doorway. "My aunt had the service upgraded to two hundred amps about five years ago when she got the new refrigerator and stove, so there's more than enough for whatever electronic toys you brought with you. The service even runs out to the barn."

"Well, then, I can just hook up that CD player and

serenade the wild cats you mentioned." Georgia grinned.

"Mommy, Corri found an old can in the barn that has a momma mouse and babies in it!" A breathless Ally flew into the house through the back door.

"She didn't bring it in here, did she?" Delia, who'd been leaning over a box of table linens on the dining room floor, stood up and appeared to cringe slightly.

"No. But she wants to take them home," Ally said wide-eyed. "Can she do that?"

"No!" August and India responded in unison.

"We have plenty of mice of our own in Devlin's Light," India told Ally. "Tell Corri to put the can back where she found it, and then come in to get cleaned up to eat."

"And both of you leave your shoes out on the back porch," Laura called after her daughter, who was fleeing toward the barn to relay instructions.

"Take a can of mice babies back home!" India shivered. "What will that child think of next?"

"Georgia, what do you want me to do with these tablecloths you brought with you?" Delia asked.

"There are tons of things there in the sideboard," Laura pointed out. "Leave your things packed and use Aunt Hope's."

"Oh, I wouldn't want to do that," Georgia told her. "Besides, I'm not planning on any social event more formal than this little feast we're having this afternoon. Nope, after today, it's that lovely little nook in the kitchen for me, where I can watch the birds—"

"Damn. I meant to buy some birdseed for those feeders." Laura made a face to express her displeasure at having forgotten.

"I'll get some tomorrow," Georgia said.

"Go into Tanner's right in the middle of town," Laura told her. "Tell Mr. Tanner you're living here and that you want to set up an account."

"What's Tanner's?" Georgia stepped around India on her way to the sink to fill the coffeepot with water.

"It's the general store in O'Hearn. It carries just about everything, including hardware, videos and books, and food—human and livestock. You can't miss it. It's in a big red building that looks sort of like a barn."

"Speaking of barns, I think I'll go on over and get the two girls," India said.

"I'll go with you." Nick put his arm around his wife. "It will give us an opportunity to look around the rest of Georgia's new domain."

"Aren't they just perfect together?" Zoey sighed as she watched her brother and sister-in-law wander down the drive. "And isn't India perfectly adorable with that little baby-tummy?"

"Does India know whether she is having a boy or a girl?" Laura asked.

"No." Delia shook her head. "She wants to be surprised."

"Another little girl in the family would be fun," Georgia mused. "Maybe with India's blond curls and Nicky's soft brown eyes . . ."

"Or a little boy with dark hair like Nick's, and India's sweet smile . . . ," Delia offered. "What fun to anticipate. I love both of my granddaughters dearly, but they both came to me after the fact, so to speak. This is the first time I've been able to dream over a baby that's on it's way, and I rather like it."

Delia pushed aside one of the living room curtains and watched as Corri and Ally spilled from the barn door and ran toward the edge of the back field where Nick stood with his arms around his wife. Corri—the adopted daughter of first India's brother, then of India when her brother Ry had died—had become her granddaughter when Nick had married India. That she was not of Delia's blood had made no difference to her. The child was Nick's and India's, and therefore she was Delia's, as well. Delia had found Ally when her private detective had located Laura. Finding her firstborn had been nothing short of a miracle to Delia, and finding Ally had been the icing on the cake. Delia watched the children from the window of the old farmhouse and felt her heart swell. There was nothing—nothing that could take the place of a close and loving family, and she thanked the heavens for the joy of sharing a day in the country with her loved ones.

Smiling at her good fortune, Delia hummed as she went in search of her jacket. She would join the children outside and perhaps do a little exploring with them. Ally had mentioned a special tree that grew in the middle of the back field, and Laura had spoken of a pond. The clouds of the morning had been burned off by an unseasonably warm sun. It would be a good day to walk with her granddaughters and see what they could see.

Delia found her jacket on the back of one of the dining room chairs, and swung it over her shoulder as she walked through the kitchen on her way outside. Laura, Georgia, Zoey, and Ben were trudging down to the basement in search of some of Hope's preserves, and Delia could hear their arguments over what kind to open. She smiled at the sound of the good-natured bickering and sighed happily, so content on this day. She paused in the kitchen, then poured herself a fresh cup of steaming coffee to take along on her walk, reflecting on recent events.

Delia had been initially concerned about Georgia's decision to back away from dance, and needed to assure herself that her youngest child was making a decision she could live with for however long she chose to stay away. Georgia's announcement had been unexpected, but it was not necessarily a bad thing.

Georgia had chosen to deny herself much of her childhood, had all but skipped her teen years to concentrate on her love for the dance. If she felt she needed to explore her options, then explore she should. And Pumpkin Hill was a grand place for such reflection, with its wide fields and fresh air and peaceful solitude of the very best sort. A person could think here, could turn their sights inside and see what they were made of, where they had been, and where they wanted to go. Yes, Delia conceded, Georgia would be fine here, for however long she needed to stay.

Reaching across the kitchen table for the sugar bowl, Delia's sight fell upon the photos lined up across the window ledge. She lifted the one closest to her, the one of Matt and Hope, much as Georgia had done. Not for the first time, she regretted never having met Hope Evans Carter.

"You watched over one of my daughters for many a summer," Delia whispered to the weathered face in the photograph. "Would it be too much for me to ask for you to look after another one of my girls now?"

Delia returned the photo to its place on the ledge, her eyes lingering on the image of Matt Bishop's smiling face.

"And as for you, my fine fellow," she said softly to the photo, "don't you think for a minute that we'll let you remain outside the fold for much longer. Sooner or later, one of us will find a way around that barrier you've erected, and we'll draw you in. It's cold out there alone, Matthew, and there's lots of love here to be shared. And you may not know it now, but we will need each other if we are to help Laura over the months ahead. There's something . . . *something* not quite right, I see it in her face. So you see, my boy, it's really only a matter of time. . . ."

Matt dragged one hand through his dark hair and made a mental note that he'd gone far too long between haircuts. It was eleven-thirty on Saturday night and he was tired clear down to the bone. Up at three A.M. following a frantic phone call from a breeder of Lhasa apsos whose champion show bitch had gone into a troubled labor, he'd driven through a nasty storm to get to the breeder's home in time to whelp the litter, only two puppies of which had survived. From there he had gone into the clinic, stopping first at a local convenience store only long enough to grab a large coffee to go and arriving just in time to see his first appointment, a collie with chronic hepatitis.

The day had spun past at a dizzying pace. Because

it was Saturday, his last patient had been scheduled for noon. Unfortunately, he'd already been running a half hour late when his eleven-thirty appointment— routine inoculations for a springer spaniel—was interrupted by a motorist who'd struck a Gordon setter about a quarter mile down the road from the clinic and wanted help for the setter, who was still lying where he'd been hit. Matt made his apologies to the owner of the springer and drove the pickup to the scene of the accident. The setter was badly injured and required immediate surgery. Fortunately, Liz had been able to track the dog's owner from the address on the tag that hung from the collar, and Matt had the permission he needed to start working on the dog. He'd been in surgery for four hours. Once finished, he had just enough time to run home, shower and change, and drive a half hour to attend the local SPCA's annual fund-raising banquet, where he'd given a speech about responsible pet ownership.

Now, as the clock neared midnight, Matt was drained. Too tired to read, too tired to talk. Too tired to move. He fell asleep in his favorite chair and slept until Artie woke him to be let out at six in the morning. Matt stood in the doorway, looking out over the yard behind his rented house. Dense fog hung like fat damp clouds over the grass and cast an eerie glow over a quiet Sunday morning. Even Artie was subdued, going about his business in an efficient manner, for once not pausing to sniff at places where others might have been during the night, and returned to where his master stood without even waiting for Matt to call him.

Padding back through the kitchen on quiet feet still wrapped in dark blue socks, Matt paused to open the refrigerator and study its contents, and was pleased to find a forgotten bowl of leftover spaghetti on the second shelf behind a container of sour cream.

"Ah, the breakfast of champions," he beamed as he reached for the bowl of spaghetti, which he ate cold.

Feeling better but still tired, he walked back through the living room, unbuttoning his dress shirt from the night before. The light on his answering machine was blinking, and he hit it as he passed by. The only message of any note was one from Laura, telling him that she'd found a tenant for Pumpkin Hill and Matt could call her for the details. Matt paused in midstride. He didn't need details; a tenant was a tenant. Matt had not been the least bit happy over the prospect of renting out the family farm, but after the break-in at the barn the week before, he had been forced to face the fact that leaving the property vacant could well be a heartache waiting to happen. Although he tried to drive out to O'Hearn once a week, his responsibilities at the clinic sometimes prevented him from making the trip.

But there was another trip on his agenda once a week, one that nothing ever deterred him from taking. And this morning, he would take that trip out to Riverview to see his mother. Hopeful that perhaps this week she'd know who he was, Matt pulled off his shirt and headed for the shower.

Matt stood in the dayroom of the nursing home— the brochures called it a "total care facility"—and studied the delicate face of the woman who sat staring out the window, and he felt his heart break just a little more. He'd come to know by the look on her face what to expect from any given visit. Today, he knew, she was in a world all her own. He wished that she could take him there with her. Anywhere with his mother would have been welcome, if only just for a little while. He inhaled sharply and stepped into the room, making his way around the other residents, who sat in no particular order in wheelchairs here and there around the dayroom.

"Mom," he said as he knelt down next to her chair.

She blinked, then turned and looked at him blankly. "Hello," she said pleasantly.

"It's me, Mom. It's Matt."

Just as pleasantly, she said, "Oh. Hello, Matt."

His heart sank. He hated when she didn't know him, hated the fact that he could be anyone stopping by and he'd get the same response from her. He hated the disease that had taken his mother and left this stranger in her body. He knew that, if she could *know*—could be aware of what had happened to her—that she would have hated it, too.

"Did you have your breakfast yet?" he asked as he pulled up an orange plastic chair to sit close to her.

"No." She shook her head.

"Would you like me to ask the nurse to bring you something?" He took her tiny hands and rubbed them gently with his own.

"That would be nice," she said and smiled, melting his heart.

"You wait right here, and I'll see if I can find someone." He patted her hands and placed them in her lap, where she left them.

"Excuse me," he flagged down an attendant in the hallway. "I was wondering if I might get some breakfast for my mother."

"Everyone's already had breakfast," the young male orderly told him.

"My mother says she hasn't."

"You better check with the nurses, then." The young man pointed to the nurses' station down the hall.

"Excuse me . . ." Matt approached the desk.

The pretty brunette nurse looked up and smiled. Matt smiled back.

"I'd like to get some breakfast for my mother."

"Breakfast was served at eight this morning," she told him.

"My mother said she hasn't eaten. . . ."

"Who's your mother?" she asked.

"Charity Bishop."

"Mrs. Bishop ate in the small dining room with Mrs. Hanson and Mr. Samuels and a few others," she told him, then added gently, "It isn't unusual that she'd forget."

"But are you sure . . . ?"

"Oh, positive. I saw her there when I came on my shift at eight. She definitely ate. She has an excellent appetite, I might add."

Matt thanked her and, shoving his hands into his pockets, walked back down the hall to the dayroom.

"Mom, the nurse said you ate breakfast with your friends earlier," he told her as he sat down.

She frowned. "I don't think I did. No, I'm certain I did not."

She was so sincere that, for a moment, Matt thought perhaps the nurse had made a mistake. But then he recalled how many other things she had forgotten—like the names and faces of her children—and realized that she simply could not remember.

"She'll bring something in a while," he told her, patting her hands again.

"Thank you." She smiled sweetly.

"In the meantime, while we wait, how 'bout if I get you some tea, and we can visit for a while?"

"That would be very nice." She nodded.

He went back into the hallway, down two doors to the small snack bar where he purchased two overpriced cups of tea and some shortbread cookies in a red plaid wrapper. *Maybe she had eaten, but if she feels as if she had not,* he rationalized, *perhaps she's hungry.*

He took the tray back to the dayroom and placed it on a nearby table. Her eyes had a faraway look, and he bit his bottom lip to hide his disappointment.

"The tea will be cool enough to drink in a few minutes," he told her as he sat down. "Now, I'm sure it isn't as good as the tea that Hope used to make—"

"Who?" she asked.

"Hope." He sighed. "Your sister."

"Oh."

"Do you remember Hope?"

She looked confused, and did not answer.

"There was a break-in at the barn," he told her, waiting to see her reaction to the news.

"Oh?"

"Yes. Nothing was stolen—actually, it was just a

bunch of kids who got in through a window that Laura left open. They climbed a ladder to the second floor and spent the night drinking beer and having a little party for themselves." He paused. When she did not respond to this news, he added, "Chief Monroe has convinced Laura and me that the best thing to do would be to rent out the farm. So that's what we're doing. There will be a tenant living at Pumpkin Hill, Mom."

"Do you live there . . ."

Matt could tell that she was struggling, so he told her his name again. "Matt."

"Matt," she repeated, adding, "That's a nice name."

"Thank you." He smiled weakly. "I live in Shawsburg. With Artie. Do you remember Artie? My dog?"

"No," she told him, her eyes brightening just a little. "But someone . . ."—she appeared to struggle, then shrugged it off—"has birds here. Would you like to see them?"

"I'd love to. Where are they?"

She frowned. "We'll have to find them. Would you like to push me in this . . ." She tapped the arm of the chair, searching for the word.

"Wheelchair," he helped her out.

"Yes." She pointed to the door. "I think the birds are out there somewhere. Maybe they'll be singing. I do love it when they sing. . . ."

All the way home, Matt thought about a canary a neighbor had given to him on his seventh birthday. That bird sang from the second that Charity removed the cover from its cage in the morning until she covered it up again at night. Nonstop. All day. Every day. It drove everyone crazy. Except for Charity.

"It's all that poor thing can do," she would tell them when they complained. "All it knows is how to sing. And as beautiful as his song is, as much as I love to listen to him, I can't stand to see him in that cage. I wish Mrs. Carsen had asked before she bought it for you. It bothers me to keep wild things in a cage."

Charity would linger for a moment at the side of the cage and watch him. The bird would watch her, its head bent slightly to the side as if it understood that she was the one who not only appreciated his music, but sympathized with his captive plight. Then the bird would begin to sing again. It wasn't long before Charity was letting the bird out of the cage for a few hours every day. And it wasn't long after that, that the bird had flown straight out the front door when Matt had come in after school one day.

Matt thought of that now, of how she had offered to buy him another birthday present to replace the bird, but she had never apologized for having set it free.

He thought of the days after his father had died, when he had watched her wander up onto the beach at Bishop's Cove, where she would walk along the water's edge—a shoe swinging from each hand, the wind whipping her hair around her head—lost in her grief.

Charity had been a woman who had appreciated freedom for all things, and who had celebrated her own. That she was now restricted to the confines of a room or two, with only an occasional trip outside, brought tears to his eyes. It seemed so unfair that age and disease had taken so much of what she once had been; of all she had loved and treasured.

The only good thing, he realized, was that she had no idea of how much she had lost. If she did, he suspected, it would probably kill her.

chapter eight

Upon waking early that first morning in the front bedroom at Pumpkin Hill, Georgia had been slightly unnerved by the unfamiliar sounds that enveloped her new surroundings. In place of the street noise she'd become accustomed to back in Baltimore—the cars, the sirens wailing off in the distance signaling that some unfortunate soul was on his way to jail or to the nearest emergency room—she heard only birdsongs that wafted into the room on a morning breeze. All in all, she thought, it was not a bad trade.

She lifted her arms over her head in a healthy stretch, then sat up, dangling her legs over the side of the ancient poster bed with its lumpy mattress and feather pillows that felt as if they could have been original to the farmhouse. Standing, she tried to work out the kinks in her neck and in her back, mulling over the inevitability of buying a new mattress, even if she was planning on staying at Pumpkin Hill for

143

only a limited time. She couldn't start every new day feeling as if she'd slept on the floor.

Leaning on the wide ledge of the side window and looking out at the first minutes of the new day, she grinned, lured by its prospect. The sun had risen gently—certainly not with the spectacular flair one might find on the beach at Bishop's Cove—but with the same promise of a fine day ahead. The weather report had predicted temperatures would rise close to sixty—a veritable heat wave—which would be just right to do some exploring. She changed into jeans and a flannel shirt and sat on the edge of the bed to put on her sneakers. She groaned, swearing she could feel the bed rails through the quilt.

She would definitely have to look into a new mattress.

Breakfast was coffee and two of Mrs. Colson's biscuits left over from the night before. She would have to drive into O'Hearn and do a little food shopping before lunch, she thought as she dribbled some of Hope's delicious apple butter onto first one, then the other biscuit, or lunch would be a repeat of breakfast.

Unlocking the back door, Georgia stepped outside and inhaled deeply, filling her lungs and sighing with the sheer pleasure of that first cool rush of fresh morning air. She sipped at her coffee as she strolled down the path leading from the back door, then stopped and frowned. The garden gate stood open again. She walked toward it tentatively, then peered over the fence. It startled her to see the plants that Laura had braced up with sticks only the day before lying broken and trampled on the ground.

The vandals had returned while she had slept alone in the farmhouse. The realization made the hairs on the back of her neck stand straight up.

She went back into the farmhouse and searched for the telephone book, which she found in a drawer in the front hall table. She called Chief Monroe, who promised he'd be around as soon as the morning rush hour was over. Georgia was tempted to ask how many cars constituted a traffic jam in O'Hearn, Maryland, but decided against it.

That someone had sneaked back onto the farm— maybe even walking beneath the windows of the very room she had slept in—had annoyed and puzzled her. How had someone managed to accomplish this without her having heard? Even if they had come on foot, she'd slept with the window partially open, and was a very light sleeper. Back in Baltimore, she'd often be awakened by the sound of the elevator landing on her floor, even though her apartment had been three doors down from the lobby and her bed was in the far back room.

Maybe Ben was right. Maybe she should think about getting a dog.

She refilled her cup with the last of the coffee and went outside to wait for Chief Monroe.

Early spring really was the best time of the year, she decided. There was a newness that had settled on everything at Pumpkin Hill, and it cheered her even as she paced the farmyard, waiting for the police to arrive.

Maybe it would be fun to have chickens, she thought as she wandered by the old chicken house. Maybe she would plant something in the big vegetable garden that Laura said her aunt always planted out behind the barn. Tomatoes, maybe, and maybe some green beans. Zucchini was a favorite. And cantaloupe . . .

She rounded the corner of the barn and stopped in horror. The devastation in the flower garden was nothing compared with the mess she found in the vegetable garden. Everything that had remained from last year's planting had been ripped out by the roots, and the flattened stalks of dried vegetation lay scattered everywhere. She could do little more than stand and stare. Why would someone do something like this?

Maybe, she rationalized, *there were homeless people living in the woods*. But then, wouldn't they have moved into the obviously vacant house? Or at least sought shelter in the barn?

The sound of the police cruiser's tires crunching on the stone drive drew her to the side of the barn, where she waited for Chief Monroe, wondering what he'd think of this latest bit of vandalism.

"Now, that does beat all." He scratched his head. "And no footprints that I can see. Must be some kind of animal. That'd be my guess. Maybe a raccoon, though I've never known one to make this sort of mess. Deer will raid a garden, but I've yet to see one open a gate. I'll ask around when I get back to town and see if anyone else has had a similar problem. And I'll check in with the kids we picked up the other night. They swear they went nowhere near the garden, but won't do harm if I ask again. Maybe see where they were last night, while I'm at it. In the meantime, just make sure you keep the doors locked and the phone handy. Don't hesitate to call me, now."

Chief Monroe patted her on the back as he walked toward his car, whose radio had begun to squawk. "A dog might be a good idea," he called over his shoulder.

"I'll think about it," she told him.

"County SPCA always has some nice ones," he added as he got in the car. "And don't forget to call Laura and let her know."

That would wait, she decided. Laura had enough to worry about. For now, Georgia would clean up the mess in the garden behind the barn, then she'd make that trip into O'Hearn for groceries. Then, if there was any time left, she'd relax in that wing chair in the living room and read the book on fortune-telling she'd found on one of the shelves before she went to bed last night. She'd been too tired to read through that marked section on reading tea leaves, but tonight she wouldn't be.

Georgia unlocked the barn using the padlock key that Laura had given her, and poked her head in just to make sure that no one lurked within. Satisfied that she was alone, she stepped in and took a sturdy rake down from the wall, where it hung alongside other implements used for turning over the earth. She knew what the hoe and the shovels were for, but some of the other implements looked more like weapons than garden tools. She locked the padlock behind her and set off for her first task of the day.

By the time she realized that she lacked the most important tool for the job at hand—a good pair of gloves—her palms were already red and chafed, her soft hands just about to erupt into the blisters she could feel working beneath the surface of her skin. She looked around to gauge the morning's accomplishment. She'd gathered up all of the tall dried stalks and piled them high for the trash, then raked up the lesser debris. Not quite pretty, but certainly much tidier than how she'd found it. Mentally she added trash bags onto her shopping list, and absently brushed the dirt from her hands onto the seat of her pants.

Not so bad for my first morning, she nodded, grateful for the feeling that for the first time in days, she had accomplished something useful.

Maybe just a quick tour of the farm, she thought. *Laura said it was ninety-something acres, but so far I've only seen the area around the house and the barn.*

In the field behind the barn, the ancient tree with the enormous canopy stood proudly. *The wishing tree,* Laura had called it. Georgia headed for the tree, picking her way through the furrows left in the dirt by the last plowing, wondering what had been the last crop Hope Evans had planted there, and wondering when these fields might be planted again.

The wishing tree was an impressive sight from far away, but even more so from directly under its sprawling, leafless branches. The bark was deep gray-brown and closely ridged, like a freeway design gone wild. At its base, roots twisted just slightly from the ground, and the first spring grass sprouted from the spaces between the gnarled elevations of tree root and earth. Georgia sat on one of these outcroppings of root, and gazed around at her new home.

The tree stood like an oasis in the middle of the field that spread back to woods on two sides. Off to her left, a pond lay nestled in the fuzzy remains of last year's cattails. Straight ahead were the farmhouse and its outbuildings, as close to a living postcard as anything she'd ever seen. Laura had told her that by the end of the summer, the apple, peach, and cherry trees would be laden with fruit. Maybe, she mused, she could find Hope's recipes and she could make jams to line the cupboard in the basement, to replace the ones Laura had taken back to the inn. Just for this one summer, she could learn to make apple butter and raise her own vegetables. She pictured herself at the end of the summer, tanned and lean from farm-work, and she smiled.

Georgia leaned forward and hugged her knees, tingling with an unexpected flush of contentment. *This is a good place,* she told herself, *the right place for me to be. A person could find herself here—could heal here—could learn and grow here.*

Hopeful that she would, in fact, be able to do just that, she stood and brushed off the back of her jeans then headed toward the farmhouse. She'd make that trip into O'Hearn now, and when she got back, she'd make a list of things that she wanted to accomplish while she was here at Pumpkin Hill. A favorite Chopin piano concerto began to play in her head as she walked the narrow rows, and she began an extemporaneous dance. A *soubresault*—a sudden leap straight upward and forward—followed a *pirouette*— no small accomplishment in running shoes—and she giggled at the very thought of how she must look in her jeans and flannel shirt as she danced across the field, choreographing her steps to the silent tune playing out in her head. Her arms reached upward in perfect form *en haut*—high above her head—while her feet found it difficult to *glissade* through the clumps of dirt. By the time she reached the edge of the field she was laughing out loud at her clumsy efforts.

Georgia walked through the back door of the farmhouse in search of her car keys and the cell phone, sobering as she sought to remember the last time dancing had been such fun.

Having spent several hours with his mother, Matt felt drained to his soul. It was all he could do to maintain a cheerful attitude while he was with her. Leaving her there in the care of strangers bothered him in ways he'd never been able to express. This was the same woman who had reached in and rescued him from hell; the woman who had taught him who he was, how to love. Every time he walked through the front doors of Riverview, he felt physically ill and depressed. How could he turn his back on her, abandon her to strangers, after all she had done for him?

On a strictly intellectual level, Matt recognized that neither he nor Laura was equipped to deal with their mother's special needs at this stage of her illness. Somehow, even that knowledge didn't make him feel better; did not, in his eyes, let either of them off the hook. All it did was to serve to confuse him even more. He drove back to Shawsburg with the windows of the pickup down, hoping that the March breezes would clear his head and let him forgive himself for leaving Charity behind. They did not. There was only one thing that would.

He stopped at his house only long enough to pick up Artie before making the drive to Pumpkin Hill.

The old farm never failed to restore him, and he figured he could use a little rejuvenation right now. He was tired and ornery and wanted nothing more than a few hours alone with his dog and the wind that would blow across the empty fields of his family home. Anxious to get there, he stepped on the gas, grateful that it was, after all, Sunday, and traffic would be light. He'd reach his destination in less than thirty minutes, and he'd have the entire day to himself.

Matt pulled the pickup all the way to the end of the drive, and turned off the engine. Eager to romp, Artie flew out of the cab and off into the fields, while Matt checked out the barn. Satisfied that the kids who had broken in had meant no real harm, he checked the padlock before going up the steps to his apartment. He paused on the landing and looked back down. The barn was quiet without the rustle of his aunt's pygmy goats. Someday soon, he hoped, they'd be able to bring them home. And someday, he'd set up his own veterinary clinic right here at Pumpkin Hill.

He closed his eyes and, for the thousandth time, pictured in his head the way the farm had been when his aunt was still alive, with animals in the barn and every field and garden alive with growth. There was something disturbing about a silent barn, about fallow fields, and gardens where weeds were taking over. Someday, he promised himself, Pumpkin Hill would once again bustle with life. Someday. He would see to it.

Unlocking the door to his apartment, Matt stepped into the quiet rooms beyond. He paused in the kitchen to open the window, then made a quick round to make sure that nothing was amiss. Grateful that this very private space—his since he had claimed it right out of high school, his all through college— had not been violated by strangers, he opened the bedroom windows to bring in fresh air, then stripped off the shirt he'd worn that morning and folded it neatly before placing it on the end of the bed. He opened a dresser drawer and pulled out an old sweatshirt, then changed from his khakis into a pair of well-worn jeans. Feeling better, he went down the steps, whistling for Artie.

Matt walked to the farmhouse and let himself in with his key. A faint scent of something led him into the kitchen, where he was surprised to find a half pot of coffee in the coffeemaker, and a cup on the counter. Frowning, he checked to make sure that the pot was turned off. It was. Without a second thought, he rinsed out the cup in the sink. His hands on his hips, he walked through the dining room, where boxes sat here and there on the floor, then into the living room, where more boxes were piled and several books had been left on the footrest near his favorite wing chair near the fireplace.

He frowned again. Laura had said that she'd found a tenant, but not that said tenant had moved in.

He picked the books up from the stool and idly

glanced at the titles. *Secrets of Gypsy Fortune-telling. Crystals and Card Reading.* Aunt Hope's books.

The tenant was reading Matt's aunt's favorite books—while sitting in Matt's own favorite chair—and Matt didn't like it one bit.

He replaced the books on the shelves and walked to the bottom of the steps and called upstairs. "Hello? Is anyone here?" No reply.

"Is anyone up there?" Silence.

He wondered what room the tenant had claimed, and hoped it wasn't his. Or his aunt's. Or Laura's for that matter. Feeling foolish for caring, Matt took the steps in long strides and peered into each doorway until he found the room with the open suitcase on the foot of the unmade bed. Grateful that the tenant had at least had the good sense to choose the guest room and *not* sleep in someone else's bed, he almost forgave him—or her, he didn't know which, he realized—the fact that the quilt was hanging half off the bed. He was sorely tempted to make the bed, but he fought the urge and went back downstairs. The tenant was obviously elsewhere.

He locked the back door and whistled for Artie, who came flying around the corner of the barn, a happy grin on his big, silly dog-face.

"Ah, you're happy to be back too, aren't you boy?" Matt bent down on one knee and gave Artie a scratch behind one ear. "How 'bout if we take a walk down to the pond and see if the ducks are back?"

Artie was sniffing maniacally around the small fenced-in garden. Matt peered over the fence and sighed in disgust at the mess. He could have sworn that Chief Monroe had said that the kids hadn't gone near the house, but Aunt Hope's kitchen garden had clearly been the object of some kind of tear. He'd make sure he mentioned it to the Chief when he stopped down at the police station later on.

"Come on, boy." He called to Artie, who sped past him, nose to the ground as if on a scent, and set off across the field. Maybe he'd make a stop at the wishing tree, though he knew in his heart that the things he had wished for that day could never come true.

It would be enough, Matt reasoned, if a few hours at Pumpkin Hill would take the heaviness from his heart. More than enough, if he left later that day having found just a touch of that serenity that had always been there for him over the years. He whistled to Artie, who'd taken off toward the woods, and the dog ran back to him, chasing down to the pond where his sudden appearance startled the flock of Canada geese that had wintered over at Pumpkin Hill. Artie scolded them for trespassing, barking fiercely. When the geese had all sought sanctuary at the opposite side of the pond, Artie lay down on the muddy bank, pleased with his success, and rolled onto his back so that Matt could rub his stomach.

"Oh, you are so proud of yourself, aren't you?" Matt laughed. "Scared those birds clear across the pond. You're some fierce guy, you are."

Ragged fronds of last year's cattails lined one side of the pond, and it was there, Matt suspected, that the ducks hid from Artie. Too early in the season for frogs, he knew, and too soon for the turtles to have emerged from hibernation beneath the warming mud. Before too long there would be both, along with minnows and all manner of pond life. As a boy, Matt had spent endless hours here, sifting through the layers of life that gathered in, on, or near a country pond, from tadpoles and water-skimmers to dragonflies and the occasional heron, raccoons, and deer. Over the years, he'd come to know them all. His love for the wildlife that populated Pumpkin Hill had been influential in his decision to become a veterinarian.

"Come on, Artie." Matt leaned down and patted his dog on the back to get his attention. "Let's take a walk."

With Artie at his side, Matt walked the width of the back field, noting the proliferation of weeds—most noticeably dandelions—that had sprouted up where his aunt's market crops—potatoes some years, soybeans some others—had once grown. Hope would be getting the soil ready for seeding, had she lived for one more spring. She'd be cleaning up the equipment—the tractor and the tiller—that would be used to plow under whatever might have sprung to life where the cash crops would be sowed. She'd dig deeply, turning over the soil, making sure the earth was warm and ready for planting. In another month or so, Matt pondered, she'd have close to sixty-five acres set in seed, the other acres being comprised of pond, woods, and the area close to the road where the house and the outbuildings sat.

He missed Hope, just as he missed his father, and his mother. Dr. Espey wouldn't be around forever, either, and Laura . . . well, he was losing her in a different way. The thought that sometimes life seemed like little more than a series of losses swept over him and pinched him around the heart. He was still thinking about life and loss as he wandered toward the old tree. Without thinking twice, he sat down and leaned back against the trunk, trying to focus more on the many happy days he'd spent right here in this spot. It relaxed him a little, and he braced his hands behind his head, entwining his fingers, and closed his eyes. He smiled to himself, recalling how Laura had always repeated the local legend about how if you fell asleep under the wishing tree, you'd see the face of your one true love when you woke up.

"Not hardly," Matt mused. "Unless we count Artie . . ."

Artie found his master fast asleep and lay down beside him, his head on Matt's lap. And there Artie stayed, until he heard the tires of the Jeep crunch on the stone drive. He sped off to investigate the intruder.

Georgia pulled up next to the farmhouse, as close to the back door as she could get. As Laura had promised, Tanner's had everything. She had purchased a week's supply of groceries along with a pair of sturdy canvas and suede garden gloves, a large bag of birdseed, and several boxes of extra large plastic lawn and leaf bags. She had called Laura on her cell phone and was telling her just that, as she turned off the engine and reached for the door handle at the exact second that the black beast attacked her car.

"Oh!" She screamed and backed away from the driver's side window. "Oh!"

The dog—it *was* a dog, she felt pretty certain, though it was acting more like a vicious bear—

snarled and barked and growled through the glass. Thoroughly frightened, Georgia screamed again.

"Georgia! Georgia!" a terrified Laura yelled into the phone. "What is it?"

"Oh, go away! Go away!" Georgia was shouting.

"Georgia! What—"

"Oh, Laura! It's horrible!" Georgia unhooked her seat belt so that she could back away from the window and the snarling jaws of the killer beast. "It's the most horrible big black dog! He's trying to eat his way into my car! And it must have rabies, it's drooling and slobbering all over the window. I'm going to hang up and call Chief Monroe. . . ."

"Wait a minute," Laura said. "Did you say *big black dog*?"

"Yes!"

"How big?"

"Oh, enormous-big! The biggest, fiercest dog I've ever seen!"

"Tell him to sit," Laura instructed her. "Open the window and tell him."

Georgia was certain she had not heard correctly. "What?"

"I said, open the window and tell him to sit."

"Are you *crazy*? Laura, if I open this window, he'll get me."

"Georgia, trust me. Just open the window a little and tell him to sit."

"Laura . . ."

"Do it."

Georgia rolled the window down just a hair. "Sit," she whispered.

The dog lunged at the window.

"See?" she shrieked into the phone. "He wants in. He wants to bite me—"

"Georgia, that little whimper of yours would not get the attention of a child. Now, you tell that dog in no uncertain terms that you are the boss."

"Laura, I'm not the boss! He is! You should see this thing, it's bigger than I am!"

"I know he is, sweetie. That's why I'm trying to tell you how to control him."

Georgia paused. "How would you know?"

"It's Artie. Matt's dog. He'll intimidate for a while—for as long as you will let him, or until he tires of the game."

"Artie the water-dish Artie?"

"Yes."

"He thinks this is a game?"

"Absolutely."

"Bully the blonde?"

"Every chance he gets," Laura laughed. "Now, say, 'Sit, Artie.' "

Putting a name to the beast made it a little less fearsome.

"Sit, Artie." Georgia opened the window a little farther.

In mid-lunge toward the window, Artie cocked his head to one side.

"Again, louder. More forceful."

"Sit, Artie," Georgia commanded sternly. And to her amazement, Artie sat.

"Hey, it worked!"

"Tell him he's a good boy."

"He's not a good boy. He's slobbered all over the side of my car and he scared me to death."

"Georgia, do you want to spend the rest of the day in the front seat of your Jeep?"

Georgia rolled the window down a little more and peered down into the face of the beast. He was panting, watching her curiously.

"You're a good boy."

"Say it like you mean it," Laura prodded her.

"You're a very good boy."

"*Artie.*"

"*Artie,*" Georgia repeated. "You're a very good boy, *Artie.*"

Artie's tail thumped the dirt.

"What's he doing?" Laura asked.

"He's wagging his tail and his tongue is hanging half out of the side of his mouth."

"Good. Give him a reward."

"Reward him for attacking me?"

"No. Reward him for stopping. What did you buy at Tanner's?"

"The closest thing to wild-anything food that I have is birdseed." Georgia turned and leaned into the backseat, poking through bags, and frowned. "No meat, of course. Salad stuff. Eggs." Georgia paused, her hand on the egg carton. *Do dogs eat raw eggs?*

"Carrots?" Laura asked.

"Oh, sure. I have carrots." She reached into the closest bag and drew out the large bunch of organic carrots that sported their long leafy tops.

"Oh, good. Break one and call him to the car."

"I really don't think it's carrots he's after. I think he'd rather have my forearm."

"Offer him the carrot." Laura laughed. "Trust me."

Georgia rolled the window down a little more.

"Here, Artie," she called tentatively. "I have a nice carrot for you. . . ."

The eager animal jumped up to the window, and Georgia tossed him the carrot, lest he get too close. His tail wagging merrily, he went around the front of the car and lay down on the grass, munching his prize with obvious relish.

"How 'bout that?" Georgia grinned. "Who'd ever believe it? A vegetarian rottweiler."

Laura laughed. "Artie is a very special dog. I'm sorry he scared you, but he was only protecting his home from an intruder. You'll be fine now."

The crisis having passed, Laura was suddenly struck with the obvious: Artie. Matt.

"Ah, Georgia, I think I should warn you . . . ," Laura began hesitantly.

"Oh, I think we're okay now."

Having dispatched the carrot, Artie returned to the window, and Georgia handed him an apple. The big brown eyes of the dog glazed over with ecstasy as he returned to his spot on the grass. "I think he'll let me out of the car and into the house, don't you?"

"Oh, Artie will be fine. You're his new best friend. But, Georgia—"

"Oh, Artie, you are such a handsome boy." Georgia opened the door cautiously. "Such a good boy."

The dog's tail smacked the turf. Mashed up chunks of apple dribbled through his big smiling dog-mouth.

"Piece o' cake," she told Laura. "Thanks for the help. Right now, I'm going to unload the car. The danger's past. I'll give you a call tomorrow."

"But Georgia—" Laura sighed as she realized that Georgia had already disconnected the call, thinking all was well at Pumpkin Hill. A snarling Artie was nothing, Laura knew, compared to a snarling Matt.

Artie could be beguiled by a carrot, tamed with an apple.

It was going to take a lot more to maneuver past Matt.

chapter nine

The sun had dropped lower in the sky when Matt awoke and found himself beneath the tree in the middle of the field, his neck miserably crinked from being held in so awkward a position. He muttered a curse and tried to massage the back of his neck only to find that one arm had fallen asleep in protest of having spent the past two hours tucked behind his head. Matt stood up and tried to shake the blood back into his left arm while he rubbed his neck with his right.

"Artie," he called when he realized the dog was nowhere in sight.

He whistled, long and loud. Once, twice, then looked around, expecting to see the big black dog streaking across the field in his direction. Nothing moved except a few low-hanging branches of the tree as a bit of breeze stirred up.

Concerned when the second whistle brought no more response than had the first, Matt walked with brisk apprehension toward the farmyard, fearful that

Artie had chased something across the road and was, at that moment, off and running to parts unknown. He was still rubbing the back of his neck when he reached the grassy area between the barn and the old chicken house. What he saw stopped him dead in his tracks.

A tiny, trim blond woman tossed a stick halfway across the drive, with Artie in hot pursuit of the prize. From the distance, Matt could hear her laughter as Artie jumped into the air and caught the stick like a Frisbee. She patted her blue-jeaned knee and the dog trotted back happily to her, wagging his tail as he presented her with the stick to be tossed again.

It was the blonde from the inn. Matt was certain of it, even without seeing her face. Her hair—palest silk in the late afternoon sun—hung almost to her waist as she gathered it with one hand, catching it in something that held it in one long sweet line down her back. She moved with the same grace with which she had crossed the parking lot that day at the Bishop's Inn, effortlessly flowing like an easy stream on an April morning. She had made him think of music then, and now, for some odd reason, she made him think of a jewelry box Laura had gotten for Christmas one year. It had been made of pink leather, and inside stood a tiny dancer that twirled to tinny music when the lid was opened.

Matt's heart sank when he realized that he was more than likely still sleeping under the tree. A woman like this didn't cross your path twice in real life—except in dreams.

Artie strutted across the yard, cheerfully showing off, nuzzling her hand and wagging merrily when she bent down and scratched behind both of the dog's ears at the same time.

Matt watched in fascination as his dream woman—a fairy princess, if ever he'd seen one—continued to play toss-the-stick with his dog.

Several minutes passed before Artie spied his master and decided to include Matt in the game. The dog raced up the drive, stick in mouth, then stopped about five feet from Matt, challenging him to chase him and try to take the stick from his mouth. Matt had taken no more than two steps toward Artie when the dog turned and raced back toward the blonde.

What could Matt do but follow?

Besides, in dreams, he was thinking as he chased his dog toward the farmhouse, *the beautiful princess always showed up, sooner or later.* He was halfway across the drive, wondering if he appeared to be running in slow motion the way people always did in TV dreams, when his left foot rolled over a large stone, causing his foot to twist and sharp pain to shoot through his ankle.

That's when it occurred to him that maybe this wasn't a dream. After all, things weren't supposed to hurt in dreams, and here he was, going down on one hand with knives of heat running up his left leg.

"Are you all right?" The princess was rushing toward him.

"Oh. Fine. Sure." He gritted his teeth and smiled up into eyes green as spring grass and shiny as new dimes. "It's just a little twist."

"Are you positive?" she was asking, her voice like soft bells.

"Yes." He felt fortunate to have gotten that one word out.

She was beautiful enough to take a man's breath away, and for a long moment, it seemed to Matt, she had taken his.

"Maybe some ice . . ." she was gesturing toward the farmhouse and saying something that his brain—struggling as it was with the effects of both pain and something else that was registering at a point equidistant between infatuation and lust—wasn't quite comprehending.

"You live here?" he asked, understanding seeping through.

"As of yesterday." She nodded.

Their tenant? The princess was their tenant? *Yes!*

She took his arm gently and asked, "Would it help if you leaned on me? I can help you to the back steps."

He wanted to tell her that he wasn't really hurt *that* badly, but her arm was already around his waist, surprising him with its strength for one so slender.

Matt knew he should remind her of the dangers of permitting a stranger to get so close, but she smelled of sunlight and new grass and her red-and-white flannel shirt was soft against his bare arms and he couldn't get the words out. Of course, actually leaning on her was out of the question, she being barely five three or so and he being close to six feet, but he felt compelled to let her think she was helping. After all, she looked so anxious, so sincere.

"If you think you can get into the house, we can prop your foot up and maybe put some ice in a towel," she offered.

"You know, you really should not do that." He couldn't help himself. Women who looked like that—who smelled like that—really shouldn't be so naive.

"Do what?"

"Offer to take a strange man into your home." He frowned. What if he'd been up to no good? "It's dangerous. Didn't your mother ever warn you about strangers?"

"Every chance she gets." The princess laughed and held the door open for him. "But you're not a stranger."

"I wouldn't think that carrying your bags for you at the inn would make me less of a stranger." He followed her into the kitchen, his frown deepening.

"You're Laura's brother, Matt." She smiled sweetly and pulled a chair away from the kitchen table, motioning for him to sit.

He did, earning himself a fine view of the back of her jeans as she leaned over to get a dishtowel from a nearby drawer.

"That's right." He nodded, his head filling with the buzz that had been set off inside his head when she had smiled at him.

It was, the scientist in him observed, the same kind of inner ear noise you got when you stayed underwater for too long. Something told him that no amount of head-shaking would shake off this buzz.

He continued to admire her as she took a white box filled with ice from the freezer and set it on the counter next to the dishtowel, which she opened and layered with ice.

She handed him the towel with one hand and

swung another chair around to face him with the other, saying, "You can prop your leg up on this chair and leave the ice on your ankle for a few minutes. It'll help to keep it from swelling."

"Thanks." As if he hadn't suffered a million injuries over the years, from the sandbox to the football field.

"I made iced tea this morning. It's herbal. Would you like a some?"

"Yes, that'd be great. Thank you." He watched her reach into a near cupboard to take down two amber colored glasses. Without thinking he said, "My aunt always used those glasses for iced tea in the summer. There was a pitcher that matched, and she always made iced tea in the pitcher and served it in the glasses."

The princess smiled as she opened the refrigerator door. "You would be referring to this pitcher?" she said as she lifted it from the top shelf and placed it on the counter.

"Yes." He nodded, pleased in some unexplainable way to see her using things that he himself had used.

"I found it in the closet." She pointed to the tall built-in closets at one end of the room. "I hope you don't mind. Laura said I could use what was here."

"No, I don't mind at all."

She poured the tea into the first glass, which she handed to him, saying, "I hope you like this. It's cranberry with some fresh lemon in it."

He sipped at it. "It's great." It could have been hemlock for all he knew at that moment, held as he was in the spell of those moss green eyes.

"Oh, good, I'm glad you like it." She poured her own glass, then leaned back against the counter.

"So, Laura told you about me, did she?" As he watched the princess move toward the table, he blessed his sister with ever fiber of his body. He owed Laura big time for this.

"Yes, she did."

"What did she tell you?"

"Well, she told me about Artie—actually, I was speaking with her on my cell phone when I drove up and Artie attacked my car." She pointed to the Jeep that was parked near the side of the house.

"Artie attacked your car?"

"Laura said he was just being territorial, this being his place and all. He was jumping up at the driver's side window and snarling."

"I'm so sorry. Did he scratch your door?"

"No, I don't think so." She shook her head and her hair shimmered like gentle waves with the movement. "He was really bouncing more against the glass than he was the side of the car. Scared me half to death at first, though."

"I guess he can be pretty fearsome sometimes. I'm sorry if he frightened you, but he's pretty protective."

"He makes a very impressive watch-beast."

"So what else did Laura tell you about her little brother?" Matt knew he was flirting. He also knew he couldn't remember the last time he'd enjoyed it this much.

A look of wariness crossed the delicate features of her face.

"Well, she said that you probably wouldn't be too happy about finding me here. . . ."

"Oh, I know I was reluctant to rent out the farm. I have to admit that I resisted the idea at first. But I've come around to the idea. And Laura's right, we've left the place vacant for longer than we should have. I guess we're lucky that there's been no real damage done to the place." He paused, then asked, "Laura did tell you about the barn being broken into last week?"

"Yes. Actually, I was at the inn when Chief Monroe called to tell her about the kids sneaking into the barn to have a little party."

"Well, then, you know that it was probably time for us to do this. Nothing personal, but I don't think either of us felt comfortable handing over the keys to our mother's family home to a complete stranger, but it had to be done."

"I'd feel the same way, I'm sure—but then again, I'm hardly a stranger, either."

He looked at her blankly, and in that moment, she understood.

"Laura didn't tell you who your tenant is, did she?" she said slowly.

He shook his head. "No. Just that she found someone who could move in right away."

She stretched her hand out to him and he took it, cradling her small palm in his and liking the feeling.

"I'm Georgia Enright."

For a very long moment, he was certain he had misunderstood. Then with the resignation of one who had known all along that it had been too good to be true, he repeated flatly, "Georgia Enright."

"That's right," she nodded.

"Well then," he said from between clenched teeth

as he dropped her hand unceremoniously, "I guess that explains why Laura neglected to tell me the name of the tenant, doesn't it?"

"Why does it make a difference who I am?" she asked.

He ignored her, choosing to dump the remains of his tea into the sink without bothering to answer.

"Well, I wouldn't get too comfortable here if I were you, Miss Enright," he said without looking at her.

"And why is that?" she asked, her cheeks beginning to flush as her oh-so-carefully controlled temper began to rise.

"Because you won't be staying." For a brief second he considered rinsing out the sink where the tea had splashed against the porcelain, then decided against it.

"Excuse me?" Her hands rolled into fists, her nails biting against her palms.

"I said, you are not staying here. This is as much my house as it is Laura's, and I don't want you here. We'll find another tenant."

"May I remind you that Laura and I have an agreement?" she asked with much more calm than she was feeling.

"Un-agree." He brushed her aside as he limped through the back door, across the back porch, and down the steps.

Georgia's fists found their way to her hips as she marched behind him. "I moved out here in good faith—"

He turned to her and said, "I'd like you to be gone by Wednesday."

"That's ridiculous." She planted both feet firmly

on the ground and stared him down. "I'm not going anywhere."

"By Wednesday, Miss Enright." Matt whistled for Artie, who had been sleeping in the grass near the garden fence. "Come on, boy."

The dog headed for Georgia and, in spite of her anger, she bent down to give the dog a good-bye rub under the chin.

"Artie, come!" Matt yelled without turning around as he headed toward his pickup. When he reached the cab, he opened the door and waited for Artie to jump in before climbing in himself and closing the door. He started the engine and turned the truck around in a narrow arc at a higher rate of speed than he should have, causing stones to fly and the tires to grind out cranky groans as he sped toward the end of the drive.

"Wednesday!" he shouted curtly as he passed by in a cloud of dust.

Georgia fought the urge to make an obscene gesture in his direction.

"Wednesday," Matt struggled not to yell into the phone. "Wednesday, Laura."

"Matt—" Laura sighed heavily. She'd been expecting this. "Matt, calm down and let's discuss this."

"Laura, there's nothing to talk about. I don't want anyone named Enright living in our house and sleeping in our beds. Period. Get rid of her."

"No, Matt." Laura said calmly. "No, I won't. Georgia and I have an agreement—"

"Laura, I don't want her there. Tell her she has to leave."

"No. We needed a tenant, one we could trust . . ."

"I don't trust her."

"You don't know her, so your opinion doesn't count."

"Well, I don't see where you could know her very well, either. How long have you known her, a couple of months?" he growled, then added, "You had no business leasing our farm without my consent."

"I don't need your consent, Matthew. That farm belongs to Mother, and I have sole power of attorney over all of her affairs. My advice to you is to steer clear of Pumpkin Hill for however long Georgia stays, or get used to the idea of her being there, because she's not leaving."

Ignoring her, he said, "I want you to call her and—"

"Apologize for you being a horse's ass?" Laura shot. "I already have."

"You what?"

"I said, I already apologized to her for your behavior. Thankfully, she is more gracious than you are."

"I don't need anyone to make apologies for me. I'm perfectly capable of making my own when—"

"Then I suggest you do exactly that."

"—when I feel it's warranted. Which in this case, it is not."

"Matthew, you are acting like an obnoxious child. If I didn't know you better, I'd think you were jealous."

"Jealous? Of what?"

"That I have found my birth family."

"Laura, let's get one thing straight. I know where I came from, okay? I don't want to go back—hell, I don't even want to look back there."

"Matt, you can't compare the two situations. . . ."

"No, you can't. And while I'm sure that the woman who gave birth to you is nothing like the woman who gave birth to me, the fact remains that you don't really know her, Laura."

"If you had your way, I never would."

"I just think you're moving way too fast where these people are concerned."

"What's that supposed to mean?"

"I mean that out of the blue, this woman turns up. Tells you she's your birth mother. Trots out the half siblings. Everybody's happy-happy."

"So what's wrong with that?"

"What's wrong is that they can leave, as quickly as they came."

"That is such an awful thing to say. If you knew them, Matt, you'd never say that."

"I don't have to know them to think that you're way too trusting. Sometimes people have to earn trust, Laura. I don't think that a woman who abandoned you thirty-five years ago is worthy of your trust just because she shows up one day and pays off your mortgage."

"That was a cheap shot. Delia did that because—"

"I don't need to know why she did it. It's between you and her. The point is that she—and the rest of her family—are essentially strangers to you. I'd hate to see you have your heart broken because you gave it blindly like you . . ."

"Go ahead, Matt. Finish it."

"Laura . . ."

"This is nothing like that, Matt. How can you even compare my mother, my family, to *him*? How could

you compare *anyone* to him? How dare you—"
Laura's voice rose sharply.

"I dare because I love you, Laurie. The last time
you needed someone to look out for you, I let you
down. This time—"

"Is that what this is about, Matt? Your guilt? You
think that somehow you could have stopped me from
marrying Gary? Or that somehow you could have
figured out what he was doing?" Laura sighed
deeply. "Matt, trust me when I tell you that there was
nothing you could have done. I never saw that side of
him. I swear it. I never knew, up until the day he was
arrested. How could you, in college a hundred miles
away, have known what he was really like, when I
lived with him, day in and day out, and I never
knew?"

"Maybe if someone had warned you to take things
slowly, things would have turned out differently."

"I doubt it, Matt. It's just my nature to jump in with
both feet. I can't help it. I appreciate your concern. I
love you for it. But I know what I'm doing. You don't
have to worry. The Enrights will be around for a long,
long time, so you're just going to have to get used to
the idea. Just like you're going to have to get used to
the fact that Georgia is living at Pumpkin Hill."

"That's different, Laura. It's our family home." His
voice softened, and in it she could hear the unspoken
plea.

Ah, so that was it.

"Oh, Matt . . ." Laura shook her head. How could
she help him to understand that embracing her new
family did not mean that she was turning her back on
her old one?

"Look, I have to go," he said abruptly. "I promised Doc Espey I'd stop in and see him tonight. I'll be talking to you."

He hung up the phone as soon as he realized that he was sweating. He was afraid, pure and simple, for her, and for himself.

Didn't she understand that the closer she allowed these people—this new family—the more it would hurt later, if and when the time came that they all drifted back to their own lives and decided not to take her with them?

And lately, the thought had crossed his mind that if he lost Laura to them—if she was an *Enright*, would she cease to be a *Bishop?*—he would lose his last connection to the family they had made with Tom and Charity, and then who would he be? Would he not become, once again, the boy who had no one?

The thought of it brought back memories drenched in shadow, shadows that had held uncertainty and fear of the places where he'd been deserted for hours—sometimes days—on end. The child who had lived in those shadows had never forgotten, had never gotten over the fear that someday, someone might realize that perhaps *that* was where he really belonged, and would send him back, alone, and those same shadows would claim him again.

Matt fought back the shadows and dropped the phone onto its base, his palms sweating, wishing he could have found the words to tell Laura, but his voice had frozen, refusing to let the words out. After all, if he spoke his fears aloud, might they then have life? Might they have power?

Matt cleared his throat and whistled for Artie. In

spite of his still throbbing ankle, he would walk to Doc Espey's. The afternoon had clouded up and a brisk wind had started to blow from the east, bringing with it the promise of a hard-driving, cleansing rain. With any luck, it would help clear his head.

Georgia locked the back door to the farmhouse and turned on the back porch light. She walked through the rest of the downstairs, turning on the lights in the front hall and the one over the front door, then one in the little sitting room. It was just starting to get dark, and she was feeling uneasy, wondering if the vandals would be returning again tonight. She shook the fear off, telling herself that there was not much left in the garden to destroy.

It had been nice having the dog there, though. A big, ferocious dog who could be mean if he wanted to.

Much like his owner, she thought dryly as she turned back to the stove, where she was heating up some vegetable soup she'd found in the freezer.

Matthew Bishop was a real piece of work, all right.

If he hadn't been quite so obnoxious, she mused as she stirred the soup, *I might have liked him.*

She unwrapped the foil where she'd stored the leftover biscuits and took out two, noting there were still several left. Mrs. Colson must have made more than one batch.

All right, I did like him. At least, I did at first.

She next searched the cupboard for a suitably sized soup bowl, trying to ignore the thought that she had more than liked Matthew Bishop.

Okay, fine, I was starting to like him a lot.

Seeing his smiling face in the photographs lining the windowsill didn't make it any easier.

"Okay, so you're a hunk of the first order. Maybe the sexiest, handsomest, hunkiest man ever to cross my path. That doesn't make you any less of a jerk," she said aloud to the photo as she slid into the chair he had sat on earlier. "The only nice thing about you is your dog, mister. And your sister. It's hard to believe that you and Laura are sister and brother. . . ."

It was then that Georgia recalled that only by having been adopted by the same parents had Laura and Matt become siblings. She buttered a biscuit, trying to call up the details of Matt's adoption as Laura had once mentioned. Something about his having been abandoned by his mother and being brought into the Bishop home as a four-year-old who had not yet learned to speak. . . .

Well, he sure had had plenty to say *that* afternoon. Georgia's eyes fell upon the photo of Matt with a laughing Ally on his back, and she felt an unsolicited stab of envy.

The truth was that she'd been really attracted to him. That he'd activated all those bells and whistles she'd always read about but had never believed in. It had started the minute she had looked up to see him coming across the farmyard—and ended with the dark look that had crossed his face as soon as she had introduced herself to him.

No, it didn't end there, a tiny voice inside her protested. *If it had, you wouldn't be sitting here right now thinking about him.*

Well, it hardly matters, she reminded herself, since he's a crazy man.

A crazy man who wishes my entire family and I would disappear and never come back.

With any luck, he'll stay away and I won't have to deal with him.

Georgia turned his picture facedown on the sill and, determined to not waste another thought on Matthew Bishop, resumed eating her dinner.

chapter ten

There was never any question but that Georgia would totally ignore Matt's demand that she pack up and leave.

She ignored him early the next morning, when she awoke to her second day at Pumpkin Hill, determined to finish cleaning up the mess in the garden, and she ignored him as she sat that night in his favorite chair and read his aunt's books on fortune-telling.

She ignored him again on Tuesday when she sat on the back step, Aunt Hope's book on fortune-telling in one hand and her teacup in the other, trying to decipher the little blobs of tea leaves left behind in the bottom of her cup. And she ignored him later that day when she pushed aside the furniture in the living room in the hopes of carving out a space big enough for dancing and was disappointed that there was only sufficient room for some very limited exercise.

She was still ignoring him on Wednesday when, determined to find a place large enough in which she could *really* dance, she dragged first the broom, then the vacuum cleaner up to the second floor of the barn to clear away the cobwebs and the many years of ancient dust from the floor. It had taken her all morning, but by one o'clock in the afternoon, the old hardwood floor had been thoroughly cleaned as it had never been cleaned before. She had even brought up a wet mop, making countless trips back to the first floor for clean water. When she had finished and the floor had dried, she walked the length and width of it, searching for splinters and other such hazards. Mentally noting those spots best avoided, she lugged the bucket back down the steps for the last time, and went off in search of her portable tape player and her box of music tapes.

Later, dressed in pale pink tights and leotard, dark green leg warmers, and pink leather ballet shoes, her equipment tucked into Mrs. Colson's picnic basket for easy toting and her pointe shoes slung over one shoulder, she had marched defiantly across the farmyard to the barn.

Just let him try to run me off.

In her head the music she had selected was already playing as she all but ran up the steps to the second floor. She went to the outlet she'd located earlier and plugged in the tape deck, but did not turn it on. There was one more thing to be tended to.

She stood in the middle of the floor, contemplating the fact that there was no barre. Well, then, she'd use a chair. Off she went to the house where she grabbed one from the kitchen and carried it over her head up to the second floor of the barn. After setting the chair on the floor near the window, where the light was best, she turned on the tape, straightened her shoul-

ders, and, holding on to the back of the chair, began
her warm-up exercises at the makeshift barre. Starting with *pliés*—leg bends—to stretch all of the leg
muscles, she ran through what had been for years her
normal routine. First *demi-pliés*—the knees bent halfway; then *grand pliés*—the knees completely bent;
through each of the five classic ballet positions, first
on one side, then turning the other side to her
"barre" to repeat all of the exercises. Then on to the
second set of exercises, those intended to limber the
hip joints, improve turn-out, and stretch the calf
muscles. Finally, on to the last of the barre exercises,
ending with a *grand écart*—a split so complete that
the entire length of both legs touched the floor.

Pausing only long enough to change the tape,
Georgia brushed the beads of perspiration from her
brow and moved to the center of the room, where she
began the progression of floor exercises—from *port
de bras en fondu* through *saut de chats* and *pirouettes*—
pausing only long enough to change the tape. When
the floor exercises were completed, she sat on the
chair and peeled off the flat pink leather shoes and
replaced them with worn satin pointe shoes, which
she tied around her ankles with satin ribbons that
had begun to fray.

Returning to the chair, she worked without music,
then turned back to the room to complete her round
of exercises, the stiffness of the toes of the shoes
welcomed against the calluses she had long ago
formed. She worked her way across the floor in a
series of movements intended to move a dancer
across a stage. When she had gone as far as the
outside wall, she turned around and went back across

the floor again, repeating the movements over and over. When her calf muscles had begun to plead *no more,* she grinned and granted herself a ten minute break. She lifted the lid of the picnic basket and brought out a bottle of water, from which she drank slowly.

It felt so good to work. Even if no one ever saw her dance again, it felt so good to go through the steps, to work her body the way it had been trained to work. She straddled the chair and sipped at the water, her muscles, unused as of late, springing back to life to complain loudly. She would ache tomorrow, she knew, but she shrugged it off. It was her own fault for not having kept up with her exercises. Well, she would get back into shape and she would stay in shape.

Every day, she promised herself. *I will do this every day.*

As if to test her resolve, she pulled the chair to one side of the room and set the bottle on it. Turning to the basket, she rummaged for the tape she wanted, then slipped it into the player and turned up the volume.

If she was going to dance, she would dance only to her favorite music. She would dance all of those roles she would never get to dance on stage, and it would not matter that no one but she would know that she had mastered every step. She would dance to please herself, for the sheer joy of it, and there would be no one to say that she was not good enough; no one to judge her. She could be Giselle, she could be Columbine, she could be Cinderella or Sleeping Beauty. She knew all of the classic ballets by heart, though she had never had an opportunity to dance the leads. Now she would.

Today, however, called for impromptu dance. She would dance from her heart. The tape she had selected was a mixed collection of Chopin's works that she had recorded herself from several longer tapes. Georgia had always felt the composer's piano pieces—much of it written during his affair with a popular romance novelist of the day, George Sand—reflected both the romance and the heartbreak of his life, the perfect thing for impromptu dance. The lively strains of the *Mazurka in B Major* was a good warm-up number, and she followed it with the *Waltz in C Sharp Minor*, swirling and leaping and gliding across the old pine floor of the barn. She had just finished a labored routine to her favorite *Ballade in G Minor*, when unexpected applause from the top of the steps startled her.

"Wonderful! Oh, Georgia, that was so wonderful!" Laura cried. "I knew you were a professional dancer, but I had no idea of how . . . well, incredibly talented a dancer you are!"

"Aunt Georgia, you are a real ballerina!" An awe-struck Ally pointed to Georgia's feet, which were still poised on their toes. "Can you teach me to do that?" Ally spun around awkwardly, demonstrating a jump. "I want to dance like that, too!"

"I had no idea I had an audience." Georgia blushed, disturbed to find that she had not been alone after all.

"Oh, I'm so sorry. We didn't mean to intrude or to

spy on you. We just followed the music. . . ." Laura realized, too late, that for Georgia, the afternoon's dance had been something more than mere exercise.

"It's okay. I was just finishing up."

"Oh, I wish I had known you were going to dance," Ally pouted. "I could have danced, too."

"Next time, bring your ballet slippers, and we will dance together," Georgia told her.

"Can I come tomorrow?"

"Don't you have school tomorrow?" Georgia laughed.

Ally's face fell.

"Then how 'bout Saturday?" She brightened again. "I don't have school on Saturday."

"I think you should ask your mom if she'd be willing to drive you out here again on Saturday." Georgia suggested.

"I don't mind the drive at all, but, Georgia, are you sure you want to?" Laura asked.

"I'd be delighted to teach her. It will be fun for both of us."

"Can I bring Samantha, too?" Ally asked.

"Who is Samantha?" Georgia sat on the floor and began to untie her shoes.

"She's my friend. She used to take dancing lessons with me until our teacher stopped."

"Sure." Georgia shrugged. "The more the merrier."

"Yippee! This will be fun! Wait till I tell everyone that I get to take dance lessons again!" Ally jumped up and down.

Georgia laughed. "Well, keep in mind that this is a pretty makeshift arrangement here, kiddo."

"That's okay. It will be fun anyway." The issue of her dancing lesson having been resolved, Ally proceeded on to the next item of business. "Can I go down to the pond now and watch the ducks?"

"Sure. We'll join you in a few minutes."

Ally raced down the steps and slammed the barn door behind her.

"Here, I'll get that for you." Laura grabbed the chair and lifted it with one hand. "What else do you need help with?"

"Nothing, really." Georgia returned the tape player and her pointe shoes to the picnic basket. "If we can just take a minute to stop at the house, I'll put sneakers on." She pointed down to the thin leather ballet slippers on her feet. "These weren't made for traipsing through fields."

Laura paused at the top of the steps and looked back at the wide expanse of room behind her. "What a great place to dance. Too bad the lighting isn't a little better."

"The lighting's not too bad close to the window," Georgia noted. "A few skylights would make it better; a few fluorescents would make it better yet." She grinned and added, "Of course, a smoother floor would be nice—I'm going to be digging splinters out of my toes for the rest of the week, despite my efforts to avoid the rough spots. But that's a small price to pay to have such a wonderful place to dance in."

They walked down the steps, side by side. When they reached the door, Laura pushed it open and allowed Georgia to pass through.

"Do you have everything?" Laura paused and asked.

"Yes," Georgia replied.

"Then I'll lock up now, so that I don't forget later." Laura set the chair on the ground and padlocked the door.

"So, how was your day?" Laura asked as they walked toward the farmhouse.

"Ah, I get it." A smile spread across Georgia's face. "Thank you, Laura, but it wasn't necessary."

"What wasn't necessary?"

"You didn't have to drive all the way out here to check up on me. I can handle your brother."

Laura had all intentions of pretending that she hadn't realized that it was Wednesday—the same Wednesday that Matt had demanded Georgia be gone by—but knowing that Georgia was already on to her, she dropped the pretense. "I was hoping you wouldn't hear from Matt."

"And I haven't," Georgia assured her.

"I'm sorry that he's being so unreasonable . . . embarrassed that he's been so rude to you—" Laura's cheeks flushed red. "I think at the heart of it is that he just feels really threatened right now, by Delia, by you . . ."

"I can understand him feeling threatened by Delia, because I'm sure he feels protective of his mother. Your mother. But by me? I'm hardly a threat to anyone."

"I think he's afraid of all of you. Zoey, Nick . . ."

"You mean your new siblings, collectively." Georgia nodded slowly. "A whole new family that doesn't include him."

"Matt and I were always close—"

"And now he's afraid he'll lose you; that you have

other sisters, another brother. But he has only you. I can understand why he'd feel jealous."

"I don't really think it's jealousy." Laura shook her head. "In spite of his actions, Matt doesn't have much of a mean or jealous streak. I think he's just so scared that what little family he has left will be taken from him. He came to us from a really bad place when he was just a little boy, Georgia. I think he's just trying to keep you away so that he doesn't have to deal with it. Regardless of whatever else he says . . ."

"What else does he say?"

"He thinks that—well, that maybe, after a time— you and Delia and everyone will just go on back to your lives before . . ." she hesitated.

"Before Mother found you?"

Laura nodded.

"That's so incredibly stupid. That anyone would think—" She shook her head in disbelief. "Laura, you don't believe—"

"Not for a second. Matt just thinks I should take more time to get to know everyone."

"I'm so sorry for him. Sorry that he feels so threatened. It must be a very uncomfortable place to be in, where he is right now. Maybe in time he'll see that we're not trying to take you and Ally from him. I understand why he doesn't want me here, and if it would make things easier for you, I'll leave. Do you want me to leave, Laura?"

"Absolutely not." Laura shook her head. "Matt will come around in time. He's going to have to."

"Well, then, that pretty much settles it." Georgia took Laura's arm as they approached the back porch. "And I'm glad. I don't want to leave, Laura; I like it here. I liked it here the very first time I pulled up and parked my Jeep right over there by the barn. I like it more every day. There's something about Pumpkin Hill that is just peaceful and . . . I think *comforting* is the word I'm looking for. I feel *comforted* here. I don't know how else to explain it."

"That's Pumpkin Hill." Laura nodded vigorously. "I've always felt that way about coming here. So does Matt. It's where we've always come to lick our wounds and think things through. It's always been here when we've needed it, and—hey," Laura stopped at the kitchen table and picked up the book Georgia had left there. "Aunt Hope's book on reading tea leaves! Don't tell me you've been digging into this."

Georgia laughed. "I thought I'd try to learn a new skill while I was here."

"Have you?"

"I think I'm starting to get the hang of it." Georgia picked up the cup in which she'd had her morning tea and tilted it sideways. "The problem is acclimating your eyes to seeing little tiny shapes or pictures in the leaves around the sides and bottoms of the cup. You sort of have to train yourself to see something more than just a blob of tea leaves."

"What do you suppose that is supposed to be?" Laura peered inside the cup and pointed to some leaves that were stuck near the rim opposite the handle.

"I think it sort of looks like a pipe."

"Like a pipe you would smoke?" Laura turned the cup around to get a different perspective. "You know, I think you're right. It does look like a pipe."

"Which is a good thing." Georgia grinned. "According to your aunt's book, a pipe signifies the need to take a break; to step back and contemplate your position in life and to regroup."

"Why, that's incredible!" Laura exclaimed. "That's exactly what you are doing!"

"I laughed out loud when I read that this morning. I know it's just a coincidence—I mean, I guess you could interpret the pattern of the leaves in different ways, though the book tells you to go with your first impression. My first impression was of a pipe. We'll have tea later and maybe I can take a look and see what's in your future."

"I'm not sure that I want to know." Laura looked wary.

"Well, since I am so new at this, there's no guarantee that I'll be able to see anything at all, but I'll try. It's kind of fun—a sort of harmless game. I've been amusing myself for the past few nights, reading your aunt's notes."

"Aunt Hope had notes on reading tea leaves?"

"Several pages of them." Georgia nodded. "She kept a record of what she must have considered noteworthy or significant readings. Oh, and she was apparently interested in reading about some type of magic that had to do with plants, too."

"What do you mean, magic?" Laura frowned.

"I found a journal on one of the shelves in the living room. In it is a detailed list of which plants are believed by some to have whatever different magical properties."

"That's ridiculous." Laura waved away the thought. "Why, my aunt was the most practical, no-

nonsense, both feet on the floor woman you'd have ever met. The book must have belonged to someone else. . . ."

"Sure. I'll bet there were lots of women living around O'Hearn named Hope Evans Carter." Georgia nodded.

"Her name is in the book?"

"And the writing is in the same hand as the notes she made on tea leaves."

"How very odd." Laura shook her head. "I just can't see Aunt Hope believing in magic. She never gave us a clue. . . ."

"Oh, I don't know that she necessarily *believed* in magic. My overall impression from reading through the notes was that she was reading more out of curiosity, that it may have been something she mostly entertained herself with."

"That would make more sense. I know she did experiment with growing unusual plants. Some she referred to as heirloom plants. Old varieties that you don't see so much anymore. She kept the seeds in little envelopes in her desk. But I never heard her mention anything about any of them being capable of *magic.*"

"I think she merely amused herself with the possibilities." Georgia grinned and pointed to the small bundle of dried plant material that was nailed to the wall. "That, for example, is dried aloe. Her book said it drives away evil and brings good luck."

"How can you tell what that is? It's dried beyond recognition."

"Because in her journal, she talks about replacing

the dill that had hung over the back door with aloe. I guess she decided aloe had stronger powers. Or maybe she used different plants for different seasons. And look, here—" Georgia opened the pantry closet and took out a small glass jar containing something that looked like dried grain. "Alfalfa."

Laura looked at her blankly.

"You put it in the pantry to protect from poverty."

"I suppose that was in the journal, too?"

"Page thirty-two." Georgia nodded.

"Well, this all sounds more like old wives' tales than magic potions."

"Oh, she had all sorts of recipes for potions, and some very detailed descriptions of spells. Some of which she apparently had tried out just for fun, judging from her little comments about what worked and what didn't."

"For pity's sake, Georgia, don't let Ally hear about it. That's all we need is for her to decide that her great-aunt was a witch." Laura grimaced.

"It's really an interesting book, Laura. Do you know, for example, that if you want to attract elves to your garden, you should grow rosemary?"

"That's it. I don't want to hear another word." Laura pushed Georgia toward the back door. "Let's go get Ally and we'll come back and have our tea. No more talk of spells or magic. Fairies, of all things!"

"Oh, no, I said elves," Georgia giggled. "Now, if it's *fairies* you want, you have to plant primroses. Preferably blue and red."

"Out." Laura laughed and followed Georgia down the back steps.

"Oh, Laura, I almost forgot—" Georgia paused midway across the yard—"I want you to look at the garden."

They leaned over the fence. In the distance, geese were squabbling loudly.

"What am I looking at?" Laura asked.

"See the holes in the ground?" Georgia pointed toward the ground. "They weren't there yesterday. I spent part of the afternoon cleaning up these rows, and this morning, there were all those holes in the ground."

"It almost looks as if someone or something was digging around, looking for something." Laura frowned.

"Every day there's something else, some other evidence that someone's been poking around at night. But I never hear a sound. And for someone to sneak past a light sleeper like me is a real feat."

"Did you call Chief Monroe?"

"I've called him just about every day that I've been here. He doesn't even bother to come out anymore. He just adds each new complaint to his list. He's pretty sure it's some kind of animal, but I can't imagine what."

"Maybe I should have Matt leave Artie here for a few days. . . ."

"Oh, of course. Why didn't I think of that? I'm sure that Matt will be more than happy to send his dog here to protect me." Georgia rolled her eyes. "Fat chance."

"Sorry. For a moment I forgot what a bozo my brother is sometimes." Laura turned back to the garden. "Maybe if you tied the gate closed with a really intricate knot it will deter whatever's doing this from coming back. Though what they could possibly be coming back *for* is a mystery to me."

"Mommy! Aunt Georgia!" Ally came racing around the side of the old chicken house. "I saw a fox! A red fox! He was out in the field!"

"And he's probably halfway to Cambridge by now," Laura told her.

"No! He's not. He went toward the woods. I didn't scare him, honest. He was creeping toward the pond—" Ally's eyes were round as dinner plates and almost as large—"'cause there were ducks on the bank. Near the cattails. And then some of the geese spied him, and they all started yelling at him, and he ran away. But I didn't chase him. He didn't see me."

"Ah, I thought I heard the geese scolding a few minutes ago. I guess he was out looking for an early dinner."

"Not so very early," Georgia turned Laura's wrist to check the time. "Why not stay and have dinner with me? Unless you are needed at the inn."

"Actually, right now we have only Gordon Chandler and two people who are apparently going to be working with him. I'm sure that Jody can take care of the three of them, if, in fact, they are dining in tonight. Let's go inside and I'll give her a call. I'm sure she would appreciate one unexpected night off this week."

"What are you making for dinner, Aunt Georgia?" Ally asked.

"I was planning on making a mushroom and broccoli stir-fry. Do you think you might like that?"

Ally looked skeptical.

"Do you like broccoli?" Georgia asked.

Ally nodded.

"Do you like mushrooms?"

"Sometimes. If they don't have those little dark spots on them."

"I'll tell you what." Georgia took a bag of mushrooms from the refrigerator and handed it to her niece. "You go through this bag, and you pick out the mushrooms you would like me to use. I will need about eight of them, so you count them out and line them up on the counter there for me."

"Okay," Ally brightened, "but I can count past eight."

"I thought you could. But tonight, we only need eight mushrooms." Georgia ducked back into the refrigerator to gather carrots, onion, and broccoli, then turned to Laura and asked, "Would you like that tea now?"

"Yes." Laura nodded.

Georgia placed a pot of water on the stove to boil for the Chinese noodles that would accompany her stir-fry, then set about chopping vegetables while Laura put water on for tea.

"I read someplace that there are different kinds of vegetarians. What kind of vegetarian are you?" Laura asked as she munched on a piece of celery.

"I'm a lacto-ovo, meaning I do eat cheese and other dairy products and I also eat eggs. And on very rare occasions, I have been known to break down and have a piece of fish. *Lactos*, on the other hand, don't eat eggs, and *vegans* don't eat anything that has animal origins."

"Why did you become a vegetarian?"

Georgia shrugged and tossed the vegetables into the electric wok she'd brought with her and had installed on the counter. "It just seemed healthier to me. People do it for all different reasons. Plus after you do it for a while, meat loses its appeal."

"Matt always talks about it, but I think he's too lazy. He says it bothers him to heal animals during the day, and then eat animals at night, but that cooking vegetarian meals is too complicated."

Georgia laughed. "I hear people say that all the time. It really isn't any more or any less complicated. It's just a matter of rethinking how you eat and how you cook."

The tea kettle screamed and Laura turned off the burner and took down two cups.

"You know, you and Matt really have a lot in common," Laura mused.

"Oh, I'm sure we do," Georgia said dryly.

"No, really. You both respect animals, you both love Pumpkin Hill . . ."

"And we both love you and Ally. And that's about it. Now, let's get dinner on the table and then after we eat, we'll read our tea leaves and see if there's a tall dark stranger in either of our futures. . . ."

Dinner was delicious. Even Ally had cleaned her plate. Before the meal was over, Laura had asked Georgia to jot down a few of her recipes for Jody, so that the inn could expand its vegetarian offerings to its guests. Dessert was pound cake served with plums that had been put up by Hope the year before, and warmed on the stove.

"Okay, Laura. Let's take a look at that cup." Georgia said after the dessert plates had been cleared.

"Can you see anything?" Laura held the cup on its side for Georgia to take a look.

"Not so fast. There's a ritual involved here. I'm too much of a novice to take short cuts." Georgia laughed. "Ah, good, you didn't drink it all."

"No, there's still a little left in the bottom. I remember that my aunt always said you had to have enough tea left to move the leaves around the cup."

Georgia nodded. "I think that's enough. That looks like about a tablespoon, and that's what the book says you're supposed to have. Now, you rotate the cup three times, holding the handle in your left hand."

"Clockwise or counter-clockwise?" Laura asked. "I forget, but I do remember that it made a difference. Men turn the cup one way, women turn it the other."

"Ummm, I think counter-clockwise." Georgia thought for a minute. "Yes, that's it. Men turn the cup clockwise, women counter-clockwise. Go head, turn it."

"Three times?"

"Right." Georgia nodded. "Okay, that's three. Now, let's see what kind of patterns you have there. . . ."

Georgia lowered her head and peered inside the cup. "Now, the handle represents you, as the person whose leaves are being read."

"I remember that, too, from watching Aunt Hope read." Laura nodded. "She always said that the symbols nearest the handle were the most important or the most immediate." Laura pointed into the cup and said, "And those little dots . . . the tiny little pieces of tea leaves . . . I think they meant that whatever symbol they are closest to is the most important."

"Maybe not the most important symbol," Georgia murmured as she turned the cup this way and that, "but they add emphasis to the meaning of that symbol."

"Do you see anything?" Laura frowned.

"I do. I'll tell you what symbols I see, then we'll go to Hope's book and look up what they mean."

Georgia pondered the dark flakes on the inside of the cup, then leaned toward Laura and said, "Here, near the rim—also significant, because the closer to the rim, the stronger the message is said to be— here's a triangular shape. My first thought was a pyramid, so that's what we'll call it."

"Is there a difference between calling something a triangle and calling it a pyramid?"

Georgia frowned. "I don't know. I just know that the book says go with your first impression, and *pyramid*, not *triangle*, is what came into my mind. And there are lots of little dots nearby, so it must be important, whatever it means. And down there," Georgia pointed to the bottom of the cup, "there is an odd shape . . . I don't know, but it kind of looks like a horse's head to me."

She held the cup up for Laura to take a look.

Laura nodded. "Yes, I can sort of see a horse's head, too. Okay, we'll call it that. What are those other little things?"

Georgia turned the cup around several more times,

looking at the patterns from different angles, then shook her head. "I'm not getting any other impressions. Just the pyramid and the horse's head."

"Okay. Let's look those two things up."

Georgia flipped through Hope's handwritten pages of notes, then stopped and smiled and said, "Oh! Good news, Laura. The horse's head means that a lover is coming."

Laura blanched, then grabbed the cup. "Let me see that thing again. You know what, on second thought, I don't think it looks at all like a horse's head. I think it looks like a blob. What does the book say a blob represents?"

Georgia laughed. "There's nothing for blobs, and we already agreed that it was a horse's head. And since it's on the right side of the handle, it's a positive thing."

"I sincerely doubt that." Laura, still strangely white, motioned with her hand to a puzzled Georgia to proceed. "Okay, forget about the horse's head for a minute. Go on to the pyramid. What does that mean?"

"Hmmm . . . let's see . . ." Georgia scanned the pages, then grinned. "Here it is. Pyramid. It means a great secret will be revealed."

Laura coughed and went a shade or two whiter.

"It's something that has held you back in some way, but its revelation will let you move on . . ." Georgia looked up, startled to see just how pale Laura had become. "Whoa, Laura. Are you all right?"

"Of course I am." Laura paused, then asked, "That secret would be finding out that Delia is my mother, right?"

"No, I'm sure that's not it. That's no longer a secret." Georgia shook her head, then picked up the cup again and turned it toward the light. "No, I think that this is a secret that has yet to be revealed."

Laura took the cup from Georgia's hand and took it to the sink to rinse it out.

"I always thought this was silly. We've had our fun for the night. Ally!" Laura called into the living room where Ally was busy lining up chess pieces along the windowsill. "Put those away, honey. It's time to go."

"But, Mommy . . ."

"You have school tomorrow, Ally," Laura reminded her gently.

"Okay." Ally frowned. "But I do get to come back on Saturday to dance."

"Yes, you do."

"With Samantha."

"If Samantha's mom agrees."

"She'll agree." Ally nodded confidently, then turned to Georgia and said, "And can we have that music you had?"

"The Chopin. Yes," Georgia assured her, all the while watching Laura's face as Laura gathered up Ally's things in the manner of one preparing to flee a burning building. Whatever had set her off?

"What's a good time for you, Georgia?" Laura asked without looking at her.

"Ten, eleven. Whatever works. Why not give me a call on Saturday morning and let me know how your day is going?"

"Fine. We'll do that." Laura grabbed Ally's jacket and tossed it to her, saying, "Here, sweetie. Put this on. It's chilly out."

"No, it's not." Ally looked at her, puzzled.

"Well, I feel chilled . . ." Laura met Georgia's eyes from across the room, then shrugged nonchalantly. "Maybe it's just me . . . okay, got everything? Georgia, thanks for a wonderful dinner . . . don't forget to write down the recipe for me to give to Jody." Laura kissed Georgia on the cheek as she blew past her in the kitchen doorway.

"Thank you, Aunt Georgia." Ally waved, and Georgia grabbed her long enough to plant a quick smooch on the child's upturned face. "I can't wait till Saturday." Ally's voice trailed out the back door, and Georgia followed her.

"Laura—" Georgia called from the back steps. Laura was already at the passenger's side door and had it open for Ally to jump in.

"I'll talk to you on Saturday," Laura called back as she walked hurriedly around the car.

Now what, a wide-eyed Georgia wondered, *was that all about?* Why, Laura acted like someone being pursued by banshees.

It had been the horse's head that had set her off, Georgia recalled.

Closing the back door behind her and locking it, Georgia sat at the table and picked up Hope's book once again, wondering if she had perhaps made a mistake. She closed her eyes, trying to envision the symbol that she had seen in Laura's cup. That had been a horse's head, all right. She opened the book again and read the meaning of the symbol aloud. "A lover will be coming into your life."

She turned the pages back until she located the pyramid.

"No mistake." She shook her head. "It clearly says a great secret will be revealed, one that has held you back in some way. Once the secret has been revealed, you will be able to move forward. . . ."

Two potentially good things, from Georgia's point of view. A lover and a secret . . .

From Laura's perspective, however, the reading had obviously meant something entirely different. And whatever its meaning, it had driven her from Pumpkin Hill like one pursued by demons.

Or an unwanted lover.

Or a secret . . .

chapter eleven

It wasn't cool enough for a fire, so the logs that Matt had set upon the fire grate remained unlit. He really wasn't much of a drinking man, so the beer he'd opened when he returned home from the clinic remained on the kitchen counter, where he'd left it. The stack of mail he'd pulled out of the mailbox sat in a tidy pile on the table in front of the old, dark blue plaid sofa he'd had since his college days, and the TV remained on, the volume turned all the way down, while Matt sorted his options. He could slip his video copy of *The Scarlet Claw*—just maybe the best Sherlock Holmes movie ever made—into the VCR. Or he could finish reading *The Final Problem*.

Or he could call Pumpkin Hill and . . .

And what? he asked himself.

Ask Georgia Enright why she's still there after he'd told her that he expected her to be gone by today?

And there was absolutely no doubt in his mind that she *was* there. That calm but certain defiance that had smoldered in those green eyes until they had burned with emerald fire—that snap set of her bottom jaw—that solid hands-on-hips, try-and-make-me stance.

Oh, she was there all right.

Nothing about the woman had said *Yes sir, I'm on my way, sir.*

All day his nerves had hummed with the frustration of knowing that it was Wednesday, that she was still most certainly at Pumpkin Hill, and that he had no means of forcing her to leave. Even Laura had not backed him up, though he had suspected she would not. And wasn't that part of the problem, part of what was eating at him now? That Laura had taken Georgia's side, against him?

Yeah, and who did he have to thank for putting Laura in the middle?

"Me," he said aloud.

Artie raised his head and looked up at Matt.

Matt looked down at Artie. He sighed with the resignation of knowing that he had made a total ass out of himself by making a pointless demand on Georgia and imposing childish expectations on his sister. Laura would not go back on her word to Georgia, and his own sense of fair play made Matt grudgingly admit that she should not. Like it or not, Georgia Enright was living at Pumpkin Hill, and there she would stay until she decided to leave. The only way to avoid her would be to stay away, and that was one thing he could not do. Pumpkin Hill was his haven, his sanctuary, a place that had always offered peace, a place where he could relax, a place where he could dream and plan for the future.

And besides, he had great plans for that barn. Someday it would be home to the Pumpkin Hill

Veterinary Center, complete with the most up-to-date surgical facilities. He reached under his chair and pulled out the leather binder that held the plans he had drawn up for his animal hospital. The first floor would have treatment areas as well as housing for ailing farm animals—horses, sheep, goats, cows—and state-of-the-art equipment. The second floor would have offices and a sort of big, open conference area, where vets from all over could come to discuss new modes of treatment, and those who were on the cutting edge in the areas of nutrition and holistic veterinary medicine could share their knowledge. If he closed his eyes, he could see it. . . .

He closed his eyes, but all he could see was a delicate face framed in hair the color of candlelight.

Muttering a mild curse to dispel the vision, he reached for the remote control and turned on the video. He'd deal with Georgia Enright on the weekend. Right now, there was *The Scarlet Claw*. Basil Rathbone as Holmes, Nigel Bruce as Doctor Watson. As good as it gets. He settled back to enjoy murder and mayhem as the famed detective journeyed to Canada to investigate the death of Lady Penrose. . . .

Saturday's noon appointment—routine shots for an Airedale—having been canceled due to illness on the part of the dog's owner, Matt closed the clinic at twelve-twenty and headed home to pick up his dog.

"Now you listen up, Artie," he said sternly as he backed out of his narrow driveway, "no more fraternizing with the tenant, you hear? We're going to keep this all very businesslike, okay? She's the tenant, we're the landlord. We're not going to play fetch with her and we're not going to let her scratch behind our ears, you hear?"

Artie drooled onto the scuffed leather seat, then turned his head to look out the window.

"Yeah," Matt muttered. "That's what I thought you'd say."

It was just a little past one when Matt drove up next to the barn and parked his pickup. He swung the door of the cab open and hopped out, then stopped in midstride and asked Artie, who had leapt past him to water the nearest tree, "Do you hear what I hear?"

Matt took two or three steps, then stopped, frowning. "Classical music, that's what it is. And it's coming from the barn."

He took off across the yard—a man with a mission—and went through the open door and up the steps. The music grew louder as he approached the second floor, and when he neared the top, he stopped, dumbfounded.

The woman was dancing in his barn. Right where his conference tables would be.

Anger bubbled up inside him and was about to boil over. But just as he opened his mouth to yell, just before his *What the hell do you think you're doing in my barn?* could roll out, he was spotted by his niece.

"Uncle Matt! Uncle Matt!" Ally fairly flew across the floor, a look of sheer joy on her face. She, too, was dressed all in pink and looked like a gumdrop. "You came to watch me dance!"

She flung herself into his arms, and habit caused him to hoist her over his head.

"Aunt Georgia is teaching me how to dance," Ally told him breathlessly. "She is a real ballerina. And she's teaching Samantha and Mary Beth, too. She said 'the more the merrier,' so I could bring friends. Want to see what I can do?"

"Sure, sugar." He set her down on the rough wooden floor, trying to avoid the eyes of one Ms. Enright. She had looked over her shoulder when Matt had come up the steps, and it had seemed to Matt that she had looked mildly amused when she'd seen how quickly Ally had defused him. He met her gaze from across the distance and said, "Sure. Let's see what you can do."

Recognizing a challenge, Georgia raised one eyebrow and pointed to a folding chair where he was, he assumed, expected to sit.

"All right, girls." She directed her attention to her three little students, who lined up next to three folding chairs. "Let's do that again. Right hands on the back of the chairs . . . now, First Position. Heels together, toes out, legs stretched straight. Your feet should look like what, Samantha?"

"A straight line." Samantha responded boldly.

"That's right. A straight line. Very good, all of you. Now, let's move our arms into position . . . very nice, girls. Lovely. Now, can you move into Second Position? Does anyone remember where your heels belong?"

Georgia smiled as the little girls watched each other, trying to recall.

"Very good, Ally. Now, open your arms just a little more, Mary Beth, yes, like Samantha has done."

Ally and her friends were adorable and eager to learn. Georgia was enjoying herself—or had been, before Darth Vader had shown up.

"Back into First . . ." Georgia told them, demonstrating, "then again into Second . . ."

A black streak darted across the floor and pounced upon her from behind.

"Artie!" She cried, laughing as the dog nearly knocked her off her feet. "I'm glad to see you, too!"

Matt rose from his chair to grab the dog, trying not to look at her face, with its joyful smile as she patted the dog's big head, nor at her body, which he couldn't help but notice was trim where it should be and full in all the important places. He crossed the floor to retrieve the dog, commanding his eyes not to fall beneath the level of her chin. It was better this way, he rationalized. Anything below her chin was trouble.

Then again, those eyes could do real damage to a man, and those lips, curved as they were into a smile as she grabbed the dog's collar and passed it to Matt, seemed to draw him like a magnet and cause him to tingle in places he was better off not thinking about.

"Come on, Artie." Matt tugged at the dog's collar.

"Uncle Matt, aren't you going to stay and watch us dance?" Ally called.

"Ah, no, sugar. I think I need to . . . to take Artie out." Matt backed toward the stairwell, aware that he was dangerously close to staring at those shapely petite legs. As a matter of fact, he realized, there was no place where it *was* safe to look, when the woman was wearing little more than that little pink thing.

Being a man who knew when to cut his losses, Matt figured the best place for him was someplace other than where he was.

He forced himself to take the steps at a decent pace. Closing the door behind him, he stepped into the sunshine and exhaled.

Ballet in his barn.

Then again, it was for Ally, and she had seemed to be having one hell of a good time.

"Hey!" Laura rolled down the window of her car and waved as she drove up and parked behind Georgia's Jeep.

"Hey, yourself," he shouted back. He wasn't sure why, but he really didn't feel like talking to his sister right now. He knew he'd end up yelling about the whole Georgia thing all over again and just didn't feel up to it. He wished he could just go right on back up the steps and through the door into his apartment. Why hadn't he done that while he was up there and had the chance?

He knew why. He'd ignored his own good advice and permitted his eyes to drop below her chin. The sight of that trim little bottom in that little pink thing as she'd walked away from him was almost enough to make him forget that she was merely a presence to be tolerated on a strictly temporary basis.

Almost.

"Did you see Ally?" Laura was asking.

"Yes." He cleared his throat. "Yes, I did."

"Isn't she too cute?" Laura got out of the car and crossed the grassy distance between them. She leaned up and kissed his cheek. "I'm glad to see you came around. You won't be sorry, Matt."

He started to tell her that he hadn't exactly "come around," when the door behind him blew open and the three little dancers came bolting out, each carrying something to the house.

"Mommy, Uncle Matt got to watch us dance." Ally stopped and pulled her feet into First Position again. "We did First and Second Position, and if we practice all week and remember next Saturday, Aunt Georgia is going to teach us Third and Fourth Positions!"

"Well, pretty soon you'll be dancing up a storm," Laura laughed.

"Oh, no, Mommy. There are lots of things to learn before you can dance up a storm," Ally told her earnestly. "It takes a long time to become a real ballerina like Aunt Georgia."

"Did you have fun?" Laura smoothed back the hair from Ally's face, which was flushed more from excitement than from exertion.

"Oh, yes." She spun around and lost her balance, tipping over onto the grass. "I love to dance. I'm going to be a dancer just like Aunt Georgia when I grow up."

"Hey," Matt said, "I thought you were going to become a veterinarian and work with me."

"I can do both," Ally answered without a second thought. "I will dance and I will be a veterinarian." She turned to her companions and said, "Let's go get something to drink, then we'll go down to the pond."

"Ally!" Laura called after her as the three girls sped toward the house. "Change your clothes first!"

Ally was already up the back steps.

"I better go make sure they change," Laura told

Matt as she took off after her daughter. "Stop on over at the house and have a cup of coffee with me."

He was about to call after her that he'd rather not, when he heard the sound of the door behind him slamming into the outside wall of the barn. Startled by the sound, he turned in time to see Georgia step out, folding chairs under each arm. With her left foot, she was attempting to close the door. Chivalry and animosity warred within him.

Still, his mother had taught him better.

"Here, I'll take those," he said curtly as he reached to take the chairs from her arms. *Not below the chin*, he reminded himself.

Too late.

"I have them." She smiled mechanically, making a point of not looking at him.

"Fine. Suit yourself." Matt could almost hear his mother's reprimand. He sighed. "I'll get the door."

"Fine." She headed toward the farmhouse awkwardly, the chairs being too tall for her to comfortably carry under her arms, but not for one minute inclined to admit it.

"Thank you," she said without turning around.

"You're welcome," he called to her back as she walked away.

Not below the chin didn't count if he couldn't *see* her chin, he rationalized, and for one long, sweet moment, he watched those killer legs carry the rest of her across the farmyard.

He crossed his arms over his chest and tried to think of what to do next. He had thought perhaps he'd try to talk her into leaving, but recognized the sheer futility of that. She wasn't going anyplace. There was no point in even discussing that. He'd seen the look on her face. Hell, he'd seen the look on Ally's face. He may not like it, but he wasn't stupid enough to think he could actually do something about it.

Okay, fine. She was staying. He'd just have to find things to do while he was here that would keep him out of her way.

Like . . . like . . . he looked around, searching for possibilities.

Like painting the old henhouse.

He went into the barn in search of a ladder and some sort of implement that would scrape off the old paint.

"Matthew Bishop, what the hell are you doing?" Laura demanded from eight feet below the ladder he was standing on.

"I'm scraping old paint off the henhouse," he replied calmly.

"Why?"

"Why?" He looked down and frowned. "Because I can't paint it until I scrape off the old, loose paint."

"I meant, why are you painting the henhouse? We haven't had chickens in there since Aunt Hope died."

"Well, now's the best time to paint it. While there are no chickens living in there."

Laura shook her head as if to clear it. "We're getting ready to leave, so come down from there and say good-bye to Ally. And try to be pleasant to Georgia, please. I don't want you to upset Ally."

"Why would my being less than pleasant upset Ally?" he asked, even though he knew the answer. Worse, he knew that Laura *knew* that he knew.

"Matt . . ." Laura sounded exasperated.

"Okay." Conceding defeat, he climbed down the ladder and stuck the scraper in his back pocket.

"Uncle Matt, will you come to my birthday party?"

Matt knelt down so that Ally could jump onto his back. "Now, when have I ever missed a birthday party?"

"Never. You never have." She hugged his neck.

"And I never will." He twirled around so that her head dropped back and her hair, now out of its ponytail, spun around, and she laughed heartily. His niece had never failed to touch his heart. One day, he knew, she would break it by falling in love with someone her own age, but not yet, he reminded himself. Not yet.

"You promise?"

"Of course, I promise." He lifted her over his head once more before setting her feet on the ground. "How could it be time for your birthday again?"

She giggled and nodded. "It is. In two weeks."

"Two weeks? That's not possible." He frowned. "Didn't you just have a birthday?"

"Last year, silly." She hopped into the car.

"Well, then, I guess I'll see you in two weeks at the inn." He closed the car door, reaching through the window to tweak her nose. "Anything special you might want this year?"

"Ballerina Barbie," she answered, nodding enthusiastically. "But my party won't be at the inn. It's here, at Pumpkin Hill. All my friends are coming!"

She leaned halfway out the window so that he could kiss her cheek. "And we're all going to dance!"

Matt heard laughter, like the tinkling of fairy bells, behind him. He didn't have to turn around to know who it was.

"And Aunt Georgia said that next Saturday, Jamie and Carly can come dance with us, too!"

Laura looked across the hood of the car. "Georgia, you can still change your mind. It's good enough that you're willing to take a few of her friends from Bishop's Cove. You don't have to add kids from O'Hearn, too. . . ."

"It will be fun. I'm really enjoying it." Georgia dismissed her concerns.

"I'll talk to you later." Laura waved and drove off, three little girls in the backseat calling "Thank you!" as she drove away.

The car left the drive, leaving both Matt and Georgia painfully aware that they were alone.

"Well, I guess I'll go back to scraping paint," he said awkwardly.

"You do that," she told him and walked off toward the garden.

He couldn't help but notice that she had changed into jeans and a shirt. He liked the pink thing better.

It was almost dark when he decided it was safe to come down from the ladder. He'd just go right on up to his apartment, take a shower, then run out and grab some dinner.

His stomach growled, reminding him that he hadn't eaten since breakfast.

Maybe he'd run out for dinner first.

As he lowered the ladder, it occurred to him that if

his arms were covered with paint chips, his face probably was, too. And he probably had lots of it in his hair, too. He'd have to shower or settle for some fast food. He hated fast food.

He put the ladder away, then whistled for Artie. The dog was nowhere to be seen. Laughter drifted from the open windows in the kitchen of the farmhouse, and he'd bet anything that *that* was where his traitorous dog was. He went to the back door and listened.

"Artie, you are so cute," he heard Georgia say. "Now, sit, and I'll give you another carrot. Good boy."

Matt's stomach growled again.

He knocked on the screen door, which was open. He could see her as she walked toward him, looking more graceful, more elegant in jeans than most women did in designer gowns.

"I was looking for my dog," he explained.

"Oh. Come on in. He's having a snack. I hope you don't mind."

"I usually don't let him eat between meals. It's not good for him," Matt said, pretending not to see the *Liar, liar, pants on fire* look on Artie's big slobbery dogface.

"Oh. I'm sorry. I won't do it again."

Artie's look changed from accusatory to displeasure. Matt continued to ignore him. Just as he was trying to ignore the aromas that wafted around him, teasing his nose and tantalizing his stomach.

Matt couldn't help himself. Without wanting to, he gazed beyond her to the stove, the source of the wonderful smell of curry, one of his favorites spices. His nose betrayed him by sniffing.

"That smells like—"

"Curry." She nodded, and turned to the stove to lift the lid off one of two saucepans. "I'm making curried vegetables with rice."

"It smells great." He had to call 'em as he saw 'em.

"Would you like some?" she asked without turning around.

"Ah, no, that's all right," he backed away from her, wishing he could look away from her trim little self leaning against the stove. "I have to get cleaned up and get back to Shawsburg."

When she turned around, he was still standing there. There were little flecks of paint in his hair, and a trace of tiny white speckles across the bridge of his nose like albino freckles. It was all she could do to keep her fingers from brushing them away.

"Was there something else?" she asked.

"Ah, no. Well, actually, yes. I was wondering if I could just go down to the basement and grab a jar of plum jam."

"Sure." She unlocked the basement door and turned on the light. "Of course. It's your basement, your jam . . ."

He tried to avert his eyes on his way downstairs, but that faint scent of spring flowers mixed with curry teased him as he passed her, and he couldn't help himself. His eyes lingered on her face. It was a hard face for a man to turn away from, and it held him for what seemed like a very long moment.

"I'll just . . . go on—" he heard himself mumble

when he realized how long he'd been staring—
"downstairs . . ." His feet made brief thumping
sounds as he ran down the steps.

When he came back up, he was empty-handed.

"Did you change your mind?" she asked. "About
the jam?"

"I couldn't find it."

"Plum?"

He nodded.

"I know there's some there. I saw several jars last
week." She dried her hands on a towel and motioned
for him to follow her back down the steps.

He followed.

She turned the small light on in the corner of the
basement and opened the cupboard doors. She knelt
down and began moving jars around on the second
shelf.

"Here," she said, handing up two large jars of
peaches, "hold these so I can look around in here.
You moved things a bit."

"I might have." He stepped up close behind her,
taking the large glass jars from her hands.

"Ah, here they are. You must have pushed them
toward the back." She swiveled around a bit and
started to rise, not realizing how close he was. When
she stood up, she found herself just below his chin,
her hands and the jars skimming his chest.

She looked up at him, struck by the depth of his
dark brown eyes, the long lashes like so much thick
fringe. The proximity of his face startled her. She
tried to move back, but the cupboard was behind her,
and she was trapped between it and his body. There
was a very male presence about him, and her reaction

to it caught her breath in her throat. For the first time in a very long time, Georgia was speechless.

Matt looked down into her face, and fought back the bad angel who had come from nowhere to perch upon his shoulder and whisper in his ear. *Kiss her. Kiss her now.*

"Ah . . . I'll take . . ." Matt reached for the jars of jam she held, only to realize that he was still holding the larger jars.

"Oh. Right. Here. I'll take the peaches . . ." She seemed to be fumbling as much as he was, and they made an awkward exchange of the jars in a tight space.

It hadn't occurred to Matt that he could have just backed up.

It hadn't occurred to Georgia to ask him to.

"Well, then." He cleared his throat. "I guess we're done down here."

"Right." She turned her back and bent down to replace the jars of peaches on the shelf.

When she stood back up, he still hadn't moved. "Matt? Was there something else you wanted?"

"What?" The bad angel, who had been at that moment comparing the sight of her butt in jeans to that of her butt in her leotard, encouraged Matt to respond in a manner guaranteed to win him a smack across the face.

"Oh, no. No. This is fine." Matt slapped a hand over the bad angel's mouth and opted for the high road. "Thanks."

Georgia closed the cupboard door and turned out the light. For a moment, she was lost in the darkness. With his free hand, Matt reached out, seeking her face, just to make certain that she had not, somehow, disappeared before his eyes. The fingers of his right hand found bone, and they lightly traced the line of her cheek before pulling back.

"You're welcome."

The sound of her voice broke the spell, and somewhat nonplused, Matt stood aside, motioning for her to go ahead of him to the steps.

She climbed them softly, and he followed closely, the bad angel filling his mind with randy thoughts as they ascended to the kitchen.

"Are you sure you wouldn't like to stay?" she asked.

"I . . . um . . . really have to get back," he muttered. "To Shawsburg."

If he didn't leave, he'd be drooling as pathetically as Artie was. And not necessarily just from the curry.

"Oh. Okay." She lifted the lid again and tossed in a handful of raisins, then a handful of green onions.

"So, thanks." He opened the door and walked through it as quickly as he could.

"For what?"

"For . . . for feeding my dog." He slapped the side of his leg and Artie caught up with him.

From the doorway, Georgia watched Matt cross the yard to the barn, where he went up the outside stairs to his apartment. She was still watching as the lights appeared in the rooms she knew to be his kitchen, his bedroom, his bath.

Unconsciously, her fingers followed the path his had taken along the side of her face.

She had instinctively known that there was no good reason why he had to rush back to Shawsburg.

In spite of the spark that had passed between them—his hand to her face—it was obvious that he wanted to avoid being anywhere near her. She had known that he didn't like her, didn't want to get to know her, so it shouldn't have come as a surprise, but it had.

It shouldn't have hurt, but it did.

chapter twelve

The sun had not quite risen the next morning when Georgia was awakened by the muffled sound of leaves rustling somewhere beneath her window. She crept from her bed and stealthily pulled the curtain aside to take a look. There, there in the shadows near the garden, something lurked. Was it crouched near the gate, perhaps trying to undo the string she had tied there?

She tiptoed back into the bedroom, where she quietly lifted the telephone and dialed the number—which she now knew by heart—for the police department.

"This is Georgia Enright at the old Evans farm. The person who's been vandalizing the gardens out here is back, he's out there now and I would like someone to come out and arrest him." She whispered into the phone, as if the intruder could hear her from her room on the second floor.

Assured that someone would be right there, Georgia threw off her nightgown and jumped into her jeans and a sweatshirt, and tied on her old sneakers. She wanted to be there to confront him, whoever he was, and give him a piece of her mind. As the lights from the patrol car eased slowly up the drive, she ran down the steps and unlocked the front door.

"He's right out back," she told the young police officer as he pulled over onto the grassy spot near the house. "Inside the fence . . ."

"You stay here, Miss, in case he's armed," the officer told her protectively.

"Okay." She nodded vigorously, following him to the corner of the house, where she could watch. She wanted to see the perpetrator apprehended. And once he was in custody, Georgia would have a few choice words for her midnight vandal.

"Come out with your hands up," the officer announced from the corner of the house.

There was no response from the garden.

"I know you're in there. Just walk on out through the gate with your hands over your head," the officer called.

There was a faint, indistinguishable noise from the other side of the fence. The officer crept forward to investigate, his gun drawn and his eyes keenly focused on the garden gate.

"Oh, for crying out loud," the officer exclaimed.

"What is it?" Georgia whispered loudly, venturing a brave step from the safety of the shadow of the house.

"I think you should come take a look."

Georgia joined the policeman at the fence.

"There's your intruder." He pointed into the far corner, where a small figure crouched.

The figure was grunting.

"What is it?" She peered more closely over the fence, just as the dark figure sprang forward.

"That's a pig. A Vietnamese potbellied pig."

"A pig?" She frowned and looked down at the animal that was vainly attempting to poke its too-wide snout through the narrow space between the fence posts.

"We see them abandoned from time to time," the officer explained as he leaned over to scratch the area between the pig's eyes. "They used to be real popular as pets about ten years ago. People get tired of 'em, though, just like they sometimes get tired of a dog or a cat, and they turn them loose to fend for themselves."

He continued to scratch the pig's head. The pig closed its eyes and drifted off to heaven.

"It looks tame," Georgia observed.

"Oh, yes. This breed of pig used to be so popular, they used to call 'em Yuppie puppies. They used to sell for big money. A thousand dollars and up, some of them. Lots of big celebrities had 'em. I saw a picture one time of Julia Roberts walking a pig just like that one. Had it on a leash."

Georgia knelt down near the fence to get a better look. The pig stood up as if looking her over at the same time. It was small and black, swaybacked, so that its stomach was near to the ground. It poked its wide, dark nose through the wooden slats and grunted softly.

"I guess if it's been abandoned, it's been coming to the garden to look for food."

"That would explain why the plants were uprooted." The officer knelt down next to Georgia. "I guess you're hungry, aren't you, Spam?"

Georgia laughed at the name. The pig grunted with slightly more vigor.

"Well, I'll take it to the SPCA over in Salisbury." He stood up. "If they're still taking these pigs."

"What will happen to it?" Georgia reached tentative fingers through the fence to touch the snout. The pig's skin was cold and tough, and it nuzzled its face against her hand.

"Well, they'll try to find a home for it. There are some rescue organizations that take in abandoned potbellied pigs, though I've heard that lately, they're turning away more animals than they can take, leaving the local SPCAs to . . . dispose of them however they can."

"Oh, poor Spam," Georgia whispered, and as if to plead its case, the pig made an effort to climb up the side of the fence, causing Georgia to laugh. "Oh, I don't think you're built for climbing. Your legs are far too short and far too much of your weight is too close to the ground."

She stood up and reached over to open the gate.

"Come on, Spam," she called, and the pig trotted out.

As if assessing its chances of survival, the pig looked over both the officer and Georgia, then rolled the dice and flung itself toward Georgia and nudged her knees.

"It likes me!" Georgia exclaimed.

"They say they're real social animals. Lots of folks even had them as house pets."

"You're kidding?" Georgia laughed. "I can't imagine keeping a pig in my house."

She scratched the sides of the pig's head, and the pig appeared to swoon. "How long do you think the SPCA will keep it before they . . . do whatever it is they'll do?"

"A few days, if that. I don't think there's much call for these critters anymore."

"That's so sad, to just turn an animal out like that."

"Especially when most of them this young are probably the product of several generations of domestic breeding. They don't have the survival skills of the wild pigs." He leaned over and, with his flashlight, illumined the pig's left flank, where deep scars gave evidence of some sort of attack. "Looks like something's had at it."

"What do you suppose did that?" Georgia leaned forward to investigate, and the pig lowered itself to the ground and rolled over like a dog wanting its tummy rubbed.

"Dog, maybe. May be a few wild ones out in the woods, there." He pointed out beyond the barn, then stood up. "Come on, Spam, it's time to go. I'll just get some rope out of the car, and we'll be on our way."

The pig rolled close to Georgia's feet, and she leaned forward to scratch its stomach. The pig turned its head toward her and grunted contentedly.

"You're pretty cute," Georgia told it, "for a pig."

"It is, isn't it, in its own peculiar way," the officer chuckled as he came back with the rope. "Let's try this around the neck, like a leash."

The pig rolled over onto its back and pulled itself up from the ground, clearly aware that something was about to happen. As the rope was tied about its neck, it began to squeal faintly, as if appealing for mercy.

"What if I kept it here for a few days?" Georgia heard herself ask. "Maybe it wasn't abandoned. Maybe it's lost. Maybe its owner is looking for it."

"Not likely." The officer shook his head.

"Well, how 'bout if I were to put up a few signs, like at Tanner's?"

"That might work. If it's a lost pig, and if it's from around O'Hearn, the owner might see the sign. Sure. I don't see any harm in you keeping the pig. Just as long as you understand that it isn't likely that it's going to be claimed."

"That would be okay. He can stay in the barn." Georgia slipped the rope from around the pig's head, and the pig nudged at the calf of her right leg.

"Actually, I think it's a 'she,'" the officer said.

"Oh. Well, then, she can stay in the barn till her owner shows up."

"If her owner shows up."

Georgia bent down and petted the top of the pig's head.

"I think I'll get her some breakfast. What do you suppose I should feed her?" Georgia looked up. "You don't suppose they make pig chow, do you?"

The officer nodded. "Well, they make every other kind of chow. I'd try Tanner's—they sell all kinds of livestock supplies. If we're done here, I'll go on back and write up my report. I'm sure Chief Monroe will be happy to find out that we collared your intruder."

Georgia laughed and called her thanks as the officer climbed back into the patrol car.

"Well, then, Spam . . . I think we'll keep that name, it's kind of cute." Georgia stood, hands on her hips, talking to the pig. "I think I'm going to go in and get my breakfast. You can wait over here in the garden . . . come on."

She walked to the fence and opened the gate, the pig trotting along behind her as if it knew it had just gotten a reprieve, and was determined to follow orders.

"I'll be back out in a while and I'll bring you something. Don't know what, but I'll find something for you."

The pig replied with a grunt as a laughing Georgia turned back toward the house.

Later, after she'd filled an old pan with water and taken it out to the garden, she told her new companion, "I'm going to run into Tanner's now, and see what kind of food they have for pigs. In the meantime, you can munch on these carrots—look, I even saved you the tops—and you can stay here in the garden till I get back. Feel free to root around all you want, because there's nothing left here that you haven't already eaten. And be a good little piggy while I'm gone."

It amused her, she realized, to have taken in the little pig. Zoey and Ben had pups—adorable golden retrievers named Diva and Dozer (short for Bulldozer), and the Devlin home had a cat. Delia had a big old cat named Gracie, a barn full of horses and ponies, and several dogs. Up until now, Georgia was the only member of the family who had no pet.

At least I'll have a little company when I'm outside, she

thought as she strolled the rows of animal chows, finally locating what she needed. She found herself wishing she could have called Matt to ask him about what to feed Spam and if there was any special care one needed to give a potbellied pig. Surely he'd know. She dismissed the thought as quickly as Matt had dismissed her the week before, bolting and running from the kitchen as if he couldn't get away from her fast enough. She'd been bothered for days by the look in his eyes as he had backed away from her, as if she were tainted.

I guess as far as he's concerned, I am, she sighed absently as she approached the cashier. *I'm an Enright.*

She had several bags of pig chow loaded into the back of the Jeep along with two large-sized dog bowls—one for food, one for water. On her way out the door, she pinned the index card with the FOUND: VIETNAMESE POTBELLIED PIG notice to the bulletin board inside the front door. If in fact Spam was lost, surely her owners would want to know where she was and how to find her.

"Well, let's see what you think of this," Georgia told Spam as she poured the packaged pig chow into the just-purchased bowl and set it on the ground.

Spam approached it, sniffed it, then attacked her meal with gusto.

"Spammy, you eat like—well, frankly—like a pig. When you're done, we'll take a stroll over to the barn and see if we can find some accommodations that suit you."

It was obvious that Spam did not like the barn. She peered curiously into the empty stalls, then bolted for the door and raced back to the house. When a laughing Georgia caught up to the pig, it was lounging near the porch steps.

"Sorry, but no," Georgia said aloud. "There will be no pigs living in my house."

Spam sighed and plunked her head down onto the ground.

"Well, maybe you could sleep on the back porch there. At least it's enclosed and you'd be safe from things that might think you look like a pork chop."

Georgia opened the screened door at the top of the steps and went inside the porch, which was enclosed by windows on three sides. It might work . . .

The phone was ringing in the kitchen, and she answered it on the sixth ring.

"I was just about to hang up, *cara*."

"Lee! I was thinking about you just yesterday! I miss you!" Georgia cried.

"And being psychic, I knew that. And I miss you too, Georgey. Now, tell me, how's farm life?"

"Oh, I love it! Pumpkin Hill is wonderful. I wish you could see it, Lee. I know you'd love it too."

"Well, you just might get your wish. I was thinking about driving up over the weekend and bringing your rent check. Adam moved in on Monday, and I asked for two months in advance plus a month's security."

"Wow. That's terrific! Thank you." Georgia quickly calculated three times the agreed upon rent and realized that her own rent plus food money was covered well into the future, the condo in Baltimore having demanded a loftier price than the nominal sum Laura had asked for the farmhouse.

"You're quite welcome. Adam is thrilled with the

location, and loves the apartment. He told me to tell you that if you ever decide to sell it, he'll be first in line with an open check book."

"That's good to know, though I haven't thought that far ahead. I am just enjoying each day here as it comes. Oh, and Lee! I have a pet!"

"Oh?" He asked.

"You'll never guess," she giggled. "I have a pig."

"Sorry, *cara*, there must be something wrong with the connection. For a minute, it sounded like you said you have a pig."

"I did. I do. I found her just today. Her name is Spam and she's a Vietnamese potbellied pig. We think she was abandoned."

"Ah, and you took her in. Well, I've heard they're wonderful pets. You know, years ago, I had friends in Connecticut who had several miniature potbellied pigs. They were litter trained, like cats, and were kept in the house."

"I cannot bring myself to have a pig wandering through the house. But I'm thinking I might let her sleep on the back porch at night. It's enclosed, though not heated. Maybe I can find some old blankets someplace for her to lay on."

"Well, I can't wait to see her. And you. I haven't had a day off in months, and I thought that Saturday I'd try to steal a few hours and drive out to spend them with you. That is, of course, if you're free . . ."

"Of course, I'm free! What time would you like to come?"

"Would sometime in the afternoon be convenient?"

"Yes. Oh, I'm giving ballet lessons to my niece and

a few of her friends at eleven. You can come early and watch, if you like."

"Ballet lessons? *Cara,* have you opened your own studio already?" Lee chuckled. "Ah, I knew you couldn't stay away from it."

"I wouldn't exactly call it a *studio.* And I've only just started. But it's such fun, Lee. Ally and her little friends are so enthusiastic, so happy to learn every new little step. And I'm dancing every day now, for several hours. Just for the sheer fun of it. I'd forgotten how much fun it can be."

"I'm delighted for you, Georgey. You haven't had near enough fun these past few years. It would appear that walking away when you did may have been the best thing for you."

"What are they saying about me?" She asked. "I mean, people in the troupe."

"Nothing of any relevance, I'm sure." He said off-handedly. "Now, I will need directions . . ."

Georgia gave Lee instructions for finding the farm, and hung up the phone with a smile on her face. She hummed as she went back outside to give Spam some chunks of apple. Next she would change into her leotard and dance for a while. Maybe today she'd dance something modern, something bold and inter-pretive.

She searched the stack of CDs she'd left on the coffee table in the living room, hoping to find a song with a tempo to match her mood. Ah, this one. Tori Amos. "These Precious Things." Perfect.

Humming the tune, she took the steps two at a time, anxious to get on with her day.

* * *

Laura was a half-hour late on Saturday, Georgia having just decided to call the inn when the dark blue van arrived. Out poured Ally and not two, but four friends, all giggling and toting small canvas bags.

"I'm sorry, Georgia," Laura told her, "but this thing just seems to keep snowballing. It seems that our Ally had mentioned at lunch yesterday that she was having ballet lessons and the more the merrier— you really do have to watch what you say around children, Georgia, they take you literally—and the next thing I knew, Missy and Lydy were getting dropped off at the house at nine this morning, all ready to dance. Their moms all said to send them the bill for their lessons. Do you mind terribly?"

"I don't mind at all," Georgia laughed. "Besides, there are only five of them. That's no more of a problem than three were last week."

"Well, I think if you are going to continue to do this, you should decide how much you are going to charge their mothers for the lessons."

"I never thought of doing that." Georgia frowned. "I really was doing this for Ally."

"And Ally now has half the girls in her kindergarten class ready to sign up. And since it seems that you're a girl who can't say no, you're likely to end up with a dozen or more girls here some weekend soon. I think you need to decide what exactly you want to do here."

Laura unlocked the back of the van and started unloading folding chairs. "I know you don't have enough of these, so I brought a few extras for the girls to use. Ally," Laura called to her daughter, who was pointing out all of the farm's points of interest to her friends, "I want you girls to take these chairs to the barn and set them up. Two girls to a chair, please."

The girls divided up the chairs and headed off to the barn, still giggling and chattering.

"Georgia, I need to ask a favor." Laura's eyebrows knit close in concern. "Would you mind terribly if the girls stayed for a few hours after their lesson? One of the nurses from Riverview called just as I was ready to leave the inn. She said my mother is having a bad morning. She keeps asking for my father, and is becoming somewhat argumentative. I'm so sorry, I hate to impose on you, but . . ."

"For heavens sake, Laura, it's no imposition, and there's no need to apologize. Just go."

"I was hoping you'd say that. I brought some stuff to make lunch for the girls. I thought they could have a picnic." Laura pulled a large brown paper bag from the back of the van and balanced it on her hip. "There's bread and peanut butter—I didn't bring jelly, but I know you have tons of that—apples, some cookies . . ."

"Sure. It's not a problem. Give me the bag, and get on your way. The girls will be fine."

"I didn't say anything to Ally," Laura said as she walked to the driver's side. "I just told her I might go visit Grandma while she's dancing. I left a message on Matt's answering machine, so I expect he'll meet me out there." She climbed into the van and closed the door, saying, "I just hate what this disease is doing to my mother. I just hate it."

"I'm sorry, sweetie." Georgia reached through the window to give Laura's arm an encouraging squeeze. "Don't worry about the girls. They can stay all day, if necessary. That is, if the other mothers aren't going to worry."

"I told them I wouldn't be back till later this afternoon. No one objected," she said with a wry smile. "I have a vision of all the other moms heading for the nearest mall to do a little unencumbered shopping and meeting their friends for lunch."

"My friend Lee is driving down from Baltimore today, so we'll have a picnic and we'll do some exploring. We'll be fine."

"Thanks, Georgia." Laura started to drive away, then stopped for a moment and looked back. "The girls won't be in your way, will they? I mean, did you want to be alone with your friend?"

"No, no." Georgia laughed. "He's not that kind of friend. We'll be fine. Go. Take care of your mother. We'll be here when you get back."

Hoisting the bag upon her hip, Georgia carried it to the house and was just about to take it inside when Lee's spiffy little sports car buzzed into the drive and stopped on a dime. She set the bag down on the back steps and went to meet him.

"*Cara!* You're a sight for sore eyes!" He hopped out and hugged her warmly.

"Oh, I missed you, too." Georgia hugged him back.

"Your color is terrific," he told her, "and that pinched look is gone from around your eyes. I'd say country life suits you very well."

"It does. I feel very good."

"Aunt Georgia—" Ally poked out from the barn door and stopped when she saw that her aunt had a visitor.

"I'm coming, sweetie. I'll be right there. Are the chairs all set up?"

Ally nodded.

"I'm on my way." Georgia turned to Lee and said, "You're just in time. My niece and her friends are ready for their dance lesson. Come watch." She tugged on his hand.

"I wouldn't miss it," Lee grinned. "Who knows, there might be a budding Pavlova or Fontayne . . ."

"Or at the very least, five little kindergartners who love to dance."

Georgia's dance class was a rousing success, and all five girls begged to be permitted to come back the following week.

"You will be back," Ally told them. "It's my birthday party, remember? And we're all going to dance!"

"Then the time after that," one of the girls said, tugging on Georgia's sleeve. "Can I come the time after the party?"

Georgia paused, thinking about what Laura had said. Maybe she should give some consideration to setting up a more organized program, and charging for it. There did appear to be a demand, and she had certainly enjoyed the time she spent with the girls.

"Why don't I speak with your mother and see what we can work out?" Georgia said.

"Will you talk to my mother too, please?" Samantha asked.

"And mine!"

"And mine, too!"

"All right," laughed Georgia. "I'll speak with all your mothers. Now, I think we'll leave the chairs here for next week. But take your bags and we'll go back to the house so that you can change. We're going to take Lee on a tour of the farm. Oh, and I have a surprise to show you!"

She remembered Spam, who was at that moment lounging in the garden, probably sleeping contentedly in the warm spring sun.

The girls raced down the steps as Georgia gathered up her music.

"So, what did you think?" she asked Lee.

"I think you are a natural teacher. I think you have a gift, *cara*." He told her. "I think your greatest contribution to dance may well be your ability to share it with others. You were wonderful with the children, and your face just glowed the entire time."

"I was having fun."

"And it was obvious. I would definitely give some thought to teaching, if I were you. And you know," he looked around the big open space, "this could be a wonderful studio. Why, a few skylights, a few mirrors . . ."

". . . a few less splinters in the floor," Georgia laughed. "But I don't really know how long I'll be here. It wouldn't be worth it to make such an investment."

"So you skip the skylights. How much can a few mirrors, a barre and a floor sander cost?"

Georgia shrugged.

"I think it's worth looking into," Lee said.

"You may be right. Maybe I should talk to Laura and see what she thinks."

"Well, while you debate your employment options, why not give me that tour I was promised? And where's this little piggy you told me about?" Lee took her arm.

"Oh! Spam! I left her in the garden. And it looks as if the girls have found her." Georgia took off across the yard ahead of her guest. "Ally, don't scare her, okay? She's a little on the timid side."

"Where'd you get her? Is she yours? Can we keep her? What's her name?" Ally jumped up and down excitedly.

"Her name is Spam . . ."

"Spam!" Five giggly girls repeated in unison.

"Here, Spam, it's okay," Georgia crooned. The little pig crept to her, a wary eye on the others. "See, she's very sweet, but she's a little overwhelmed. There are so many of you, and only one of her."

"Can we touch her, Aunt Georgia?"

"Why not take turns just letting her sniff your hand until she gets used to the commotion?"

One by one, the little girls poked little fingers gingerly through the fence.

"Oh! Her skin is rough!"

"Ugh! She licked my finger!"

"Does she sleep in the barn?"

"No," Georgia stood up, watching Lee, who had walked to his car and opened the trunk. "She sleeps on the back porch."

"Does she have a bed?"

"No, but I do need to find something. I think pigs sleep in straw, but I don't want to litter the back porch with that."

"How about this?" Lee was on his way back to the garden, a large basket held high over his head.

"Oh!" Ally cried. "It's a big dog bed! With a plaid cushion like the one Aunt Zoey got for Diva!"

"Oh, Lee, for heaven's sake . . ." Georgia laughed out loud.

"Think she'll like it?" Lee asked.

"I think she'll love it. Here, bring it in and let's see if she can figure out what to do." Georgia opened the gate.

"Here you go, Spam," Lee said softly as he lowered the wicker bed to the ground and patted the cushion. "What do you think of this?"

The pig hesitated for a moment, then investigated the basket with her snout. In the blink of an eye she had climbed in and rolled onto her back, much to the delight of the children.

"She loves it, Lee," Georgia hugged him. "What a clever gift."

"I'm glad she likes it. I wanted to get you a house warming, and couldn't think of anything that you didn't already have."

"It's perfect. Thank you. Spam thanks you. Now, girls, run inside and change into play clothes. And wash your hands really well, because we're going to make peanut butter and jelly sandwiches and pack a lunch for a picnic down by the pond."

Five pairs of small feet headed to the house.

"They must be hungry," Georgia mused. "I only had to tell them once."

"Georgia, are you expecting someone?" Lee asked.

"No, why?"

"Because you keep watching the drive as if you're waiting for someone."

"Do I? I didn't realize." She shrugged. "No. I'm not waiting for anyone."

But later, as they strolled back from their picnic, the girls running ahead with Spam, Lee noticed the black pickup truck parked near the barn right about the same time Georgia did. He saw the look on her face, and the color rise to her cheeks as her eyes scanned the yard from side to side.

"Whose truck is that?" Lee asked casually.

"Truck?" she reddened. "Oh, that truck. That belongs to Laura's brother."

"Now, would that be your half brother?"

"Oh, no. We're not related." She answered much too quickly, Lee thought. "Laura was adopted by a family named Bishop. Years after they adopted her, they adopted a little boy."

"I see. And how old is this little boy now?"

"He's about my age. Maybe a little older. I'm not sure." She shrugged as if to show that the age of Laura's brother—that Laura's brother himself—was of no consequence.

Lee smiled to himself. To one who knew her well, she was as transparent as glass.

"What's he like?"

"What's who like?"

"Laura's brother. What does he do?"

"He's a veterinarian. In Shawsburg." She poked him in the ribs. "And he's not your type."

Lee laughed. "But I would venture a guess that he might be your type."

"Why would you say that?"

"Because you are blushing to the very tips of your

fingers, a phenomenon I have only witnessed once in all the years I've known you."

"Matt is . . . he's . . ." She tried to come up with words that would describe how she felt about him, but wasn't doing a very good job of it.

". . . quite a handsome young man." Lee nodded in the direction of the barn, where Matt was coming down the side steps behind his dog.

Matt whistled to get Ally's attention, and she skipped across the yard to throw herself into his arms, while Artie sped across the grass.

"Lee, Matt has not been quite as welcoming as Laura."

"Really?"

"Really. As a matter of fact, he doesn't want me here at all. If he had his way, I would just disappear and take my whole family with me."

"Now, why would you say that?" Lee glanced down at his beeper as it went off, then frowned as he read the number which flashed across the small screen. "Damn. It's the restaurant. I hope nothing's wrong. May I use your phone?"

"Sure. It's on the wall right inside the kitchen door." Georgia said, seemingly unaware that her eyes had never left the dark-haired man who was swinging Ally around by her arms.

Dropping Ally carefully onto her feet, Matt looked past her to where Georgia strolled with Lee. The look on his face was not the look of a man who gazed upon someone he wished would disappear.

A squeal of terror startled them both.

"That's Spam . . . oh, no. Artie!"

Georgia took off across the yard.

"Artie, no, no!" She called to the dog, who was in the process of backing the terrified pig into the fence. "Good dog, Artie. Here, Artie."

Artie wagged his tail. He knew he was a good dog. He was also a pleased dog, having backed the strange-looking creature into a corner.

"It's okay, Spam," she said as she knelt down next to the frightened pig. Only Spam's low-slung profile kept her from climbing into Georgia's lap. "Artie, you have to be nice to Spam."

"Spam?"

She looked up to see Matt, who had raced to discover the cause of the commotion.

"She's my pet." Georgia told him without looking up.

"She's one scared little hambone." He leaned down and placed one big hand on the pig's neck as if taking her pulse. "Artie, come here."

The dog, who had been busy making friends with Lee, bounded over. Immediately, the pig began to scream.

"Artie, sit. Be nice." Matt told him.

Artie sat.

"Do you mind?" He asked Georgia as he reached for the pig. She handed Spam over.

"Aw, it looks like something almost had you for dinner." Matt gently examined the scars on the pig's hindquarters. "I'll bet it was a big dog like Artie, wasn't it? Is that why you're so afraid of him? Aw, poor girl. It's okay, Artie won't hurt you, will you, Artie?"

Artie lay down on the grass and looked innocent.

"She's in pretty good shape, it would seem," Matt was saying, "except for the scars. Where'd you get her?"

"She just showed up. As a matter of fact, she's our garden-mauler. I found her raiding the garden at about five in the morning a few days ago."

"Someone turned you out, didn't they?" Matt said, and Spam, knowing a friendly voice when she heard one, grunted.

"So, then, what are you going to do with her?"

"What do you mean, what am I going to do with her? I'm going to keep her."

"You'll forgive me, but you just don't strike me as the pig type. A bichon frise, maybe. Or a silkie. A papillion. Maybe even a Persian cat. But a pig?" He shook his head. "It just doesn't seem to fit."

"You couldn't be more wrong." She gathered her pig to her side. "Spam is exactly the right pet for me, aren't you, girl?" Georgia gave Spam a tickle under the chin and the pig rolled over happily, if somewhat warily, Artie still being clearly too close for Spam's peace of mind.

"Georgia, are you going to introduce me to your friend?" Lee had been watching the exchange from the top step with great amusement. He couldn't remember when he'd ever seen Georgia blush like that. Or the last time he'd seen a man fight harder not to notice than Matthew Bishop at that exact moment.

"Lee, this is Laura's brother, Matt. Matt, this is my good friend, Lee Banyon."

Matt offered Lee a reluctant hand and a scowl.

Lee smiled broadly. Unless he was mistaken, that scowl was warning Lee to back off.

Interesting. Very interesting.

"Georgia, I'm so sorry, but I have to go back to the restaurant. It seems the cook sliced off half a finger and if we're going to be serving dinners tonight, it appears that I will be cooking them."

"Oh, I was hoping you could stay . . ." Georgia was clearly disappointed.

"Next time, I promise. Now, let me say good-bye to those adorable little dancers of yours, and to you, of course, Matt, nice to meet you." Lee gathered Georgia into his arms and kissed her soundly.

Behind her, Lee noticed, Matt's knuckles were turning white.

Ah, so that's how it is, is it? Lee mused as he kissed the top of Georgia's head and swung an arm around her as they walked to the car. He could feel Matt's eyes boring holes through his shirt. Georgia, however, appeared to be totally unaware.

"I'll call you, Georgia."

"Do. I want you to come back."

"Nothing could keep me away." Lee started his car. "Think about what I said, Georgey. About the dance studio."

"I will." She nodded.

"Bye, Lee," the girls tumbled out of the house.

"Bye, girls!" He waved as he turned the car around and sped down the drive to the road.

"Aunt Georgia, can we go back down to the pond?"

"Sure. Just try not to get too muddy."

The girls ran off in a pack of pigtails and sneakers.

Georgia started to follow, a pacified but still some-what wary Spam at her feet.

"Just a minute." Matt grabbed her elbow.

"What?"

"I don't think you should be making plans to have your boyfriend come to stay if Ally is here with her friends. I don't think it gives her a very good message."

"I think you assume too much," was all she said, distracted by the pulsing bits of fire that were spreading from his fingers to her upper arm and across her chest and back like an electrical current. "If you'll excuse me, I need to keep an eye on the girls."

Matt stood with his hands on his hips watching her walk through the field, Spam trotting at Georgia's heels while keeping a watchful eye on Artie, and tried to deny to himself that he wished he was walking with them. That seeing her again hadn't been the real reason he'd made the trip to Pumpkin Hill. That it didn't bother him a whit that there was a man in her life for whom she obviously cared greatly. That he hadn't felt a gnawing at his insides watching the sway of her hips as she disappeared over that first rise that led down to the pond.

"Matt!"

Laura touched his shoulder and he started.

"Matt, didn't you hear me calling?"

"No. I was, um, looking for Artie. He, ah, took off someplace." He mumbled, not willing to admit that he'd been distracted to the point of deafness.

"I guess you didn't get the message I left on your answering machine earlier today."

"No, I didn't go back to the house after I closed up the clinic."

"Artie will find his way back. He always does." Laura took his arm gently and turned him back toward the house. "Let's go inside and have a cup of tea. We need to talk, Matt, about Mother . . ."

chapter thirteen

The back road between Shawsburg and O'Hearn was old and bumpy, the result of too many potholes gone far too long without repair. Having made the trip so often over the years, Matt knew where the worst of the craters lay, yet today, his attention being diverted by other things, he somehow managed to hit just about every one of them. He cursed under his breath as his right front tire bounced into a particularly nasty patch of broken macadam head-on, causing the cab to swerve momentarily toward the center of the road. The jolt on the worn out shocks slammed his back teeth into his tongue.

He should have seen that one coming. He'd hit it once before, some months earlier, but since then had been successful in avoiding it. Until today. Of course, the last time he'd driven this way he hadn't quite as many distractions fighting for his attention.

Matt sighed and leaned back against the worn leather seat, his right hand absently reaching over to pat Artie's back in time to the music on the truck's radio. He'd been in the mood for oldies that afternoon, but the radio was acting up again. He settled for a static-y version of Van Morrison's *Brown Eyed Girl* and tried to force himself to relax. It had been a very tough week, and this weekend was not likely to make things any easier.

He eased up on the gas pedal, reminding himself that he had no good reason to want to get to Pumpkin Hill any sooner than necessary. If it wasn't Ally's birthday, he wouldn't be going at all, having decided that, after today, he'd keep his visits to the farm at a minimum for as long as Georgia was there. Something about the woman worked on his nerves in strange ways, and he knew enough to know the less *that* territory was explored, the better off he'd be, all things considered. He hoped that he wouldn't have to see too much of her today, because he really wasn't in much of a social mood. Daily visits to Riverview over the past six days had totally drained him emotionally. The news hadn't changed from one day to the next. His mother was deteriorating, and it was breaking his heart.

He just didn't have much left to deal with Georgia Enright.

With any luck, his contact with her today would be minimal. He wondered if her friend—had his name been Lee?—would be there. The thought soured his mood even more—another bit of business he didn't feel like thinking too much about right now.

There were more cars than he'd expected already parked along both sides of the drive leading to the farm, and Matt had to weave between a dark green mini-van and a long Mercedes sedan to get to his usual spot under the oak tree back near the barn. He glanced at the sedan as he walked past, wondering which of Ally's friends had parents prosperous enough to afford such a vehicle.

Music from the barn's second floor told him that the dancing lesson portion of the festivities had already begun. He stood near the barn door debating whether to go up and watch or to sneak into his apartment via the outside steps. He would have loved to skip the rest of the afternoon completely, but this was Ally's day, and she would want him to see her dance.

"You sit, Artie. Stay right here till I come back. And don't go chasing after that little porker, hear?" Matt told the dog, who flopped under a nearby tulip poplar tree and watched with soulful eyes as his master walked away.

Matt blew out his resignation in a long thin stream of air and opened the barn door. Once inside, the music was loud and full, and he started up the steps reluctantly.

Matt didn't know much classical music, but he recognized the piano tune that had been playing the first time he'd barged into Ally's dance class. The tempo had segued from lively and spirited to light and delicate, and halfway up the steps he almost stopped, knowing *she'd* probably be wearing that pink thing. He wasn't sure he wanted to subject himself to that again. He just didn't think he was up to it.

But it was Ally's birthday, and she was expecting him.

When he reached the top of the steps, he was surprised to see how the old barn had been transformed. There were folding chairs—with pink and lavender balloons tied onto their backs with long strings—in a semicircle around the makeshift dance floor, and upon the chairs sat the mothers of a few of Ally's friends, and a few other adults Matt did not recognize. There was only one seat left, that being next to a kindly looking older woman in her mid-sixties with straight salt and pepper hair who turned upon hearing Matt's footsteps. She smiled at him pleasantly as she removed her sweater from the vacant chair and patted the seat, inviting him to sit. On her right sat a pretty and obviously pregnant woman with masses of blond curls pulled back from a delicate face, and next to her, a dark-haired man who appeared to be in his early thirties who watched the ballet lesson with mild amusement. Laura sat near the opposite end of the row whispering something to a woman Matt recognized as the mother of one of Ally's friends from Bishop's Cove.

From her place behind her chair where she had lined up in third position, Ally bounced up and down with glee when she realized that Matt had arrived.

"Hey, Uncle Matt! You were late and we had to start without you!" She cupped her hands to her mouth and stage whispered.

"Sorry, sugar. I got a late start." He whispered back.

"It's okay. You're here now and you can watch me!"

"I'm watching, Ally." He leaned forward and rested his forearms on his thighs, his hands dangling between his knees, and tried to pretend that he did not see Ally's ballet teacher.

He had been right. She was wearing the pink thing, only today she also wore a light pink chiffon-y wrap skirt thingy that tied around her tiny waist. She had piled her hair atop her head, but it was too thick and too heavy to stay there. Long tendrils had escaped to flirt with the back of her neck and the sides of her face, which was flushed as pink as the leotard that was leaving little to the imagination as far as that petite and perfect body was concerned. Matt decided he was better off keeping his eyes on the students and away from the teacher.

There were a dozen or so little dancers who had been invited to spend the day with Ally, and they all hung on Georgia's every word. Surprisingly, there was no horseplay and very little giggling while the steps were being taught, nor any later when each of the girls had a turn to perform the positions along with the teacher. All of the adults, on the other hand, ooh'd and ahh'd at the girls' efforts. In particular, Matt noticed a handsome looking woman with short, soft hair the color of champagne sitting five seats away who beamed with pleasure as she watched the dancers follow their instructor around in a circle to end the performance. The small audience applauded the efforts of the children as the class came to an end.

"And that concludes our lesson for today," Georgia bowed first to the audience, then to her class, telling them, "Girls, there's a cooler over here with popsicles if you'd like one . . ."

She laughed then, as the small sea of sprites in various colored leotards engulfed her, and she opened the cooler and took a few steps back to permit the children access to the treats. As she did, she caught Matt's eye. She'd known he'd been watching her, had felt his eyes on her before she'd been aware of his arrival. She tried to smile at him as a sort of peace offering, to make him feel at ease, surrounded, as he was, by Enrights and near-Enrights, but he appeared to be making polite conversation with August Devlin, who was seated on his right. Georgia wondered if Matt knew how close to the enemy camp he had been sitting, then realized that he had no way of knowing that many of those in the audience were members of her immediate family.

"Is there anything more *earnest* than little girls who are just learning their first ballet steps?" The woman who sat next to Matt patted his arm. "Aren't they just delightful?"

"They are cute, yes, ma'am," Matt nodded.

"And have you ever seen anyone more graceful than Georgia?" The woman shook her head slightly in admiration, then added, in Latin, *"Vera incessu patuit dea."*

It took a minute or so for his four years of high school Latin to kick in so that he could translate the phrase. *By her walk the true goddess was revealed.*

He smiled wryly and asked, "Virgil?"

"Good for you, my boy." The woman laughed. "I'm afraid I forget myself at times. I taught Latin for more years than I care to admit to, and old habits, you see, do indeed die hard." She said as she stood, dropping the forgotten sweater. Before Matt could respond, she asked, "Now, did I hear Ally call you 'uncle'?"

"Yes," he said as he bent down to pick up the sweater, earning him a smiled thanks as he handed it to her. "Ally is my niece."

"Then you must be Matthew. Laura's brother." She touched his arm softly with the fingers of her left hand.

"Yes," he nodded.

"I'm very pleased to meet you, Matthew," she said with a smile that revealed dimples in her softly lined face. "Laura's told us so much about you. And of course, we've all been looking forward to meeting you."

"I'm sorry, ma'am, but you are . . . ?"

"Terrible of me." She flustered. "I'm August Devlin."

The name rang familiar but not familiar enough for Matt to readily identify it. His blank expression gave him away, and she laughed again, saying, "Which tells you nothing, I would guess. I'm India Devlin Enright's aunt."

"Oh," he said, not quite sure of who India Devlin Enright might be, other than to know she was a part of Laura's life that did not include him. "Nice to meet you. If you'll excuse me, I just want to see my sister for a minute . . ."

Matt's head had begun to pound as he walked toward Laura, the barn walls closing in upon him. How many of the people surrounding him were members of her new family, and why hadn't she prepared him? He stopped halfway across the scuffed pine floor and caught Georgia's eye. He wanted to pretend he had not seen her, but there was something in her expression—a wary, uncertain welcome—that spoke to him whether he wanted to listen or not, and for a moment he felt as if he had read her mind. The unexpected intimacy spooked him, and suddenly, speaking to Laura did not seem so very important after all. He turned and walked toward the stairwell, fishing in his pants pocket for his keys. By the time he had reached the door to his apartment, the key was in his hand and slid into the lock in the blink of an eye.

Georgia's eyes were on him every step of the way.

He's fled like one in fear—or in pain, she thought. *Perhaps a bit of both . . .*

She bit her bottom lip, wondering whether to follow her first instinct—to follow him—or to let it go.

"This was lovely, darling," Delia approached Georgia from behind and kissed the side of her daughter's face. "What a wonderful place for a dance studio, such wonderful space. Although you really do need some mirrors and a real barre. And you really should do something about the lighting."

"What?" Georgia, whose mind had not been on her surroundings, tuned back in. "Oh. Yes. Well, you know I'm only staying month to month for the time being, so I have to make do."

"Maybe you should think about looking for a more permanent spot. Your little dancing school has tremendous potential. All the mothers are talking about signing their daughters up for regular lessons. You could have quite the lively business going. I can just see the sign out front," Delia mused. "Ballet in the Barn . . . at Pumpkin Hill."

Georgia laughed. "Why, thank you, Mother. If I

decide to open a real dancing school, I just might use it. It does have a certain flair, doesn't it?"

"You are a wonderful teacher, Georgia." Zoey joined them. "You had those little ones eating out of your hand. And you looked like you were having such a good time."

"I was. I really enjoy working with them more than I ever imagined."

"Well, I for one am very impressed." Delia said. "Your little students are adorable, and you look better than I have seen you look in years. I had the same feeling I used to get, watching you dance so long ago. You look, well, *happy*, Georgia."

"I am happy, Mother." Georgia's eyes kept returning to the door in the wall at the top of the steps to see if Matt had reappeared. He had not.

Georgia handed Delia the tape deck and said. "Mother, would you take this down with you? We're going to need these chairs outside for the party— some of the mothers are staying plus there are so many of *us*—so I want to get Nicky and Ben and Zoey to help carry them. Oh! And there's Gordon Chandler. Ally must have invited him."

"Gordon Chandler . . . ?" Delia's eyebrows knit together in concentration, as she tried to place the name.

"Oh, Mother, you've met him. At a book convention or something a few years ago, he mentioned it. He's a ship salvager . . ."

"Of course! I remember him." Delia smiled. "Fascinating man."

Georgia grinned and her eyes began to sparkle. She

leaned close to her mother's ear and whispered, "Intelligent. Handsome. Witty. And he's a widower."

Delia laughed and took the tape player from Georgia's hands. "I'll certainly be interested in seeing him again. Now, did you want this in the house, sweetie?"

"The girls might want to play some music later, so I guess you can leave it on the big folding table that Laura is setting up in the yard." Georgia turned and called to her brother, "Nicky, there are four more chairs along the wall there . . ."

The children had taken off down the steps, headed for the house where they would change into play clothes, the mothers who had attended following behind, all enthusiastically discussing their plans to not only sign up their daughters for regular lessons, but to talk Georgia into having an adult class as well. The chair brigade had formed and was on its noisy way toward the ground floor. Georgia watched as the Enright crew passed by.

Nick. India. Aunt August. Zoey. Ben. Corri. Mother. Me.

It must seem to Matt that there are so many of us.

And only one of him.

She paused at the top of the steps, her hand on the light switch. Matt would still be in his apartment, right behind that door.

He must be feeling so alone. So overwhelmed . . .

Without a second thought, Georgia knocked lightly on the door, which swung partly open at her touch. When Matt did not answer, she pushed the door open the rest of the way and stepped into the small kitchen.

Matt stood at the sink, a glass of water in his hand, his gazed fixed upon the farmyard below.

"Excuse me," she said softly from the doorway. "May I come in?"

"It looks like you already have."

She smiled wryly, then took a few steps into the room that was rapidly filling with tension. She took a deep breath.

"Ally is having a wonderful birthday," she began. "She was so afraid you wouldn't come."

"I have never missed Ally's birthday." He said somewhat stiffly, trying to ignore the faint trace of honeysuckle that seemed to accompany her. He knew the scent well, it being the only fragrance his aunt had ever worn. "She knew I would be here."

"I'm glad you are."

Georgia took another tentative step toward him, as if approaching a rabbit that was likely to take off at any minute. Searching for the right thing to say, she followed his gaze to where the strangers gathered below.

Perhaps, she thought, *if the strangers had names . . .*

"That's August Devlin, in the blue and white dress. The woman you sat next to during the dance class."

"She introduced herself."

"Then you know that she's India's aunt."

"Yes."

"India is that beautiful young woman with the honey-blond hair. She's married to my brother, Nick. She's pregnant."

"That would explain the maternity clothes."

Georgia ignored the sarcasm.

"Nicky is the man in the yellow sweater."

Matt did not respond, so she took a step forward, and continued.

"Nick's a marine biologist. He and India live on the Delaware Bay with their daughter, Corri." Georgia ventured close enough to put a finger to the window pane. "Corri is the little girl with the long brown braids. We're also celebrating the finalization of Corri's adoption today. She had been adopted previously by India's brother, Ry. India kept her when he died. She's a wonderful little girl, and we all love her so much. And she's so thrilled to find that she has a cousin. She and Ally have become fast friends."

He recalled the look of total joy on Ally's face when she had announced excitedly that she had a *cousin*. Just like all her friends.

"Now that tall, dark-haired woman who looks so much like Laura—surely you noticed the resemblance—is my sister, Zoey. She's a sales host on a TV shopping channel. The tall man with the dark hair speaking with August is Ben Pierce. He used to race cars. Grand Prix. He and Nicky were best friends as children. Now he and Zoey are engaged."

"Well, now, it sounds like you're just one big happy family."

"We *are* one big happy family, Matt, and whether you like it or not, you're a part of it," she told him gently, touching his arm with her right hand. When he did not pull away, she sought his hand, and slowly began to entwine her fingers with his. "As much as August Devlin and Corri and India . . . as much as any one of us."

She waited for his protest, and when it didn't come, she continued. "Matt, I know this has not been easy for you. I know how close you and Laura have always been. No one wants to come between you.

We're not trying to take her away. Look, I know that accepting major changes in your family is a very difficult thing."

"And what might you know about that?"

She took a deep breath and told him something she had shared only with Zoey.

"I know how I felt when I found out about Laura. I felt . . . betrayed, that my mother had kept this secret from us all these years. Realizing that her secret had been the cause of our father abandoning us so long ago. That I had a sister I had never met, had never even heard about. It was so hard, meeting Laura that first time—sisters meeting as adults—and trying to get to know her. To find out what she was like, what kind of person she was. I was so afraid to meet her, that first time . . . ."

"Laura is a wonderful person. I've always been proud to be her brother." Matt rose to Laura's defense.

"Yes, she is a wonderful person, and you've every reason to be proud of her. I can honestly say that knowing her has enriched my life greatly. I adore her. But if I'd held onto my fear, my prejudices, I'd never have discovered how wonderful she is. Look at all I would have missed, if I hadn't given her a chance."

He continued to stare out the window. Nick was carrying Corri on his shoulders, and Ben was chasing two golden puppies across the lawn.

Finally, smiling reluctantly, he told her, "You're not very subtle, you know."

"It was the best I could do in a pinch." Georgia watched his face hopefully. "Please give us a chance, Matt. For Laura's sake. And for Ally's."

And for your own.

And for mine.

"Maybe you won't like us. Maybe you will. But you'll never know if you don't at least try to get to know us. We're really a very nice family. Laura is very much a part of it, now and always. So in a way, you are too."

He wished he could tell her that it wasn't her, it wasn't her brother or her sister or even her mother that he thought he wouldn't like. Watching them from the window, the easy way they interacted, with lots of laughter, he was starting to think he probably would like them. But at some point during the hours he'd spent at Riverview over the past week he'd lost all hope that his mother would ever regain any semblance of the woman that she had been, and he mourned her. How could he embrace this new family of Laura's and still be true to the family they had once had, especially now, when their mother was slipping away from them forever?

Then, as if reading his mind, Georgia said softly, "It's not a choice, you know. Not either, or. It's *both.* Laura knows that. I wish you did, too."

She stood on her tip toes to kiss the side of his cheek, then dropped his hand, turned and left quietly. He could hear the padding of the soft leather soles of her ballet shoes as they raced down the steps. The barn door swung shut with a bang, and he watched her walk across the drive.

By her walk the true goddess was revealed.

Her candor had stunned him, and it took him a moment to recover from her words as well as from the lingering wisp of her perfume, the softness of her lips on his skin, the gentleness of the touch of her hand, all of which had set his senses on edge. He'd had no defenses against her rationale or the emotions she had stirred up in him.

It isn't either, or . . .

Knowing that he'd been bested on all fronts, Matt sighed.

Who was he to refuse the wishes of a goddess whose touch was both light and searing, who smelled of honeysuckle and was wise enough to temper his inner chaos with her tender logic? Maybe for today, he could put it all aside—his confusion, his uncertainty, his fears for Laura as well as for himself—for Ally's sake, for Laura's.

He emptied the remains of his glass into the sink, then went off to find Ally's gift.

Later, Matt reflected, joining the lively group outside had been so much easier than he had anticipated. Georgia had been right, the Enright's *were* a nice family. There had been more than enough warmth and laughter and good cheer to go around. And, he admitted, it had fed his own family pride to show off Pumpkin Hill to people who admired and appreciated it.

"Georgey, you're the luckiest person in the world," Zoey had sighed with contentment as she stretched her legs out on the grass, an enormous wedge of birthday cake tipping perilously close to the edge of a paper plate. "It is so beautiful here. Look at all those daffodils and all those tulips! Gorgeous!"

"It's just heaven early in the morning," Georgia told her, "when the sun first comes up and it's so quiet, you just can't imagine. And then the birds start singing . . ."

"We'll have to come back and spend a weekend," Nick sunk to the ground between his sisters. "After the baby has been born."

"Oh, I can't wait to see this baby, Nicky."

"Neither can any of the rest of us, Zoey." Delia beamed. "After all, this will be our first baby. I am so sorry that I missed Corrie and Ally's babyhoods. I'm really looking forward to the whole experience."

"We'll see how much she appreciates the 'experience' the first time we drop the baby off for a long weekend," India winked at her husband.

"I will be more than happy to baby-sit. Anytime." Delia laughed. "August and I will be watching every move this child makes, won't we, August?"

"Absolutely *every* move," August nodded vigorously. "Do feel free to plan a long trip. The baby will be in excellent hands."

They were easy with each other, as those who know each other well, who understand each other's body language, tend to be. In spite of himself, Matt found that he envied the closeness of the group. In truth, he had to admit that they had all made an effort to include him in conversations, and had all applauded him heartily when he had defeated Ben, the odds-on favorite in the pie eating contest that Ally had insisted on. Having recently read a story set in the early part of the century, Ally had become fascinated by the descriptions of the games the children had played, and so, along with the pie eating contest, had set her heart on sack races and an egg toss, in addition to the traditional Pin the Tail on the Donkey.

When the games had concluded and the candles on the cake had been lit and blown out to a spirited chorus of the birthday song, some of the young guests had departed and the sun had begun to dip lower behind the trees. For the first time, Laura's entire family—except for Charity—sat together on the grass, savoring the remaining hours of what had been a very pleasant afternoon.

"You know, Pumpkin Hill reminds me a little bit of Mother's place when we were little." Nick said.

"It does," Georgia nodded. "It even has a pond like the one we had."

"Ben, remember when you used to teach me how to catch frogs?" Zoey leaned back against him lazily, her eyes closed, a slight smile on her lips.

Before he could answer, Ally jumped up and cried, "Aunt Zoey, you know how to catch frogs?"

"Are you kidding?" Her eyes still closed, the smile slid across Zoey's face into a grin as she held up her hands and said, "These hands are feared by frogs from here to Pennsylvania."

"Would you show us how?" Ally jumped up and down. "Me and Corri and Samantha and Carly? Now?"

"Sweetest, the first thing you have to do, if you want to catch frogs, is to be very, very quiet."

"We can be quiet." Ally whispered.

"And you have to be barefooted."

Four little girls hit the ground and started to take off their shoes and socks.

"Zoey, they're going to be covered with mud." Delia pointed out.

Zoey sat up and shielded her eyes from the afternoon sun and asked, "Is there a hose?"

"Right on the side of the house." Georgia pointed to it.

"Then it's a-hunting we will go." She kicked off her sandals and stood up. "Now, let's get in a nice, straight line. We need to creep up on the frogs, remember."

Zoey made the motion of zipping her lips.

The girls nodded wordlessly, zipping their lips as Zoey had done.

She motioned for them to follow behind her, and the train of frog hunters headed for the pond with exaggerated stealth.

Ben and Nick exchanged a look of pure mischief.

"So, Ben," Nick asked, "how long you suppose it's been since you gave my sister a good pond-dunk?"

Ben pretended to ponder the question before responding. "Has to have been at least seventeen, eighteen years . . ."

"My, my," Nick grinned, "has it been that long?"

Without another word, the two men immediately began taking off their shoes and socks and set off toward the pond.

"If you go around from behind the barn," Matt called to them, "she won't hear you coming."

Both men grinned.

"We owe you one, Matt." Ben called over his shoulder as they set off for the barn.

"They were full of mischief as boys, and they're still full of it," Delia shook her head. "As bad now as they were when they were twelve and thirteen. Poor Zoey . . ."

India laughed. "I'm willing to bet that 'poor Zoey' can take care of herself. I'd go with them, but it's hard to creep up on someone when you're almost seven months pregnant and rolling like a bowling ball."

"You hardly look like a bowling ball. I never looked as good as you do when I was pregnant with Ally." Laura sat down on a nearby chair, balancing a plate of grilled vegetables on her knee. "And before I forget, Georgia, I want you to feel free to plant up that flower garden, and the vegetable garden behind the barn."

"I've been meaning to ask you about that. I've thought of it. Being a vegetarian, I like the idea of growing my own food."

"What would you grow?"

"Oh, maybe some green beans, squash, peppers, eggplant, and of course, tomatoes. Cantaloupes. Strawberries."

"You know, there are apple and peach trees right along the fence, there." Matt ventured to join the conversation.

"I noticed. I'm looking forward to summer here in a very big way."

Matt had a sudden vision of a tanned Georgia in shorts and a tank top, her long blond hair pulled atop her head in an untidy ponytail, sitting on the top rail of the fence biting into a fresh peach, the juice sliding down her chin and onto her throat, and he almost choked. He tried to blink the vision away, but it was mighty slow to leave.

"Well, if you're going to plant, you need to decide

soon exactly what and where. The ground will need to be turned over, though, so let me know if I can help. That's a lot of work." Matt offered, wondering if it would help if he tried to make the vision wear one of those long things people used to wear over their clothes in the rain. What were those things called? A poncho . . . ?

"I'm not afraid of a little hard work." She told him. "And I love working outside. I spend a lot of time out here. Just me and my little piggy."

She scratched a weary Spam on the snout. The pig had had an active day, avoiding the pups, running from the children, and hiding from Artie. It was enough to wear out any girl.

"Maybe you could plant some extras for the inn," Laura suggested hopefully. "Like Aunt Hope used to do."

"Lee hinted the other day that I should grow herbs for his restaurant," Georgia said offhandedly.

"Lee was here?" Delia asked. "How is he?"

"He's fine." Georgia told her, and appeared to be about to say something else on the subject when India told her, "I think your phone is ringing."

Georgia excused herself and raced toward the steps.

Delia had not been blind to the fact that Matt's eyes had followed her, and that those same eyes had narrowed and clouded at the mention of Lee's name.

Oh, my, here's an unexpected twist, Delia mused.

"Who is Lee?" Laura was asking.

"Lee Banyon is Georgia's best friend from Baltimore," Delia told her, turning her head slightly to ensure that Matt heard every word. "He took her under his wing when she first joined the Baltimore troupe, and more recently, he helped her to leave it."

"Oh, he's a dancer?" Laura noted.

"A former dancer. Lee had been quite well known and highly regarded. He has performed with several troupes over the years." Delia settled back, knowing that Matt was listening. "He quit a few years back when David died."

"Who's David?" Laura asked.

"Oh, sorry." Delia smiled apologetically. "David was Lee's companion. They'd been together forever."

"You mean Lee is . . ." Matt noted, the light beginning to dawn.

"Yes," Georgia told him as she rejoined them and sat back down. "Lee is gay."

"Lee is gay," he repeated flatly.

"Yes. Does that bother you?" Her eyes narrowed as readied herself to defend her friend.

"No, it doesn't bother me at all." He cleared his throat to mask the relief that washed over him at that moment.

"I was just about to say that when David died, Lee quit the troupe and took over David's restaurant."

"How is the restaurant doing?" India asked.

"It's doing very well. Of course, Lee thinks of David every time he walks through the door. And so do I, quite frankly."

The rest of the day had seemed even easier after that, as if an obstacle had been rolled out of the way by a large unseen hand, and Matt had relaxed and had even begun to cautiously enjoy himself. He and Nick and a very soggy Ben—Zoey had not gone quietly into the pond—had folded the chairs and tables and returned them to Laura's van. He had built a fire in the living room of the farmhouse and they had all gathered around it for coffee and the last of the homemade ice cream that August had helped the girls to make after dinner. A sort of comfort had settled over the entire afternoon and evening, as if he had been embraced by wide arms that had folded around him and pulled him inside. The warmth of it had lightened his heart. He was too tired to analyze it, too weary to protest. Scrutiny could wait.

Laura's new siblings—the whole extended family, for that matter—were a caring, lively, fun group. Even Delia had been nothing like he had imagined. There was an elegance about her, that much had not come as a surprise. But the woman had seemed to possess a true warmth, a way of listening to you that made you feel that there was nothing more important in the world at that moment than what you were saying. He had to admit that she was a compelling and fascinating woman, and that he didn't know how he would feel if he learned, after all these years, that she was his birth mother.

Matt was beginning to understand how it had been so easy for Laura to have fit so effortlessly into her new family. He had a vision of the entire Enright clan lined up side by side on an ever extending park bench, cheerfully sliding over to make room for one more. For Laura's sake, he hoped with all his heart that it was more than a temporary accommodation. Having seen firsthand how easy it was to slip into their stride, Matt's heart squeezed at the thought of how very painful it would be for Laura if his worst fears for her materialized, and they all vanished, one by one, from her life.

It had all gone really well till right there at the end, when Delia was leaving—she had a stop to make, she had said—and Laura had carved out a large square from the lower right corner of the enormous birthday cake, the piece with "Ally" written on it in blue frosting, and placed it on a large plate.

"This piece goes to Grandma, Ally," Laura had said, and Ally had handed the plate to Delia, who had leaned down and kissed Ally on the forehead and whispered something in her ear.

It had been a family tradition started by Laura, continued by Matt and later Ally, that the piece of cake bearing the birthday name would be presented to Charity. That Laura could blithely pass on the honor to Delia had struck Matt like a sharp blow to the head.

Matt had offered a curt goodnight. Calling for his dog, he headed for the barn, putting the day and the Enrights behind him once again.

chapter fourteen

Georgia pulled the hood of her old gray sweatshirt up over her head. The light sprinkle of rain that had been falling when she left the farmhouse was turning into a steady downpour, and she headed for the big elm tree in the middle of the field for shelter.

"Come on, Spam, hurry." She called to the pig who had wandered in the general direction of the pond. Upon hearing Georgia's voice, Spam waddled at her top speed—which wasn't very speedy— toward the tree.

Seating herself upon one of the gnarled roots that had long ago pushed above the surface of the earth, Georgia wiped beads of water from her face and shivered as a few strays slid down her throat and onto her chest. What, she wondered, had happened to yesterday's beautiful weather?

Seems it disappeared as quickly as Matt's pleasant disposition had the night before, she thought, trying for the hundredth time to figure out what could have caused him to close off and flee so suddenly.

Everything had been fine. Better than fine. Matt had seemed to be getting along with everyone— everyone liked him—and he even seemed to almost like them. It had appeared that even Delia had started to win him over. Then bam! out the door he went without so much as a fare-thee-well.

Even Laura had been at a loss to understand what had caused him to bolt like that, and Ally had been crushed that he had left without kissing her goodbye.

Georgia traced small circles on the ground with the toe of one foot, then leaned over and picked the small purple flower she had unintentionally torn from its plant. Violets had always been a spring favorite, so she picked a few more and tried to recall what Hope's flower book had said about violets. Something about offering protection against wicked spirits. And that mixed with something—was it lavender?—they were a powerful love stimulant and something about arousing lust.

She twirled the flowers around on their stems between two fingers, pondering their reputation and wondering just what exactly one *did* with them that could inspire love—to say nothing of lust—from another.

Several clumps of dandelions, their flowers having already gone to seedheads, grew around the base of the tree. When she and Zoey were little, they had called the milky white globes of seeds *wishes*, and had spent many a spring and summer afternoon contributing to the plants proliferation by blowing countless wishes to the wind to ensure that they would come true.

Georgia had never wished for material things, or for beauty, or for love. She had wanted only to become a dancer, to dance upon a big stage in a beautiful costume, to feel the music invade her body and to move with it. It had been her constant wish, her only wish, and eventually, it had come true.

Maybe there's something to these things after all, she mused.

Hope's book had listed many magical uses for dandelions, and Georgia tried to remember them all as she picked one, causing it's sticky juice to cling to her fingers.

If you blow the seeds off the head, the remaining number of seeds will be equal to the remaining number of years of her life.

She blew, and the seeds scattered. There were lots of seeds left clinging, though, too many to count, so she figured she was good to go for a few more years.

She picked another one.

Blow three times and the number of seeds left will tell you what time it is.

After the third puff she paused and counted. Seven seeds remained. It had been about eight-thirty when she left the house. Close enough.

Amused now, she picked another, and tried to recall another of the entries in Hope's book.

Blow the seeds in the direction of someone you love, and they will receive whatever message you send.

The rain had slowed, and Spam grunted loudly. She might be cold from the dampness, Georgia frowned, and having read something about taking care not to let your pig get chilled, she said aloud, "Okay, we'll go back and you can curl back up on your little pig bed and sleep away a rainy Sunday. Which, actually, is not a bad idea . . ."

Thinking about the pleasures of a hot cup of tea and a good book, Georgia pulled back the sweatshirt hood and followed a straight furrow to the end of the field. Realizing she still held the last dandelion in her hand, she pointed the stem in the direction of the barn and blew. She stood for a long moment, watching the tiny white seed heads drift upwards toward the second floor, wondering if, in fact, her message had been received.

Matt stared out his living room window, his eyes fixed on the small figure walking toward the farmhouse. If things had gone otherwise last night, he might have pulled on a parka and joined her on her early morning walk. In his mind's eye, he could almost see them as they followed the deeply cut rows, walking closely enough for their shoulders to occasionally tap as they navigated the muddy furrows. Then maybe they'd sit in the farmhouse kitchen for a cup of coffee and some easy Sunday morning conversation. He scowled and turned from the window, picked up his coffee cup, and sat down at his own table to drink it, alone.

He glanced at the clock, the hour hand of which approached nine. He'd flown out of the farmhouse last night and jumped into his truck, banged the key into the ignition and . . . nothing. His battery was dead. Clear as day, he could see cables on a shelf in his garage back in Shawsburg, right where he'd left them the last time he'd cleaned out the truck. He'd been forced to wait until morning to call a local service station to come out to give him a charge. The delay in leaving was frustrating him even further. He had wanted to be at the nursing home early this morning. And Doc Espey had asked him to stop over this afternoon around two—there was something he'd wanted to talk about—and Matt promised he'd be there. *Probably wanted an update on the success of that new canine antibiotic we've been using,* Matt thought as he drained the last bit off coffee from the cup just as the tow truck pulled into the drive. He ran down the steps and out into the rain to go about the business of getting his truck running.

Later, after the service truck had done it's duty and returned to O'Hearn proper, Matt washed the cup and the plate from breakfast, then rinsed out Artie's water dish before turning out the light and heading for his bedroom, where he repacked his clothes, made his bed, and whistled for his dog. He locked the door behind him, then paused there on the landing, to stand in the rain and look across the yard.

There was a light in the kitchen. He wondered what she was doing, and wished he could have felt free to join her. A crack of thunder from someplace out beyond the woods shook the ground beneath his feet. Calling to Artie, he opened the door of his truck, threw in his overnight bag, and hopped in after the dog. Whatever Georgia Enright was doing on this stormy morning, it had nothing to do with him.

It had saddened Matt in ways he could not express

to have seen Delia Enright take his mother's place the night before as Ally had presented her with what had traditionally been reserved for Charity. It had only served as yet one more reminder of what they had lost as a family that had always been so close, of what Charity had lost of herself. He had wished that his mother had been there, for Ally's sake, certainly, but mostly for Charity's sake. She had so loved Ally, had always made such a fuss for Ally's birthday, helping Laura to plan her parties and make certain that all was perfect for her only grandchild's special day.

Whatever had made him think he could integrate these people into his life, Delia especially, who was obviously all too eager to step into his mother's role? And Laura's words—"This goes to Grandma."—still rankled. Had Charity's absence been felt by no one but him?

He played with the radio dial, searching for something other than Sunday morning sermons or hip-hop, which grated on his nerves. He lingered for a moment over the station that was playing gospel. Charity had loved gospel music. He left the station on, hoping that perhaps a little of the optimism of the music would have a positive effect on his state of mind. He hated being gloomy when he arrived at Riverview. It didn't help his outlook, and surely couldn't help Charity's, for him to be on edge and miserable.

"I won't be too long, Artie," Matt said as he parked the car under the sheltering canopy of a large tree in the visitors lot. "I'll leave the window partly down on your side if you promise not to keep sticking your head out into the rain. And don't bark at anyone unless they try to open the door, okay? Some of these folks might be late sleepers . . ."

Out of habit, Matt locked his door, even though he knew that the chances were slim that anyone would steal his truck with a one hundred and thirty pound rottweiler sitting on the front seat. He tried to put a little life in his step as he walked toward the one-story white clapboard building that overlooked the river below, but his feet felt leaden and his spirits sagged. He pushed open the door and walked through the lobby, which on this rainy morning smelled musty and tired.

A glance into his mother's room told him that she was already dressed and up for the day, her bed neatly made. He followed the hall leading to the morning room where he would be most likely to find her at this hour on a Sunday. Chapel having concluded for those who felt up to attending, there was often a social hour after the service. Matt could hear the chatter of the residents as he rounded the corner and poked his head through the door. There by the window Charity sat, a frail doll-like figure dressed in white, in her wheel chair. Pink and purple balloons were tied on long pink strings from the back of her chair.

The sight slowed Matt's step, then stopped him, midstride, halfway across the room.

At one of the long tables, a young nurse's aid was slicing a large wedge of cake into thin pieces and serving it to the residents.

On Charity's lap, a square piece of birthday cake rested on a pink paper plate that was held by thin fingers. The cake's frosting was deep pink, and even from ten feet away, Matt could clearly make out the letters. A L L Y.

Matt pulled a chair close to his mother's and stared at the plate.

This goes to Grandma.

"I have cake," Charity looked up and told him happily.

"I see that you do." He cleared his throat. "Is it good?"

"It's delicious," she nodded. "You should have some. It's someone's birthday, though I don't remember whose . . ." She paused, looking confused, then brightened, pointing to the nurse and saying, "I think it's *her* birthday."

"I see you have some balloons," he noted.

"Well, of *course* I have balloons. It's a birthday party." Her voice rose, slightly strident, as she stated the obvious.

"Mrs. Enright brought the balloons in last night," the nurse's aide called to him, "but don't worry, we'll take them off the back of the chair before anyone gets the idea to pop them or to eat them."

"Mrs. Enright?" he said, although he had already known.

"She dropped them off with the cake last night. It was too late for her to read, but she said that . . ."

"Read?" he asked, confused.

The aide nodded, her brown ponytail bouncing up and down. "She usually comes in once during the week to read aloud to Mrs. Bishop and some of the others, and she sometimes stops in over the weekends, too."

"Delia Enright . . ." He got up from his seat to approach the table.

"Young man," Charity grabbed his sleeve as he passed her, "Edna did not get her cake."

"I'll get her a piece," he patted her shoulder gently. To the perky young aide, he said, "Are you talking about *Delia* Enright?"

"Right. Mrs. Enright. She said that she talked to some specialist in New York who told her that lots of times, even though Alzheimer's patients lose the ability to read themselves, they enjoy being read to. So she comes in—usually on Wednesday afternoon around two—and reads. Everyone looks forward to her visits."

"Does my mother know who she is?"

"You mean, does she know that Mrs. Enright is a famous writer? I don't think any of them realize that. She's just the book lady to them." The nurse went on. "She's been real nice. She brings in autographed copies of her books for the staff. I figured you knew. I mean, we all figured she must be a relative or something, since she arranged for Mrs. Bishop's private night nurse and . . ."

"What?" The word exploded from between his lips.

"Well, you know, Dr. Bradshaw said that pretty soon Mrs. Bishop would be needing someone to stay with her at night, 'cause she had been sleepwalking again, so Mrs. Enright told us to arrange for someone to come in every night at seven and stay until change of shift at seven the next morning. She said to get the best person available and to have her start right away." The nurse looked confused. "Didn't you know?"

"No," he said quietly. "No, I didn't know."

Beyond the window, the river ran high and muddy and swift after the night's storm. From over toward Salisbury lightning cracked the sky in two. The clouds seemed lower, the mist thicker, the air heavier. Another storm was brewing, and Matt felt it both within and without. He thought it would be best to leave before either storm could break.

Matt left a gentle kiss on his unsuspecting mother's cheek and left the room, back to the hall, through the lobby to the front door and beyond, where big splats of rain were beginning to fall hard on the concrete steps and thunder began it's rumble from somewhere down the road. That the weather matched his mood was not lost on him. He unlocked the truck and hopped in, and without his customary greeting to Artie, drove off, hoping to sort through it all between now and Wednesday, when he'd be back for the story hour. He and Delia Enright had things to talk about.

As if he hadn't had enough on his mind, Matt would take one more hit that Sunday afternoon.

He'd arrived home a little before one, with enough time to take a shower and change before driving over to Doc Espey's. He stood beneath the blast of a relentless stream of hot water, hoping to burn out the chill and clear his head. He'd been caught off guard by the sight of Ally's birthday cake on his mother's lap, caught even more so by the news that Delia had arranged for a night nurse to watch over his mother.

He was torn between gratitude for her kindness and anger over her presumption. Generally confused, he thought this was not the time to call Laura and try to discuss the situation. He was afraid of what he'd say.

And besides, he'd be spending the next few hours with Doc Espey, and didn't want to spoil it by getting into a yelling match with Laura, and that's just what would happen if he confronted her right then. He needed time to mull it over, time to sort it all out. Better to set it aside, and see what was on Doc Espey's mind.

In retrospect, a shouting match with Laura might have been easier to take than Matt's meeting with his old friend.

"Matthew," Doc Espey had said when he entered the room, "come and sit. No, not that chair." He pointed to one closer by. "Come sit by me."

Matt sat where he was told.

"Turn that light on, son," the old vet instructed. "It's so dark in here, what with this storm. Would you like anything? Tea? Coffee? Eva is in the kitchen . . ."

"No, I'm fine, thank you." Matt's eyes narrowed. There was the slightest air of unfamiliar formality that caused a faint tickle of suspicion to run up his spine.

"Out to see your mother today, were you?"

"Yes."

"Is she any better?"

"No. No, she's not." Matt leaned back in the chair and said, "I think we're at the point where we're just beginning to understand that, with Alzheimer's, you don't get better. You only get worse."

"I'm sorry, my boy. I really am so sorry. It isn't easy watching someone that we love grow old." Espey shook his head slowly. "And it's not easy to accept certain things about ourselves as we get older, Matt. It's not easy, growing old."

Matt watched the old man's face, and his chest constricted. Something was about to be said that he wasn't going to like, any more than he liked finding out that Delia Enright had taken it upon herself to hire a nurse to care for his mother.

"The rain. The cold. The dampness." Doc leaned back in his chair. "All of it takes its toll, you know. When you get to be my age . . ." He waved his hand vaguely, and appeared to be struggling with his words.

The old doctor met Matt's eyes, and he smiled. "You know," he said, "I'm trying to look for an easy way to say this, but I can't. So you'll just have to forgive my bluntness, Matthew. I've decided to move to Arizona to be closer to my sister. Eva and I will be leaving June first."

Surrounded by the silence that followed in the wake of his announcement, the old man watched the face of the younger as the words sank in.

"You're leaving . . ."

"Yes, son. It's time," Espey said quietly.

Matt stood and paced, wound tightly as an old watch, his mind reeling.

"Have you changed your mind about Shawsburg? You know that my first choice would be to turn my practice over to you."

"Thank you, Doc. I appreciate that. I like Shawsburg, and I've really enjoyed working here. I'm grateful for the opportunity, but it's always been my dream to open a clinic at Pumpkin Hill."

"I know that, Matt, but I wanted to give you the choice, in the event that you'd changed your mind."

"Thank you, but no," Matt said quietly, "I haven't changed my mind."

"I had a feeling that you'd say that," Espey nodded slowly. No surprises here. "I have had an offer from Greg Dannon to buy the practice."

"Then, by all means, you should sell it to him. Greg's a good vet. He'll serve the community well."

"That's what I thought."

"How soon . . ." Matt could barely get the words out.

"Well, he said he'd send one of his assistants out to take over as soon as we signed the deal and he could get some equipment ordered."

"What equipment could he possibly need?" Matt frowned. "There's nothing here that's more than two years old, and everything is state of the art."

"I'm selling him the building and the practice, but not my equipment." Espey leaned forward. "The equipment goes with you, to Pumpkin Hill."

"That's very kind of you," Matt said softly. "But I'm afraid I'm just not in a position to buy the equipment any more than I could afford to buy the practice."

Matt thought of the many thousands of dollars the vet had spent on the latest X ray equipment, CAT scans and lab and surgical equipment. It would take Matt years to be able to afford such tools. His heart sank. He'd have to go work with another vet for a while.

He'd been saving money, but he was far from being able to afford to open a clinic of his own.

"The best I can afford right now might be a few of the examining tables," Matt tried to force a smile.

"Matt, I'm not offering to sell you the equipment," Espey told him gently. "I'm giving it to you."

"Doc, you don't just give away thousands of dollars' worth of equipment . . ."

"I replaced everything over the past few years with the thought that one day you'd take it with you when you left."

"Doc, I couldn't accept it . . ."

"Oh, but I'm not giving you a choice, son. It's what I planned all along. Think of it as my last gift to you, Matt."

Matt raised his eyebrows. "Doc, you've given me so much over the years. There's no need for you to give me anything more."

"I appreciate that you feel that way. I do. But this isn't negotiable. All of the equipment, all of the supplies, will be loaded on a truck and delivered to your farm. It's already been arranged."

For the second time that day, Matt was caught up by emotions that conflicted and collided.

"I don't know what to say," he whispered.

"There's nothing you need to say."

Eva appeared in the doorway with two cups of tea.

"Ah, you're just in time, my sweet," Espey beamed. "Matt and I could use a little refreshment."

"Will you stay for dinner, Matt?" She asked as she placed his cup before him.

"Yes, of course he'll stay," the old vet answered for the younger one. "We have a few more details to discuss, and I want him to read the results of the research project that Denton faxed down from the University of Pennsylvania yesterday. Did I show you my new fax machine, Matthew? It works on my computer, look here . . ."

Later, his head still reeling, Matt drove over rain soaked streets to his little rented house at the edge of Shawsburg. He parked in the driveway and unlocked the front door with little thought to his actions. He fed the dog, then slipping the leash onto Artie's collar, went back out the same way he'd come in.

Over the past few hours, the temperature had risen and the rain had settled to a steady, fine drizzle. Fog was growing from the warming pavement like mushrooms in a dank cellar. Matt walked past the closed and shuttered shops, past the library and the fire house, past the town's one funeral home and the community swim club, which wouldn't open for another month. Few cars passed and no one else, it seemed, had ventured out on such a night. The fog grew along with the silence, and soon the only sounds Matt heard were his own footsteps and the scraping of Artie's claws on the sidewalk. He lost track of how long he had walked, and where. It was almost midnight by the time he arrived back at his own front door, his thoughts no less jumbled than when he'd set out.

The red light on his answering machine flashed once, twice, three times. His beeper hadn't gone off, so he knew there were no animal emergencies. So, he felt he could ignore his machine. He walked past it into the kitchen and turned on the light. There was no one he felt like talking to, no one whose voice he wanted to hear. His nerves were stretched to their limit and his emotions had been beaten raw.

He took a beer from the refrigerator and went back into the living room and turned on the television. Sorting through his stack of Sherlock Holmes videos, he found the one that matched his mood.

The Hound of the Baskervilles.

He slid the tape into the VCR and settled back, hoping to lose his inner turmoil somewhere amidst the mists that drifted across the moors surrounding Baskerville Hall.

chapter fifteen

After Sunday's storms, Monday's warmer temperatures and sunny skies were welcomed. By Tuesday afternoon, the mercury in the thermometer that was nailed to the side wall of the farmhouse had risen all the way to seventy-eight degrees. It was spring and it was warm, and Georgia's thoughts had turned to planting. A trip into Tanner's for pig chow had resulted in her purchase of several flats of cool weather vegetables: three kinds of lettuce, some spinach and some Swiss chard. First, she thought as she unloaded the plastic trays from the back of the Jeep, she would have to decide where to plant them, then take an hour or so to do the actual planting. For years she'd watched old Tom Larson, who often helped her mother with the gardening back in Westville, and he'd always made it look so easy.

Inspecting each of Hope's old garden locations, Georgia decided that the best place for the vegetable garden might be the larger garden behind the barn where it was sunny all day. Now all she had to do was turn the soil over, and she could stick the little plants right into the ground. She grabbed a shovel from the wall inside the barn. Matt had said he'd help, but, she knew, after the way he took off the other day, best not to count on *him*. She'd start today, and she'd do it herself. How hard could it be to plant a few flats of vegetables?

Once she had chopped up the soil and tucked in her new plants, she mused as she walked to the field behind the barn, she could just throw seeds in for the other vegetables she wanted to grow. Pleased with the thought of having several months of eggplant parmigiana and zucchini bread made from her own crops, she began to whistle.

She stood at the edge of last year's garden, envisioning the yield come July and August. Mentally, she placed her selections in neat rows. Zucchini there, broccoli there, maybe some cantaloupe here. Green beans and sugar snap peas . . . pole or bush? And she could put in several rows of carrots and lots of tomatoes, there was so much room. *Acres* of room. Today she would dig it all up. Tonight she would sketch out where she would plant everything. Tomorrow she would put the new plants in the ground and go back to Tanner's to buy seeds for everything else.

Optimistically, she broke ground for the little trench she'd use as the border for her garden.

"Marigolds," Georgia said aloud to Spam. "I read in one of Hope's journals that if you plant lots of marigolds around the perimeter of your garden, they will keep out deer and rabbits. I think I'll plant marigolds in this little trench." She paused and looked down at the pig that was now rolling in the dirt she had loosened. "Unfortunately, I'm not sure how effective they are on pigs."

This will be so much fun, she was thinking at three in the afternoon.

By three thirty-five, she recognized the task for what it was.

Backbreaking.

Georgia slammed the tip of the shovel into the ground and leaned upon it's handle.

"Spam, I love you for the porcine cutie that you are, but right now I'd have to admit that I'd be tempted to trade you for the first mule that came strolling by." She momentarily went cross-eyed watching a line of sweat roll down her nose. "Oh, my kingdom for a tractor!"

The tractor! Yes, of course! The tractor! Why hadn't she thought of it sooner?

"Because I foolishly thought that digging a few hundred square feet of dirt would be a walk in the park." She said aloud. "Come on, Spam. There is a better way . . ."

Dragging the shovel—which now weighed close to thirty or forty pounds, she was certain of it—she returned to the barn, Spam grunting a protest at having had her little siesta in the sun disturbed. Georgia walked around first one, then the other tractor, then hoisted herself onto the seat of the smaller of the two.

Hope had driven it all the time. Laura had driven it, too. Why couldn't she?

First, of course, she would have to figure out how to turn it on.

She tried to recall what Laura had done the day she

had started up the equipment. Something with this switch here . . .

The rattle and roar of the engine startled her, and she drew her hand back as quickly as if she had touched a hot wire. The seat wobbled under her rear end and the whole machine sort of shook.

Spam bolted for the door.

Georgia placed her hands on the steering wheel and braced herself against its vibrations. Turning the stiff wheel first to the left, then to the right, she leaned over and watched the movement of the big front tire as it responded to the wheel in her hands.

I think I could drive this thing, she nodded. *And Laura did say that I could use whatever was here . . .*

She studied the pedals near the platform beneath her feet. *That* must be the fuel pedal, and *that* must be the brake. Which means *this* would be the clutch.

Testing each of the foot pedals tentatively with her sneakered feet, she repeated aloud, "I can drive this thing."

The large first floor of the barn held little more than the tractors. She looked over her shoulder. A small plow was attached to the back of the tractor, but other than that, there seemed to be little that could get in her way. She depressed the clutch, which was slightly stiff, then moved the gearshift back and forth, confirming the gears. From neutral to drive. Did this thing have different speeds? She leaned closer to inspect. The small letters at the base of the stick shift spelled out, "first, second, third, fourth, reverse."

Just like that ancient Mercedes sports car that Mom used to have, she mused.

If I could drive that, I can drive this.

She downshifted into first gear, and stepped on the gas.

"Holy mother!" she yelled as the tractor lurched forward toward the back wall of the barn. She hit the brake, bringing the machine to a sharp stop.

Well, it had been a while since she had driven that car . . .

She pulled forward a few more feet, more slowly this time, then stopped it again. Start, then stop. Start, then stop. She made a slow arc around the inside of the barn. Once. Twice. Three times, then pulled the tractor back to where it had been.

What, she wondered, controlled the plow?

She tested this lever and that until she found the one that lowered and raised the plow blades.

She began to whistle again, the theme song from *Oklahoma!* coming to mind.

"Tomorrow I will plow up that little bit of field, Spam." Georgia announced as she hopped down from the tractor, "just like Hope used to do."

Confident that she was up to the task, and knowing somehow that Hope would have been proud, Georgia turned off the light and headed to the house to sketch out her garden plan. Matt Bishop could stay in Shawsburg. She wouldn't need his help.

Matt had rescheduled his Wednesday afternoon appointments so that he'd be able to leave the clinic no later than one. Unfortunately, a Pekinese with skin allergies arrived—unannounced—at twelve-forty-five, and kept him till close to one-thirty.

"The best laid plans," he muttered to Artie as he arrived home and stripped for a quick shower. The peke had shed loose fur all over him, and he needed to be rid of it.

Finishing in record time, he pulled on a short sleeved olive green shirt and a pair of jeans, and whistling for Artie—who'd been lounging on the sofa, moving only when he heard Matt's footsteps drawing near—headed off for Riverview.

He still had no idea of what he was going to say to Delia, but he figured it was time. He wasn't even certain of how he felt about her anymore.

On the one hand, he had been touched almost to tears that Delia had taken the prized piece of Ally's birthday cake not for herself, but for Charity. That small act had spoken volumes to Matt of Delia's kindness, of the generosity of her spirit.

That she had taken it upon herself to hire a private duty nurse to care for his mother, *that* was something else entirely.

He had deliberately not mentioned it to Laura, though he wasn't exactly sure why he had avoided doing so. Maybe because Delia was, after all, Laura's birth mother, she might feel obligated to defend her, to explain on her behalf. Matt wanted to hear it from Delia herself why she felt she was entitled to make such a decision. If Delia had conferred with Laura first, Laura may have chosen not to discuss it with him for any number of reasons, not the least of which being that she might have been afraid he'd tell where Delia could put her money.

Or, on the other hand, maybe Laura was feeling a little bit torn between the two women. It was, he concluded, a complicated situation.

The visitors lot was almost filled when Matt arrived

at Riverview at three-twenty. Even so, there was no way to have missed the Mercedes sedan. It stuck out from between a Honda and a Subaru station wagon like a red rose in a vase full of white carnations. He parked the truck, gave a verbal reminder to Artie about minding his manners, and went into the nursing home.

The hall leading to the dayroom was quiet, and the soles of his Nikes squeaked softly on the tile floor. As he approached the room, the sound of a woman's voice became audible. He paused in the doorway and took a look around. There were twenty or thirty residents gathered around the chair where Delia sat, her glasses perched on her nose, her legs, in tailored navy blue slacks, crossed at the knee. Her voice was clear and animated. Matt took a step inside and listened as she read from the hardcover book which she held open with both hands:

" 'The bucket that had hung from the frayed rope was gone, the rope cut cleanly. She leaned over the edge of the old well, wondering if the wooden bucket had fallen down, down, down past the old stone walls.' "

"When I was a little boy, we had a well on our farm," an elderly man sitting to Delia's left interrupted her.

"So did we," another nodded.

"I lived on a farm, once." It was Charity's voice. "And we had a well. My father covered it up when my sister Faith fell in and drowned."

Matt's chest constricted. That his mother would remember that! Charity could not have been more than six or seven at the time her older sister had died. It had been years since she had talked about Faith.

"The water in our well was very cold," the old man continued as if he had not heard. "It was sweet to drink on a hot summer day . . ."

"Faith had yellow hair," Matt heard his mother say. "The yellowest hair I ever saw. My mother used to braid it in two fat plaits. On Sundays she let us wear ribbons in our braids, me and my sister Faith and my sister Hope."

"Faith, Hope and Charity," an old woman seated next to Charity said in the kind of loud voice used by people who are themselves hard of hearing. "That was in the Bible."

"Now, do you want to chatter," a gentleman wearing a blue cardigan sweater and a slouched straw hat stood up, "or do you want the book lady to read a little more?"

"Oh, read more, please!"

Delia shifted slightly in the chair, gave everyone a few seconds to reposition themselves, then continued on with her reading.

Matt sat down on a chair just inside the door, studying the back of Delia's head. Several times she had raised a hand to the back of her neck and rubbed it slightly, as if to rub away some stiffness, but she kept reading until the clock in the hallway chimed four bells. She had been interrupted several more times by members of her geriatric audience when their memories had been jogged by something she read, but she never seemed to mind. She simply waited patiently until they were ready for her to continue. Then she would read some more until someone else had a flash from the past and spoke up to share it.

When the bell rang, Delia finished the sentence she was reading and closed her book, saying, "And that's all till next week."

Several in the group groaned their displeasure that reading time was over for the day, but most simply nodded. The aides stood and prompted everyone to "Thank Mrs. Enright."

"Thank you, book lady," several said as they passed Delia on their way out of the room.

Charity wheeled herself past Matt without looking at him.

He stood and leaned against the wall, debating whether or not to speak with Delia now, or if perhaps he should wait for her by her car.

He had taken too long to decide. Delia turned toward the door unexpectedly. If she was surprised to see him, she hid it well.

"Matthew," she greeted him with a even smile.

"Mrs. Enright." He nodded to her.

She stopped to speak to one of the aides, then gathered a light jacket from the back of her chair. Folding the jacket over her arm, she handed the book to the aide and said, "Why not keep this here until next week?"

"Do you mind if I finish it between now and then?"

"Not at all," Delia smiled, "as long as you don't give away the ending."

"I promise." Looking pleased, the aide hugged the book to her chest.

"Well, Matthew," Delia looked up at him when she reached the door, "are you going my way?"

He nodded. "I suppose I am."

They walked together through the lobby, Delia waving at this one or that, employees and residents, all with the same friendly greeting. As they neared her car, she said, "I'm guessing that this was not a coincidence, that you just happened to stop by today . . ."

"I knew you would be here."

"Then I take it you have something to say to me." Her voice was soft, not challenging, not apologizing.

"First, I want to thank you for the kindness you have shown to my mother . . ."

Delia smiled wryly, as if mildly amused.

"The birthday cake, the balloons . . . ," he said.

Delia waved a hand, as if it was all inconsequential. "Ally was upset that her grandmother would not be there this year. She said she always gave her the piece of her birthday cake that had her name on it. I thought she should still have that."

"Well, I appreciate your thoughtfulness."

Again, that amused smile.

"But . . . ?" she prompted him.

"But I think you went too far when you hired a private nurse without consulting me or Laura." His jaw set hard and his eyes narrowed. "I'm assuming you didn't tell Laura . . ."

"No. I didn't discuss it with Laura."

"How did you get them to do that, bring in a nurse without getting Laura's permission?"

"Laura's permission wasn't needed. The doctor agreed that it was absolutely necessary."

"Who does she think is paying for it?"

"There's a special fund that's been established at

Riverview to provide extra services to residents who need them. Others benefit as well, not just your mother."

"Let me guess who funds this 'fund.'"

"I believe the donors are anonymous." Delia averted her eyes.

"Look, Delia, this is very generous of you, and I think I understand why you did it, but all the same . . ."

"Do you?" She looked up at him in a way that suggested that perhaps he didn't understand at all. "And what do you think you understand?"

"I'm guessing it might help to help ease your guilt."

"My *guilt?*" Delia's eyes flashed, but her voice remained steady. "And what guilt might that be?"

"Giving away Laura." His quiet words faltered. He hadn't wanted to be so blunt, wished she hadn't made him say it.

Delia shook her head slightly. "You'll have to do better than that, Matt. I stopped feeling guilty the day I met Laura in the library in Bishop's Cove."

He stared at her, clearly not understanding.

"You feel *guilty* when you feel you've done wrong. As soon as I met Laura, as soon as I saw what a lovely person she was, I knew that I could leave behind whatever guilt I had felt. She had obviously been brought up well, with a great deal of love. I knew then that I had done the right thing. Of course, until I saw her, I didn't know that, all those years . . ."

"You don't regret having given her up?"

"Ah, *regret* is something else entirely. I believe we

were speaking of *guilt.*" Delia smiled slightly. "It took me years to understand, but once I accepted the fact that nothing I could have done or said would have made any difference, it was a lot easier to forgive myself."

"I don't understand."

"The decision to give Laura up for adoption had been made by my parents, Matthew. I had just turned seventeen. They took it upon themselves to arrange for my baby to be immediately turned over to her adoptive parents upon leaving the hospital. I was not told until it was time for me to leave, and I waited for them to bring my baby to me . . ."

Delia's bottom lip trembled almost imperceptibly.

"I'm so sorry," he heard himself say.

"It took me a very long time to sort through it all. For years I hated my parents for what they did to me."

"How could you forgive someone for doing that?"

"Forgiveness is yet another issue." She smiled wryly. "Let's just say that in time I came to understand what motivated them to do what they did. It was the nineteen-sixties, and things were very different back then. I was the only child of a prominent minister of a prestigious church in a wealthy community. My parents reacted in the only way they knew—to make the whole episode go away and then pretend that it had never happened."

"It's ironic, isn't it, that Laura married a minister?" Matt said.

"Oh, the thought's occurred to me. But my father meant well, Matt. He thought he was doing what was best for me—and of course for him and my mother, as well. He may have been misguided, but he wasn't evil. Now, Laura's husband . . ."

Matt met her eyes, and realized that they were in total agreement on that one subject.

"Anyway, to put that aside for a moment, anything I may do for Charity has absolutely nothing to do with guilt."

"Then why . . . ?"

"Let's just call it honoring a debt." She said simply. "Because she adopted Laura."

"Because she *loved* her so selflessly, and gave her the home that I could not give her. Because she was there for her, because of everything she gave Laura over the years, all those things that have gone into making Laura the wonderful woman that she is today."

"Do you think that's enough reason to go behind our backs and interfere with her care?"

"I'm sorry, Matt. I didn't think of it as interfering. Charity needs someone to stay with her at night. She mustn't be in a situation where she might fall or injure herself." Delia took a breath and looked up at him and said, "And besides, I felt that this was between Charity and me."

"She's our mother, Delia. She's our responsibility."

"Are you in a position to take on that additional bit of responsibility?" she asked kindly.

He bit his bottom lip but did not respond.

"I know that Laura has her hands full right now with the inn and with Allie. I thought that if I just took care of this one little thing, it would be one less thing that Laura had to worry about."

"Why not just ask?"

"Because people always feel obligated to say *no* when you offer to spend money on their behalf. If they do 'permit' you, they feel beholden. I didn't want that. I just wanted Charity well cared for, Matt. I just wanted her to be safe." Delia paused, and when she looked up, Matt saw tears in the corners of her eyes.

"Why should it be so important to you?"

"There is a bond between us, between Charity and me." Delia tried to smile but her eyes clouded and the tough twitch of her lips betrayed her. "Every night for thirty-five years, I tried to picture what my daughter looked like. I tried to picture her as a baby held close by loving arms, being rocked to sleep to a lullaby I would never sing to her. I tried to picture her as a toddler, with a thousand questions that someone else would have to answer for her. I tried to see her starting school, her hair pulled up in a ponytail that someone else's hands had tied up with ribbons . . ."

Her voice caught and her the hot tears fell like fat snowflakes but she appeared not to notice.

"And all the time I prayed that her mother would love her every bit as deeply as I did, would do all those things for her that I wished I could do. Charity was the answer to all of my prayers, Matthew. She was everything I had prayed for, and more."

Matt took the carefully folded cotton handkerchief from his back pocket and handed it to Delia. She dabbed at her face gratefully, then continued.

"When I was here last week, I overheard one of the nurses talking about your mother walking in her sleep. It's apparently not uncommon for someone in her condition. Of course, I became alarmed that she might fall and injure herself. I asked how they would prevent her from sleepwalking, and there didn't seem to be much of a plan, other than some type of restraint to keep her from getting out of bed. It occurred to me that perhaps if someone was with her through the night she would be safer, but when I checked around and found out how expensive it was to have someone come in to stay, I thought . . . well, I thought I would like to do that for her. For any of the residents who need special care. So I set up a fund. It is no hardship for me, Matt, but it would be a hardship for Laura. Perhaps it would be for you as well. So I thought I would just take care of it. I figured it was just between Charity and me."

"Do you always just take it upon yourself to 'take care of things' for everyone?"

"Yes," she smiled somewhat sheepishly. "I'm afraid that sometimes I do."

"Mrs. Enright. . . ."

"Delia."

"Delia, I think I'm beginning to understand why you did this, and I appreciate the fact that you cared enough to step in. But the fact remains that our mother is our responsibility."

"Might I propose a solution?" She touched his arm lightly. "I have all intentions of continuing this fund. It's benefitting several others. But if it would make you feel better, supposing I keep track of the expenses for Charity's nurse. Then, perhaps, you might start paying me back a little at a time, whatever you can afford."

"That's pretty generous of you."

"It's the very least I can do. For Charity. And for Laura." *And for you, too, for all you may not want my help.* "Of course, there is something I would ask of you in return."

"That being?"

"I would like you to put whatever prejudice you have toward me and my family aside for a while. Try to keep a more open mind. Give us some time to prove to you that we've no intentions of hurting Laura . . . nor do we want to take her from you."

"How could you know how I feel?" His throat tightened unexpectedly.

"Matthew, we share something very precious, whether or not you realize it. Something besides Laura's love. We both cherish our families. I might very well have the same concerns, if strangers invaded my family."

He met her gaze.

"You need time to learn to trust, Matt. I don't blame you. Just don't be so afraid of losing something that you have, that you overlook the precious things you might gain." She folded her arms across her chest. "Give us six months to get to know us, Matt. That's not so very much to ask."

"And in the meantime, I'll be paying on the loan for the night nurse . . ."

"Yes. That arrangement will continue, regardless of what you decide at the end of six months. Charity's well-being should have nothing to do with how you feel toward me."

It was a hard offer to walk away from. His mother did need the night nurse, and Delia had been generous enough to provide for the needs of other residents as well. And Laura was having enough trouble holding up her share of the monthly bill from Riverview as it was. Right now, the last thing his sister needed was one more big bill to worry about each month.

"Mrs. Enright—Delia—you are a very generous, very thoughtful woman. If you would draw up some sort of agreement, I'd be happy to sign it."

"I'll take care of it today. Shall I mail it to you in care of the inn?"

"No," he thought it over for a long moment. Delia was right about not wanting to worry Laura. Any correspondence to him from Delia was sure to evoke curiosity on Laura's part, and Delia was probably right about not worrying Laura right now. And then, after his recent chat with Dr. Espey, he wasn't sure about how much longer he'd be in Shawsburg. "Send it to me at Pumpkin Hill, if you would. And Delia, maybe we could keep this between us. Right now, Laura does have a lot on her hands . . ."

"Then between you and me this shall stay." She extended her right hand to him, saying, "Deal?"

"Deal." He took her hand, smiling at the firmness of her grip. Delia Enright was a woman of substance in more ways than one.

"You know, we could work out our agreement right now. I just remembered that I have a laptop in the trunk of my car." She searched her purse momentarily, withdrawing the remote which unlocked all of the car doors. Opening the trunk and sliding out the leather computer case, she said, "Matt, be a dear and open the glove compartment. There should be a box of Godiva chocolates . . . yes, that's it. Now, let's just walk down to that picnic area and we'll type up our agreement. And then, if you're not in too great a hurry, I'd like to share with you some information I recently received concerning that despicable man Laura married. Oh, and bring the chocolate, if you wouldn't mind. We may be a while . . ."

chapter sixteen

Matt had been fighting the urge all the rest of that week and over the weekend.

On Tuesday he caved in.

Oh, he told himself that it was the barn space that he needed to take a good look at. Hadn't Doc Espey suggested that before Matt abandoned his dream of opening a clinic at Pumpkin Hill, he should try to figure out what it would take to convert the old barn into a modern veterinary facility? Didn't he encourage Matt to see if it was doable, and then to approach one of the local banks to obtain a loan to cover the renovations? Sure, he had, and good advice it was. Why, Doc had even offered to co-sign the loan.

That Matt would most likely run into their tenant had nothing to do with the fact that he left Shawsburg right after his three o'clock appointment, that he'd planned ahead and brought Artie with him that morning rather than run home after work to fetch him, or that he'd worked through lunch to make sure he'd get out on time.

But heck, if he *did* happen to run into their tenant, he'd try to find a way to explain why he'd left Ally's birthday party so abruptly. Okay, he'd even apologize. And somehow he'd work into the conversation that he'd had a long chat with her mother last week, and that maybe he'd misjudged her. Maybe he'd misjudged all of them.

Not for the first time, Matt wondered if Georgia knew about the arrangements Delia had made on Charity's behalf. He guessed that Delia probably hadn't bothered to mention it to anyone.

It had taken him a few days to sort through it all, but in the end, he realized that Delia had done what she had done from the purest of motives. Certainly, he'd had all intentions of demanding that she back off and permit him and Laura to take over the night-shift problem. Then Delia had pulled up the nurse's last billing statement on her laptop computer and he'd had to struggle to maintain his composure when he realized just how expensive Mrs. Grayson's services were. Taking that over right now would wipe out that college fund—however small it may be—that Laura had managed to start for Ally a few months ago. College tuition would be astronomical by the time Ally was ready to start applying to schools, though the thought crossed Matt's mind that Delia, being Ally's grandmother, might find a way to take care of that, too.

The terms Delia had offered Matt for the repayment of Mrs. Grayson's fees had been very generous, and consisted of a small monthly payment—an embarrassingly small payment for the time being—but it was all he could afford right now. Delia had seemed pleased with the arrangement, provided, she had said, that Laura didn't know about it. They had both agreed that Laura had enough on her plate right then.

No, this would be Matt's responsibility alone. After all, his sister had her inn and her daughter and their mother's basic expenses to meet. If Matt could get his clinic up and running, he would eventually be in a position to take over the nurse's salary from Delia and Laura would never be the wiser.

It sounded like a good plan to Matt.

And besides, he promised Delia that he'd do his best to get to know her family. What better place to start than with the one who was right there, at Pumpkin Hill?

Now, he thought as he pulled up the drive toward the barn, he'd just take a look inside the old barn and try to satisfy some questions that had poked at his own mind all week. Should he keep a section of the downstairs area in stalls for farm animals he might be called upon to treat? After all, there were still some farms in the area, and it would not be implausible that he might have call to use the stalls on occasion. If he converted the entire first floor, he'd lose that option. On the other hand, if he kept those stalls, and kept some room for the tractors, just how much space could he count on for examining rooms?

The last song he'd been listening to on the radio— The Who's "Behind Blue Eyes"—stayed in his head and he found himself whistling along with it as he opened the cab door and stood back to allow Artie to jump out. He slammed the door and pretended he wasn't looking for the Jeep, but there it was, parked just across the drive from his pickup. He wondered what she was doing, if she had heard the truck and maybe paused to pull a curtain aside to see who was there. Would she come out to say hello, or having been burned by his abrupt behavior, would she let the curtain drop back and just go about her business?

He turned to look for Artie, but the dog had dashed through the open double doors of the barn.

It took Matt's brain a few seconds to register this information.

Why would the big double doors both be open? Hope had only opened them when she was taking out a piece of large equipment.

Frowning, Matt followed the dog and walked through the open doorway. There was an empty space where his aunt's favorite tractor—the 1956 John Deere model 60—should have been parked.

"Son of a bitch!" He yelled to the rafters above.

Someone had broken into the barn and stolen one of their tractors!

He stomped toward the farmhouse to call the police and to interrogate their tenant. Wasn't that the reason she was here? To keep an eye on things? What the hell had she been doing when the damned thief was stealing the tractor? It wasn't like it hadn't made some noise, for cryin' out loud. You don't fold up a piece of farm equipment and tuck it unobtrusively into your pocket! Why, the racket that that sucker made when it started up was enough to raise the dead. It was loud, it was . . .

Matt stopped midway across the drive and tilted his head to one side, listening to the sound that drifted on the afternoon breeze from somewhere beyond the barn.

The loud whiney rattle of the old John Deere.

Had Laura rented out the fields to a local farmer to plant?

Puzzled, he followed the sound of the tractor until he stood twenty feet out into the field, where he stared at the tractor and its improbable driver.

Even in the oversized T-shirt and jeans shorts, big round sunglasses and wide brimmed straw hat, there was no mistaking who was at the wheel.

Lord have mercy. Barbie meets John Deere.

"Hey!" she shouted and waved when she turned the tractor to the right and started to make her way down the next row.

"Hey, yourself!" he shouted back.

She drove the tractor steadily if not expertly, and pulled within a few feet of him before cutting the throttle and bringing the tractor to idle.

"What do you think?" She grinned, pointing to the plowed sections of the field. "Pretty good for a novice, no?"

He pretended to inspect her efforts, then nodded, "Not bad."

"Not bad?!" Georgia hooted. "I'm doing a damned fine job."

Matt laughed. "You are doing a damned fine job. Who taught you how to handle this thing?"

"I taught myself."

"You taught yourself?" He repeated almost dumbly. "Damn. I was twelve before my aunt let me drive a tractor, and that was after several hours of instruction and years of watching her drive."

"Well, I admit if Laura hadn't started it up one day, I might have had a problem figuring out how to get it running, but other than that, it just took some practice. It's really not much more difficult than driving a stick shift, though someone should consider selling these babies with power steering. A little clumsier than a sports car, maybe, and I'd sure hate to see this thing doing eighty on a freeway, but it really wasn't such a big deal, once I got the hang of it." She slid off her sunglasses and cleaned them with the long end of her shirt. "It sure beat trying to dig up this section of field."

"I told you I'd help."

"Well, Matt, quite frankly, after the way you tore out of Ally's birthday party, I thought I'd be wise not to wait for your assistance." She stood on the tractor with one hand on her hip, the other on the steering wheel.

"I can't say that I blame you." He rubbed the back of his neck, as if perhaps that motion could somehow prevent the flush of red from spreading upward toward his face. "Georgia, I'm sorry. I overreacted to . . . well, it's a long story. But it never should have happened."

"I think the person who deserves the apology is Ally. It was her party." Georgia had folded both arms across her chest.

Matt knew enough about body language to know what *that* meant. The last thing he wanted now was for her to close him out.

"You're right, of course. I've already spoken with Ally and I think she understands. I was hoping that maybe, if you and I could talk over dinner, maybe you'd understand, too." He knew he was holding his breath, waiting for her answer, and was trying his damnedest to act as if he wasn't.

"I'm in the mood for pizza today. That's what I was planning on having tonight."

"No problem." he told her, relieved. The Italian restaurant in O'Hearn was an upbeat sort of place, with an old fashioned juke box and a steady stream of locals. It might be easier to say some of the things he knew he'd have to say in an atmosphere like that.

"Actually, I make my own," she was saying. "I already made the dough. You're welcome to join me."

So much for the old safety in numbers defense.

"Thanks. I'd like that. What's a good time?"

"Six should be about right. I want to get the rest of this side plowed up, then I'll need a little time to get cleaned up."

"Are you sure you wouldn't rather go out to eat?"

"Positive."

"Well, then, could I give you a hand with the rest of the plowing?"

"Nope," she grinned and slid the dark glasses back onto her face as she turned and pulled herself back up onto the tractor. "I'm doing just fine."

"Well, then I guess I'll see . . ."

Matt's words were drowned out by the roar of the tractor.

". . . you around six." He tried to shout over the engine.

She touched the brim of her straw hat in a sort of salute, then went on about her business.

"Six it is," he said aloud, knowing that she had not heard, since she had already turned the tractor around and headed off down the next row.

Matt tried to whistle for his dog who had taken off in pursuit of a few crows, but found his mouth was dry. He tried to look away, but it was near impossible not to notice just how fine Georgia looked astride that wide black leather seat, her back ramrod straight, her hair stretching down her back in a straight line under the hat.

Very fine indeed.

It should, he conceded as he set off to find Artie, make for a very interesting evening.

The first thing that Matt noticed when he came into the kitchen at six on the nose was the intriguing combination of aromas that met him at the back door—garlic and basil and honeysuckle.

The second thing he noticed was that Georgia had changed into a soft, sage-green clingy little number that looked like what he supposed a leotard might look like if it ended in a long skirt. He did later recall that when she turned around to greet him, he'd thought how her eyes were almost the same color as the dress.

The third and last thing he remembered—for a

while, anyway—was the sound of his heart hitting the floor when she smiled up at him.

"You look . . ." he was aware that he was stammering, but couldn't figure out how not to.

". . . less dusty?" She finished the sentence for him. "Cleaner?"

"I don't think that was what I had in mind, but we'll let it pass." He cleared his throat, and tried to appear nonchalant. "That's a great dress."

"Thanks," she smiled again. "Are you hungry?"

"Sure."

"Dinner's just about ready." She started to open the oven. "I'll be drinking iced tea, if you wouldn't mind getting the pitcher out of the refrigerator. And I think Ben left a six-pack of beer on the bottom shelf, if you'd rather have that."

"Iced tea is fine."

"The glasses are in that cupboard. I moved them." She pointed to the cupboard next to the sink.

Georgia opened the door and pulled the rack out slightly. "Looks like dinner is ready."

With a spatula she slid the three small pizzas onto a serving tray, and placed it on the kitchen table. Her every movement, it seemed to Matt, was both graceful and efficient.

"Must be all those years of dancing." He was appalled when he realized he'd spoken aloud.

"What's that?" She pulled out a seat for him and motioned for him to sit.

"Ah . . ." he found himself clearing his throat again. "You, ah, move like a dancer."

"I am a dancer," she whispered, as if confiding a

big secret, then grinned and pointed to the pizzas. "I probably should have asked you if you like artichokes."

"I do."

"Oh, good." She seemed relieved, then placed the largest of the rounds on his plate. "I'm not sure that everyone would like this combination."

"What is it?"

"Artichokes and tomatoes and red onions with a little mozzarella cheese on top."

"What's the green and white stuff on the bottom?" He tried not to appear to be inspecting the offering as closely as he felt compelled to do.

"Cream cheese and spinach."

"Oh."

"It tastes better than it sounds," she assured him, "but if you don't like it, I have some tofu lasagna from last night . . ."

"No. No, this is fine. It looks great." Matt smiled and cut his pizza into quarters.

Tofu lasagna?

He'd take his chances with the pizza.

"So. What are you going to plant out back of the barn?"

"Oh, all kinds of things. Lots of vegetables and herbs. I'm really excited about it. For the past few years, I've been buying organic vegetables from a market in Baltimore. Now I'll be growing my own." She was clearly pleased.

"What did you decide to do for water?" He asked as he took the first brave bite into the artichoke pizza.

"What?" She looked puzzled.

"Water. To water your plants." He took another bite. "You know, this is really good. Very good. Really."

"Thank you. I'm glad you like it." She frowned, then asked. "Isn't there a hose?"

"There's a water hookup in the barn that Aunt Hope used to run the irrigation system from, but I think it might be overkill to set all that up for a small garden area."

"I thought I could just use a hose." Georgia looked a little flustered. Her right index finger began tapping on the table.

"You'll need about a dozen of them to reach from the inside of the barn to the place where you're plowing."

"Can I do that? Just get a bunch of hoses and hook them together and water the plants that way?"

"I guess that could work." He nodded. "It might take the water a while to travel all that distance. And it would be very awkward to move all those hoses around."

"As long as it works." She said thoughtfully. "Damn. I didn't think about that—about getting the water out there."

"Well, you know, your garden is actually closer to the old chicken house than it is to the barn. At one time, there was a separate water line that fed out to that building. If you like, I'll take a look at it and see if it's still hooked up."

"Oh, would you? That would be wonderful." She beamed, and Matt knew right then that she'd have an easy source of water if he had to dig her a well with his bare hands. All she had to do was smile like that, and he'd dig clear through to China, if that's what it took.

"Would you like some dessert?" Georgia asked when the last of the pizza had been eaten. "I bought some raspberries in Tanner's yesterday. They're perfect. And we're having a special on birthday cake this week. Ally left me with a slab . . ."

He put his fork down quietly. This was his opening.

"Georgia, about Ally's party. I'm sorry I walked out. It was rude of me."

"You know, all week long I was trying to think of what I might have said or done that caused you to leave so suddenly."

"What *you* did . . . ?"

"You seemed to be having such a good time, seemed to be getting along with everyone. I figured maybe I said or did something that upset you for you to leave without saying good-bye."

He reached across the table and touched the tips of the fingers of her left hand with his own.

"It was nothing that you said or did. It was my reaction to something that I didn't fully understand." Matt watched her fingers spin the spoon around and around, and in that moment wanted nothing as much as he wanted to take that tiny hand in his own. So he did. "You know that my mother is in Riverview . . ."

"Yes, of course. Laura told me. I'm so sorry, Matt. I can't even begin to understand how difficult it must be for you and Laura and Ally. I don't know how I'd cope if my mother was in that situation."

"Lately, it's been more and more difficult, because

her disease is progressing, and we know now that recovery is not an option. We all miss her, we mourn her, almost as if she's already passed away, in a sense. Her body is still there, and for the most part, she still *looks* the same, but there is really so little left of the woman we knew. All the things that made her so unique have been devoured by her disease. We all want things to be the way they used to be, but we can't bring her back. Ally's birthday was a hard time for us. Birthdays have always been very important to my mother."

"I'm sure you missed having her here."

"I did." Her sincerity and concern touched him, making it easier for him to continue. "Do you remember when Laura told Ally to give the piece of cake with her name on it to Delia?"

"Not really. I think I might have been in the kitchen trying to sweet talk the old coffee maker into doing its thing."

"Laura handed the plate to Ally and said, 'This goes to Grandma.'" Matt wondered if the truth made him sound as petty and foolish as he was, at that moment, beginning to feel. Not a good enough reason not to continue, he knew. If he was going to tell her why he had left, it would have to be the truth. "We had always given the 'name' piece of birthday cake to our mother. Laura and I always did it, Ally did it, too. It was just sort of an honor, we thought."

"And you thought that Laura was passing that honor to Delia," Georgia said softly, squeezing his hand lightly to let him know she understood. "Which of course, has other implications—Delia being Laura's birth mother."

"Let me guess. Psychology major." He said wryly.

"No," she shook her head, "I never went to college. Too busy dancing."

"That's a shame. You'd probably make a great psychologist." His fingers entwined with her smaller, delicate ones.

"Actually, it's on my list."

"Your list?"

"Of things I might want to explore." She tugged on his hand impatiently. "We're getting off the subject. You thought that Laura was giving Delia something that you felt was rightfully Charity's, and you resented it."

"You would definitely make a great shrink," he repeated. "That's exactly how I felt. I know it sounds petty, but that's exactly how I felt."

"It's not petty. Yours is a difficult position to be in. I don't know that I'd feel any differently. And I admire your loyalty and your devotion to your mom. And besides, you apparently didn't know that my mother was going to stop at Riverview and drop the cake off for your mother."

"Not until I arrived at the home the next morning and saw the cake." He frowned. "But how did you know?"

"Laura had mentioned it earlier in the day, before Ally cut the cake. I'm surprised that you didn't hear her."

"I wonder if that was when I went out to my truck to look for matches for the candles." He tried to recall, but could not. "Well, for whatever reason, Laura's remark just set me off. I just wanted out, and away from all of you."

Matt knew he had to go on and finish the job. "I felt like you all were Laura's family now, and that her other family—Charity's family—didn't maybe matter so much anymore. I realize that it sounds so stupid . . ."

"I don't think it sounds stupid. I think I'd probably have felt the same way."

"Did you know that your mother goes out to Riverview at least once a week—sometimes twice— to read aloud to the residents?"

"Yes."

"You don't find that odd, that someone like your mother would travel all that distance to read to people she doesn't even know?" he couldn't help but ask.

"No, I don't find it odd, knowing my mother," she appeared to bristle slightly. "But I'd sure like to know what you mean by 'someone like my mother.'"

Matt wasn't oblivious to the rise in her voice and the snap of annoyance that brought those green eyes down a shade or two.

He chose his words carefully.

"I only meant that someone who has your mother's . . . *celebrity* might find other ways to spend her time than reading to a group of Alzheimer's patients in a backwoods nursing facility in Maryland once or twice a week."

"My mother has never been concerned with her *celebrity*, and I suspect that she does not consider Charity to be just another Alzheimer's patient."

"That's pretty much what she said."

"You've discussed this with her?"

"Last week. I ran into her at Riverview. She's quite an amazing woman."

"Yes, she is."

"I'm beginning to realize that I have misjudged her. She seems to be sincerely concerned about my mother's health and well-being. She came as quite a surprise to me, I don't mind admitting it."

"Now, how did she manage to win you over in one short afternoon?" Georgia leaned forward, curious.

Matt debated on whether to tell her about the nurse, then decided against it. He and Delia had agreed to keep it between them for the time being.

"I guess I just had to see for myself what she's really like." he said, not bothering to mention that he had promised to do exactly that for the next six months.

"I would venture to guess that you only saw the very tip of the iceberg. My mother is loving and giving and kind and caring and generous to a fault." Georgia grinned and added, "And we all adore her anyway."

"I guess I'm glad for Laura that she found Delia," he spoke the words slowly, the admission was not an easy one. "And I'm glad that Ally will at least have one grandmother as she grows up."

"What happened to her other grandmother?" Georgia gave his hand a last squeeze before releasing her fingers from his so she could begin to stack the dinner dishes.

"What?" The question was unexpected, and Matt wasn't certain he'd heard correctly.

"Ally's father's family." Georgia stood and carried the dishes to the sink to rinse them. "And while we're on the subject, where's Ally's father?"

"Don't you know?" He couldn't believe that she didn't know.

Georgia shook her head. "The few times I asked Laura about her husband, she snapped shut like a clam. She has made it very clear that that is one topic she does not want to discuss."

"And your mother didn't tell you . . . ?"

"No. She said that Laura would probably discuss it when she felt she could. Which I thought was an odd choice of words, but my mother didn't seem inclined to elaborate." Georgia waited for Matt to volunteer some information, and when he did not, she prodded him. "So . . . ?"

"So . . . ?"

"So, what happened to Laura's husband? Where is he?"

"He's in a federal prison."

Georgia suspected that the thud she heard was her jaw hitting the kitchen floor.

"Prison?" Georgia sat back down. "What did he do?"

"Stole money from his church." There really was no way to pretty it up.

"He stole *money* from a *church?*"

"Not just *any* church. *His* church."

"You mean he was a *minister?*"

"Yep. The Very Reverend Gary J. Harmon was pastor and spiritual leader of the New House of God."

"Yow." Georgia's eyes were growing larger. "Wait

a minute. The New House of God . . . why does this sound familiar?"

"You might have seen it on the news when the story broke a few years ago. Gary was a young, handsome, Bible-toting man of the cloth. He had a large ministry that went out over the airwaves every Sunday morning and every Wednesday night. And every Sunday morning and every Wednesday afternoon, he was appealing for contributions for the poor in our midst . . . 'the souls entrusted to our care by none other than God Almighty Himself . . .'" Matt's voice lowered and took on the tone of a deeply sincere and concerned humanitarian. ". . . and on Monday and Thursday mornings he was on the phone to his bookie."

"You mean he gambled with the church's money?"

"Every last red cent, near as we could figure out."

"I can't believe that Laura would fall in love with someone like that."

"You would have had to know Gary, Georgia. Handsome, as I said, and with the most humble, down-to-earth, sincere manner you'd ever want to see. He was as charming a man as you'll ever meet."

"But for Laura to marry someone like that. A con man!"

"Oh, I think he did his best con job on her. I don't believe she ever saw through him. That's what made it such a shock to all of us. None of us ever saw it coming."

"How could you not know?"

"Georgia, all you ever really see of anyone else is

that which they want you to see. He played the role of a totally devoted husband, totally committed man of the cloth to perfection."

"How was he caught?"

"One of his congregation saw him in a casino in Las Vegas. He was supposed to be attending a retreat in the desert." A look of disgust crossed Matt's face. "He was retreating, all right. Straight to the blackjack table. A drink in one hand and a showgirl in the other."

"Oh, poor Laura! She must have been devastated!"

"Totally. She could not believe it. Did not believe it, even when the congregation formed an audit committee and started going through the church's books and found a tangled mess but no money. Laura stood by him until the evidence was so overwhelming that even Gary didn't bother to deny it. And as humiliating as it must have been for her— living in the town she'd grown up in, married to a man who'd fleeced half the community, hell, half of Maryland!—I really think the worst part for her was the deception. Finding out that her life with him had been nothing more than a sham. That the man she loved really did not exist. That she was married to a total stranger."

"But she's still married to him, isn't she? She said something one time about being separated, not divorced . . ."

"Well, that's another problem. It seems that the longer Gary stays in prison, the more he's starting to believe his own press."

"I don't understand." Georgia asked as she filled

the teakettle with tap water and placed it on the stove.

"He always maintained that he was a devoted man of God. One that had sinned and sought redemption, but still a man of God. His little speech before he was sentenced was carried on a lot of the news programs, and to give the devil his due, Gary was quite convincing. He is a compelling speaker, Georgia. Mesmerizing. He had been tempted, he confessed, he had succumbed to temptation, but he had seen the light and was stronger in his faith because of it. He's become a bit of a celebrity there in prison. He 'ministers' to the prison population now, leads them in prayers and teaches them how to redeem their souls, so he claims. I understand he has a totally devoted flock there at the Gray Bar Hotel where he is presently incarcerated. And he really does seem to believe that he is a true and anointed man of God. He's become frighteningly devout."

"That's an odd choice of words," she frowned. " 'Frighteningly' and 'devout' shouldn't go together."

"No, they shouldn't, but in his case, it fits." Matt recalled the conversation with Delia and the information she had shared. "I've heard that his ministry has spread from prison to prison throughout the country. Something about the thought of an entire network of hardened felons devoted to Reverend Gary scares me."

"Have you seen him?" She turned the knob for the first burner, then leaned sideways to make sure that the gas flame appeared.

"I saw him last year when he came up for parole.

While they say he is a model prisoner, the parole board did not feel that his sentence should be cut short. He took money from a lot of hard-working people, and a good number of them wrote letters to the hearing board asking that he not be paroled."

"Did Laura go with you? To the hearing?"

"No. You know, for all of her reluctance to divorce him, she seems almost frightened to even see him. I went to the hearing because I felt that a member of the family should be there and I did not want Laura to go when she clearly did not want to. She really has not been able to put this whole thing behind her, I'm assuming that it's because of Ally, but I'm still not certain that *that's* the whole story. In any event, I went to the parole hearing, over Laura's protests. She hadn't wanted me to go either. Afterward, I was glad that she stayed home."

"Why's that?"

"Gary seemed . . . different."

"Different how?"

"I couldn't put my finger on it. It bothered me a lot at the time. The way he was looking at everyone, as if everyone in that room was totally . . . *insignificant*. As if he was amused somehow by it all."

"I wouldn't think that having my chances for parole being shot down would be terribly amusing."

"Oh, well, I'm sure he hadn't expected that. And of course, the denial of parole wasn't announced then and there. But there was certainly something about him that had changed."

"Why doesn't Laura just divorce him and get it over with?"

"I don't have a clue. She started proceedings a few years ago, then dropped them. She wouldn't discuss it, other than to say that she thought it was for the best."

"I've noticed that Laura is very good at avoiding topics she wants to avoid."

"Well, I can't figure it out. She's a beautiful woman, she's got her own business, a wonderful child, she should be getting on with her life. I can't for the life of me understand why she would want to stay tied to the likes of him."

"Do you think she still loves him?"

"No. Not a chance."

"Maybe it has something to do with Ally . . ."

"I used to think that, but it doesn't feel right. Ally has never even seen the man. She was born six months after he was sentenced. He's never laid eyes on her."

"Poor Laura." Georgia sighed as she measured loose tea into the silver ball and dropped it into one of the cups. "She deserves so much better than that."

"I couldn't agree with you more. You know, last year I tried to fix her up with a vet I know from Ocean City and you know what she said? She said she couldn't date. That she was still married and couldn't go out with anyone."

"But at the same time she doesn't see him and has no contact with him and never talks about him."

"Right."

"I see what you mean about people only letting us see what they want us to see. Laura's never given me so much as a hint." Georgia chewed on the inside of her bottom lip. "I never in a million years would have guessed at any of this."

The kettle began to whistle and she turned off the burner, then poured hot water over the tea ball, recalling Laura's reaction to the reading of her tea leaves. A lover. A secret to be revealed. Well, that much came true. Her secret had been revealed to Georgia.

"I wish I could get her to talk to me about this. Maybe together, we can find a way to help Laura move forward. Maybe she just has a fear of starting over." Georgia said softly. "And really, all things considered, starting over isn't so very bad. Change can be very good."

"You're doing well here?" he asked although the answer was evident. Georgia glowed of good health and contentment.

"Very well. I am very happy here. Every day is totally new and there's always something to do."

"Plowing. Pig farming . . ."

"Don't laugh. It's been fun, though it's definitely a very different lifestyle for me. It's making it easier for me to see what direction I might want to follow." She went to the refrigerator and returned with a bowl of raspberries which she sat between them on the table. "Help yourself," she said as she popped one into her mouth.

"And that direction is?"

"I really love dancing, Matt. It's been my life. But for the past year or two, I really haven't been very happy. Not the way I have been since I've been here.

I've had the best time teaching, and I think I'm good at it. I've had calls this week from several of the moms who were here for Ally's birthday . . ."

"Wanting to sign their daughters up for lessons?"

"And wanting to take lessons themselves. Word has spread very quickly. There's no other ballet school in the area to compete with, so I already have enough adults—via word of mouth—for one class, and enough children to do two beginner classes each week. And I haven't even done any advertising!" Her eyes were glowing as the words tumbled out. "Oh, I know it's only temporary, only for a few months, I've told everyone that. But they want to come anyway."

"And from here?" He asked tentatively.

She shrugged. "I'm not sure. Right now, I'm enjoying farm life and dancing."

"That's such an odd combination."

"But it's perfect for me." She added a little more hot water to each of the teacups. "You know, you never did tell me what brought you down here today."

"Oh." He couldn't bring himself to tell her that he'd come to measure the barn for his clinic. That that exact spot where she set up her little row of chairs would be a wall that separated one of several examining rooms from the operating room. "Just wanted to check on a few things. Pick up some mail."

"I'm glad you did. I'm glad you're here."

"So am I." He glanced at the clock. It was almost ten. He had surgery scheduled first thing tomorrow—removing tumors from the shoulder of a cocker spaniel—and he still had to drive back to Shawsburg. "It's later than I thought. I need to be getting back home."

He stood and held the back of her chair as she rose.

"Where do you suppose Artie is?" she asked.

"Probably sitting at the bottom of the steps, waiting for his dinner."

"I could give him a few carrots."

"Nah, he can wait."

Matt opened the back door and stepped out. The evening air was crisp and fresh and laced with the scent of tulip and iris. The moment brought back memories of other spring evenings, and for just a moment, he thought he could almost see Hope at the window, looking out.

It was only an illusion, of course, but a comforting one.

"Well, thanks for dinner," Matt said.

Georgia had followed him outside, and stood on the top step. With Matt on the bottom step, they were almost the same height.

"It was very much my pleasure. I hope you'll come back."

He hadn't planned on it, but before he'd given it so much as a passing thought, he found his mouth moving down to meet hers. Her lips were soft and sweet and were like no lips he'd ever kissed before.

"I didn't mean to do that." He heard a voice say. It took a few seconds for him to recognize the voice as his own. "I'm sorry," he added.

"Matthew," she whispered, her hands still on his shirt collar drawing his face slowly back to hers, "don't ever apologize to a woman for kissing her. She might think you didn't like it."

Without apology, he bent and kissed her again. And again. And for a long time it seemed that there was nothing else under the moon that night but Georgia, and lips that tasted like raspberries and invited him to feast, arms that wound around his neck like soft, fragrant vines and that sweet body that was soft in all the right places.

There had been, he thought as he drove down the dark road back to Shawsburg some time later, nothing sorry about it.

chapter seventeen

S ee you on Saturday," he'd turned and called back
to her across the hush of the late spring night.
"Early afternoon. We'll see what we can do about
getting that water hooked up."

Georgia watched from the top step until the tail-
lights of Matt's truck disappeared as he turned on to
the road at the end of the lane.

See you on Saturday.

She settled Spam onto the porch for the night and
locked the back door behind her, then went back into
the kitchen and absently began to rinse the dinner
dishes. It wasn't until she dropped the second fork
that she acknowledged the fact that her hands were
shaking. Raising her fingers to her lips, she traced the
path of his kisses, still feeling the pressure of his
mouth on hers.

She tried to remember if she'd ever been struck
dumb by a kiss before and thought perhaps that this
had been a first.

Grinning, she turned the water back on and rinsed

the saucers of the small splashes of tea that had run down the side of the cup. She reached for the cups and was just about to run them under the swift stream of water when she stopped, set the cups down on the counter, and went off to get Hope's book.

Let's see, she thought, I had the cup with the tiny chip on the handle.

She looked inside at the small amount of liquid left.

Just right, she smiled. Swishing it around, she turned the cup around three times—counter-clockwise, of course—and tilted it into the light so that she could see the tea leaves left within.

Hmmm. I'd call that a cat's head, there by the handle. And down there a little farther, that sort of looks like a hat. And down at the bottom, some sort of bird with wide wings. A hawk, maybe . . .

Georgia leaned over the counter and paged through Hope's book, looking for notes that might correspond with the images that she saw.

"Well, the cat is an easy one. Domestic comfort, and I certainly have that." She murmured aloud.

Hat. Let's see. She skimmed the precise handwriting and neatly drawn figures. There was a hat that looked almost exactly like the one in Georgia's cup. A new project or challenge. Well, that was certainly on the money.

And the last, the bird . . . danger. A predator.

Georgia frowned and looked at the tea leaves again, trying to see something else in the configuration at the bottom of the cup. It still looked like a broad winged bird.

She set the cup down and looked into Matt's cup. Could she read his tea leaves if he wasn't there to go through the ritual of turning the cup around? She turned it this way and that to see if there was any discernible image in the leaves.

There was.

A key shape near the handle. An egg nearby.

Georgia flipped through Hope's book. The key meant that there would be important decisions to be made about the future. Perhaps a new path to be taken.

The egg—beneficial changes, new projects, success.

All good things.

She turned the water back on to rinse the cups, and saw the image at the bottom of Matt's that she had missed.

A broad-winged bird.

Thinking she had picked up her own cup, she lifted the other cup and looked inside. The same image rested in almost exactly the same place in both cups. A shiver ran up her spine and she rinsed both cups out quickly.

It would be silly to take this too seriously, she told herself as she turned out the kitchen lights. *After all, it's only spots of organic matter in the bottom of a teacup. And I don't even know if Hope really knew what she was doing. For all I know, she could have made it all up as she went along.*

Still, the feeling of unrest stayed with her as she changed for bed, slipping the soft jersey dress onto the hanger and sliding the oversized T-shirt over her head. And still as she turned on the small lamp that sat on the bedside table and turned off the overhead light. It didn't start to fade until she was five or six pages into the novel she was reading—a historical romance recommended by the cashier at Tanner's, where you really *could* buy just about everything—and wasn't completely forgotten until her head began to nod and her eyes began to close and she heard the promise of that soft, sexy voice—*See you on Saturday*—as she drifted off to sleep and to dreams where strong arms held her and sweet kisses set her heart pounding out of control.

There was a delivery truck parked in Matt's usual spot under the tree on Saturday afternoon, and he slowed down to inspect it as he crept past it in the pickup. The back doors of the white truck stood open, as did the door to the barn. Matt hopped out of the truck behind Artie and followed the dog to investigate.

"Hello?" Matt called into the barn.

"Matt?" Georgia leaned over the second floor railing. "Oh, Matt, come *see!*"

She was all but dancing up and down with delight when he reached the top step.

"Look, they finally came!" She grabbed his hand with one of her own, the other pointing to several long cardboard boxes from which two young delivery men were removing a long wooden pole that they placed on the floor next to several other equally long, round poles.

"What are they?" Matt frowned, allowing her to lead him across the floor.

"They're barres. For my dancing classes. And of

course, for me, too. They're only temporaries, of course. They fit on these metal stands so they can be moved around, and I can take them with me when I go to . . . to wherever I eventually go." She lifted one end of the long smooth pole. "But they'll be wonderful! My students won't have to use those silly folding chairs anymore. Not that they were much good as far as a barre was concerned, but they did help the little ones to balance."

"Here, I'll do that." Matt grabbed the opposite end of the barre. "Now what?"

"We set it right on here," she directed him to follow her to one of the heavy metal stands, "and we just put it right in here." She placed her end of the barre on the stand and appeared to be searching the floor for something. "Ah, there it is . . . and we just put these long screws through . . . there."

"Isn't it wonderful?" She sighed.

Matt took the screwdriver from her hand and proceeded to affix the barre to the stands at the designated intervals.

The last of the barres having been brought up to the second floor, Georgia pulled a crumpled bill from the pocket of her short jeans overalls and offered it to the delivery men in thanks for their assistance. She walked them part of the way down the steps, then, after they had gone, came back upstairs and asked Matt again, "Isn't it wonderful?"

He laughed and agreed that it was just that.

"Now, all I need are some portable mirrors to put along this wall and that, and I'll have the makings of a real ballet school."

"Why do you need mirrors?" Matt asked, catching

her by her tiny waist as she danced past, pulling her close within the circle of his arms.

"So that you can check your position," she told him, wrapping her arms around his neck. "You can't correct something if you can't see that you're doing it improperly."

"Is it that important, to see every move, to make every movement perfect?" He lowered his face to hers, and without apology this time, kissed her mouth, drawing in her sweetness, letting the feel of her flow through him.

She stood on her tiptoes, and still his arms had to lift her slightly to return his kiss, the heat of which sped through her veins like live current. For a long minute she understood what the poets meant when they spoke of a fire in the blood, because hers was certainly starting to boil. His hands had lifted her to him, holding her body closely to his, her body crushed against him. For a long time she seemed to drift in the fog that had surrounded her, blocking out everything but Matt and the eagerness of his seeking tongue, his firm body that had come alive so suddenly to stir feelings in her that she wasn't sure she'd ever felt before. Georgia found herself responding on instinct, with seemingly no input from her brain, and it was only when he began to set her feet back on the floor that her senses began to return. Slowly. And not completely.

"Ah . . ." his teeth nipped at her bottom lip before he released her and said, "you were saying, about how important the right movements are . . ."

"Oh. Right. Yes. Position and movement." She felt her face flush scarlet and her legs wobble as she stepped back from him, and she hoped it didn't show. She cleared her throat. "For a classical dancer, yes, correct position is critical. And it is very important for the little ones to see where their feet should be, where their arms should be. It's the only way they'll learn."

"How are your classes going?" He needed to distance himself from her before he did something that could embarrass them both, she had filled him so totally and so suddenly that it had taken him completely off guard and left him shaken inside.

He looked for a distraction.

She had been anxious to move all the barres into place, so he folded up one of the no longer necessary chairs and leaned it against the wall, then folded another one.

"They are truly wonderful, and I'm loving it. Teaching ballet is such a happy thing to do." Georgia took a deep breath and ordered her respiration to return to normal. "You missed Ally and Laura this morning, by the way. I told them you would be here this afternoon, but they couldn't stay. Ally had a birthday party to go to."

"How many little friends did she bring this morning?" Matt asked, and Georgia laughed.

"Eight. Last week there were ten, but two of them were twins who were going out of town this weekend." She folded up the last of the chairs and started to arrange the barres in a straight line. "I could probably do three classes of children each week and at least one class of adults. Someone stops me to ask about classes every time I go into Tanner's and the phone rings at least once a day. Ally's birthday party sparked a lot of interest here in O'Hearn as well as in Bishop's Cove."

"You're kidding?"

"Nope. I wasn't kidding when I said there was no competition. The closest ballet school is in Salisbury."

"Well, then, since you're enjoying it, and the demand is there, why don't you schedule a few more classes and hang out a shingle?" *And why don't I shut up, since the shingle that goes up is supposed to read Pumpkin Hill Veterinary Clinic. Matthew T. Bishop, DVM.*

"I really haven't felt that I could do that—charge people to teach them when the arrangements are so makeshift. But now with the new barres, if I can find a few mirrors, I think I can schedule some paying classes." She scuffed one toe along the worn wooden boards. "Of course, the floor is in bad shape in spots, but they rent sanders in Tanner's, so I'm thinking of renting one and seeing if I can smooth it out a little, maybe put one of those non-slip finishes on it."

They finished dragging the last of the barres into place and Georgia stepped back to admire the scene, her eyes shining. She went to one and placed her right hand upon it, straightened her back, and made what looked to Matt like a deep knee bend.

"You really are pleased, aren't you?" He smiled, her joy was so infectious.

"Yes, I really am. Oh, I know it's only temporary," her own smile dimmed slightly, "but for now, it will be wonderful. I can hardly wait until tomorrow morning when I can try out my new barres."

"Why not now?"

"Because now we have to look for water." She ran her hand along the length of the barre till she reached the end, then took his arm and pulled him gently toward the steps. "Though maybe I will sneak back in later with some new music I've been dying to dance to."

She turned off the light and they went down the steps side by side.

"Do you dance every day?" he asked.

"Every day. Every morning." At the bottom of the steps, she held the door open for him and closed it behind her after they passed through, hand in hand. "You know, dancers all over the world follow the same basic routine. Classes every morning, rehearsals in the afternoon. I spent years of my life at the barre from ten in the morning till one or two in the afternoon. I still do. Only now, I choreograph my own dances. I can dance every role I ever dreamed of."

"You don't miss the other dancers? Isn't it hard, doing it all on your own?"

"Well, in some respects. I mean, you can't very well do a *pas de deux* with one person." She grinned. "But I love the freedom of having the music to myself. At least, for now, I do. That might wear a bit thin after too long a time, but for now, I welcome the solitude. I guess I needed time off more than I suspected."

They had reached the old chicken house—the one Matt had started painting a few weeks earlier—and stood staring at the front, where the old mesh fencing had contained the many chickens that had once lived at Pumpkin Hill.

"The building's bigger than it looks," Georgia

noted. "I always think of a chicken house as just a small place for a half-dozen chickens."

"Not in Maryland," Matt told her. "Chickens are a big business down here. Grandfather used to raise poultry to sell to the retailers for the supermarkets—hence the larger building—but for the past ten or so years, my aunt only kept enough chickens for eggs for the farm and for a few of her friends."

Georgia followed him around back—Artie and Spam trailing along behind, the pig still keeping a wary eye on the rottweiler—and stopped when he did. There was a metal spigot sticking out of the back wall, and he bent down to twist the handle. It didn't budge.

"I think I might need a wrench. I have one in the truck. I'll be right back."

Georgia hadn't meant to stare, but there was just something about the way he wore those jeans that kept her eyes glued to his back as he sauntered across the grass and down the drive.

Not nearly the troll I once thought him to be, she mused as he opened the door of his pickup and leaned in to reach under the seat.

Not even close, she thought as he walked back toward her.

"I think this should do it," he told her as he approached the chicken house. "And if it does, we can drive into Tanner's and buy a couple of hoses. Two will probably do."

"I already bought them," she said as he fitted the wrench onto the pipe.

"You did?"

"I figured, either way, I'd use them."

"Good thinking." Matt stepped back as brackish water began to spurt from the old spigot. "It's a little rusty, but it should run clean in a minute."

"I'll go get the hoses," she brightened and sprinted off to retrieve the hoses that she had left near the back steps, "and we can hook them up and see if they reach the field."

"They'll reach," Matt told her as she returned with a green vinyl hose looped over each shoulder. "They'll be just right."

He turned the water off and fitted the hose to the spigot while Georgia fitted the second hose to the first. They straightened out both sections, and turned the water back on.

"That's perfect!" She beamed. "I can water all my little plants without using the watering can. I can tell you, that became a bit tedious this week."

"You've been carrying that old watering can all the way from the barn?"

"Sure. It was the only way to get water back there."

"Completely filled, that can has to weigh almost as much as you do."

"Not quite, but it did get heavy after a while. But I really am stronger than I look." She flexed her biceps and offered her right arm for his inspection.

"Solid," he nodded appreciatively. "And hard as a rock."

"The dancing keeps me in pretty good shape."

"You can say that again." He muttered as he bent over and picked up the wrench, which he stuck into his back pocket. "Well, we have that problem solved and the afternoon to spare. What would you like to do with the rest of the day? Assuming you haven't made other plans, of course."

"Oh, no other plans," she smiled up at him. "Except I did think it might be fun to have a picnic down by the pond. If we had time, that is. Which we do."

"That sounds great." He was pleased—touched—that she had planned ahead and that she had included him in her plans.

"Great. Come back to the house with me and you can help me carry the stuff."

The stuff proved to be an old quilt, a large thermos of iced tea, and an old wicker basket into which she loaded several prewrapped and packaged items. He was curious as to their contents. What does a vegetarian pack for a picnic? Whatever it was, it was still slightly warm and smelled wonderful.

"I have to ask, " Matt said, lifting the basket higher and sniffing as they walked down the back steps, "what smells so good?"

"Oh, it could be one of several things, but it's probably the guacamole on the sandwiches. It always smells better when it's warm." She told him, obviously pleased.

"What's in the sandwiches?" he asked cautiously.

"Oh, I made my favorite." She increased her stride slightly to keep up with his longer legs as they made their way across the yard. "It's grilled portobellos with red onions, lettuce, tomatoes and bean sprouts. Oh, and the guacamole, which I made myself."

His own step slowed and his eyebrows knit closer together.

Could she be serious? Mushroom sandwiches?

"Mushrooms." She nodded.

And mushrooms are a *fungus,* he inwardly grimaced.

Fungus and sprouts. With guacamole. Homemade. Matt could hardly wait.

"Actually, this is quite delicious," Matt heard himself admitting after he'd eaten the first half of the sandwich, which was on a fresh whole wheat roll. "I suppose you made the buns, too."

"Yesterday," she told him.

Matt put his sandwich down on the paper plate. "I was kidding."

"I'm not." She grinned. "I couldn't find any I liked that didn't have tons of preservatives."

"You know, you should probably consider doing a take-out business, or a line of prepackaged and frozen foods. Or, at the very least, a cookbook. Anyone who can make a mushroom sandwich taste this incredible obviously has something going for them."

"It's on the list."

Matt leaned back against the trunk of the weeping willow tree that tilted toward the bank of the pond, its thin arms just starting to drip with pale green fringe.

"Well, so now we have a possible degree in psychology and a line of vegetarian specialties on the list. What else?"

"Just my dancing school."

"That's a lot."

"Maybe I won't do them all at the same time. Maybe I will." She grinned and pulled her legs up

Indian-style and leaned her elbows on her knees. "The state college about fifteen miles from here offers a degree in performing arts with a concentration in dance. I called and spoke with someone in the department last week, and I may be able to get several credits for certain courses based on my professional experience. I could take dance as a major and psychology as a minor, or vice versa. I also learned that there's a teacher's training workshop this summer in New York, that I'm thinking about signing up for. It's only for a week, but I think that would be beneficial."

"How could you fit it all in?"

"I can dance in the morning, attend class in the afternoon or evening, and schedule my dance classes for the afternoons when I don't have school. And classes on Saturday mornings, for Ally and her friends, of course."

"That sounds like a pretty ambitious schedule."

"After years of following exactly the same routine, I love having the freedom to try new things. I think I can balance teaching and going to school."

"And farming."

She laughed. "Right. Let's not leave that out."

"Where do you see yourself in ten years?"

Georgia shrugged. "Well, by then, certainly, I hope to have my degree. And maybe a master's, too, who knows? And of course, I'll still be dancing."

"And farming." He added.

"A girl's gotta eat." She grinned. "How 'bout you? Where do you see yourself in ten years?"

"Here." He answered without hesitation. "At Pumpkin Hill."

"You're planning on living here?"

"I always have. It's been my dream for as long as I can remember to open a veterinary clinic here in the barn and live in the old farmhouse."

"That's a lovely dream," she said softly. "Pumpkin Hill is a special place. There's both peace and energy here, it's hard to explain."

"I've always felt it. It's what always draws me back. I've never wanted to settle anywhere else."

"Then why are you living in Shawsburg?"

"Ah, that's a long story." He sat up and reached for the second half of his sandwich. "Doc Espey was one of my instructors in vet school. He's a wonderful man. A truly dedicated vet, an innovator . . ."

"How so?"

"For example, for years he's been developing dog foods that have lower fat, sodium, and animal products." He grinned. "Sort of a quasi-vegetarian approach, if you will."

"Ah, that explains why Artie is so partial to carrots."

"Exactly. Doc Espey has been trying his formulas out on Artie for years. And the dog has thrived, as you can see." Matt motioned with his head in the direction of the dog in question, who was at that moment, his nose to the dirt, following the hopping motions of a small frog as it fled toward the safety of the pond. "And he's also encouraged the use of chiropractic treatment and other nontraditional methods of treating animals."

"He sounds like someone I'd like to know."

"I think you would. There's a lot that we just don't know about disease. I think a holistic approach, using a variety of modalities, may be the ultimate answer, for humans as well as animals. And I admire people like Doc Espey who aren't afraid to investigate and utilize other techniques beyond conventional practices."

"But you won't be staying with him . . ." She sensed that there was something more coming, and tried to ease the way.

"I interned with him. He's had several strokes since then, now he's mostly retired. I stayed on to help him to keep up his practice for a while."

"That's very nice of you. Considering that you would rather be running your own practice here."

"Well, not so totally altruistic. For one thing, I couldn't afford to start up my own clinic when I first got out of school. For another, he taught me so much, that I just felt I owed him. Now, more than ever, I owe him . . ."

"What do you mean?"

Matt told her about Espey's decision to sell his clinic and his gift of equipment to Matt for the clinic at Pumpkin Hill.

"Oh, but that's wonderful!" Georgia clapped her hands together, startling some ducks who napped in the shade of some nearby cattails and causing Artie to mosey over to investigate the movement. "Then you'll be able to open your clinic and move back to . . ."

She stopped midsentence, realizing the implications. "Oh. Of course. I'm in your house. My dance studio is in your barn," she said flatly.

"Look, it's not going to happen tomorrow. I haven't even figured out what I'll need to do to reconfigure the barn. Then I still have to see if the bank will give me a loan to get started. It will take a few months."

An awkward silence settled in and hung over them for a few long minutes.

"Well, you know, I have an apartment here, I have a place to stay," Matt told her. "It's not like I'm going to throw you out. Besides, for a while after I get my practice set up, it may be easier for me to just stay in the apartment anyway. Especially since I might have farm animals staying there that might need care in the middle of the night." He was rationalizing and they both knew it, but he didn't want her to think that he was anxious for her to leave. On the contrary. The thought of her leaving Pumpkin Hill disturbed him.

"Well, that's nice of you to say. We've had a fairly open-ended sort of arrangement, and I think I've let myself ignore the fact that this is a temporary situation for me because I've been so happy here. I just will have to make more of an effort to remember just how temporary this is."

"Where would you go? If you left?"

"*When* I leave . . . I don't know." She opened the picnic basket and took out a bowl of fruit and set it between them. "Maybe I'll look for another place to lease in the area. Maybe I'll look around Bishop's Cove. I like this part of the state, and I'd hate to leave my dance students high and dry."

"You can stay on in the farmhouse and find a place in town for a studio." He suggested, suddenly as concerned about her options as he was of his own. "We'll work it out somehow."

There had been a For Rent sign on that storefront

two down from Tanner's. While it wouldn't be the quite the same—she'd have to drive into town every time she felt like dancing—it could work. She didn't want to think about that now. She was here, and so was Matt, and the sun was warm on her skin, the air was sweet with wild hyacinth and the day felt ripe with promise.

"It's not a decision I'm going to make today," she told him. "Besides, it's a beautiful spring day, one to lean back and watch the clouds."

And she did just that, dropping back to rest her head on the ground, her hands shielding her eyes from the sun. "Look, there, Matt, there's an alligator . . ."

He put his half-eaten apple down on his plate and laid down next to her, following her finger that was directing his gaze to the left.

"Alligator?" He frowned. "No, no. That's a snake. *Definitely* a snake."

"A snake? Snakes don't have legs!"

"Where do you see legs?"

"Right there, see . . . ?"

"Nah, those aren't legs. Those are the weeds the snake is crawling through."

He caught her hand as it stretched upward, encircled it with his own, and let them both rest on the quilt in the space between their bodies. Georgia tucked her other hand behind her head and turned sideways to look at him.

Her eyes are almost as green as the new grass, he was thinking, right before he raised himself up slightly and, drawn to her mouth like a bee to a flower, kissed her. Her lips were pliant and soft and welcoming, just as they had been earlier that day. His free hand caressed the soft cheek and traced a line from her temple to her chin before sliding through the silken stream of hair that had eased onto her face. His fingers slid through the warm shimmer of it, and bunched it gently into a fist. From the first moment he'd seen her, he'd wanted to do this, to send his fingers through the golden wave and feel its silk, tangle in its thickness and measure its weight. His teeth scraped across her bottom lip and he felt her tongue meet his own to take those first tentative steps in a slow dance of seduction. He traced the inside of her mouth before plunging into it, and he knew that for the first time in his life, fantasy had met its match in reality. The hand that he had held found its way free and was making its way around his waist, and her other hand sought the back of his neck to draw him closer still. She arched her back and strained against him, and he covered her body with his own, thinking that she was every bit as sweet and soft and yielding as he had dreamed she would be. Her fingers twisted in the back of his shirt and he raised himself onto his elbows and slid his mouth down the side of her jaw, teasing her skin with his tongue and his teeth until he reached her neck. Drawing the soft skin between his lips, he inched his way to her throat, his breathing matching hers in short quiet gasps.

"Matt," she whispered, "kiss me again . . ."

His mouth found its way back to hers, and was just about to do her bidding when he heard it.

Beepbeepbeep. Beepbeepbeep.

The sound didn't immediately register, but then she asked, "Matt, are you wearing a beeper?"

He groaned and rolled over and, pulling the small electronic device off his belt, held it up to read the message.

He rested his elbow on the ground and his chin in his hand. "The Gilberts' sheep dog is in labor."

"And this means . . ."

"She had a tough time with the last litter and almost didn't make it. I promised I'd be there this time."

"Then you have to go," she told him without hesitation.

"You don't mind?"

"Oh, yes," she grinned, "I mind. But I'll be here when you get back . . ."

"It might be late."

"I'll be here," she said softly.

"Then I'll be back." He pulled himself up before offering her a hand and helping her to her feet. "I'll call you when I'm on my way back."

"You don't have to," she stood on her toes to kiss his neck and repeated, "I'll be here waiting . . . if it takes all night."

chapter eighteen

It was ten-fifteen when Georgia heard the truck tires creep softly up the drive and stop behind her Jeep. It had been some hours since Matt had left, but she would have waited for days if she had to. He had been in her head since the first time she'd met him in the parking lot at the inn and had charmed her, before he had known who she was. She had felt a pull toward him that day, had always known instinctively that someday there would be more between them than animosity or casual conversation. It had only been a matter of time before he recognized it, too.

Must have been the dandelion wishes, she mused as she heard the slam of the pickup's door.

Smiling to herself, she got out of the old arm chair and called to Artie, who had gone on full alert at the sound.

"It's Matt," she said to the dog. "Shall we go meet him?"

Artie got up and sped to the back door, where he

348

stood wagging his entire hindquarters in anticipation of his owner's return. Georgia opened the back door and the dog pushed past her to the porch door. The intrusion roused Spam, but only briefly. The pig flopped her head back onto her bed and went back to sleep even as Artie bounded down the steps to meet Matt as he rounded the side of the house.

"Did you take care of Georgia while I was gone? Good boy, Artie."

"How's the sheep dog?" Georgia asked from the doorway.

"Nine healthy pups," he told her. "Mother and babies doing well."

"Then I'm glad you went." She stepped back into the dim light from the kitchen and he followed her. "Gladder still that you came back . . ."

"Me, too." He folded her into his arms and kissed her full on the mouth. "We have some unfinished business to tend to."

"I was hoping you'd say that," she sighed between kisses.

She pushed over the door to close it with one foot, and reached behind her to close over the latch. That was as much locking up as the house would get that night. Everything else—the downstairs lights and the open kitchen window—would have to wait.

Wordlessly, Matt followed her up the steps.

"Which way?" he paused to ask.

"The front bedroom."

He'd known that, of course, but didn't figure this was the time to discuss the fact that he had investigated on his own when she had first moved there. Back in the days when he'd resented the fact that there was a stranger living in his house. When she had been a stranger, and an unwelcome one at that. It hadn't taken her long to win him over. There was something in her that had drawn him to her in a way that no woman ever had. Georgia was beauty and sweetness, strength and passion, joy and music, goodness and laughter, and if he was smart enough, *wise* enough, lucky enough, she would be his, tonight and always.

How had he been blind to the fact that just looking at her caused the blood to pound in his veins and his breath to quicken? Had there ever been a time when he had not wanted to bury himself inside her and never seek the light of day again?

Moving onto the old double bed, Georgia pulled him down to her, pressing herself against him, knowing she'd never wanted a man more than she wanted Matt Bishop at that moment, had wanted him in ways that had made her blush just to think about it. Easing herself back onto the pillow, she took him with her, touching him with loving restless hands, her body urging him to touch her in return, and he did, with hands that plied and teased and stoked the heat within her until it threatened to erupt. His mouth took forever, it seemed, to make its way from her lips to her throat, from her throat to her breasts, building the fire and coaxing it on. He heard—felt—her soft moans as she opened to him and helped him inside, felt himself slip into the slick heat of her smoothness, into a deep sweet place that was warm and wet and waiting for him, only for him. He met her cries and matched them, and urged their bodies onward, tumbling them both into a bottomless well of pleasure so deep and so unexpected that it rocked him to his very core and knocked the breath from his lungs as he shattered inside her.

And that, he thought as he lay in the dark and stroked her back with gentle hands, unable to trust himself to attempt to put feelings into spoken words, *was as close to heaven as I will ever get.*

The clock on the bedside table ticked softly, and in the dark, Matt could see the hands were just past the twelve and on the two. Remembering where he was and the joy that had filled his heart that night, he reached for Georgia, just to touch her skin. Just to prove to himself that she was real, that it had not been a dream.

There was nothing there.

Matt's arm stretched to the opposite side of the bed.

Nothing.

He sat up, tilting his head slightly, listening. Perhaps she was down the hall, in the bathroom . . .

But there was no sound.

Without turning on the light, he crept down the hall, whispering her name.

"Georgia . . ."

Nothing.

Panicking, he returned to the front room, and pulled on the shorts he had worn earlier. As he leaned forward to grab his sneakers, he glanced out the window.

Rising slowly from the bed, his shoes now forgotten, he went to the window and looked out at the moonlit meadow just beyond the old farmhouse, and fell on one knee, in awe at the sight.

She danced in bare feet to music only she could hear, her golden hair aglow, her thin pale pink nightgown flowing around her body like the very moonlight. The perfect tilt of the head, the graceful arms raised over her head, the palms opened as if holding the moon in her hands, the lifting of her body as she rose onto her toes and turned, spun gently and leaped effortlessly to the sky—every movement took his breath away and left him numb and weakened and humbled. It was as if the night itself had come to life and celebrated itself, gliding across the meadow in joyful leaps in the form of a goddess and casting a spell upon any mortal who dared to watch.

As if he could have looked away.

On and on she danced, as if aware of nothing but the music within her and the need to set it free. Elegant, supple, grace and energy defined, the dance was a proclamation of joy, of wonder. It was as if something had been released in her that night that had lurked within her for a lifetime, and was now expressed in the only way she truly understood.

One last series of spins, of turns that molded the thin fabric to her body, and caused her hair to ripple like a golden river around her slight form, and she crumpled to the ground, a pale moonlit heap that had fallen with the crescendo of whatever music had played in her head. The spell almost broken—almost, but not quite—Matt rose and went down the steps. A stream of sweet-scented air drifted in through the open front door. He picked his way carefully across the grass in bare feet to the place where she rested on the ground.

Without a word, he lifted her, and cradling her against his body, carried her back to bed.

In the morning, the goddess was, once again, a woman, one whose natural modesty was somehow incongruous with the passion of the preceding hours, and who hesitantly offered to make breakfast for the man whose heart she had captured the night before.

"My turn." Matt told her. "You always cook for me. Let me make you my world famous breakfast of French toast and bacon."

A look of horror crossed her face.

"No!" He tried to cover up. "Not bacon. Did I say bacon? I meant that soy stuff that only looks like bacon."

She laughed in spite of herself, gesturing her head toward the porch door. Spam peered through the screen, watching from the other side. "In this house, b-a-c-o-n is a four letter word."

"What an insensitive clod!" He smacked his forehead with an open palm. "Not only are you a vegetarian, but of all things, it had to be *bacon*. Sorry, Spammy." He called toward the screen door.

"I'll think of some way to let you make it up to me later. Right now, however, French toast sounds wonderful. Oh, and we can have blueberry syrup with it. I bought some at Tanner's the other day. Someone made it locally and they had a display of . . ."

A sound from the drive drew her attention to the window, and she looked out as a dark green Jaguar rolled slowly to a stop in front of her Jeep.

"Were you expecting someone?" Matt asked.

"No." Georgia peered through the curtain on the back door, and watched the couple emerge from the sleek automobile. "I can't believe it! It's my mother and Gordon Chandler!"

She began to giggle. "Matt, my mother is wearing jeans!"

"What's so funny about that?"

"My mother *never* wears any kind of pants that aren't perfectly tailored trousers. She just *doesn't*. She's never even owned a pair of jeans before." Georgia watched curiously as Delia and Gordon strolled leisurely in the direction of the house. "I wonder what they're doing at this hour of the day."

"That's probably going to be the exact question your mother will be wondering when she sees me," Matt grimaced.

"Well, it's certainly too late to hide you," Georgia grinned, "so damage control would appear to be in order."

"So what do you propose we do?"

"Act like it's the most natural thing in the world for you to be in my kitchen at nine o'clock on a Sunday morning making French toast." She winked and opened the back door. "Mom," she called as she ran out in bare feet, "I'm so glad to see you! And Gordon! What a surprise! You're just in time for breakfast. Matt's making French toast . . ."

"Matt . . . ?" Delia's eyebrows raised only slightly higher than her daughter's had when Georgia realized who her mother's early morning companion was. It would appear that Matt may have taken her request to get to know her family more seriously than she had intended.

"Yes. He drove down for the weekend. He's found a source of water for my vegetable garden. Wait till I show you. Oh, Spam, I forgot to let you out."

The pig stood impatiently at the top step until Georgia lifted her and carried her down to the ground.

"Her legs are too close to the ground—as is her stomach- so she can't negotiate the steps."

"Hi, Delia," Matt said casually from the back door.

"Matthew," Delia's eyes narrowed as she tried to search for a logical explanation for his presence there without jumping to a possibly erroneous conclusion. "Have you met Gordon Chandler?"

"Of course." Matt came down the steps and offered his hand. "Good to see you."

"Thank you, Matt. Beautiful place," Gordon gestured with an outstretched arm as if to take in Pumpkin Hill in its entirety.

"Thank you." Matt folded his arms over his chest, well aware that all was under careful scrutiny at that moment. Of all mornings for her mother to drop by. "So. Would you folks like to join us for breakfast?"

"Thank you, Matt, but we already had breakfast on our way down from Westville . . ." Delia began. Flushing slightly when she realized just how much she'd given away, she offered a hasty excuse. "Gordon wanted to go to the Devon Horse Show, and it got somewhat late, and of course, Devon being so close to my home . . ."

"And I thought today would be a perfect day to take your mother to watch the bird migrations on the Delaware Bay," Gordon said smoothly, "so of course we would have to get an early start . . ."

"The Delaware Bay is an hour and a half northeast of here. If you're going from Westville to Delaware, you've taken one hell of a wrong turn," Georgia pointed out with some amusement. She was unaccustomed to seeing her mother flustered.

"Yes, well, we took a little detour to have breakfast in St. Michael's at a dockside place Gordon is fond of." Delia shoved her hands into the pockets of her lightweight jacket.

"Well, then," Matt cleared his throat, grateful that he was not the only one who felt as if he was dangling from the end of a hook, "maybe just coffee, or tea . . ."

"Actually, a cup of tea might be nice," Delia nodded, and taking Georgia's arm said, "Now, Laura's been telling me that you're swamped with calls from prospective dance students. That's wonderful, darling. I'm so happy for you."

"I'm not sure that *swamped* is the word I'd use, but yes, I've been getting lots of calls."

Matt and Gordon followed mother and daughter into the kitchen.

"You look wonderful, Georgia," Delia was saying, "you actually look as if you've put on a few pounds."

"Seven," Georgia's face turned white at the admission.

"Sweetie, it's okay." Delia took her daughter's hands in her own and squeezed them gently. She was well aware of the tirades Georgia had endured over the years where her weight was concerned. "You look better—healthier, stronger, happier—than I've seen you look since you were twelve years old," she said with conviction. "You needed those few extra pounds, Georgia. Why, you've lost that gaunt look. Sweetie, you've never looked more beautiful."

"Well, I have to agree with your mother," Gordon interjected. "Now, when I met you on the beach that day, I thought, there's an exceptionally beautiful young woman, but even with all those heavy clothes on, I figured you were good for another ten pounds. But now, after a few months in the country, you have a real glow about you."

"I guess Pumpkin Hill agrees with me," Georgia blushed and started to prepare tea.

Something certainly does, Delia's eyes narrowed, *but I'm not certain it isn't more than just the country air . . .*

"So, when will you be putting up your sign?"

"My sign?" Georgia frowned.

"'Ballet in the Barn, at Pumpkin Hill,'" Delia reminded her.

"Oh," Georgia bit her bottom lip, "well, that may not happen here."

"What do you mean, sweetie?" Mother studied daughter's face. "I thought we just established that the demand is there, you're enjoying teaching . . ."

"Matt will be moving back to Pumpkin Hill soon. He'll be opening a veterinary clinic in the barn. Isn't it wonderful?" Georgia placed steaming cups of amber tea in front of her mother and Gordon. "It's what he's always dreamed of, and now the opportunity is there . . ."

"But I thought . . ."

". . . Georgia is welcome to stay at Pumpkin Hill as long as she likes," Matt interrupted her.

"I can stay here at the house, Mom, and rent a place in town, maybe, for studio space. I haven't had time to give it much thought yet. But I did get my portable barres this week," she sat down next to her mother. "I can take them wherever I go."

"That was a wise idea." Delia sipped at her tea, trying to digest this late-breaking news.

"Gordon, how's your salvage operation going? Any luck with the *True Wind*?" Matt asked to change the subject. He had a few ideas of his own that had only just then begun to formulate. He tucked them away for future scrutiny.

"We're right on schedule. I was one man short, but Delia came up with someone who is working out quite well." Gordon told them.

"Mom, who do you know in the salvage business?" Georgia asked curiously.

"Well, not exactly salvage, but ships and diving and that sort of thing." Delia set her cup down on the saucer. "Do you remember Tucker Moreland? Captain Pete's son?"

"Sure. He drove the boat out to Devlin's Light when Nicky and India got married." Georgia nodded. "As I recall, he spent most of the way out and most of the way back staring at Laura . . ."

Ignoring that comment for the time being for reasons of her own, Delia continued.

"Well, Tucker was a Navy SEAL. When he retired last year, he returned to Devlin's Light to give his father a hand with his charter business and consider his options."

"How do you know all this?" Georgia asked.

"August Devlin. She and Captain Pete are . . ." Delia chose her words carefully, ". . . old friends."

"I thought there was something between them," Georgia nodded, looking pleased. To Matt, she said, "You met India's Aunt August at Ally's birthday party."

"I remember her very well. Lovely lady. Friendly. Charming. Tested my memory."

"In what way?" Georgia looked amused.

"She quoted something in Latin and I had to scramble to translate it." He grinned.

"Ah, yes," Delia laughed. "August sometimes forgets that everyone was not one of her high school Latin students, though it seems that just about everyone in Devlin's Light was, at one time or another."

"What was the phrase?" Gordon asked.

"Oh. It was a quote from Virgil." Matt flipped over the French toast in the pan on the stove. "*'Vera incessu patui dea.'*"

"You'll have to translate for me," Georgia shrugged. "I never took Latin."

He turned loving eyes to her and said softly, *"'By her walk, the true goddess was revealed.'"*

"Oh." It was the look that passed between them, more than the words, that caused Georgia to blush again.

Delia's left eyebrow rose almost imperceptibly.

Georgia cleared her throat and continued. "Anyway, India told me that August and Pete were sweethearts a million years ago when they were in high school."

"Careful, sweetie. August is only about ten years

older than I am." Delia tapped a manicured finger on her daughter's arm.

"Sorry," Georgia laughed. "Anyway, August went away to college to become a Latin teacher and Pete stayed in Devlin's Light and became a sea captain and ran charters and when she didn't come home he married someone else. He and his wife had several sons—Tucker's the oldest—and a few years ago, his wife died. He and August have sort of, um, resumed their friendship."

"When Gordon mentioned needing someone with expert diving skills, I thought immediately of Tucker," Delia told them.

"We drove up to Devlin's Light a few weeks ago," Gordon continued, "and I met with Tucker and discussed the project I'm working on. He's exactly the man I was looking for. I made him an offer and he accepted."

"He's commuting from Devlin's Light every day?" Georgia asked as Matt placed a plate of French toast—the top slices slightly darker than the rest—on the table. She hadn't missed Gordon's we.

"Oh, no," Delia shook her head, "he's staying at the inn."

"Really?" Georgia grinned. "Well, isn't that convenient."

"What's that mean?" Matt stood in front of the cupboard taking plates down. "Are you sure you won't join us, Delia? Gordon?"

"Thank you, no." Delia smiled, knowing exactly what Georgia was thinking about Tucker's stay at the inn. The very same idea had occurred to her.

Georgia took the teacups and placed them in the

sink. Then, on second thought, she moved them to the back of the counter, off by themselves, careful to note which cup had been whose. The teacups, with the remnants of tea and shards of tea leaves in their bottoms, sat on the counter like gifts she couldn't yet open.

'What's convenient about this diver staying at the inn?" Matt repeated as he sat down at the table and helped himself to French toast.

"Tucker seemed very fond of Laura." Georgia said evenly. "And he seemed like a really nice guy."

"He's a great guy," Gordon nodded his head. "Terrific."

"Laura has met a lot of nice guys. A lot of terrific guys." Matt noted. "She wouldn't give any of them the time of day."

"Perhaps they gave up too easily," Delia stirred her coffee slowly. "Somehow Tucker strikes me as the type of man who might not."

Maybe I need to make a trip to Bishop's Cove and check this situation out, Matt thought as he took another bite. *Maybe I should see firsthand just what this Tucker Moreland's all about . . .*

Later, as Delia and Gordon prepared to leave, Georgia walked arm in arm with her mother to the car. "Mom, why didn't you tell me about Laura's husband."

"I thought if she wanted you to know, that she should tell you. I take it that Matt . . ."

"I think he was so surprised that I didn't know, that it sort of blurted out. Mom, if this man had deceived you as totally as he deceived her, wouldn't you divorce him?"

"Divorce is the very least I would do to him," Delia said dryly.

"Why do you suppose Laura won't file for divorce?"

Delia worried her bottom lip with her top teeth for a long minute. "There's something I can't put my finger on, Georgia. I believe that at one time she had filed, then let it drop. I've asked her and she makes vague comments." She paused, then asked, "My gut feeling?"

Georgia nodded.

"I think she's scared somehow." Delia seemed to choose her words carefully.

"Scared?" Georgia asked. "Scared of what?"

"I think she's scared of him. Of Gary."

"But he's in jail, and his request for parole was turned down."

"For the time being . . ." Delia said thoughtfully.

"Is there any way of finding out when he's eligible?"

"In two years he can apply again."

"You have already checked?"

"Of course."

"What else?"

"What do you mean, what else?"

"What else have you found out about him?" Georgia watched her mother's face for a sign that there was more. She was pretty sure there would be.

"It seems Reverend Harmon has quite an active little ministry there in prison. He has many devoted followers. A regular little network from one prison to another."

"That's what Matt said . . . oh, I see. Your private investigator . . . ?"

"Jeremy Noble is the best in the business," Delia assured her. "He's been keeping an eye on Reverend Harmon and his little band of merry men. As luck would have it, the warden in the prison where Harmon is incarcerated happens to be an acquaintance of Jeremy's, and he seems to feel that Harmon has almost a Svengali-type hold over some of his fellow inmates. A frightening thought." Delia appeared to shiver.

"Do you really think that Laura might be interested in Tucker Moreland?"

"I think she's more interested than she wants to be. But first, we have to get her to agree to dissolve that sham of a marriage. She'd never pursue another relationship while she is still married. Even if it is only a legality. We'll just have to work on her. Tucker isn't the type of man who happens along every day."

"Mom, you're not playing matchmaker . . ." Georgia cautioned.

"Of course I am, sweetie," Delia put her arms around her daughter and hugged her. "And if you hadn't done so well on your own, I'd be actively matchmaking on your behalf, too. Matthew really is a fine young man. I'm not certain I could have done better myself."

"Matt is wonderful, Mom," Georgia said simply.

"Good. Let's hope he stays wonderful so that I don't have to track him to the ends of the earth." Delia turned toward the car, an arm around Georgia's shoulder.

"Mother . . ."

"Georgia, you are my baby." Delia kissed her lightly on the cheek. "My last child. I want only happiness for you. I love you very much, my precious girl."

"I love you, too, Mom." Georgia whispered. "And I want you to be happy, too."

"Oh, but darling, I am happy." Her eyes followed Gordon as he walked around to the driver's side of the car. "I am very happy. I have everything a woman could ever ask for. Absolutely everything. I am blessed beyond measure, Georgia."

"And you deserve every last bit of it," Georgia hugged her mother.

Delia turned to get into the car as Georgia went to say good-bye to Gordon. Turning back to Matt, she touched his arm. Her eyes bore the slightest glisten, like the last trace of dew on a summer morning.

"I see you've taken my request to get to know my family to heart," she said softly.

"Directly to heart," he replied.

"Don't let her be caught in . . . in whatever other concerns you might have, about me, about the situation," she pleaded.

"This is between Georgia and me," he told her.

"Matthew, in my family, when one is wounded, we all bleed." Delia whispered. "Take care with my precious girl."

"Always." The simple word was his most solemn promise. "Always."

chapter nineteen

T"hank you so much for solving my little water problem," Georgia toyed with the collar of Matt's shirt and bit the inside of her lip to keep from smiling.

"Hey, it was nothing," he leaned back against the truck and took her with him. "My pleasure. I think maybe I should stop back on Friday night to make sure it's still working. A system that sophisticated is real high maintenance."

"I thought it might be, seeing how it's so high tech and all." She grinned and pulled his face to hers.

"Hey, you never know when one of those hoses might spring a leak." He kissed her solidly. "And besides, I really do need to measure off that barn space."

"Then I'll look for you on Friday night."

"Dinner will be on me." He opened the door to the truck and Artie jumped in.

"No cheating with take-out," she warned him.

"I hate take-out."

"Me too." She laughed. "My sister, on the other hand, couldn't exist without it. She has a different take-out menu for every night of the week."

"Well, I'll make something. I'll come up with something good." Matt paused, then asked tentatively, "How do you feel about Sherlock Holmes?"

She recalled the memorabilia in his apartment.

"Elementary, my dear Matthew," she grinned. "He's the quintessential detective."

"I'll bring videos." He gathered her into his arms for one last kiss, one that lingered, one that he hoped would carry him through till Friday, though he knew he'd barely be out of the drive before he'd wish he could kiss her again.

"Um, dinner and detectives," she said as she backed away from the truck door as he closed it behind him. "Sounds like a great night."

"A great weekend," he promised as he started the engine and turned the truck around, slowing to wave before heading on down the drive.

Georgia stood for a long time with her arms folded tightly across her chest, staring at the end of the drive. Finally, she turned and walked back to the house, Spam at her heels.

"He'll be back in five days, Spammy," she sat on the bottom step and spoke aloud to the pig. "Five days."

The pig sat at her feet, looking up.

"You don't mind Artie so much anymore, do you?" She scratched the back of the pig's head. "Which is a good thing, since he'll be living here too."

Georgia absently toyed with the pig's ears, thinking about all the news Matt had shared with her over the weekend. He'd be moving here soon, maybe as early as next month.

It was a good news–bad news kind of weekend.

"That would be a good thing," she said aloud, grinning at the prospect of seeing him every day.

He'd be taking the barn space.

"Not as good, but I can probably find space for the studio in town. Not my first choice, but all things considered, like the fact that it *is* his barn, not so bad. I'll work it out."

Then there was the matter of Laura's husband.

"Not good. Not good at all." She shook her head, wondering how she could help her sister when Laura wouldn't confide in her, and oddly, didn't seem anxious to resolve her predicament.

"But then there's Tucker . . . and Spammy! Looks like Mom has a gentleman friend!" She giggled and the pig rolled over on her back. "What a perfect thing. Mom and Gordon Chandler! I'm going to call Laura . . ."

Georgia went back into the kitchen and dialed the inn. She left a message for Laura with Jody, who was, at that moment, preparing dinner for seventeen guests.

"Full house," Georgia murmured.

She opened the refrigerator and contemplated her dinner possibilities.

Cauliflower soup, she decided, and took the ingredients out and placed them on the counter. The teacups—her mother's and Gordon's—still sat along the back near the wall. She paused momentarily, then grabbed them to look inside. There was still a bit of liquid in the bottoms of each.

Taking both cups to the kitchen table, she sat down and peered first into Delia's.

Clouds near the handle, with several dots nearby. Dots, she knew, emphasized the importance of the closest symbol.

Farther down, what appeared to be a candle.

She set the cup on the table and lifted Gordon's, turning it around three times, clockwise, on his behalf.

A fish. Something that looked vaguely like an old Roman soldier's helmet, and next to it, a vase.

Humming, Georgia opened Hope's book, which she now kept in the kitchen for handy reference, and studied the symbols.

"Candle, candle," she muttered.

A symbol of one who does good deeds.

"Nothing could be closer to the truth," she exclaimed. "That's my mother to a 'T'!"

The clouds, however, were harder to define.

A dark period . . . have courage, have hope . . .

The dots nearby added urgency to the message.

It could mean something else, Georgia told herself. *There's probably lots of different meanings, depending on who you ask . . .*

Putting her mother's cup aside, she checked Gordon's once more to make sure that the images still looked the same to her, that no other shape was more accurate. The fish, helmet, and vase all looked the same. She would go with those and see how Hope had interpreted those objects.

She looked for a fish shape, and found one.

Good fortune. Your endeavors will prosper.

Finally, some good news.

She searched for a helmet through the pages and pages of hand-drawn symbols.

The protector. *You are in a position of trust.*

A vase. *You will be of service, of strength, to others.*

"Well, then, that's nice for Mother," Georgia mused. "Maybe those last two together mean that Gordon will be there for Mother, that for once, she'll have someone to help her, instead of her being the one who always helps everyone else. Not that she ever seems to need help . . ."

She closed the book on that upbeat note, pushing aside the darker suggestions she'd found in the leaves over the past several days and the question of what help her mother might require.

"Matt, supposing you tell me what planet you're on so that we can join you there." Liz leaned over the end of the desk and waved a piece of paper under Matt's nose. "That's the third time today you tuned me out."

"What do you mean?" He attempted to tune back in without appearing that he'd actually been gone, a futile effort. Liz was far too sharp.

"Don't give me that stuff." She smacked him lightly with a thin file. "You have no idea of what I just said to you."

"Ah, sure I do." He glanced down at the file in her hand—*Henson: feline*—then beyond her to the waiting room. "You said the Hensons were late bringing in their cat."

"You're good, you know that?" She laughed and smacked him with the file again. "But I asked you if you'd mind if I left a little early today so that I could pick my grandson up at nursery school. My daughter has the flu."

"Oh, sure," he grinned. "Not a problem."

"Matthew Bishop, if I didn't know you better, I'd think you were in love."

The flush spread slowly up from his collar.

"No!" she whispered loudly. "When did you find time to find a woman?"

He reached around her for his coffee cup which he had set on the corner of her desk. Trying to ignore the question, he asked, "Does Chery have the day off?"

"Don't you even try to waltz away from that one," Liz crowed. "Look me in the eye and tell me that there isn't a new woman in your life."

"Ah, well, there is someone . . ."

"Well, then, who is she?" Liz demanded.

"She's my sister's sister . . ."

Liz appeared to think this over before asking quietly, "Isn't that against the law?"

"No, no. Georgia is my *sister's* sister, she's not *my* sister." He stopped when he realized that didn't sound much better. "My sister and I were both adopted by the same couple, but we're not related by blood. Georgia is Laura's half sister. They have the same birth mother. But I don't. With either of them."

"I see," Liz nodded, though it was clear that she was still working through it in her head. "How does your sister feel about you being in love with her sister?"

"She doesn't know yet. I'm just finding out myself."

The front door opened. The Hensons with their cat.

"By the way," Matt whispered as he waved a greeting to his patient, "do you happen to have any good vegetarian recipes you could share with me? It's my turn to cook this weekend."

Matt ushered the Hensons into the first examining room.

"I'll see what I can come up with," Liz replied. "And Matt—"

He turned in the doorway as the Hensons passed by with their cat.

"It's about time."

Matt chuckled and started to close the door.

"Nothing with tofu, though," he called back over his shoulder. "I really don't like tofu . . ."

The week had shaped up nicely for Georgia. By Wednesday, the catalog she'd requested from the nearby state college had arrived, and she had pored over the course requirements for a dance major. She figured she was good for credit worth at least a minor in performance arts, and decided to make arrangements for a performance exam upon which her advanced standing would be based. She could also probably take a proficiency exam in English. Cheered that she could start out with some credit behind her, she called the college and arranged for her dance proficiency to be evaluated, and was given a date in late June. She wrote a check for the summer dance instructors' seminar and stuck it on the pile of mail she'd take to the post office when she drove into town later that day. She tended her new tomato plants and babied her dill and basil seedlings, then watered all with the hoses that Matt had hooked up for her.

On Friday morning, she'd heard a car come up the drive and was delighted to see that Lee had driven down for a surprise visit. He wore gray shorts and a T-shirt with the DRA—Dancers Responding to AIDS—logo and carried worn black ballet slippers in one hand and an enormous bouquet of white lilies in a white porcelain vase in the other.

"When you called the other night to tell me about your new barre, well, nothing would do but that I help you christen it," he'd told her when she flew down the barn steps and raced across the yard to spin him around with a bear hug.

"Oh, Lee, we haven't danced together in years," she kissed his cheek. "Oh, come on, I can hardly wait!"

She dragged him by the hand to the second floor.

"Well, this is an improvement," he pointed to the portable barres. "And with some mirrors, some better lighting, a decent floor . . ."

She held up a hand, palm first. "Please, no more. I've mentally redone this place a thousand times. All in vain."

"What's that supposed to mean?" He slipped off his loafers and pulled on the ballet shoes.

"Matt will be moving back soon and he's going to be renovating the barn . . ."

"Wonderful!"

". . . for a veterinary clinic."

"You mean, as in animals, birds, reptiles . . ."

She nodded.

"It's okay, though. I can stay in the house. I just have to look for another place to dance in."

"Pity. This place is ideal." Lee tested the spring of the floor. "Sanded and finished, this floor would be perfect."

"It would be." Georgia moved to the barre and began her stretching exercises.

"You don't seem very upset." Lee took a place a few feet away and began to stretch along with her.

"I'm not."

"Why? I would think you would be."

"Because it will mean that Matt's here all the time."

Lee digested this while doing a series of *pliés*.

"And this would be significant because . . ."

"Because I think I might be falling in love with him."

"Georgey, we've been out of touch for far too long. Fill me in with all the details. And don't leave out any of the good parts."

Georgia laughed. "You want to know all my secrets."

"Well, you have to admit it's been a long time, *cara*."

"Since Alexi went back to Moscow." She nodded grimly.

"There was Sebastian," he reminded her.

"He liked you better than he liked me," she quipped, and they both laughed.

"We need music," she said after a few quiet minutes of stretching and bending.

"I brought something for you," he told her, "wait here . . ."

He dashed down the steps and was back up in minutes, holding out a handful of CDs. "Here we have some Chopin—I know he's your favorite—and for when we are done warming up, the music from the second act of *Giselle*."

Touched that he had remembered the role that she had so long coveted, then felt compelled to reject when it had been offered to her for all the wrong reasons, she put her arms around him and they held each other, two old friends who loved each other and loved to dance.

"Thank you," she said.

"Well, then, come," he held a hand out to her. "Let's dance . . ."

He led her into the first *pas de deux* from the second act, followed by Giselle's solo, then the final duet, during which they both blundered a series of steps. When they had danced to the point of exhaustion, they folded to the floor to drink bottled water and laugh about their shaky performances and gossip about mutual friends.

"Want to see my garden?" she asked as they finally descended the steps.

"Sure."

"It's back behind the barn," she pointed in the general direction. "Let me just run over to the house to get Spam, and I'll show you."

Spam rolled across the yard behind Georgia like a small hairy tank on tiny legs, greeted Lee with grunts and stayed between them as they walked to the field.

"Nice," Lee nodded his approval when she showed him her little patch of crops.

"I plowed it up myself, and I planted everything

myself," she told him proudly. "Matt helped me hook up the water, but I did everything else myself."

"Do you have to be so perfect?" he teased. "Is there anything you can't do?"

Georgia laughed. "I'll have you know I worked very hard out here every single day. I spoke with a couple of the old farmers who hang around Tanner's—that's the general store in town—and they gave me some tips. You know how methodical I am, Lee. I never do anything halfway. If I was going to farm, I was going to farm right. And it's paying off. My little truck patch is thriving."

"Wonderful." He bent to inspect the herbs, rubbing different varieties between his fingers to release their scent. "Beautiful lemon basil. Lots of dill. Oregano. Italian basil. Parsley. Georgia, what were you thinking when you planted all this? You have enough here for about twenty households."

"I do?"

"Cara, you can make pesto till the cows come home and you'll never run out of basil. I guess you'll just have to sell some to me for the restaurant."

"I wouldn't sell it to you," she told him. "If you want some, I'll gladly give it to you. And actually, Laura wanted some for the inn, so I planted lots . . ."

"You planted lots all right." He leaned over to inspect the yellow flowers on the tomatoes, harbingers of fruit. "I'll bet these will be wonderful when they all come in and ripen. What else did you plant?"

"Zucchini, yellow squash, green beans, eggplant, cantaloupes . . ." she walked him around her garden, pointing here, then there, at this variety and that.

"Georgia, you will have vegetables coming out

your ears," he laughed. "Let me be a customer. Let me buy your surplus."

"Nah. I'll give you what I don't use and what Laura doesn't need. But you have to come to pick it up yourself. That way I'll get to see you at least once every other week or so."

"Deal. And when the critics stop into Tuscany and rave about the vegetables, I'll tell them where it all came from. By this time next year, you'll have half the restauranteurs in Baltimore banging on your door to buy your produce."

"Who knows where I'll be this time next year? But in any event, I guess I don't need to worry about running out of career options."

"Now show me what you're doing as far as flowers are concerned."

"Oh, back toward the house." She paused and looked around for Spam. She spotted the pig rooting in something behind the small barn and called to her. Reluctantly Spam left whatever prize she'd found and fell in step with Georgia and Lee.

"Hope—the woman who used to own the farm, she was Matt and Laura's aunt—used to have a big flower garden here," Georgia pointed to the area surrounded by the white picket fence, "but I've been using it for Spam when she's outside and I can't be out with her."

"That's a pretty fancy pig pen, Georgia." Lee looked over the fence. "It looks like you have some flowers coming up along the side. Maybe you should find another place for the piggy and plant this area back up again."

"I'll think about it."

"You'll have some lovely roses there," he pointed to the back of the fence. "And tons of lilac."

"Want some to take back with you?" she asked. "The bushes have been in bloom for a week now, and I know it doesn't last forever. I have it in bowls and vases and tureens all over the house, and there's still tons of it."

"I'd love some. I love the fragrance. I'll put some in the restaurant."

"Then let me get the clippers and I'll cut some big bunches. A trade for the lilies."

She had filled two large plastic pitchers with bowers of deeply fragrant blooms and still the ancient trees were thick with flowers.

"I think I'll take some to Laura for the inn," she said as she handed the containers to Lee, who took them inside to fill the bottoms with enough water to get them back to Baltimore without wilting.

"How's my tenant doing?" she asked.

"He loves your condo. He'd buy it in a snap. As would I, if you ever wanted to sell it."

"I thought you loved your townhouse."

"I do. But the longer I stay there . . . since David . . ." He didn't have to finish the sentence.

Georgia took his arm as they walked to his car, each of them carrying a container overflowing with lilac. "If I decide not to move back to Baltimore, you'll certainly be the first to know."

"I'd be happy to get an appraisal or two of the property for you. I know several people in the business. And I'm sure the condo is worth much more than you paid for it. Real estate in that part of the city has really sky-rocketed in value."

"Hmmm." She tucked the thought away. "That's good to know. I haven't made any long-term plans as yet, though I am thinking about going back to school this fall."

She told him about her call to the local college.

"Well, it sounds as if everything is falling into place for you. You left Baltimore and found love and happiness at Pumpkin Hill." Lee smiled as they tucked the flowers into the back of the car. "And I couldn't be happier for you. I can see my fears were totally unfounded . . ."

He paused, and looked as if he was about to bite his tongue.

"What fears?"

"Oh, you know, sometimes when you don't see someone you're close to for a while, you start wondering if they're okay." He shrugged it off and gave her one last hug and kissed her cheek before getting into the car. He put the key into the ignition and said, "You know what a mother hen I am at times."

"I'm fine. I've never been better." She stepped back from the car as he eased onto the gas. "Thank you for the visit. And for the flowers . . . the music . . . the dance . . ."

"My pleasure, *cara*," he made a U-turn in the drive and slowed down as he passed her, tempted to ask her if the farmhouse had smoke alarms, if there was a local fire department that came out as far as Pumpkin Hill. But then he'd have to tell her about the dream that had shaken him and sent him to see with his own eyes that she was all right, that there had been no fire, no danger, that no dark forces threatened her. Pumpkin Hill was a place of peace and positive energy. There had been no hint of anything dark or sinister.

He'd simply been mistaken this time, he told himself as he waved and headed for home. This time, perhaps it had just been a bad dream, one that had no deeper meaning, unlike some of the others he'd had over the years, which had, in their time, become reality. His own car accident three years earlier, David's illness and death.

Sure, he told himself, this time there's nothing to worry about. Georgia's fine. She's happy, she's in love. All is well.

Convinced, he slipped a CD into the dash and accelerated, hoping to get the lilac to the restaurant while it was still fresh and fragrant.

chapter twenty

S hoo!" Georgia charged the crows feasting in her new garden, waving her arms about and swatting at the birds with her wide-brimmed straw hat. "Out . . . of . . . my . . . *garden!*"

Assisted by Spam, who did more harm than good by gleefully chasing the intruders through the fledgling green beans, Georgia stood with her hands on her hips and contemplated the age-old problem of keeping pests from her garden.

"Starting with you, Spammy," Georgia frowned and gently stood the mangled green bean vines back against the wire frame she was using to train the plants to grow upward, thus saving space. "The marigolds are doing a decent enough job against the bunnies and the ground hogs, but flowers haven't proven much of a defense against your . . . er . . . *dainty* feet. And I don't know what to do about the birds."

She repeated her lament later to Laura.

"Aunt Hope used scarecrows. She had wooden

380

forms that she dragged out every year and dressed. I think she kept them in the barn." Laura suggested. "You might want to take a look."

"What did she put on them?" Georgia asked. "For clothes?"

"Oh, she had a different theme every year. She had the cleverest scarecrows you'd ever want to see. They always appeared to be in costume." Laura laughed. "There are some boxes of old clothes in the attic; she used to take stuff from there. Go on up and take a look. You're welcome to use whatever is there. No one's likely to wear any of those clothes again."

"Maybe I'll do that. It irks me that I worked so hard and spent so much time getting that garden in, only to have the birds come pecking along for the seeds."

"They are pesky. But a good scarecrow might buy your seeds some time. By the way, did you speak with Delia yet today?"

"No. I've been outside all morning, and I haven't checked the answering machine yet. What's up?"

"She's decided that we should have Zoey and Ben's engagement party now, rather than in July, because she thinks that we should do it before India delivers. She's planning a big party for the baby's christening, and doesn't want the two events too close together."

"Mother never misses a good excuse for a party." Georgia thought back to India and Nick's engagement party. Hadn't that been the night that Georgia realized that Zoey and Ben had found each other again after so many years? "I guess she'll have her caterer going crazy again . . ."

"Not this time. She's asked if we could have the

party here at the inn. That way, everyone could stay over and go to the beach the next day."

"Great idea. And you'll be catering the party?"

"Jody will be. You know, for one so young—she isn't even thirty yet—Jody's very accomplished in the kitchen. She's already putting together some menus and will be going over her suggestions with Delia later in the week. It should be fun. I'm really looking forward to having a big family gathering here at the inn. I figure it's time." She paused, then added, "I only wish . . ."

"Wish what?"

"That somehow I could get Matt to come around." Laura frowned, thinking back to Ally's birthday party. "I think we almost had him turned around at Ally's birthday."

"I'll work on him," Georgia tried to suppress a giggle. Obviously Delia hadn't discussed Matt's presence at breakfast the previous weekend.

"I wish someone would," Laura sighed. "I wish he wasn't so hard-headed. I love all of my family. I want you all to love each other."

"Well, maybe he'll surprise you." Georgia bit the inside of her cheek.

"Maybe Spam will learn to fly." Laura grumbled.

"Stranger things have happened."

Grinning, Georgia hung up the phone, thinking what fun it would be when Laura realized that Matt had "come around" in a big way.

Georgia's construction of her scarecrows took most of the afternoon. Having found the wooden forms—six of them—leaning against the wall inside one of the old stalls in the barn, she dragged them outside and dusted them off before heading to the attic to search for proper attire.

"Wonder who these belonged to?" she muttered as she went through box after box of old clothes. "Laura said Hope always had a theme. Let's see what we can come up with."

Pleased with her final selections, she folded the garments over her arm and turned off the light.

All I need are a few inexpensive straw hats to complete these ensembles, and I'll have scarecrows to make Hope proud, Georgia grinned as she stood up the wooden T-shaped forms—one at each end of the garden, two on each of the sides. Over each of the forms, she draped the garments, then stood back to view her handiwork.

All Georgia's scarecrows wore housedresses, the skirts of which billowed in the light breeze. Over the arms she had slipped long sleeved blouses, the cuffs of which dangled and flapped slightly.

"You ladies definitely do need hats," she said aloud as she straightened a shirt collar.

Gathering her purse from the house, and admonishing Spam to keep out of the garden, Georgia drove over to Tanner's and looked at the selection of straw hats. She bought one for each of her scarecrows, along with six pair of neon sunglasses from a barrel near the door.

Once back at Pumpkin Hill, with hammer and nails in hand, she proceeded to the garden, where she distributed the hats and the sunglasses to her crones, as she had begun to think of them.

"Scarecrones," she told the silent forms. "Much more apropos for ladies such as yourselves."

Three nails—one on each of three sides of each pole—held on the sunglasses, and one nail through the top kept the hats from blowing off.

"You are altogether *too* charming, each and every one of you," she announced as she tied the long hot pink scarf that bedecked one of the hats. "Stay right there . . . I'm going to take your picture."

Georgia ran back to the house, grabbed her camera from the sideboard in the dining room, then dashed back to photograph her crones in all their glory.

"Now, do your job well and maybe I'll have some pretty beads to drape around your necks." She told them as she shot the last frame.

"Lord help me, I'm starting to sound like Zoey." Georgia laughed out loud, recalling how her fanciful sister used to talk aloud to the stuffed animals in the craft shop she had once owned when her stock had been more plentiful than her customers.

The phone in the kitchen was ringing when Georgia reached the house.

"Ah, there you are, sweetie. I'd almost given up on you today. Don't you ever check your answering machine?" Delia admonished.

"Oh, hello, Mother. Actually, I was going to call you tonight."

"And what have we been busy with today?"

"I was making scarecrones to keep the birds out of my garden."

"Scarecrones?" Delia laughed.

"Picture nineteen-forties housedresses and straw hats," Georgia told her. "With sunglasses and long-sleeved polyester blouses from the sixties . . ."

"Oh, I can just imagine," Delia laughed. "I cannot wait to see them."

"They are fun. And hopefully, they will keep the pests from devouring my garden. I've worked so hard, Mother, trying to get all my plants in. I'm not so generous that I want to share with the wildlife."

"Perhaps a well-stocked bird feeder will keep the birds out of the garden. And perhaps you should think about a fence to keep the deer from eating the plants as they get a little bigger."

"I've been wondering about that. I did plant marigolds . . ."

"They'll do as long as there's other plants for the animals to eat. But I wouldn't depend on them."

"I'll ask Matt this weekend. Maybe he'll have some ideas."

"Oh? Will Matt be there again this weekend?" Delia asked nonchalantly.

"Yes. He's helping me to . . ." Georgia tried to remember what it was that Matt was helping her to do. ". . . to adjust to farm life."

Delia bit her lip and tried her best not to laugh.

"I see," she said.

"Yes." Georgia cleared her throat. "You probably do."

"Well, perhaps in return you can help Matt adjust to life with the Enrights," Delia said. "I'm planning on having a party for Zoey and Ben in three weeks."

"Laura mentioned it. She said you wanted to have it at the inn."

"I thought it would be nice to ask Laura to host it. She's missed out on so many important events with us through the years."

"That was a nice touch on your part, Mother."

"Well, it would be especially nice if Matt attended."

"And who all else will be there?"

"Just family this time, sweetie—immediate and extended. Ben's grandfather and his lady friend, of course, and August . . . and certainly her friend Pete, which is convenient since his son is working with Gordon . . ."

"And of course, Gordon will be there."

"Well, he *is* staying at the inn, Georgia." Delia said casually. "We certainly wouldn't want to exclude him."

"Oh, of course not," Georgia agreed. "We couldn't do *that*. How is Gordon, anyway?"

"He's fine, dear, and if you're thinking to pry, don't waste your time."

"Mother, I have never known you to be coy."

"Yes, well, there's a first time for everything. And I don't consider myself *coy* . . . I hate that whole concept. I prefer *discreet*."

"Ah, I see, so if I were to ask you . . ."

"Which you wouldn't do," Delia laughed, cutting off her daughter, "because you were raised with much better manners. Now, not to cut you short, sweetie, but I have plans for the evening . . ."

Plans for the evening, Georgia mused as she hung up the phone. *My mother has plans for the evening.*

And I couldn't be happier. It's about time Mother had some fun and found someone who appreciated her for the extraordinary woman she is. Mother's worked so hard over the years and spent so much of her time and energy keeping up with her children, she deserves a little romance . . .

Georgia searched the tool drawer in the kitchen, where, she had found, Hope had stashed wrenches of various sizes, nails, a screwdriver or two and other assorted things with which Georgia wasn't well acquainted. Finding the clippers she was looking for, she went back outside and began to clip away at the suckers that had sprouted along the bases of the apple and peach trees.

"It's probably late in the season to be doing this," she said aloud to Spam as she inspected the thin clippings, some of which had already sprouted leaves as well as small flowers. "But it's better than not doing it at all, and I've made up my mind that every day I will do just a little. Before we know it, Spam, all of the fruit trees will be tidied up. Just think of all the apples that will just drop right off the trees and into your waiting mouth come September and October."

Would she still be here to see the apples ripen and fall?

Matt had said she could stay in the house, but what of her dancing school? She couldn't give up her plans to have a dancing school, not now, when she had students clamoring to attend and she had so newly discovered the joy of teaching, of sharing her love for the dance.

Perhaps she should find the classified section from last Sunday's paper and see what kind of space might be available to rent out. If there was nothing suitable, what would she do? Maybe someplace closer to Bishop's Cove, if there is nothing here around O'Hearn.

I guess I should call the realtor whose name is on the sign on that store front in town. There's no point in waiting until the trucks pull in the drive and Matt starts to unload his equipment.

Gathering the pruned-off apple suckers she'd dropped to the ground, she carried them to the side of the house where the trash cans sat and dumped them in a pile. Later she'd come back out with a ball of string and she'd tie them up into a neat bundle. Right now, she had a few phone calls to make.

Late Friday afternoon, as Georgia turned toward the farmhouse with the armful of iris she had just finished picking, the black pickup pulled into the drive. She'd tried to pretend all day that she wasn't waiting for him, wasn't watching for him, didn't jump every time a car slowed down, but her efforts to convince herself were futile. Matt had called the night before to remind her that he'd be making dinner for her on Friday, and it was Friday, and just about time for him to show up. And there he was, cool and handsome getting out of the truck, his dark hair tumbling down across his forehead just ever so slightly as he leaned over to get something from the floor of the cab.

And there he was, walking across the yard to greet her, his eyes looking into hers telling her everything he'd not said on the phone the night before.

And there he was, his arms closing around her and his mouth seeking hers before he'd said a word to her . . .

"I think I mashed your flowers," he said, finally, his arms easing up just a little.

"It's okay. I'll stick them in water and they'll be fine." She was looking up at him and so was unaware that several of the irises hung at awkward angles from their stems. "I thought I'd bring a vase of flowers over . . . to your apartment, that is . . . for the table. For dinner."

"That would be nice," he smiled, thinking of the other little details he planned on tending to before she arrived later. "How 'bout if I take them over now? That way I can put them on the table when I set it?"

He took the flowers from her.

"I thought maybe we'd eat around eight. No earlier, though. I won't be ready before then."

"Won't be ready?" She laughed. "That's another hour and forty minutes from now. What on earth are you making?"

"It's a surprise. Eight o'clock. No earlier." He bent down and kissed the tip of her nose.

Tickled that he'd taken the time to plan a surprise—of whatever sort hardly mattered to her—Georgia ran upstairs to shower away the dirt from the garden. She finished drying her hair and tried to decide, once and for all, what to wear. Finally deciding on a long, floaty gauze skirt of soft rose, with a matching short-sleeve shirt to wear over a tight-fitting camisole in a paler shade, she slipped on mother-of-pearl earrings and a wide cuff bracelet of silver, then tied her hair back in a thin scarf of rose and cream silk. Not too dressy, but not farmhand casual, either. Satisfied, she went downstairs and looked at the clock on the kitchen wall.

Seven forty-five.

She had fifteen minutes to spare.

"Spam," she called out the back door, and the pig came rolling out from under the lilac bush. "Time for you to come in, girl. Oh, I know it's still light out. Now, if you were a little smarter, I'd explain daylight savings time to you, but things being such as they are, we'll just say that it's time for you to come in and let it go at that."

Spam grunted softly as Georgia lifted her and carried her into the safety of the screened porch.

"Yes, I know you'd like to come with me, but you can't. You weren't invited." She set the pig down on her bed and picked up the water bowl, taking the ceramic dish inside and rinsing it in the sink. She refilled it with cold water and took it back out to the porch. She patted Spam on the head, scratched under the pig's chin, sending Spam, momentarily, to piggy heaven before returning to the kitchen to wash her hands.

Seven forty-nine.

She pushed aside the curtains and looked across the yard. There was an odd glow from the front windows. Whatever was Matt doing over there?

Seven fifty-one.

I'm as nervous as a schoolgirl on my first date. How silly is that . . . it isn't as if we haven't . . . as if we didn't . . .

And as if I haven't been thinking about it all week . . . as if I haven't seen his face every time I've closed my eyes, or dreamed about how good it felt to be in his arms, or wondered if this is what it's like to be falling in love . . .

Seven fifty-two.

Eight more minutes.

How best to waste them?

Georgia closed the door of the farmhouse behind her and stood on the back steps. The honeysuckle was just coming into its own, and the roses that hung over the fence had just come into bud that week. The first stars had already appeared. It was a perfect late spring dusk, the sun balancing atop the trees beyond the barn and the last of the bird songs drifting across the farmyard. Pumpkin Hill was, truly, a wonderful place to be in the spring. She looked forward to spending the summer there, to rising early to water her garden and inspect the newest growth, to the rich smell of ripe tomatoes and sweet cantaloupes, to air scented with rain-drenched basil and dill and rosemary, to harvesting her own produce for the very first time in her life.

And what of autumn, of winter . . . ?

Georgia had high hopes of seeing both seasons come and go right here. There seemed to be just about everything she'd ever really needed, right here.

From a open window Georgia heard the old mantel clock chime eight bells. Exhaling deeply, she headed for the barn, and Matt, and for whatever the night would bring.

chapter twenty-one

Matt lifted the lid of the Dutch oven for the fiftieth time. *A watched pot doesn't boil*—he remembered hearing his mother saying that so many times that he thought she had authored the cliché—but it was almost eight o'clock and Georgia would be there any minute. He poked his head back into the living room where he'd set the small round table with white dishes on a blue and white checkered cloth, her irises off to one side.

And candles. Everywhere.

Tall white tapers and dozens of votives in pretty glass bowls stood on every flat surface around the small living room, all waiting to be lit. Matt ducked back into the kitchen and lifted the lid on the rice. Watched or not, it was boiling, and the stir-fry needed only a few more seconds. He turned the flame down and took a deep breath. He'd never cooked dinner for a woman before. Had never gone to such lengths to surprise a woman—to please a woman—before.

But then again, there'd never been anyone quite like Georgia in his life before.

Oh, Georgia had been on his mind, all right. All week long, she'd stayed with him, in his heart and in his mind. *Just an old sweet song*, indeed, he'd thought. It had disconcerted him at first, this always-on-my-mind thing, but he'd been unable to shake the feeling that there was more—so much more—ahead for them. He'd come to look forward to seeing her face in his mind's eye, to the vision of her in that pink leotard as she had walked away from him that day in the farmyard, to the memory of that lilting laugher and million-dollar smile. There'd never been a woman in his head before, and now that he was beginning to get used to the idea, he was thinking he might actually like it.

"Just a minute," he called out when she rapped on the door. "I'll be right there."

He paused, wondering if he should light the rest of the candles now, as he had originally planned on doing, hoping to dazzle her with the sight, or whether to wait till he was ready to serve dinner. Having decided to wait until dinner, he slipped the book of matches back into his shirt pocket and opened the door.

"Ummm," she sniffed appreciatively. "Whatever it is, it smells wonderful."

"Thanks," he grinned and stood aside to let her enter. "I remembered that you liked curry . . ."

"Oh, I love it!" She went to one of the pots and raised the lid to peek within. "Oh, yum, you made the rice with the raisins in it. My favorite."

"That's one of my favorites, too." He checked the

stir-fry, then turned off the flame. "I'm glad you were on time. Dinner's actually ready."

"May I help?"

He hesitated, then handed her a blue and white bowl.

"If you wouldn't mind spooning the rice into this bowl, I'll be right back . . ."

What is he up to? she wondered as he disappeared into the next room.

Her curiosity was beginning to get the best of her when he came back into the kitchen and took the bowl from her hands.

"Come on in and have a seat," he told her.

She followed the sound of his voice, and walked into a room alive with the soft flicker of candlelight.

"Oh, Matt, it's beautiful." She sighed. "Just beautiful. However did you think to do this?"

"Candles on the table didn't seem to give quite enough light," he grinned, "and too much light would make viewing so difficult."

"'Viewing'?" she asked.

"The film." He held out a chair for her, gesturing for her to be seated, then poured wine into a pretty stemmed glass and handed it to her. "I thought we'd have a little dinner, and watch a little Holmes."

The wide-screen TV sat at an angle to the room, and the lights blinking on the VCR indicated that the film was loaded and ready to go.

"Let me just bring in the food, and we'll be all set."

"What's the movie?" Georgia asked, pleased and flattered by the time and attention he'd given to planning this evening with her.

"It's an old British production of *The Sign of Four*."

He placed the bowl of brightly colored vegetables between them, then sat down opposite her. Filling his own wineglass, he raised it to her and said softly, "To many more evenings together."

She touched the rim of his glass with her own, then sipped at her wine, wishing she could think of something to say, but caught off guard, could come up with nothing to match the romantic spell he'd already woven around them. Instead, she merely took another sip of wine.

Matt served her first, then himself, saying, "Anyway, to get back to the movie. This one stars a British actor, Arthur Wontner, as Holmes. Now, I personally prefer Basil Rathbone in the role, but all things considered, I think that Wontner does an excellent job. This film is actually two stories in one. The first is Holmes's investigation into a death and a subsequent theft, and the second is a romance . . ."

"A romance?" Georgia tried to recall the few Sherlock Holmes films she had watched on TV on rainy Saturday afternoons. "Fascinating character though Holmes may have been, I don't think of him as being particularly romantic."

"Oh, I agree." Matt smiled, happy that his choice for the evening was prompting some discussion, some interest on her part. "Holmes was a great detective, but he was, frankly, a bit of a misogynist. He had little use for women. The romance I spoke of was between Watson—who really was a ladies' man—and Holmes's client, Mary Morstan."

"I read that someplace . . . that Holmes had a low opinion of women."

"I think he thought they were unnecessary and not

to be trusted. He says that, as a matter of fact . . . that even the best of them are not to be trusted." Matt grinned. "A sentiment I do not share, by the way, but it makes for an interesting character study."

"Have you?" she asked, "studied his character?"

"I did a paper on Holmes for an English class in college some years ago. I admit I chose the topic because I'd seen a few of the movies and figured it would be an easy paper. It was, because I enjoyed it, but I found the characters more complex than I'd given Conan Doyle credit for."

"Ah, so that's how you got hooked."

"That's how I got hooked," he nodded. "And you? Anyone in particular that you read religiously?"

"Only my mother," Georgia grinned.

"I'm embarrassed to admit that I've never read any of her books."

"What? A die-hard detective fan such as yourself has never read a Shellcroft?" She feigned horror.

"What's a Shellcroft?"

"Harvey Shellcroft is a recurring character in a series my mother wrote early on in her career. He's a wonderful character—part Columbo, part Jessica Fletcher, part Holmes. Harve was so popular that when my mother wanted to start a new series with a new detective, her publisher wouldn't let her until she threatened to kill Harvey off."

Matt laughed.

"It's the truth. So now Mom does a new Harve every eighteen months to keep his fans happy, and in between time, writes other books that make her happy."

"That's interesting, that she's sensitive to her readers."

"She is sensitive to everyone."

"I'm beginning to believe that."

"My mother is a very caring person." Georgia speared a snow pea and nibbled one end of it. "She has always devoted herself to her children and her work. I'm so thrilled to see that she is taking some time to have a little fun for herself."

"You're referring to Gordon Chandler."

Georgia nodded. "He seems like such a perfect match for her. He's interesting, active, intelligent— and he seems to care for Mother."

"I thought he was quite solicitous of her when they were here last weekend."

"So did I. I like to see that someone is taking care of her. Not that she needs it, but it's just good to see someone do the kind of little things for her that she's always doing for other people. And she seems happy to be with him. Maybe it's finally her time to find happiness."

"I hope you're right. Chandler seems to be the kind of guy you wouldn't mind having date your mother."

"And while we're on the subject of people our favorite relatives might be interested in, have you had a chance to meet Tucker Moreland?"

"Not yet. I haven't gotten out to Bishop's Cove yet. But it's on the agenda. Maybe I'll take a ride out there tomorrow. Unless, of course, you have some farm chores lined up for me . . ." he teased.

"I have my dancing classes in the morning, but I haven't any other plans. I do want to show you what I did this week, though," she said, thinking of what fun it would be to show off her crones.

"So, what do you think of my curry?" he asked as he finished eating.

"I think it's great. I'm really touched that you made a special effort to make something just for me." She reached her hand across the table and touched his wrist.

Matt made a mental note to hit the bookstore in Shawsburg and stock up on a few good vegetarian cookbooks. And maybe a Shellcroft or two.

"I like doing special things for you," he said simply, taking her hand and toying with her fingers. "And I plan on doing lots of special things for you for a very long time to come."

"You do?"

"Yes. I do. I just thought I should warn you." Matt gave her hand a squeeze, then stood up and began to clear the table. "We can have dessert while we watch the movie, if that's all right with you."

"That sounds like fun. Can I help?"

"Nope. Just get comfortable on the sofa and we'll be ready to roll in a few minutes. I'll be right back."

Georgia seated herself on the old blue plaid sofa, drawing up her legs beneath her. Artie roused himself from his place near the door and wagged his tail as he approached her, begging for an invitation to join her.

"No, you sit there, on the floor," she told him.

He sat as close to the sofa as he could get, his tongue flopped from one side of his mouth like a rumpled tie and his big head nudging her knees.

"Oh, you want a little attention, do you?" Georgia scratched behind the dog's ears.

I like doing special things for you, Matt had said. Had anyone ever said anything sweeter to her?

I plan on doing special things for you for a very long time to come. Had any promise ever made to her been more dear?

"I don't think so," she whispered to Artie.

Matt came in with a tray piled with perfect strawberries and a bowl of popcorn drizzled with melted chocolate.

"What's a movie without popcorn?" He grinned as he moved a few books on the coffee table to make room for the tray.

"Oh, that looks wonderful," she sighed, and reached for a berry.

Matt sat down next to Georgia, put his arm around her shoulders, and turned on the VCR via the remote.

"This version was made in the early thirties," he told her as the film began. "There's an earlier version—a silent one—made in the twenties, that's interesting, too, but I haven't been able to find that one to add to my collection."

A series of flashbacks to India in the beginning of the film caused Georgia to exclaim, "Oh! I get it! India! Curried vegetables! Did you match the menu to the movie?" to which Matt laughed out loud.

"I guess I'm not very subtle. I just thought it would be fun." Matt grinned broadly. It hadn't occurred to him that her candid appreciation would please him so. "I couldn't think of too many vegetable dishes that I thought I could cook, and this is one of my favorite films."

"What's special about this one?" She asked.

"Well, for one thing, I think that this story really highlights Holmes's incredible investigative skills, maybe better than the others, because it's so complex. Just watch as the story unfolds."

She did watch, munching strawberries and pop-corn.

Midway through the movie, the phone rang. Matt stopped the VCR and patted Georgia's leg as he excused himself to answer it.

"That was Laura," he told her as he came back into the room. "She wanted to tell me about a party she is hosting for Zoey and Ben at the inn in two weeks. She asked if I would consider coming and spending the weekend along with the rest of clan. I think she was shocked when I said I'd be there without her having to twist my arm."

"I spoke with her the other day. She doesn't know . . ." Georgia hesitated.

". . . about us?" Matt grinned and finished the sentence for her. "No, apparently she doesn't. And what a surprise that will be when we tell her."

"What will you tell her?" Georgia leaned back and tugged on his hand. "What will you tell Laura?"

"I'll tell her," he said as he kissed the soft skin below her ear, "that I have had a change of heart. I'll tell her that she was right," he whispered as his mouth moved to hers, "when she said that I'd love you once I got to know you . . ."

"Remind me to ask you about that later," she said as she lay back against the cushions and pulled him to her.

"Later, I'll tell you anything you want to know. But later, Georgia. Much later . . ."

Georgia slipped the shirt from her shoulders and his lips sank to her collarbone where his tongue traced a long, slow line up her neck to her waiting mouth. Hot tongues teased and tasted, trading sensation and promising more. His hands lifted her slowly, repositioning her body atop his own where he could see her, could feel her, could love her without fearing that he was crushing the life from her, as he had been afraid of doing the weekend before. She sat up slightly and pulled the camisole to her waist, bringing his hands up to cup her breasts, moaning slightly at the touch of his fingers on her anxious flesh. When she could take no more of his searching hands, his eager mouth , she reached beneath her to tug at the zipper of his jeans and freed him, raising her skirt and sinking upon him, taking him in, taking his breath away.

"You're so beautiful," he whispered, watching her face, her eyes half-closed with pleasure.

"You're so beautiful," he told her again, as she arched her back and cried out.

"You're so beautiful," he repeated after he had shattered and shivered within her and had drawn her down tightly into his arms. "Now, if I fall asleep, will you disappear again? Will you run off to dance in the moonlight without me?"

"You could dance with me," she told him. "We could choreograph a *pas de deux* . . ."

"I think we just did that," he smiled, "and if we can remember the steps, we could do it again."

"Oh, we can always improvise, you know," she whispered. "I'm great at improvisation . . ."

Georgia was, Matt found, true to her word. Any dancing she did that night, she did with him, a long, sweet *pas de deux* that lasted nearly till dawn and left her far too tired to dance alone in the moonlight even if she'd wanted to.

At nine, Georgia awoke to the smell of coffee and the rollicking music of the Rolling Stones's *Gimme Shelter* blasting from the kitchen. Rolling over to look at the clock, she groaned and sat up gingerly, trying to recall the last time she'd slept past six-thirty.

"And just think how much worse I'd feel if I wasn't in shape," she muttered.

"But you have to admit it was worth it," Matt laughed from the doorway, where he leaned against the jamb, watching her fitful maneuver to the side of the bed.

"One has nothing to do with the other," she grumbled. "I am an athlete. I should not be slowed down by normal nocturnal activities."

"Sweetheart, if that was your idea of normal nocturnal activity, one of us will be in a wheelchair by the time we're thirty."

"Well, it won't be me. Some of my muscles are just a tad . . . rusty, that's all." She swung her legs over the side of the bed, wrapping the sheet around her. It was then she saw the mug he'd set on the wide window ledge. "Is that coffee? You brought me coffee?" She sighed gratefully.

"I thought to atone for keeping you awake all night," he said, trying to look contrite.

"It'll take more than coffee . . ." She sipped at the warm dark liquid. "Although on second thought, this coffee just might do it."

"One of my specialties. French breakfast blend mixed with Colombian beans. And breakfast is in twenty minutes."

"Just enough time for me to grab a quick shower." She headed for the bathroom, then turned and asked, "What's for breakfast?"

"It's a surprise."

She took three more steps down the hall, then looked over her shoulder. "Just what *do* you do to stay in shape?"

"I joined a gym."

"Ah, that explains it," she muttered as she continued on to the shower, "all those different kinds of machines . . ."

He laughed and watched her disappear through the bathroom door.

"We never finished watching the movie last night," Georgia reminded him when she came into the kitchen, wearing the shirt she had worn the night before, along with the skirt. She wasn't sure what had happened to the camisole, but was pretty sure it was in the living room someplace. She'd look later. Right now, she had breakfast to share with Matt—so cute in bare feet and khaki shorts and T-shirt advertising a dog training school—and in little more than an hour, Laura would arrive in a van filled with aspiring ballerinas.

He pulled out a chair for her at the small table, and she sat down.

"Well, we can always try again tonight," he said as

he took the coffee cup from her hands and refilled it without her asking. "Maybe by the end of the weekend we'll have seen the entire film," he grinned and placed a perfect omelet—fluffy eggs wrapped around long tender spears of asparagus—before her on the table.

"Oh, this looks wonderful," she beamed.

"Well, actually, I planned on making this for you for dinner tonight," he bent down and kissed the back of her neck. "It hadn't occurred to me that I'd be making three meals for you this weekend."

"Curried vegetables, fresh coffee first thing in the morning, and this beautiful breakfast," she sighed, then laughed and said jokingly, "Will you marry me?"

His hands, which had been massaging her shoulders gently, stopped for a long minute, then slowly, began again.

"Yes," he said softly, "I'm thinking I probably will."

She wanted to say that it had just been a joke, but she couldn't seem to get the words out. Though the remark had been intended as a flippant one, suddenly the idea didn't seem far-fetched. Not so very far-fetched at all.

chapter twenty-two

I have to run back to the house and let Spam out—she probably wonders where I am—and change for my dance class," Georgia was saying as she rinsed off her dishes in the small kitchen sink. "Laura should be here soon with the girls."

"Leave those, I'll clean up," he told her.

"You know, I have to tell you that you are probably the neatest man I've ever met. I used to think my brother was neat, but you have it all over him."

"I got into the habit when I was really small. The only thing Mom ever asked of Laura and me was that we pick up after ourselves, so I always did."

"You can come next door and pick up after me anytime," she tugged on his collar to bring his face closer so that she could kiss him before floating through the door.

"And I probably will have to," he said to himself, recalling the dishes stacked in her sink, the unmade bed that never seemed to be of any concern to her. Georgia seemed to have different priorities. While she wasn't by any means slovenly, she seemed to go from one busy activity to another, pausing to clean up on her return trip, as it were. Breakfast dishes might be washed with those from dinner. It never seemed to matter to her, when she had other, more interesting things to do.

By the time Matt had finished cleaning up from the night before, including the drips of candle wax here and there, Laura's van was pulling into the driveway and six or seven eager little dancers were spilling out. Matt stood in the window and watched as Georgia called a greeting from the back door. She ducked back inside the house for a moment, then skipped down the steps and offered Laura a hug. Surrounded by chatty little girls, some of whom appeared to be showing off their new dancing garb to their teacher, Georgia crossed the yard with her charges. Laura leaned over to pat the pig who had waddled along behind the group and, unable to keep up, had rolled over onto Laura's feet.

Matt heard their feet tramping up the steps, heard them *ooh* and *ah* over the movable barres, and listened as music filled the old barn to its very rafters. Another car door slammed as the contingent of young dancers from O'Hearn arrived and ran noisily up the steps. The chatter died down in a minute, and the music stopped momentarily, then started from the beginning again. Matt supposed that Georgia had started class, and he fought the urge to go in and take a peek.

He hated the thought of taking that from her, of taking her ballet in the barn out from under her very feet. Well, she'd have the summer to find another place to rent for her school. He prayed it would be here, in O'Hearn. It would have to be. He couldn't even think of Georgia leaving Pumpkin Hill now. And besides, she clearly loved the farm, and seemed to belong here, as much as he and Laura belonged. She had fit in so easily, had taken to the place so completely, that he could almost fancy that Hope herself had had a hand in it.

He finished cleaning up the apartment, then glanced at his watch. Georgia would teach for maybe another twenty minutes. Laura was wandering around outside with Artie and Spam, and Matt decided to join them.

"Hey," he called to her.

"Matt," she waved. "I was beginning to think you were sleeping late today."

"Not a chance." He caught up with his sister and kissed her on the cheek. "Especially with the London Symphony playing in the barn."

"Oh. Is the music bothering you?" Laura frowned. She didn't need one more thing for Matt to hold against Georgia.

"Nah. I'm getting used to it."

"Really?" Laura looked pleased.

"Sure. A little Bach, a little Chopin, early on a Saturday morning never hurt anyone." He grinned, recalling that Laura still didn't know that he and Georgia had kissed and made up. So to speak. "Where are you headed? Anyplace in particular?"

"I thought I'd go see Georgia's vegetable garden. She was making scarecrows this week. Excuse me," she laughed and corrected herself, "she referred to them as scare*crones*."

407

"Then we'll have to take a look." He fell in step next to her. "How's everything at the inn?"

"Fine." She nodded.

"Any new or interesting guests?" he prodded, wondering if she'd mention this Tucker guy that Delia and Georgia had mentioned.

"Well, Gordon is still there. He's taken a bedroom—sitting room combination for an unspecified amount of time. I guess until he's done in Bishop's Cove, which could be a year or better, depending on how long it takes him to find something of value on this ship."

"He must have some kind of a crew," Matt went on as if it was just occurring to him. "Where are they all staying?"

"Oh, most of the crew he's hired on locally. He has brought a few specialty divers, though."

"Anyone interesting?"

"Oh, you," she shoved his arm lightly and laughed. "Who have you been talking to?"

He hesitated. He was kind of enjoying the fact that she still had yet to figure out that he and Georgia had begun to forge a relationship.

"I just happened to be here last Sunday morning when Delia stopped by with Gordon. He told me he'd hired on a diver from Devlin's Light who seemed to have trouble keeping his eyes off the innkeeper."

"I met Tucker at Nick and India's wedding. He's an old family friend of the Devlins'." Laura's eyes stared straight ahead, as if searching for something in the distance.

"Gordon said he's a great guy."

"Gordon's right. He is."

"Has he asked you out?"

"Matt, I'm a married . . ."

"Laura, don't even say it. If you are still married to that lunatic, it's only because you haven't take the steps to unload him. For cryin' out loud, what are you waiting for?"

"I really don't feel like talking about this, Matthew."

"Laura, are you staying married to him for Ally's sake? Because he's her father?"

"What difference does it make, Matt? I married Gary, we are still married. End of story."

"It's not the end, and you know it. What are you hiding?" He grabbed her arm. "Laura, you act as if you're almost afraid to divorce him."

"Matt . . ." Laura hesitated. She wanted to tell him. Wished *desperately* that she could tell him, but the consequences were too frightening.

"Look, I know that it must be a scary thought, starting over after you've been married and had a child. I understand where that *might* cause you to maybe retain some loyalty to him. And I understand that maybe after this experience, you might be afraid to start another relationship. But Laura, all men are not like Gary, though I understand why you might . . ."

"Oh, Matt," she sighed. "You understand nothing."

He had opened his mouth to protest when they rounded the side of the barn.

"Oh, Matt, look!" Laura pointed to Georgia's garden. "Georgia's scarecrones! Oh, isn't it so like something that Aunt Hope would do?"

"It is," he nodded, impressed and surprised by the display. He wasn't, however, so distracted that he was willing to drop the discussion. "Don't try to change the subject."

"Matt, the subject has been dropped." Better to let it go, she told herself she pretended to admire Georgia's bumper crop of colorful cotton and polyester. For Matt's sake as well as her own. "I've nothing more to say on the matter."

"Well, I have."

"I will say this one more time, Matt, and then it's done." Laura appeared, all of a sudden, to be very weary. "I am still married to Gary. Till death do us part. Don't ask me again, don't bring it up again, because I cannot change what is."

"*Till death do you part?*" he repeated incredulously. "Laura, this is crazy. Have you even gone to the prison to visit him since he was incarcerated?"

She shook her head No.

"Have you thought about what's going to happen when he's released from prison? Are you going to live with him again?"

"No!" She went white.

"So you have no contact with him, you don't even like the man, yet you . . ."

"I told you I didn't want to talk about this," she said harshly, pushing him away from her.

"Laura," he said softly. "We've always been so close. I love you and I worry about you and I want to help you. Something's not right, and we both know it. Why won't you tell me? Why won't you trust me with this?"

"Because there's nothing you can do to help me, Matt. No one can."

Laura turned her back abruptly and walked back toward the farmhouse.

Stunned, Matt stood amidst Georgia's thriving garden wondering what was going through his sister's head, and what could possibly motivate her to insist upon staying married to the likes of Gary J. Harmon.

"I was hoping you could find some time this weekend to stop out at the inn," Laura was telling Georgia as she loaded her passengers back into the van when class had ended. The girls had exhausted themselves chasing Spam and Artie around the farmyard. "I wanted your opinion on the table settings for Zoey and Ben's party. I can't decide which colors to use."

"I'll be driving out this afternoon," Matt said as he approached the van. "I'd be happy to give Georgia a ride."

"Oh, thanks, Matt," Georgia said casually. "That would be nice."

In spite of her earlier pique, Laura's eyebrows raised. Had that really been Matt offering to drive Georgia to Bishop's Cove? Offering to spend a certain hour or so in her company? Will wonders never cease?

Pleased by this unexpected development, Laura

smiled. "Will you both be able to stay for dinner? We've had some knock-out crabs this week. Gordon and his crew have been catching them in the bay."

"That sounds great." Matt smiled benignly. "How 'bout it, Georgia? Do you have plans for dinner?"

"Why, no, I haven't. Dinner at the inn sounds like fun."

"Great." Laura looked from one to the other, marveling at the change in her brother's attitude. *Maybe they're learning to get along. Maybe someday they'll even learn to like each other. Maybe there's hope for Matt yet . . .*

"Great," she repeated, trying not to appear too hopeful. "What time do you think you'll get there?"

"I just need to shower and change. Maybe we could leave in, say, an hour?" Georgia looked at Matt and tried not to grin.

"That would be fine." He nodded nonchalantly. "I guess we'll probably be arriving around three or so."

"Great," Laura said for the third time, thinking, as she drove away, how nice that Matt and Georgia were getting to know each other. It was the only good news she'd had that day.

On the drive to Bishop's Cove, with Artie between them on the seat, Matt repeated his conversation with Laura, asking Georgia, "Does this make any sense to you?"

"None," she shook her head. "I can't think of one reason why Laura would want to stay married to that man. It's so unlike her to behave so oddly."

"Laura is so logical about everything else, I just can't understand it." Matt slowed down as he approached the turn for the inn's parking lot.

"Well, let's see how she acts around this diver guy. I have the feeling there's a lot going on here that we don't know about."

"It should be an interesting dinner." Georgia swung the door of the cab open and hopped out. "I'm betting that Laura will be watching us as much as we'll be watching her."

Matt laughed. "Poor Laura is so transparent. She's just so tickled that we're being nice to each other."

"When shall we tell her just how nice . . ."

"Oh, not just yet. It's kind of fun, letting her think she's bringing us together. And I'm sure she's thinking, today, Georgia, tomorrow, Delia . . ."

Georgia laughed out loud, smiling at the two men they passed in the parking lot as they walked toward the back of the inn. *Interesting tattoos*, she thought at the time. *Must be some of Gordon's crew . . .*

"Laura?" Georgia stuck her head into the kitchen.

"Hi, guys," Jody waved from the opposite side of the stainless-steel counter, her light brown hair pulled atop her head in a tight ponytail that swung around her pretty face with every movement of her head. "Laura's not back yet."

"Not back yet?" Matt frowned. "She left an hour before we did."

"Oh, she's back from O'Hearn." Jody's eyes took on a twinkle. "She went for a walk on the beach."

"Oh? With anyone we know?" Georgia brightened.

"Well, she went alone. However, I did notice that a certain tall, dark and handsome diver wandered off in that direction a few minutes later."

"Really?" Georgia winked at Matt. "Well, then, fancy that."

Matt opened the refrigerator and took out two cans of soda. Handing one to Georgia, he said, "Maybe we should take advantage of this beautiful afternoon and sit on the front porch and enjoy the breeze."

"Sounds like a good way to pass some time." Georgia saluted Jody as they passed through the swinging door into the front hall.

"I heard there are crabs for dinner tonight." Matt called back over his shoulder to Jody, who was taking a knife to a large head of cabbage.

"Yep. We're setting up a picnic table in the backyard. Crabs are too messy for the dining room. At least, if they're eaten correctly, they're too messy." Jody laughed. "Brown paper on the table, mallets and paper plates. That's the only way to eat crabs, as far as I'm concerned."

"And lots of cold beer, iced tea, and a big salad." Matt held the front door open for Georgia. "Oh. I just realized that crabs are hardly vegetarian fare."

"That's okay. I'll eat salad."

"That's not very substantial. You need to build up your strength," he told her, "if you plan to watch the rest of that movie with me tonight."

Georgia laughed, then paused on her way to the seating arrangement of wicker furniture at one end of the wide front porch. Two of the chairs that stood opposite each other were occupied by the men they'd passed in the parking lot.

Georgia smiled and passed between the seated men. Matt greeted them pleasantly and they nodded to him as he walked past them. Taking seats on the settee at the end of the porch and a few feet away from the other guests, Georgia said, "I wonder where Ally is."

"Probably at a friend's house."

"She was so cute in dancing class this morning," Georgia told him, then proceeded to describe Ally's antics while at the same time trying not to stare at the forearms of the two men who sat only a few feet away, their long thin tattooed swords reaching all the way to the elbow.

A discussion then followed of Georgia's students, who seemed to have true potential as a dancer, who did not. This led Matt to think about his visit to Georgia's garden while she was teaching her class, and he complimented her on her crones. Talking about the crones reminded Matt about his conversation with Laura. And that reminded him that his sister was still down at the beach with a man for whom she professed she had no interest.

Matt turned his wrist to look at his watch. They'd been there for almost an hour already.

"Let's walk down to the beach and see what Laura and this diver are up to."

"Okay. I'm interested in seeing what you think of him. I personally think he's perfect for Laura."

The couple excused themselves as they once again walked between the two men, unaware of the long, dark look exchanged by the strangers, and of the brooding eyes that followed them down the path on their way to the beach.

The beach was almost—but not quite—vacant on this Saturday afternoon. A young woman walked her cocker spaniel up toward the dune. Down near the water's edge three small children searched for sand crabs. An athletic-looking man in his twenties jogged along the beach, and a young mother sat on a sand chair reading a novel, her twin daughters digging a circle around the chair with their hands. Down the beach toward the jetty, Laura and Tucker Moreland sat deep in conversation.

Matt called to his sister from a distance but she did not appear to hear.

"Hmmm," Georgia grinned as she slipped off her shoes and dug her toes into the sand. "It would seem that Tucker has managed to capture Laura's complete and total attention."

"So it would seem," Matt replied as he rolled up his pants legs, then took off his own shoes and, carrying one in each hand, walked toward the water where he tested the foamy wake from the last wave. "Still just a little too cold for my taste. Maybe in another few weeks it'll be warm enough to swim in."

Georgia caught up with him and walked straight ahead into the surf for a few feet. "I don't mind. I like it on the cool side."

They walked up the beach, chasing some small birds that followed the ebb and flow of the sea, hunting for snacks. They were practically on top of Laura before she looked up.

"Oh! You're here already! Hi!" Slightly flustered, she was obviously surprised to see them.

"We've been here for almost an hour now. We were wondering where you were." Georgia said, then greeted Tucker saying, "Hi, Tucker. How've you been?"

"Well, thanks," he nodded, then stood to offer a hand to Matt, introducing himself saying, "You must be Laura's brother. I'm Tucker Moreland."

At six feet four inches, Tucker stood several inches over Matt, who immediately noticed that Tucker was a man who had a firm handshake and a steady gaze.

"Good to meet you," Matt said.

"Tucker was just telling me about the dive he made this morning to the *True Wind* and what he thinks might be down there." Laura pushed back the long sleeve of her shirt to check her watch. "Oh, would you look at the time? I didn't realize it was so late! I need to get back to the inn to give Jody a hand. And I wanted you to look over some table linens with me before dinner, Georgia."

"Sure. I'm ready." Georgia shrugged, trying not to stare at Tucker. She'd forgotten just how handsome he was. *Be still my heart—no wonder Laura's smitten. And she clearly is. Why, just look at her face!*

Matt, it appeared, was doing just that.

"Well, then, why don't you go back on up to the inn and take care of business while Tucker and I sit and watch the gulls," Matt told his sister. "It will give us some time to get acquainted."

"Sounds good to me," Tucker sat on the sand and leaned back on his elbows, slid his sunglasses, which rode atop his head, down onto his face.

"We'll see you at dinner," Georgia tugged on Laura's arm and winked at Matt.

"But . . ." Laura protested, not sure she liked the idea of her brother sitting in easy interrogation distance to Tucker.

"Go on, Laura," Matt shooed her along with the

wave of his hand. "You have things to do. Tucker and I have birds to watch. We'll be along in a while."

"OK," Laura gathered up her shoes and a ceramic mug from which she drained the last few drops of dark liquid. Glancing warily at her brother, she followed Georgia across the beach to the wooden steps leading up to the sidewalk and back to the inn.

"Do you like the pale pink, or the pale green?" Laura held up two different tablecloths for Georgia's inspection. "Or maybe ivory. Which do you think Zoey would prefer? Maybe we should ask Delia . . ."

"Laura, you don't need to confer with us on every detail." Georgia sat down at the dining room table and smoothed a ripple from the creamy white cloth that Laura had placed before her. "And it seems to me you have much more experience with this sort of thing than we do. After all, you do this type of thing all the time here at the inn, don't you?"

"Yes, but this is different. This is for family, and it has to be perfect."

"It will be perfect. Relax. Do you know how many people Delia is having?"

"She said it would be less than thirty."

"Well, then, we could even do three round tables of eight or ten each in the sun room. That would be lovely, with the ivy and wisteria draping over the outside of the windows," Georgia suggested.

"That would be pretty. Let's just go poke in there and see how we might arrange things."

Laura pushed open the French doors leading into the sun room and walked to the middle of the room.

"We could move a few more wicker pieces in and move the upholstered pieces out for the party, and do the entire room in white. White wicker, white linens, white flowers. Lilies. Roses. Orchids . . ." Laura murmured.

"That's exactly what Mother did for India and Nick's engagement party," Georgia grinned. "Right down to the same flowers. That's uncanny."

"Oh," Laura looked pensive. "Then perhaps we should do something else."

"I think all white would be wonderful in here," Georgia told her. "And we can just consider all white engagement parties a new family tradition. India, Zoey, maybe someday me . . . maybe you . . ."

"I've had my shot at 'someday,'" Laura appeared to have focused her attention on refolding the linens.

"Where is it written that you only get one 'shot' at happiness?" Georgia asked. "Who told you that if it doesn't work out the first time, that you never get another chance?"

"It doesn't matter," Laura turned her back, so as to avoid her sister's questioning eyes. She appeared about to add something else, when her attention was drawn to the window, where Matt and Tucker were walking up the drive leisurely, Artie sauntering along between them, Tucker laughing at something Matt was saying.

Georgia watched the faintest flush of color spread across Laura's cheeks, watched her expression soften just a little.

"Laura," Georgia said, "would I be prying if I asked . . ."

"Yes." Laura gathered up the linens and seemed to flee the room. "Yes, you would be."

"This Tucker fellow is all right," Matt said as they drove along a dark and winding country road on their way back to Pumpkin Hill later that night. "He's quite an interesting guy. I really liked him a lot."

Artie having decided to ride shotgun and stick his big head out the window to catch some breeze, Georgia had been forced to take the middle seat. She leaned against Matt, her head on his shoulder, and said, "Well, I wouldn't start calling him 'brother' any time soon."

"Yes, I know. Laura's trying so hard to pretend that she hardly notices him, but yet she can't seem to put together a full, coherent sentence when he's in the room." Matt said thoughtfully.

"I know how she feels," Georgia ran a hand up Matt's arm to his shoulder and added softly, "Only difference is, I admit it."

There was a long moment's silence.

"OK," Matt said, "I want to hear it."

"Hear what?" Georgia yawned.

"I want to hear you admit it."

She leaned closer to his ear. "I am in serious danger of falling head over heels in love with you, Matthew Bishop. And if you play your cards right, I just might be persuaded to watch the rest of that movie with you when we get home tonight."

Matt smiled in the darkness and stepped on the gas.

chapter twenty-three

Georgia unlocked the back door of the farmhouse and went into the kitchen, tossing her purse onto the table as she passed by. She was hot and sticky and not happy after having spent the morning looking at three possible properties recommended by one of the clerks at Tanner's whose mother was a real estate agent. Feeling somewhat like Goldilocks, Georgia had found the first property too big—the space having once been used as a warehouse for farm equipment—and the second, a long narrow space with a low ceiling and two thin windows that would only get morning sun, too small. The last lacked indoor plumbing. She had not as yet gone through the storefront on Main Street, the agent who had the key being out of town for two more days. Georgia held onto the hope that this last space would prove to be just right.

Sooner or later, she sighed as she pushed the message button on her answering machine, she would have to find that just right place or settle for something less than ideal. Or move her new dance studio out of O'Hearn, which she did not want to do, for a number of very good reasons.

Starting with you, she said to the voice on the answering machine.

"Georgia, hi. It's about noon. I was just wondering how you made out with the realtor this morning, and I wanted to let you know that I got a call back from the architect I contacted last week. He can meet with me at the barn on Saturday. I told him to come in the afternoon, so that we won't disturb your dance class. We'll talk about all that later, I'll give you call when I get home tonight." Matt paused, and she could almost see that sweet half smile of his. "I miss you. A lot. I think maybe I'll have to drive down there on Wednesday and show you just how much . . ."

Grinning, Georgia saved the message to replay again later, then went upstairs to change into her old clothes. Whistling, she pulled on a pair of faded olive green shorts and a tank top, then wound her hair atop her head before heading out to the field to check her garden. She called Spam several times before the pig appeared, waddling from around the far side of the house, to trail behind Georgia like a faithful pup.

The sun was full overhead of the garden, which was doing quite nicely. The pepper and green bean plants had filled out, the vines—cantaloupe and zucchini—seemed daily to be spreading several feet in all directions, and the tomatoes were covered with small green buds that promised bushels of fruit before the summer had ended. Georgia walked the neat rows, bending down here and there to pull an unwanted weed or to investigate a blossom or a bug. Everything was thriving, and it gave her great satisfaction.

"I'll have to remember to speak to Matt about fencing against the deer," she said aloud, and Spam, who was busy rooting in a pile of leaves behind the barn, looked up momentarily at the sound of her voice before returning to her foraging.

Georgia plunged her hands into the pockets of her shorts and grinned with satisfaction. She'd done a good job here, and she mentally patted herself on the back with pride as she admired her handiwork. Her crones, whom she had come to think of as Agatha, Bertha, Clara, Dora, Edna, and Freda, stood proudly at strategic points around the garden, their house dresses swaying in the occasional breeze. The sight of them brought a smile to her face, and she always made a point of addressing them before she left their company.

"You ladies need gloves," she told them. "White gloves. I'm sure I can find them someplace. No, no, no need to thank me. Consider it a reward for keeping those bothersome birds from the garden. Thanks to you ladies, the carrot seeds grew. Just look at how many have sprouted and sent up those lacy shoots! And I think your presence here has even discouraged the groundhogs and the bunnies. No, ladies, the white gloves are definitely on me."

There was no need to water since it had rained during the night. The storm had been brief but intense, the thunder rattling the old house and wakening her with a start. But Matt had awoken, too, and by the time the storm had passed, they had found ways to reduce the thunder to little more than background music.

"I miss you, too, Matt," she said softly, her eyes fixed on the wishing tree. "Wednesday can't come soon enough."

She headed back to the house, having decided that the garden needed none of her attention this afternoon. She would spent the rest of the day dancing, setting into movement the joyful recollection of the hours she had spent in Matt's arms, the longing to be with him, the wonder of discovering her love for him.

With the warmer weather, dancing on the second floor of the barn was becoming increasingly uncomfortable. It hadn't been so bad early in the morning, before the sun had risen too far in the sky and heated things up, but Georgia was finding that later in the day, the air was stuffy and humid and still. There was no cross-ventilation, and years of storing grain and hay had left traces of dust behind that even her careful scrubbing had failed to eliminate. Georgia frowned, trying to imagine what it would be like in July or August when temperatures as well as humidity soared into the nineties. Maybe being forced to look for other quarters was actually a blessing in disguise.

"You're going to need air conditioning in the barn," she told Matt when he called early in the evening. "It's going to be hot as hell in another month. I'm wondering how many more weeks I can run classes before I have to call it off till I find another location. But if you're planning on using that second floor space, it will definitely need air."

"It's going to need heat, too," Matt replied, "so I guess that can all be done at the same time. The architect said he can refer me to a good contractor who will go over the specifications with me and draw up an estimate for me to take to the bank when I go in to apply for the construction loan. I shudder to think what all this will cost."

"Oh, but it will be worth it. It will be yours."

"It'll take me forever to pay back the loan."

"But it will be paid off eventually. And you'll be living here, at Pumpkin Hill, exactly the way you always dreamed of doing."

"Well, not exactly the way I dreamed."

"Oh? What's changed?"

"I never realized how incomplete that dream was, until I met you. I never knew how full life could be. Now the clinic is only part of something bigger. It's still a major part of my future, to be sure, but it isn't everything. Being with you, there at Pumpkin Hill, *that's* everything."

"My dreams are different now, too," she whispered, "but so much lovelier . . ."

Funny, she thought later after she'd had a late dinner and drained the last sip of tea from her cup, *how things turn out. I came to Pumpkin Hill looking for nothing more than a few months of peace and country air, and just look at all I've found.*

A rustle from the back porch drew her attention to the screen door. Spam was peeking into the kitchen, longing written all over her snout. Georgia laughed out loud, then set the cup on the counter before opening the door.

"Are you confused because it's not yet dark, Spammy? The longer hours of daylight must puzzle you," Georgia muttered as she picked up the pig and walked down the steps with Spam in her arms.

Setting the pig down on the grass, Georgia happily inhaled the scent of early summer. The flower bed that ran along the side of the house spilled over with delicate blue columbine and fat buds of daisies not quite ready to bloom. Deep red roses climbed a trellis next to the back door, and tall hollyhocks grew like weeds along the foundation of the house. She realized she was humming, and it occurred to her at that minute that she had never been happier in her life. Somehow it had all come together for her, and she had found pieces of her life she hadn't even realized were missing. Smiling, she turned back to the house, wondering what happy surprise tomorrow might hold.

Georgia's all's-right-with-the-world feeling had started to fade by ten o'clock that evening, when she left yet another message on Laura's answering machine, the third of the day. Having discussed Laura's situation with Matt the night before and decided that she would attempt to talk to Laura about Gary, Georgia was anxious to get in touch with her. One ignored message generally meant that Laura hadn't gotten around to calling her back, but three unreturned calls meant avoidance to Georgia. It being a school night, Laura would be home to put Ally to bed. As far as Georgia was concerned, Laura was choosing not to return the call, not to respond to Georgia's suggestion that they meet for lunch the next day.

"Well, if you think that not calling me back will keep me away, you are mistaken." Georgia muttered as she went up the steps to bed. "I'll call you at seven tomorrow morning, and if I have to call back every hour, on the hour, until I catch up with you, I will. But if you think that your family is going to sit by and watch you throw your life away for the sake of some crazy man you don't even *like*, then you are crazier than he is . . ."

It was seven-ten when Georgia called Laura's private line at the inn the next morning. When she heard the answering machine pick up, she frowned and hung up the phone. Tapping the toes of one foot impatiently, she dialed the main number for the inn. Jody answered on the third ring.

"Jody, hi. It's Georgia. I'm looking for Laura. Is she around?"

Hesitantly, as if choosing her words carefully, Jody replied, "Laura doesn't seem to be here."

"What does that mean?" When Jody did not respond, Georgia asked, "Jody, is something wrong?"

"I'm not really sure . . ."

"Was there something early at school today? Maybe one of those parent breakfasts?"

"Ally and I are having breakfast together this morning. She's right here with me."

Georgia paused, as the significance set in.

"Laura always makes Ally's breakfast."

"That's right." Jody said, forcing calm to avoid frightening the child. "She does."

"Ally hasn't seen her mother this morning." Georgia said flatly.

"That appears to be the case."

"Jody, you know Tucker Moreland . . ."

"Of course."

"Maybe they went out to watch the sun rise." Georgia's mind raced, seeking any logical explanation for her sister's disappearance. "Maybe they lost track of the time . . ."

"Tucker's in the dining room having breakfast with Gordon."

Georgia fought back a rise of panic.

"Jody, I'm going to give you my number here. Will you give it to Tucker and ask him to call me right back?"

"Sure."

Georgia waited for Jody to find a pencil and paper to write down the phone number at Pumpkin Hill.

"Tell him I'm waiting by the phone."

"Consider it done."

"And Ally . . . ?"

"Is fine for now. I'm getting her ready for school."

"Go tell Tucker."

"I'm on my way."

Georgia paced waiting for the phone to ring, trying to think of a reasonable explanation. There was none. Laura would not—*would never*—go off and leave her daughter. Not ever. Not for any reason.

The phone rang and Georgia jumped in spite of the fact that she was standing next to it in anticipation.

"I'm sorry to bother you," she began, unaware that her words were tumbling out rapidly, "and it's probably nothing, but I was wondering if you had seen Laura."

"Not since last night," he told her. "We sat on the front porch and talked for a while after Ally went to sleep."

"I'm sorry, I'm not trying to pry, but when did . . ."

"She went in around midnight."

"Tucker, I hate to impose on you, but would you mind walking down to the beach and just see if Laura is there."

"Georgia, what's the problem?"

"Laura wasn't in her apartment to get Ally dressed for school today, and she isn't there for breakfast. She never misses breakfast with her. It doesn't appear that she's any place in the inn, so I though maybe . . ." Georgia had been doing a fairly good job of fighting her anxiety up until this point, but her composure finally began to crack. Her voice quivered as she added, "I'm feeling really uneasy."

"I'll call you back." He hung up the phone and walked out the front door and down the steps, his eyes scanning from side to side as he went toward the beach. Georgia was right, of course. Laura never would leave Ally, even in an emergency, without telling her that she'd be gone and arranging for someone else to be with her.

Georgia was right to feel uneasy. Suddenly, Tucker was feeling uneasy, too.

He stood at the top of the wooden steps, his hands shading his eyes, and looked up the beach in both directions. Nothing. From an inside jacket pocket he pulled what looked like a miniature pair of binoculars and held them to his eyes. Though very small, the range of the glasses was extensive. There was no sign of Laura as far as he could see. A small worm of fear began to twist within him, and he broke into a jog as he hurried back to the inn, where Ally was standing in the front doorway, waiting for her mother to walk her to school.

"Tucker, have you seen my mommy?" Ally asked with a six-year-old's impatience. "I'm waiting for her to take me to school."

"No, I haven't seen her. I'll bet she went out for an early morning jog and forgot about the time."

"My mommy hates to run."

"Well, then, maybe she took a long walk. It sure is a beautiful morning."

"Sometimes she likes to go watch the sun come up." Ally said hopefully.

"Then that's probably just what she did."

"She always comes back before breakfast. She's always here when I have to go to school."

"Oh, I'll bet she just lost track of the time today. Maybe the sunrise was extra pretty this morning," Tucker said, wishing it was true.

"I have to go to school." Ally looked up at him, concern in her face. "Someone has to take me."

"I could walk with you this morning."

Ally looked anxiously in the direction of the beach.

"Look, how 'bout if I walk you to school, then when I get back, I'll walk on down to the beach to see if your mom is there."

"When you find her on the beach, will you tell her to bring milk and ice cream money to school for me? Before lunch time?"

"How much do you need?" he asked.

"Four quarters and two dimes."

Tucker dug into his pocket and pulled out a fistful of change. Holding his hand open, he said, "Let's see if you can count out what you need all by yourself."

She took two dimes and four quarters, thanked him, and relieved that lunch had been taken care of, said, "Now we can walk to school."

He held out his hand and she took it, and they walked to the first corner, which they crossed on cue from the crossing guard. At the next corner they turned right for a block to the elementary school. When they reached the front walk, Ally stopped and said, "Mommy usually leaves me here. See, there's Mr. McAfee. He's the school guard."

"Do you need anything else?" Tucker asked as he knelt down in front of her.

"Just a kiss," she grinned, offering her cheek, which he kissed softly.

"Thank you," she took off up the sidewalk, turning once to wave and call to him, "When you find my mommy, don't forget to tell her that she should not be walking late in the morning."

"I'll do that," he nodded, thinking that if he did find Laura right now, that's the least he'd say.

When he found her, he corrected himself as he hurried back to the inn. There was no doubt but that he would. He hadn't spent a lifetime looking for her, only to have her disappear now.

Once back at the Bishop's Inn, Tucker let himself unobtrusively into Laura's apartment and walked through the neat, quiet rooms, looking for something out of place. He went into her bedroom and stood in the doorway, taking in the scene before him. The bed was only mildly rumpled on one side, the pillows

431

stacked as if the occupant had leaned against them to read, and indeed, the bedside table held a stack of books. He walked closer. Laura's reading glasses were folded on the cover of a paperback novel that lay face down on the table.

Across the room, a dresser drawer stood open a few inches. Tucker peered into the deep drawer where sweaters were folded and stacked one upon the other in four piles. Three of the piles held four sweaters each. The fourth pile held only three.

He went next into the bathroom, where a nightshirt made a rumpled pile on top of the wicker clothes hamper. He returned to the bedroom and looked around, then back into the bathroom where he lifted the lid of the hamper. It held the long sleeved T-shirt she'd worn the night before, but not the jeans. Her bathrobe hung on the back of the door, and her slippers were under one side of the bed. He opened her closet door. The Nike walking shoes she wore frequently were missing.

"Laura, talk to me," he said aloud to the empty room. "Show me who was here, so that I can find you . . ."

His eyes searched the scene for something. There had to be *something*—but it was as if she had been plucked from her bed and abducted into thin air. He had all but come to the conclusion that there were no clues to be found when he noticed the open Bible pushed partly under the bed. Hesitating only for a second, he knelt down and scanning the page—the Book of Matthew—found that a section near the bottom of the page had been torn out. He lifted the book and found the scrap of paper concealed under it.

I am a man under authority, having soldiers under me: and I say to this man, Go, and he goeth; and to another, Come, and he cometh: and to my servant, Do this, and he doeth it.

Is it possible that Laura's abductor had given her time to read her Bible before spiriting her away, and had she used that time, however brief, to seek words that might provide a clue as to whom her abductor might be?

The back of Tucker's neck began to prickle as he read and reread the marked passage, all his well-trained instincts on full alert.

chapter twenty-four

Georgia paced relentlessly waiting for Matt to arrive, replaying the phone call from Tucker over and over in her head.

"It appears that Laura disappeared sometime after she went into the inn around midnight. She'd apparently had time to change her clothes and get into bed, read for however long before whomever her visitor was, arrived. There was a book on the table with her eyeglasses, and the bed was only mildly disturbed—blankets turned back, the pillows stacked up against the headboard—as if she'd gotten into it and had time to do some reading, but maybe hadn't slept in it."

"The police . . ."

". . . have been called. They don't seem to think that she's been missing long enough for them to be involved," he had said tersely.

"And you?" she had asked.

"I think it's been plenty long enough."

"I'm going to call Matt. We'll be there as soon as we can get there. And I'll call my mother . . ."

"Gordon already has. She's on her way."

The black pickup drove past the window, kicking up stones as it made an arc in the drive to turn back toward the road, and Georgia was outside, locking the door behind her, before Matt had time to come to a full stop. She raced to the cab and climbed in, slammed the door behind her even as Matt hit the gas.

"Have you heard anything else from Tucker?" Matt asked as he flew from the driveway onto the macadam roadway.

Georgia shook her head, "No. I brought my cell phone, though. I thought I'd call in another fifteen minutes or so and see if there's anything new."

Matt nodded, his jaw tight and his eyes hidden behind his dark glasses.

"The police told Tucker that it was too early to start worrying." She leaned back against the seat and idly scratched behind Artie's ears. On the seat between his humans, the dog closed his eyes blissfully, unaware of the turmoil.

"That's ridiculous," Matt scowled. "Laura isn't the type of person to just take off like this. Where do they think she might have gone?"

They rode in silence for several miles, neither of them willing to voice their deepest fears.

Finally, Georgia dug in her shoulder pack and, pulling out her small phone, said, "I think I'll call my mother's car phone and see if she's heard anything."

Delia answered the phone on the first ring.

"Mom, it's me. Matt and I are about twenty minutes or so from Bishop's Cove. I was just checking to see if you'd left yet."

"You'll beat me by about an hour. I left as soon as Gordon called. I take it you waited for Matt."

"Yes. Have you heard anything?"

"Not from Tucker. But I did make a call or two."

"To . . . ?"

"The first was to Jeremy Noble. The second was to Nick. He and India will be there in a few hours. Nicky will have called Zoey and Ben by now. Jeremy was in D.C., so he should be there before too long."

"Jeremy is the private investigator who works for you occasionally?"

"Yes. He found Laura for me the first time. I was hoping that perhaps . . ." The line went silent.

"Mom?"

"Yes, darling, I'm here. I'm just beside myself, Georgia. I know that something terrible has happened to Laura and I don't know what to do." Delia spoke slowly, as if afraid to voice her fears.

There was a brief period of heavy static on the phone.

"Mom, say it again, I couldn't hear what you were saying."

"I said, thank God for Gordon. He's going to have someone drive him to meet me in Rehoboth, so that I don't have to make the entire drive alone."

"That's so sweet of him, Mom."

"It is. Oh, there's that damnable static again. Call me back when you get to the inn."

Georgia pressed the "end" button and pushed the thin antenna back into the phone. Keeping the phone on her lap, she told Matt about Gordon driving north to meet Delia, and that the rest of the family was on their way to the inn.

"That's good. She probably needs all of you right now." Matt nodded his head, recalling Delia's words. *If one is wounded, we all bleed.*

"That's what she said. That she'd lost Laura once . . ."

"Well, we're not losing her," Matt interrupted her. "We'll find her."

"Mom's already called her P.I. He's on his way to the inn. And Tucker's a former SEAL. He must have some skills that could be useful in this kind of situation."

"What are you saying?"

"I'm saying that if the police continue to insist that she's probably just having her nails done or she's out shopping with her girlfriends, it will be good to have some investigative types around."

"Well, maybe by the time we reach the inn the police will have changed their minds and will have launched a search for her."

The police hadn't changed their tune much, as Matt and Georgia discovered when they arrived in Bishop's Cove. If anything, they spent more time thinking of excuses for Laura's disappearance than they did of possible solutions for finding her. Even the ripped section from the Bible was dismissed as inconsequential. It was as if the thought of a serious crime having been perpetrated in their tiny coastal town was inconceivable.

"Now, look, Matthew," the old chief was saying, "you don't know that your sister didn't have a gentleman friend she was visiting with last night."

"The only 'friend' Laura was with last night was me," Tucker scowled.

"That right?" The Chief's eyes narrowed and focused his attention on Tucker. "Until what time?"

"Around midnight. I already gave this information to your officer . . ."

"Well, give it to us again . . ." The Chief pointed to a chair at the opposite end of the room and said, "Why don't you just take a seat there and you and I will have a little chat . . ."

Tucker rolled his eyes in exasperation, but took the seat and waited for the police chief to join him.

Georgia looked out the window, watching for the Mercedes to make its appearance while Matt paced anxiously. Finally, Delia's car appeared and Georgia ran out through the side door to meet her. She waved as she crossed the parking lot and Delia emerged from the passenger side door. *She's let Gordon drive*, Georgia observed, thinking how unusual it was for her mother to turn the reins of control over to someone else. Gordon hopped out from behind the wheel to slam the door quickly and catch up with Delia as she strode toward her daughter.

Wordlessly Georgia gathered her mother into her arms and let her hold on. After several long minutes, Delia stepped back slightly and said, "I saw police cars out front . . ."

"They're questioning Tucker."

"Tucker?" Delia snorted. "Good grief, they don't think Tucker had anything to do with this . . ."

"I don't know that they're thinking much of anything. It's like being trapped in a bad episode of *Mayberry, RFD*. At this point, they don't seem to think that foul play is a factor. They seem to think she just up and took off for a while . . ."

"Well, I'll set them straight on that." Delia charged toward the house.

By the time they reached the front steps, they could hear Jody shouting from within.

"Laura Bishop would not leave her child. Period." With every word, Jody took one step closer to the young police officer, her brown eyes crackling with indignation, her pretty face taut with anger. The officer took one step back for every step forward of Jody's. "She would not *not* be where she is supposed to be, when she is supposed to be there, without telling someone—most likely, me—and for you to stand there and suggest that she met her girlfriends for breakfast, which just happened to turn into lunch, without bothering to tell anyone is totally *absurd!*"

"Okay, okay." The officer took off his hat and ran his fingers through his hair, front to back.

"We'll put out an APB," the chief nodded, rubbing his chin. "Get me a photo and I'll send it over to the TV stations and the newspapers. I still think it's a lot to do about nothin', and I think she'll be strolling back in here any time now . . ."

"The new brochure advertising the inn has her picture on the back," Jody ignored him. "There's a whole pile of them right there behind you on the desk."

Without waiting for the officer to move, Jody lifted a stack of brochures and handed them to him. The Chief took them and stuck the pile under his arm.

"I'll be in touch," he said as he headed through the door, turning to address Tucker. "Don't think about leaving Bishop's Cove . . ."

"Why did he say that?" Georgia asked.

"Because I was the last person to see Laura last night," Tucker told them.

"That's ridiculous," Delia waved her hand, "to even suggest that you would have anything to do with her disappearance."

"If you did, I'll . . ." Matt began, and Tucker held up one hand, to stop him, saying calmly, "You're her brother, so I'll overlook that. Now, let's use our energy to find your sister."

"You mean, start canvassing Bishop's Cove?" Georgia said.

"Unless I am very much off-base, Laura is not in Bishop's Cove." Tucker said. "Ah, Mrs. Enright, is that your investigator?" He pointed through the window at the man who was rapidly approaching.

"Yes. That's Jeremy. Did you speak with him earlier by phone?" She went to the door.

"He called from his car, just as you had asked him to do."

"Mom, do you think he can help?" Georgia asked.

"He's never failed me," Delia said as she opened the door and briefly hugged the investigator who had been her help in time of need on several occasions.

Jeremy Noble was tall and muscular and looked more like the football player he had been in a previous life than a private investigator. He wore a black sweatshirt with PRINCETON across the front in orange, and gray sweat pants.

"Are you all right, Delia?" he asked with genuine concern.

"No, I'm not all right," she appeared to be, finally, on the edge of breaking.

440

Gordon put his arm around Delia and led her to the sofa. To Jody, he said, "Maybe some coffee . . ."

"I'll bring in a pot," Jody said as she headed directly to the kitchen.

"Who's Tucker?" Jeremy asked.

"I am." Tucker stepped forward.

"Did you speak with the police?" Jeremy asked.

"I did."

"Show them Laura's 'note'?"

"They didn't think it was significant," Tucker said wryly.

"Show me her apartment, if you would . . ."

Tucker nodded, gesturing for Jeremy to follow him. Matt fell in behind them.

When they came back a few minutes later, Matt was carrying the Bible. He placed the book on the table and opened it to the page he'd been marking with one finger.

"The Bible was on the floor, and open to this page. The torn out section was under the book. In spite of what the police think, we figure that Laura left it to help us find her. Tucker thinks that somehow, she must have talked her abductor—or abductors, we don't know how many there were—into letting her read from her Bible before they took her. She must have very cautiously torn this section out and placed it under the book, hoping it would be found."

"What kidnapper would give his victim time to read the Bible?"

"Someone who thinks he's doing the Lord's work might be inclined," Jeremy said.

The room fell very quiet.

"Gary," Matt said flatly, quickly making the connection.

"Isn't he still in jail?" Gordon asked.

"Yes, but over the past few years, he's developed a following that goes from one end of the country to the other. In the past six months alone, about forty of his disciples have been released from their respective prisons," Jeremy told them.

"You think one of them abducted her?" Georgia's jaw dropped open. "Why would they do that?"

Jeremy read from the slip of paper that he'd been holding in his left hand.

"*I am a man under authority, having soldiers under me: and I say to this man, Go, and he goeth; and to another, Come, and he cometh; and to my servant, Do this, and he doeth it.*'"

A dropping pin would have sounded more like an avalanche in the wake of Jeremy's reading.

"Gary sent someone to come and take Laura someplace." Georgia whispered, wide-eyed. "But where . . ."

"What if you're wrong?" Delia grabbed Jeremy's arm. "What if you're wrong and it isn't Gary at all? What if it's someone else, some random person . . ."

"I don't believe that it is, Delia," Jeremy told her. "I've had a trace on each one of these birds as they have been released. All of them are present and accounted for. Except for two. Last seen in Virginia Beach about ten days ago."

"Virginia Beach is not very far down the coast," Jody said aloud from the doorway, a tray bearing a large white coffeepot in her hands.

Jeremy went to take the tray and she stepped

around him, saying, "I have it." She placed the tray on the low table in front of Delia and returned to the kitchen for a second tray of cups and saucers, avoiding Jeremy's gaze as she passed.

"Why were you keeping an eye on these guys?" Matt asked.

"When Delia first asked me to check up on Gary, I never expected to find anything. A minister who gambled away his church's money is probably not the most moral man in the world, but it didn't necessarily make him a dangerous person. I know the warden at the prison where Gary is incarcerated, so I thought I'd just make a quick inquiry for Delia, just finish up the file, so to speak. But when I brought up Harmon's name to my buddy, I could feel the tension right through the phone. It seems your old friend Gary has established quite a network of loyal admirers. His 'gospel' has spread from prison to prison. His ministry—which he calls the Sword of the Lamb, by the way—has become a sect unto itself."

"Like a cult?" Georgia frowned.

"Very much like a cult," Jeremy nodded, taking the cup of coffee offered by Jody, "with Gary as it's leader."

"So you're saying that Gary could have told one of his disciples to kidnap Laura?" Jody asked. "Why would he do that now, after all these years?"

"I haven't been able to figure out what triggered it," admitted Jeremy, "but I feel very strongly that's what happened."

"So what do we do now?" Matt stood and repeated an earlier question. "How do we know where to look?"

"I think we need to try to think like Gary," Jeremy said.

"There's a scary thought," Jody muttered.

Georgia asked, "Okay, let's start with, how does he see her?"

"As his wife," Jody answered without hesitation.

"From what Laura said, she hasn't seen or spoken to him in years," Tucker said.

"They haven't, but that seems to make no difference to him." Jody shook her head. "As far as he's concerned, they are married for life. *Till death do us part . . .*"

"Laura said the same thing recently." Matt frowned. "It didn't make any sense to me then, and it doesn't make any sense to me now."

"She never showed you, did she?" Jody said softly.

"Showed me what?"

"The letters she got from him."

"From Gary?"

Jody nodded. "Every week or so, she'd get something from him. Generally it's just ranting and raving, a lot of Bible stuff. Laura just threw them out."

She paused.

"But . . . ?" Jeremy walked to her and took her by the arm.

"But not too long ago she got one that seemed to rattle her. We were in the kitchen and she was opening the mail. She opened this one envelope, and she just went white and her hands started to shake. Laura crumpled it up and threw it into the trash and walked out of the room without finishing her sentence."

"How did you know it was from him?" Jeremy asked.

"Please." she rolled her eyes. "If one of your friends reads something that makes them bolt like that, you take it out of the trash and you read it."

"What did it say?"

"It was something about sin finding you out." She frowned. "It didn't make any sense."

"And there were others?"

"Yes. Every week."

"When did they start?" Matt asked.

"Laura's been getting letters from him for as long as I've been here. Three years."

"How many did you see?"

"Several," she admitted. "They were all pretty much the same."

"When did the last one come?" Jeremy asked.

"The last one that I saw was about a week or so ago. It was another weird one that made no sense. Something about the scribes and Pharisees and a woman taken . . ." She stopped, the words sticking in her throat.

"Go on," Jeremy turned to her.

"A woman taken in adultery," Delia said softly. "*'And the scribes and the Pharisees brought unto him a woman taken in adultery.'* It's from the Gospel of St. John."

"Why would he write something like that?" Georgia frowned. "Unless he thought she was . . ."

"She wasn't," Tucker stood up and repeated, in case anyone had not understood the first time, *"She wasn't."*

"But supposing he had someone watching her," Georgia turned to Tucker, "and they thought she was . . ."

Tucker stared thoughtfully at her.

"You've been staying here at the inn for several weeks now. You've taken walks together. You've spent a lot of time together," Delia said, not as an accusation, but as a statement of fact. "If Gary had someone watching her, they might have made the assumption that you were lovers."

"And that could have been enough to set Gary off." Matt frowned.

"Where would he have had them take her?" Tucker said abruptly.

The room was silent, save for the ticking of a clock in the hallway.

"The house on Manor Road." Matt stood up. "If we're assuming that Gary has this Laura-is-now-and-always-my-wife fixation, maybe he'd want her in the house they lived in together."

"It's as good a place as any to start." Tucker headed for the door.

"We'll take my van." Jeremy was right behind him. "Matt, you'll have to show us the way."

Georgia grabbed her shoulder bag and slung it over her shoulder. She leaned down, kissed her mother's cheek and said, "We'll call you as soon as we find her."

The three men paused in the doorway, then turned to look at each other, then at Georgia.

"Georgia, we're the 'we,'" Matt pointed to Jeremy, Tucker and himself. "You are not part of the 'we' who is going."

"Oh, yes I am." She started through the door.

"Georgia," he grabbed her by the elbow, "this is

not the *Movie of the Week*. This is very real, and it could be very dangerous."

"Matt is right, Georgia." Delia protested. "It would be foolish—more than foolish—for you to go . . ."

"If they've . . . if something has happened to her . . . if they've hurt her, she'll need me," Georgia said.

"Georgia has a point. But," Tucker turned to Georgia, "no crazy stuff, hear? We have to assume that these are dangerous people who think they are serving a higher power. They will not be happy to see us. Anything can happen."

"I understand. I won't get in your way. But if she's hurt, I want to be there for her." Georgia turned to her mother and said, "Maybe Ally should go to a friend's house after school, at least until things settle down here."

"That's not a bad idea." Jody stood up. "I can call Samantha's mother. I'm sure she'll take Ally home with her."

"That might be wise. Yes, that might be best." Delia nodded.

"I'll do that right now, and then I'll call the school and let them know who Ally may leave with. They're used to me calling, so no one will be alarmed." Jody headed back to the kitchen to look up the necessary phone numbers.

"We'll be back," Georgia assured her mother. "With Laura. If she's there, we'll bring her back."

The rescue party of four headed out the door.

"Maybe we should take the rest of Gordon's crew with us," Georgia said to Matt.

"What rest of the crew?"

"You know, the big bald guy with the tattoo, and his buddy," Georgia said as she closed the door behind her.

"Who is she talking about?" Gordon frowned and turned to Delia. "I don't have any 'big bald guy' on my crew . . ."

chapter twenty-five

The drive to the house on Manor Road was, for the most part, a quiet one, what little conversation there was being restricted to Jeremy's asking directions and Matt giving them. At the top of the road, just off the highway, several houses had been built since Matt had last been there. He cautioned Jeremy to slow down until he got his bearings.

"What will we do when we get there?" Georgia asked.

"What do you mean, what will we do?" Matt frowned.

"How will you know if Laura's there? If she is, she won't be by herself."

"I think we need to see what the situation is when we arrive." Jeremy pulled slightly to the shoulder of the road to let a car pass. "How much farther?"

"Just past those trees," Matt leaned forward and pointed, "on the right. It's a two story gray stucco house . . . right there. Slow down."

The house was set back slightly from the road, a

449

pleasant-looking house with black shutters and a flagstone path leading from the driveway to the front door. A trellis next to the front door served as support for a climbing rosebush upon which dozens of large red roses bloomed. Flower boxes spilled over with red and white petunias.

The foursome in the car drove past slowly.

"This is really strange," Matt said. "That does not look like an abandoned house."

"Maybe it's been sold." Tucker suggested.

"I think Laura would have mentioned that. And I'd bet my life that my sister has not set eyes on this place since the day she moved back to the inn."

"Then who's been taking care of it? The grass has been cut, the flowers in the front there are obviously newly planted." Georgia frowned as they slowly passed the house.

"Well, maybe Gary has rented it. It would give him a little income while he's in prison," Jeremy said thoughtfully.

"Someone's in there," Georgia pointed back at the house as they drove on down the road at a snail's pace. "There's a blue light—there, in the back of the house."

"Looks like someone is watching TV." Tucker turned to look. "Jeremy, find a place to turn around. Take another swing past the house."

"I have an idea," Georgia announced. "Why not let me drive, and on the way back, I'll come to a real slow stop, just in case someone's looking out the window . . ."

"Why?"

"So that when I walk up to the door and ring the

bell and say that my van just died on me and could I please use the phone to call my husband, it will look credible. That way, I'll get to see who or what is in there."

"Georgia, you're not going near that house." Matt shook his head. "Not under any circumstances."

"Matt's right. That's out of the question." Tucker turned his head to look back toward the house.

"Does anyone have a better idea?" Georgia asked.

"I thought we'd get out here, go through the woods to the house, and see what's going on." Jeremy pulled the van to a stop on the other side of the woods and turned in his seat to face Georgia. "I was figuring on having you drive, though."

"But supposing someone sees you. What if you startle someone and they get nervous," Georgia protested. "They might hurt Laura."

"And supposing *you* startle someone and they get nervous," Matt said. "They might hurt both of you."

"First things first. We need to establish who is in that house," Tucker told them, "so a little surveillance is the first order of business here. Jeremy, I think you and I will go through the woods to the back of the house and we'll see what we can see from there."

"What about me?" Matt asked.

"You'll stay with Georgia," Tucker told them as he removed his miniature field glasses from his jacket pocket. "Jeremy, do you have any equipment in this van?"

"I have some infrared glasses," Jeremy nodded. "I think that's all we'll need this time around."

"Tucker, if you think that you're going to leave me

in the van while you and Mr. Private Eye launch a big rescue . . ."

"Nobody's launching a rescue immediately. We'll be back in less than twenty minutes and hopefully by then we'll have an idea as to whether or not Laura is in that house. If she is, we'll need you to help get her out. Right now . . ."

"Right now, you're wasting time, and I'm going with you." Matt said tersely.

Tucker sighed. The last thing they needed was an inexperienced man crashing through the woods.

"Matt, it's daylight. It's going to be difficult enough for Jeremy and me to get close enough to that house to see what's going on, and we've both been in situations like this before."

"I'll just follow your lead," Matt told him, "but I'm going. I won't do anything that would jeopardize my sister."

Tucker shrugged, then turned to Georgia and said, "I don't want the van sitting here while we're gone, so I'm going to ask you to drive the van down the road for about ten minutes, waste a little time, then turn around and come back slowly. But don't drive past the house. If someone is in there and is watching the road, they might get suspicious if they saw us go by the first time. We'll meet you here in about twenty minutes."

"Okay," she nodded, and took the driver's seat as Jeremy hopped down. "Be careful, guys."

"You too." Matt leaned over and kissed her on the cheek. "Pray that she's in there."

"I will." She squeezed his arm as he got out of the van. "What do I do if you don't come back?"

"We'll be back," Tucker told her as he closed the door.

Georgia watched the three men disappear into the dense woods, then shifted the van into drive and pulled onto the road. It was twenty minutes to four on an overcast afternoon. She drove slowly down the narrow two-lane road, past several farms and a new cul-de-sac where ranch-style homes had recently been built, the development still new enough that several of the front yards were still more mud than lawn. A gas station sat across from a fruit stand where handwritten cardboard signs boasted local strawberries for sale. She pulled in to the fruit stand and bought several quarts of fresh berries, checking her watch as she walked back to the van. Three forty-seven.

Georgia drove across the road to the gas station and pulled up in front of the full-serve bay. The attendant, who looked to be no more than fifteen, came out of the small office area and shuffled across the parking lot to the van.

"Hi," she smiled.

"Whatcha need?" he asked dully, obviously annoyed at having had to get up and walk a whole twenty feet to the pump.

"Fill it, please."

Georgia watched the young man through the rearview mirror as he took his time opening the gas tank. She drummed her fingers on the steering wheel to keep them moving and give them something to do besides shake. The clock on the dash said three forty-eight. She pulled out her wallet and opened the door, hopping down and heading toward the soda machine near the door to the office. She counted out her coins and slipped them into the slot, then pushed a button to make her selection. Nothing happened. She banged impatiently on the machine.

"It don't work," the attendant told her, coming up behind her and causing her to jump nearly out of her skin. "That's nine dollars for the gas."

Georgia fought an urge to smack him. He could have told her before she plunked her last quarters into the machine. Instead, she took a five and four ones from her wallet and handed them to him before getting back into the van. Three fifty-one.

She headed slowly back down the road, the butter-flies in her stomach having turned into something more menacing and the ache in her chest causing her pain. She reached her destination with two minutes to spare. Letting the engine idle, she watched the woods with her heart in her mouth. Three minutes later, she was startled by Jeremy's appearance at her window. Followed by Matt and Tucker, Jeremy had come from behind the van, rather than the front where she had been watching.

"What's going on?" she asked as the three men got back into the van.

"Well, as closely as we can see, there are four people inside the house. One of them," he said, his dark eyes narrowing, "is Laura. She's in the kitchen, on a chair. There do not appear to be any guards outside the house, though, which will make it a little easier."

"How will we get her out?" Georgia asked. "Shouldn't we call the police and have them take it from here?"

"This is a rural area where it's unlikely the police have had experience in situations like this." Tucker shook his head. "I think our best bet is for us to get her out fast and dirty before anyone knows what happened. Jeremy, what do you think?"

"I have to agree with you. My instincts tell me that we are Laura's best bet."

"Matt?"

"Have either of you been in a situation like this before?" Matt asked warily.

"Actually, I have," Tucker told him coolly.

"Well, that probably puts you one up on the local guys—all four of them. It could take us all day to convince them that Laura's in there against her will, and another day while they figure out what to do about it. I'm with you. The sooner she's out of there, the better."

"I think we need to distract them for a few minutes while we go in through the back door." Tucker said to Jeremy.

"How are we going to do that?" Matt frowned.

"How 'bout if Georgia just drives toward the house, pretends to have car trouble, and pulls the van over to the side of the road in the vicinity of the house. Then she gets out, raises the hood, pretends to be looking at something. Maybe one of them will watch from the window, maybe even come out to offer a hand . . ."

Matt frowned. "Why aren't I driving the van and getting out?"

"Because she's prettier than you are." Jeremy said. "At the very least, I think they'll be watching her, and with any luck, it will draw their attention from the back of the house long enough for me to pick the lock on that side door."

"What happens once you get inside there?" Georgia asked. "They might have guns."

"I'm sure they do," Tucker said.

"Well, what will you do if they start to shoot at you?" She grimaced.

"Shoot back," Tucker told her calmly. "Ready, Jeremy?"

"Yes. Georgia, give us five minutes, then drive. Go really slow, start and stop a few times in case someone is looking out the window."

"Don't worry. I can do this," she said confidently.

"Great. Tucker?" Jeremy asked.

"Let's do it," Tucker slid from the side door of the van and walked toward the woods, then turned back and called softly back to the van, "If all goes well, this will be over within ten, fifteen minutes."

"And if it doesn't go well?" Georgia turned to face Matt.

"I think we're going to have to trust them," he told her.

"Jeremy has never let my mother down before. And I think that Tucker would walk through fire for Laura."

She had no way of knowing that before the day would end, Tucker would do exactly that.

Georgia drove the van slowly, stopping and starting fitfully, as Tucker had suggested. As she neared the house, she began to let it roll to a stop on the side of the road.

"Here goes," she whispered to Matt, who was in the rear, windowless section of the panel van.

"Georgia . . ."

"I'll be fine." She hopped out and slammed the door.

Lifting the hood of the van, she peered this way and that, pretending to know what she was looking at. Leaving the hood up, she stood, hands on her hips, looking up and down the road.

"How long have we been here?" she hissed through her teeth in the direction of the open door.

"About three minutes," Matt told her.

"Guess I'd better go look at the engine again."

Returning to the front of the van, she peered once again into the engine, reaching a hand in and pretending to touch or turn the various hoses and gizmos.

"I guess it would help if I knew a little something about car engines," she muttered, wiping her greasy fingers onto her jeans, and pacing back the length of the van.

"Matt, this is stupid. It doesn't make any sense at all that a woman would just pace back and forth."

"Get in and make like you're starting the engine again," he suggested.

"That oughta kill a few seconds," she told him as she swung herself back through the open door and turned the key.

"Does it look as if anyone is watching from the house?" Matt asked.

"I can't really tell. There are curtains on the windows, but without staring at the house, there's no way to know." She tapped her fingers on the steering wheel for a long moment. "If they are watching, they must think I'm a moron."

She jumped back down from the van and peeked back under the hood. She paced along the side, kicking a stone with the toe of her right foot.

A woman would not just pace back and forth. She would ask for help. If anyone is watching, they have to be wondering why I'm not asking for help.

Georgia glanced up the drive at the tidy house, trying to picture herself walking across the grass and up to the front door, ringing the doorbell . . .

She really didn't want to do that.

"I should have driven more erratically. I should have plowed over the mailbox so someone would have come out . . ." She blew an exasperated breath from her lungs.

"I think it's a little late," Matt told her.

"Matt, is Jeremy's cell phone still on the seat?" she asked.

"Yes."

"What's the number?"

"Why do you want to know?"

"Just tell me . . ."

She could hear him shuffling, moving on the floor to grab the phone without being seen from outside the van.

"555-8720."

Her hands on her hips, she paced a few more times. "555-8720. 555-8720. 555-8720 . . ."

"Matt, is the phone turned on?" She bent down next to the van, as if to tie her sneaker.

"No."

"Turn it on."

"Why?"

"So that you can answer it when it rings."

"Who do you think will be calling?"

"Someone from in there. In the house . . ."

"Georgia . . ." He sprang forward in alarm.

"Keep down!" she told him. "Listen, Matt, we have to create a distraction . . ."

"Let me do it."

"Right. And where have you been while I've been fiddling around with the cockamamie engine for the past ten minutes?" Her heart was pounding and her stomach began to knot even as she spoke. "This isn't working. Nothing is happening, and the longer I pace back and forth with nothing happening, the more suspicious someone in that house is going to get. We need to distract them for real."

"Georgia, you heard Tucker . . . you can't go in the house," he hissed at her, frustrated because what he wanted to do was jump out of the van and shake her.

"I'm not going in, Matt. I'm going to knock on the door and say that I'm having engine trouble. I won't ask to use the phone, I'm going to ask whoever answers the door to call my husband for me and give him directions to come and get me." Saying it aloud had made it sound so reasonable. "See? What could be easier? And when the phone rings, you answer it and keep them on the line as long as you can."

"It's a stupid idea."

"*Stupid* is me pacing endlessly. This is a great idea. And do you have a better way of bringing at least one of them to the front of the house? Speak now, Matt. Nobody needs this much time to tie a shoe."

When he didn't respond, she said, "That's what I thought."

"Georgia, it doesn't feel right."

"Just sound concerned when the call comes," she ignored him. "Ask for directions . . ."

"Georgia . . ."

"Five minutes, Matt. That's all this should take."

Her heart pounding like wild jungle drums in her ears, she willed her legs to carry her to the front steps of the house and up to the landing, rehearsing what she'd say. *Hi, I'm sorry to bother you. My van broke down . . .*

"555-8720, 555-8720," she whispered to herself as she rang the doorbell, then jammed her hands into her jeans pockets to hide the fact that they were shaking so badly.

There was movement at one of the front windows, a curtain moved imperceptibly. Hushed voices from behind the door. Footsteps on hardwood. The unlatching of the inside door.

A tall, thin, intense looking man dressed in black jeans and a black T-shirt stared at her from the other side of the screen door.

"I'm sorry to disturb you," she forced her most engaging smile, "but it seems my engine just cut out on me. Just stopped dead. I can't imagine what's wrong with it . . . I just stopped down the road there not a mile or so and filled it with gas, so I know it has fuel. I was wondering, if perhaps I could impose on you to call my husband for me and ask him to come get me?"

"Call him yourself." The man stepped back and opened the screen door, inviting her in.

"Oh, well, I really don't want to impose on you or your family . . ." She started to back up slightly. She hadn't anticipated this. "I'll just give you the number. It's 555- . . ."

A long, strong arm reached through the open door to grab onto her own and pull her through the front door into the foyer.

On the bottom step of the stairwell leading to the second floor sat a man similarly dressed in black. He had a rifle resting across his knees, a tattoo of a sword running up his arm, and a bald head.

"Well, well, now, isn't this a coincidence?" he chuckled without humor, his voice a fathomless baritone. "Fancy meeting you here. Step back, there, Ronnie, and let the young lady in . . ."

Speechless, Georgia stared at the man she had seen on the front porch of the inn.

"I guess you've come to visit with Mrs. Harmon," he said as he stood up. "I'm sure she'll love to have your company. Take her on back and give her a seat, Ronnie. I think I'll just stay here for a time and keep an eye on that van. I have the feeling that sooner or later, someone's going to get curious about the little lady who just popped in."

"Why are you doing this?" Georgia fought her anxiety, forcing air into her lungs and words to come from her mouth.

"Happy is the man who fears the Lord, who is only too willing to follow his orders," was the reply.

Georgia stared at the large man, whose eyes had taken on a dark fire. Her mind began to spin.

"Listen, this is not a good idea," she protested as a third man—identically dressed except for the addition of a black cap—began to pull her toward the back of the house. "For either of us. First of all, you should be smart enough to figure out that I'm not alone. There are . . . *eight* FBI officers outside. They all have guns and they're all crack shots. If you let Laura go . . . and me, too, of course . . . things will go much easier for you. You know, I'll bet . . ."

Bald Head-Tattoo slapped a piece of tape over her mouth.

"Let the woman learn in silence with all subjection."

Two strong hands lifted her, kicking and swinging, and carried her into the kitchen, where she was dumped unceremoniously onto a wooden chair with a hard seat.

"Mmurphh!" came from her throat as she hit the seat. When Black Cap pulled her arms back behind the chair and stepped to one side to bind them with thick cord, she looked across the table, into Laura's eyes, which, already filled with terror, now began to fill with tears at the realization that she was no longer the only prisoner in this nightmare.

"Mmurphh!"

Black Cap laughed, then became somber as Bald Head-Tattoo came into the room, a small black portable tape recorder in his hand.

"Silence," he told Georgia as he placed the black plastic box on the counter three feet from Laura's face.

All three men gathered in the kitchen, standing at attention, their hands folded in front of them, their eyes closed, as if in a trance. Several long moments passed, and Georgia took the opportunity to try to give Laura courage. She winked, several times, hoping that Laura would understand that she meant *Everything will be okay, help is here,* but Georgia wasn't sure that she got the message.

Suddenly the one they had called Ronnie stepped forward and turned on the tape.

Soft music played, then came the voice.

"The people that walked in darkness have seen a great light: they that dwell in the land of the shadow of death, upon them hath the light shined."

"Amen." The three captors nodded in unison.

Laura's eyes went wide at the sound of the voice, and Georgia knew that she was listening to the smooth, oh-so-hypnotic voice of the Reverend Gary Harmon.

"The Spirit of the Lord is upon me . . . To bind up the brokenhearted, to proclaim liberty to the captives, and the opening of the prison to them that are bound; To proclaim the acceptable year of the Lord, and the day of vengeance of our God . . ."

"Thank you, Master," Black Cap muttered, and Georgia shifted her eyes to watch his face, which had, she concluded, *wacko* written all over it in great big letters.

The voice droned on.

"All wickedness is but little to the wickedness of a woman . . ."

Oh, brother, Georgia rolled her eyes and tried to stretch her neck enough to peer around Ronnie to see if she could see out the window. It wasn't until he lowered his head as if in prayer that she realized the bottom half of the window had a curtain on it.

"I will show unto thee the judgment of the great whore . . ."

Laura's eyes squeezed shut as if blocking out sight would block out sound.

Okay, guys. Tucker. Jeremy. It's time. Big rescue now. Please. We're ready. Right now, before someone gets hurt—

"Mystery, Babylon the Great, the Mother of Harlots and abominations of the earth . . ."

No secret where old Gary's coming from.

"And a mighty angel took up a stone like a great millstone, and cast it into the sea, saying, Thus with violence shall that great city Babylon be thrown down, and shall be found no more at all . . ."

"They're here," Bald Head-Tattoo said softly from behind her.

"What therefore God hath joined together, let not man put asunder."

"It's time," Black Cap said.

Two of the three men left the room, but because the third was behind her, Georgia could not see who it was or what he was doing. Laura could, however. She began to rock in the chair, shaking her head, strangling sounds coming from her throat, her face reflecting sheer terror. Georgia struggled to turn in her chair, but could not.

What? What? she tried to yell. What . . . what was that smell?

Her nostrils picked up the scent long before her brain acknowledged and identified it.

Gasoline.

"Behold, I will make thee a terror to thyself, and to all thy friends . . ."

464

Georgia heard the crackle of fire and smelled the smoke at the same time she heard a door slam, a bolt slide into a lock. Laura began to sob, shaking her head, her eyes filled with apology and regret and fear. Smoke rapidly filled the small room, and the only real item on Georgia's agenda became oxygen, her neck craning as her air passages sought to flee the thick white cloud that surrounded her.

It was then that Georgia decided she wasn't going without a fight.

She looked around frantically, seeking a way out. Maybe if she and Laura could get their chairs back to back, they could untie each other's hands.

Georgia sought to scooch her chair back from the table, but she was too close to the wall. She tried to move sideways, motioning to Laura to do the same, all the while feeling the intense heat move closer to her from behind. From someplace, somewhere, she heard loud crackling sounds, voices shouting, a door slamming. At that moment, nothing mattered but that she and Laura could get close enough to each other that one could attempt to untie the other.

"*We have made a covenant with death, and with hell we are at agreement . . .*" the voice continued. "*The wages of sin is death . . .*"

They had worked their chairs almost to a point where they were back to back, when hands lifted her, chair and all, from the floor. Suddenly the door had somehow opened, and sweet, fresh air poured into the room. Georgia gulped at it greedily. She was aware of being carried, of seeing daylight, of a *whoosh* of flame behind her. Fingers worked at the sides of her mouth to remove the tape, and when it was pulled from her face, the resultant sting was as welcome to her as the fresh air had been. To feel was to be alive.

"Laura . . ."

"Tucker has her." Matt told her as he began to loosen the ropes that bound her hands.

"What the hell took you so long?" she gasped.

"Later." He pulled the rope from her feet and lifted her with one hand. "Let's get out of here before that place blows . . ."

They had almost made it to the opposite side of the road when the first explosion hit, throwing them both face first into a ravine. A second, larger, explosion, blasted the front door off. From somewhere in the distance, a siren began to wail.

"Laura . . ." She sat bolt upright, then sought to stand on legs wobbly with fright.

"She's fine. Look. There, down the road . . ."

Georgia squinted through the billowing smoke with eyes already sorely irritated by smoke. "Where's Jeremy?"

"He's here someplace. I'm sure he got out." Matt gathered her into his arms and held her. It was then that she began to cry, softly at first.

"Matt . . . Matt . . ." She was shaking all over.

"Shush. It's done, sweetheart. It's over."

"Those men were so crazy—" Shock taking over, Georgia began to babble. "They had this tape of Gary Harmon. I know it was him, I could see it in Laura's face . . . calmly reading verses from the Bible . . . And gasoline. Matt, I could smell gasoline . . ."

Matt began to rock her, rubbing his cheek on hers, his arms beginning to shake even as she had, as the reality of what had happened began to sink in. Her life had come down to a matter of seconds. He'd almost lost her. And Laura. The enormity of it rattled him to his soul.

"You two all right?" Jeremy called to him from the road, where the fire trucks and an ambulance had come to a screeching halt.

"Scared. Shaken. I think Georgia's in shock." Matt said, his mouth still dry from fear.

"Stay right here." Jeremy told him.

He was back in less than a minute with a paramedic who carried blankets in one arm and pulled a folded gurney on wheels with the other.

Matt took the blankets and wrapped them around Georgia, snuggling her into his body and holding on to her for dear life.

"Help me lift her," Georgia heard the paramedic say, "and we'll get her onto the gurney . . ."

"No, no," she pushed herself closer into Matt. "I just want to go home . . ."

"We should check your burns," the young man told her.

"I don't have any burns. I just want to go home. Or back to the inn. Matt, we need to call the inn. We need to let Mom know . . ."

"I think we need to talk to these gentlemen first," Matt told her, raising himself slightly and calling to the policeman who was at that moment getting out of a black and white patrol car not ten feet away, "Officer, please, over here . . ."

It was hours before they were able to return to Bishop's Cove and the welcome warmth of the inn.

Delia had been white-knuckled and rigidly composed when they had arrived in the wee hours of the morning, and had all but fainted with relief when she saw that both her daughters, though frightened from the horror of their ordeal, had survived. Jody had made tea and served it in the sun room, where Laura had requested a fire be built in the fireplace so that she could, hopefully, get warm. Ally had awakened with the commotion and had climbed into her mother's lap. And there by her side, every minute, was Tucker.

As the sun began to rise, Delia shooed all to their rooms for well-needed rest.

"I forgot all about Spam," Georgia said wearily. "Spam's still in the little garden. She probably needs water. I should . . ."

"I'll call a neighbor," Matt said as he helped her to her feet. "Your piggy will be fine. Go get some sleep."

"You . . ." she began, and he cut her off.

". . . will be right here."

"Jody," Georgia called to her from the doorway.

Jody turned to her, a tray tucked under one arm.

"Save the cups," Georgia said as she yawned into her hand.

chapter twenty-six

Matt sat in the wing chair, his legs stretched out in front of him, his eyes burning with fatigue, every muscle in his body aching in the aftermath of the conflagration, but still, he could not sleep. All he could do, it seemed, was stare at the woman sleeping fitfully on the bed. Occasionally he would look out the window to the sky and whisper, "Thank you," to the heavens, but other than that—and his efforts to wet his lips with a mouth still dry from terror, neither actions requiring more than a small movement of his head—he was motionless.

They had spent hours at the police station, trying to explain how a man who was incarcerated hundreds of miles away had tried, unsuccessfully, to kill two women. The fact that the accomplices had seemingly vanished into thin air had not helped their case. It had taken calls to Delia's lawyers and several old friends of Jeremy's—federal law enforcement agents— to convince the local police that Laura and Georgia were not crazy, and that neither Tucker, Matt nor

Jeremy had torched the house, and that, inasmuch as kidnapping had been one of the crimes, the FBI should become involved. They were finally released after a telephone call from the warden at the prison where Gary was housed confirmed that, in his expert opinion, the former minister was, indeed, quite capable of such action, and did in fact have a widespread following of devotees who could be called upon to do his bidding. Whether or not those suspicions could be proven, whether or not those accomplices would ever be identified or located, whether or not there would, in time, be evidence sufficient to press charges, all remained to be seen.

Matt's tired brain ticked off the highlights of the past twenty-four hours as the clock ticked quietly on the bedside table in one of the guest rooms at the inn. The uneasy feeling that had settled over him as he watched Georgia walk toward the gray stucco house. The growing fear when he realized she had disappeared inside the house and the door had closed behind her. The agonizing wait as he counted the seconds, waiting for the cell phone to ring. The cold gnawing at his gut when it did not. His efforts to leave the van undetected, to find Tucker and Jeremy without being spotted by those inside the house. The sheer terror when the smoke began to pour from the downstairs windows. The slamming of his body against the front door, with no thought to fire or weapons in his single-minded need to reach her. The crackle of gun shots—he still wasn't sure whose. The crash of the door as he and Tucker brought it down.

The suffocating gray inside the house. The search through the cloud for the two women, following Tucker, who had seen them through a side window and managed to navigate Matt through the smoke to the kitchen. His heart stopping in his chest at his first glimpse of her in the chair, her back to him, her long golden hair dancing inches above the flames that encroached from behind. Jeremy's heroic efforts to get the back door open and lead them to safety . . .

That was the long version.

The short version was that his sister had been kidnapped by fanatical followers of an obsessed psychopath, and that she—along with his future wife—had been tied to chairs in a house that had been set on fire.

. . . his future wife.

He wondered how best to ask her. When to tell her.

Georgia stirred and shivered visibly. "Matt?" She called to him softly.

"I'm here, baby. Go back to sleep."

"It wasn't a dream . . ."

"No, love, it wasn't a dream. But it's over." He got up and smoothed the soft blanket over her shoulders.

"Will you stay with me?" she asked, drifting back into welcome oblivion.

"Always, sweetheart." He repeated the promise he had once made to her mother. "Always."

It had seemed that the questioning would go on forever. When Georgia awoke, she found not only the FBI, but local police and a dozen television reporters and their accompanying cameramen waiting for her and Laura so that the questioning could begin all over again. Delia had refused entry to the reporters, and had, effectively, closed the inn to all except Gordon and his crew.

Gary, too, had been questioned extensively from the dayroom of the prison. He staunchly proclaimed his innocence in a calm, benign manner clearly intended to make both Laura and Georgia appear to be crazy to even suggest such a thing. To the horror of everyone under the roof of the Bishop's Inn, one of the interviews ran on network television late on the following afternoon.

"Your wife claims that you have a legion of devoted followers—ex-convicts, all—in every state in the union, at your beck and call," the pretty young reporter said. "That three of these men kidnapped her and attempted to kill her and her sister."

"That's absurd. Where are these men now? Who are these men? Where did they disappear to? You've told me that only my wife and her sister were in the house when they were rescued. Did these men simply vanish into thin air?"

"They've found a tunnel leading from the basement into the woods. It's suspected that they escaped through the tunnel."

He waved a hand dismissively.

"I know nothing of any such tunnel. I won't deny that I minister to a forgotten flock, and on occasion, I have made my home available to followers of my ministry. But to suggest that I would use my position to harm someone . . ." he shook his head, knitting his eyebrows together in consternation, "particularly my beloved wife . . . I cannot imagine why she would say such a thing."

"Your wife claims that on several occasions she attempted to file for divorce."

"Yes. Yes, she has filed such actions in the past, but she has always had a change of heart. However, if she now wishes a divorce, she's certainly welcome to one."

"Just like that." It was clear the reporter wasn't convinced.

"Certainly."

"You would agree to it," the skeptical reporter persisted.

"Well, I am of the belief that marriage is a holy state. That once joined by God, a man and a woman are one for all eternity."

"But you're saying you would be willing to let her have a divorce anyway."

"If she wishes it, I cannot stop her."

"She claims that you threatened her, and her mother, and her daughter . . ."

"My daughter," he reminded her.

". . . every time she attempted to initiate such proceedings."

"I'm afraid my wife is a bit paranoid," he said calmly. "Putting aside for a moment the fact that I love her, in spite of her desire to terminate our marriage, I will always be devoted to her. She is, after all, the mother of my child, the woman to whom I have pledged myself. I do believe that those joined by God—made one *in* God, by God's law—cannot then be made separate by laws of men. All those things aside, even assuming that I wished her harm, what on earth could I do to her from behind bars, several states away?"

"I believe that's exactly the issue at the heart of the current investigation." The reporter turned back to the camera. "From inside the federal prison, I'm Carole Fox . . ."

Breakfast the following morning was a very late and somber affair, after which a physician brought in by Delia examined and chatted with first Laura, then Georgia.

"Just to check things out, sweetheart," Delia had assured Georgia, "since you both refused treatment last night. I just want to make certain that neither of you are harboring injuries that need tending to."

"I'm fine," Georgia assured her. "At least, I think I will be when the questioning is finished once and for all. I see the local police chief out there on the patio with Jeremy. How could there possibly be any other questions to be asked?"

"It does seem silly, doesn't it? I don't understand why all of these different agencies can't just get together and each of them concentrate on one aspect of the investigation, then sit down and share information. As it stands, with everyone doing their own, we are subjected to the same questions over and over. Which is fine, I suppose, when you're interrogating suspects, but you and Laura were the victims, and Matt, Jeremy and Tucker were the heroes."

"Is Laura totally traumatized by this whole experience?" Georgia leaned over and touched her mother's arm.

"I can't say that I blame her if she is. It's been a terrible burden for her to have carried around, Gary harassing her, threatening her, all the time trying to go about her business, raise her child, run the inn—not to mention the emotional trauma of having her mother so very ill. I'm hoping that Dr. Jeffers will prescribe a long rest for her. Not that I'd expect her to take one."

"I think she needs the comfort of the inn right now more than she needs to go away."

"And you, sweetie?" Delia leaned over and patted Georgia's hand. "What do you need right now?"

Georgia smiled, watching Matt jog across the front lawn, Artie trotting playfully at his heels.

"Oh, I think I just need to go back to Pumpkin Hill and watch a few good movies." Georgia smiled. "And I need to dance. Dancing would definitely help."

"Are you thinking about going back? Professionally, I mean." Delia raised a concerned eyebrow. Georgia had seemed so much happier now. She'd almost hate to see her go back to the troupe. Of course, if that was what she wanted . . .

"No. Not right now, anyway. I have a different agenda right now." Georgia sat down in the chair next to her mother. "I'm registered to attend a two-week workshop for dance instructors in New York. I leave next Thursday. I'm really looking forward to it. And I'm looking for a new location for my studio. Matt will be meeting with an architect tomorrow morning to go over the renovations to the barn for the new clinic."

"What a shame. You did so enjoy dancing there."

"I'll enjoy dancing wherever I go. Matt has dreamed of opening this clinic for years. I'm thrilled and excited for him. I don't mind if I have to find another place for my dancing school. Matt's clinic is much more important. I can find a storefront."

"Well, perhaps I could help you look . . ."

Georgia laughed. "Thank you, Mom, but I think I can find a place."

"Oh, but sweetie . . ."

"I'll be able to take care of it, Mom. I have the rent from my condo."

"Will you ask for my help if you need it? I'd be happy to float a business loan, you know."

"I promise, if I need help, I will ask." Georgia glanced at her watch, then frowned. "I hope Matt comes back soon. I had wanted to be back at the farm before evening. I want to stop and pick up my pig at the neighbors'. I'm sure Spam wonders where I am. I miss Pumpkin Hill, Mom. I understand totally why Laura and Matt want to keep it in the family. I can't wait to get back."

"And I hate for you to leave. I'm almost afraid to let you out of my sight," Delia hugged Georgia tightly to her. "I'm afraid to turn my back on either you or Laura. To think how close we came to losing you both—my first baby and my last . . ."

"Don't, Mom. It's done. Gary's being watched closely and I doubt that he'll try anything else. He's said on national TV that he'll give Laura her divorce. Finally, she'll be free of him."

Delia pushed a long strand of yellow hair back from her daughter's forehead and smoothed it behind one ear, just as she had a thousand times over the course of her lifetime. The thought that that precious life had come so dangerously close to being snuffed out—along with that of the daughter who had been lost to her for so long—made Delia physically ill every time she thought of the week's events. Later she would deal with that terror and the stress it had inflicted upon her. For now, she would be strong, unflappable, in charge, the way *the Mom* is supposed to be.

"Laura deserves a chance to be happy with someone who truly cares for her," Delia said, forcing calm into her voice. "As do you, my darling girl."

"I am happy with someone who truly cares for me, Mom." Georgia kissed her mother's cheek.

"I'll have to speak with Matt. I need to know that he will take good care of you."

"Now, Mother, I'm not sure that I need someone to take care of me. I'm a grown woman," Georgia reminded her.

"Darling, we all need to know that there's someone who can take care of us from time to time. Not to lean on, certainly, but in times of crisis it's good to know that there's someone you can trust, someone to just hold you up a little till the worst of it has passed."

"And what about you, Mother? Have you finally found someone to hold you up just a little, just till this passes?"

"Perhaps I have, sweetie," Delia smiled thoughtfully. "Perhaps I have."

"Mom, you've had a rough time these past few days, too. Now that this ordeal is over, I think you should think about taking a week or two off. On an island someplace, with nothing to do except lie on a beach and listen to the water lap against the shore."

"My thoughts exactly," Gordon appeared in the doorway. From his jacket pocket he pulled an envelope. "Plane tickets."

"Why, Gordon . . ." Delia turned to him, clearly taken off guard. "Tickets to where?"

"It's a surprise." He beamed. "Suffice it to say that Georgia has the right idea. You desperately need some time away, and I'm determined that you shall have it. Pack lots of beach wear. Think tropical. Think casual. Think the day after tomorrow."

"That soon? I'll need to pack . . ."

"Then I suggest we leave for Westboro first thing in the morning."

"But, Gordon, my girls . . ."

"Are fine now." His voice softened and he touched her arm gently. "Georgia is going back to her farm, and Laura is re-opening the inn tomorrow."

"But you had planned to have a new diver start this week . . ." Delia protested.

"Tucker will be here. I think I can safely leave things in his hands. As can you, my dear. You won't need to worry about Laura with Tucker here to watch after her."

"Mother, Gordon is absolutely right. You're out of excuses. You'll simply have to go," Georgia shrugged.

"Go where?" Laura joined them on the porch.

"Gordon is taking Mom on a trip. A getaway to a tropical beach." Georgia grinned.

"Wonderful," Laura nodded approvingly. "Where are you going?"

"I don't know. Gordon planned it. It's a surprise." Delia smiled as if still getting over the shock that someone had done for her what she might do for others.

"Will the trip require a passport?" Laura's dark hair slid from the clips that held it back from her face, and she raised her hands to re-secure the long strands.

"Yes," Gordon nodded.

"It will?" Delia turned to him, her eyebrows raised in a question.

"Yes. You do have one . . . ?"

"Of course. Hmmm. A tropical beach for which I'll need a passport—Mexico, perhaps?"

"Don't bother asking. I'm not going to spoil it for you. But I think you'll love it there." Gordon said.

"I'm sure I will." The smile spread slowly across Delia's face, one side to the other. "Oh, I'm certain I will. Well, I suppose I should call Mrs. Colson and have her ready a few things for me."

Delia winked at Gordon, then kissed both of her daughters' foreheads on her way into the inn.

"That's lovely that you've planned something special for Mom, Gordon," Georgia told him. "She's always doing such things for us. It's wonderful to see the tables turned."

"Your mother is such a very special lady. And she's been through so much over the past week. I think she needs a little time away. I was hoping you'd approve."

"Approve?" Georgia and Laura exclaimed in unison.

"I for one am delighted," Georgia assured him, and Laura nodded in agreement.

"Absolutely. Now," Georgia leaned forward and whispered, "you can tell us where you're taking her. We won't tell. Promise."

"Sorry, girls," he laughed. "It's a secret."

"But what if we need to get in touch with her . . ."

"Tucker has the phone number of the hotel where we'll be staying." Gordon laughed. "And don't think you'll sweet talk it out of him, either, Laura. He's been sworn to secrecy."

"Well, I guess it would take some of the thrill out of being swept away to a secret place if your children know where you're going." Laura conceded.

"Ah, there's Tucker coming up from the beach. Excuse me, I need to go over a few things with him before I leave." Gordon crossed the front porch with an easy stride and bounded down the steps and across the lawn.

"Now, is Gordon the most incredible man?" Georgia sighed. "The most perfect man for Mother?"

"He really is," Laura nodded enthusiastically. "And he does seem to adore her."

"And she is certainly sweet on him. And oh, to have him plan a romantic vacation for her . . ." Georgia sighed again. "I'm so happy for her. She deserves the very best."

"I think she's found the very best." Laura's eyes followed Gordon as he crossed the street and stood on the sidewalk talking to Tucker.

"And you!" Laura asked, her eyes taking on a bit of a mischievous glow. "When were you going to tell me about you and Matt?"

"Oh." Georgia grinned. "I was going to tell you,

that time Matt and I came to the inn to go over the plans for Zoey and Ben's party. But then, you were so pleased that we were just being pleasant to one another, that we thought maybe we'd put off telling you for a while. Since you almost seemed to think that somehow you were bringing us together, we thought we'd play it out."

"So?"

"So . . . what?"

"Is this a fling? An infatuation?"

"I am head over heels in love with him," Georgia admitted. "Hopelessly, totally . . ."

"Well." Laura sat back in her chair, not having been quite prepared for that response. "Well."

Georgia laughed.

"Well." Laura cleared her throat. "When I said I'd hoped that someday I'd be able to blend my two families, I'm not certain that this was what I had in mind."

"Does it bother you? Are you upset?" Georgia leaned forward to touch Laura's arm tentatively. It had never occurred to her that Laura would be less than thrilled.

"No. No, not at all. I'm very happy for you. I'm just surprised that so much happened that I was unaware of." Laura took both of Georgia's hands in hers. "I couldn't be happier for you. And Matt, I take it he feels the same way about you? Well, of course he does." She smacked her forehead with her open palm. "I guess anyone could see that. Came around pretty well, for a stubborn cuss, didn't he?"

"Remarkably well." Georgia laughed. "He couldn't

resist me. Laura, it's hard to explain, but it's almost as if we belong together, as if we were waiting for each other . . ."

"And to think, that if Delia hadn't found me, you wouldn't have found each other," Laura mused. "Funny how things work out, isn't it, how one thing leads to another?"

"Mom always said that life was a long chain. Everything that happens is just another link. That good can come out of the worst situations . . ."

Laura's gaze drifted past Georgia to the end of the drive, where Tucker was packing a duffel bag into the back of his car.

Georgia watched Laura's face.

"Seems Mom's not the only one who's falling for a sea-faring man," Georgia observed.

"Maybe, once this whole thing is over," Laura said softly.

"Laura, it *is* over. Gary is yesterday's news. You talked to Mom's lawyer, he's preparing the papers for you as we speak. Your divorce will go through without a hitch this time. The FBI is tracking Gary's cronies—they've identified the man with the bald head and the tattoo—and they'll be keeping an eye on him from now on. He can't hurt you, Laura. There's nothing he can do to you. It's time to move on. Tucker is a wonderful man and he's crazy about you. He risked his life for you, Laura . . ."

"So did you."

"That's different. You're my *sister*. I'd do the same for Zoey. You don't *think* in situations like that, you just *do*, when someone you love is at risk. And you pray that it turns out all right."

"You were really brave, Georgia, to march up to that door like that."

"Truthfully, I didn't expect for anything to happen. I really thought I could just ring the doorbell, and buy Tucker and Jeremy a little time to come around the back of the house." Georgia's stomach turned at the memory of it. "I never thought I'd end up in there with you."

"I'm so sorry, Georgia," Laura's eyes filled with tears. "I never would have had you in that danger. If I had thought for one second that things would have gone that far . . ."

"Laura, why didn't you tell anyone about the letters that Gary was sending you? Why didn't you at least let Matt know? Or me? If it hadn't been for Jody fishing them out of the trash, we would never have known."

"It sounds so stupid now. I just thought that as long as I did what Gary wanted me to do—stay married to him—that I could keep my mother and Ally safe. I just didn't want anyone hurt because of me." A look of pain crossed Laura's face, marring her beauty with it's shadow. "Look what I did to you. You could have been . . ."

"Don't ever say that. You did *nothing* to me. *Nothing*. Laura, *Gary* is responsible, not you. Don't ever for a minute think that anything that happened was your fault."

"Georgia, you could have been killed."

"So could you. But at his hand. Not yours." Georgia went over to Laura's chair and leaned against the arm. She stroked Laura's dark hair. "You are not responsible for his actions. I wish you had told someone when Gary first started harassing you. Maybe it would have stopped then, before it got out of hand. Maybe not. After seeing what he is capable of doing, I don't doubt for a minute that he'd have made good on his threats against you or Ally or your mother. I understand why that was a chance you didn't want to take. But I do not believe that you could have stopped him, not this past week, anyway."

"The whole thing is so insane. I still can't believe any of it really happened." Laura bit her bottom lip. "Georgia, he's had people *watching* me all this time."

"If Tucker hadn't come along, hadn't been staying here at the inn, we may never have found that out. Gary was apparently so crazed to think that you had another man . . ."

"And I didn't, Georgia. Not in the way Gary thought I did, anyway. I've been too afraid to even look at another man."

"Well, I hope you're over that, because that Tucker Moreland is one fine sight. Just look at him, Laura . . ." Georgia pointed toward the drive. "Great body, great face, and a man willing to fight dragons for you. What else could a woman ask for?"

"Nothing." Laura shook her head. "There is nothing else anyone could ever want in a man."

"Laura, show a little enthusiasm here. We're talking about a man to die for." Georgia leaned over and tilted Laura's face upward so that she could read its expression. "Oh, no. What's that face for?"

"He just has to think I'm the stupidest woman in the world." Laura got up and began to pace.

"Because you let a psychopathic bully frighten you?"

"Because I married the psychopath in the first place."

"Laura, when you met Gary, was he outwardly manipulative?"

"No, of course not."

"Did he threaten and abuse you?"

"Certainly not. I never knew what he was really like. I never knew what he was doing . . ."

"Then why would Tucker—or anyone, for that matter—hold it against you?"

"I just feel as if I should have known somehow. That maybe there were signs that I missed, things that I overlooked . . ."

"Laura, you're being too hard on yourself. You didn't know. Let it go. Move on with your life. It's time." Georgia smiled. "The future is glorious. I read it in your tea leaves."

"When?"

"Do you remember after we got back here, after the police station, Jody brought us all tea? I told her to save the cups. She did. She even remembered which was whose. I read them this morning." Georgia hesitated for a few seconds, then asked, "So, aren't you curious? Don't you want me to tell you what I saw?"

"Okay." Laura tried to force a smile.

"Well, for starters, there was a dragon. Near the rim, which as you know is a significant placement."

"What does a dragon mean?"

"It means that there are new beginnings ahead," Georgia took Laura's hand, "that wonderful opportunities will come to you after some challenges."

"Well, I hope it means past challenges. I think I've

had all I can deal with for a while." Laura nodded. "What else did you see?"

"I saw a sun, which is a symbol for great happiness."

"Anything else?"

Georgia watched Tucker slam the trunk of the car before he headed back to the inn.

"I saw another horse's head."

"You did not," Laura's eyes widened. "You're making that up!"

Georgia laughed, then kissed her sister on the cheek.

"Meet him halfway, Laur," Georgia whispered in her ear. "Don't let him leave without knowing that he matters, that he has a place in your life."

"He does. I don't want him to leave."

"You're going to have to tell him that."

Georgia waved to Tucker and stood back to let Laura pass.

"Tucker," Laura called to him. "Wait . . ."

Whistling, Georgia went inside the inn to look for Matt. It was time for them, too, to get on with their lives, to put the nightmare of the past week behind them, and to go back to Pumpkin Hill.

chapter twenty-seven

From somewhere beyond the kitchen window, a wren was singing a long and cheerful song. Georgia leaned her elbows on the sill to listen. It was bliss to be at Pumpkin Hill early in the morning, alive and well and grateful for all of it.

Especially alive, she reminded herself as she unlocked the back porch door and stepped outside. She frowned. Matt's truck was gone. He wouldn't have gone back to Shawsburg without telling her. Georgia went back into the kitchen, and scanned the counters. Had he left a note that she had missed? The counters were empty. She was just about to go back upstairs to look for a note there, when she heard the truck drive up.

"Hey!" Matt called to her as he opened the passenger door and lifted out a dark bundle. "Spammy just had her first truck ride."

Matt placed the little pig on the ground and she raced to Georgia, grunting loudly all the way as if complaining about the fact that she'd been left with strangers and scolding Georgia for not coming to get her sooner.

"Oh, Spam," Georgia laughed and dropped to her knees, the pig trying her best to climb into her lap. "I'm glad to see you, too. I missed you."

She looked up at Matt. "I never thought I'd see the day when I'd be hugging a pig."

"This pig doesn't seem to know that she's a pig. My theory is that she's been spending too much time with Artie. I think he's been trying to teach her how to be a good dog. Maybe she should be hanging out with other little piggies once in a while so she learns proper pig behavior." Matt leaned down and scratched Spam's snout.

"I think you're right. She does become awfully indignant when we let Artie come into the house and we make her stay out on the back porch."

"Maybe you could just let her stay in the kitchen," Matt suggested. "Just give her a try. You're going to have to find a warm shelter for her come the winter anyway. She wouldn't survive the cold out there on the porch."

"Okay, we'll give her a little try while we have breakfast." Georgia picked up the pig and carried her up the steps.

Matt opened the back door, and they went into the kitchen. Georgia put the pig on the floor. Spam did not move. She sniffed at the vinyl tile floor, it's texture unfamiliar, before taking a few tentative steps. She craned what little neck she had this way and that, then, apparently not willing to stray too far from the familiar world on the other side of the screen door, backed up and sat down with a huff next to Artie and nuzzled him with her snout.

"If she could wag that tail, she would," Matt laughed.

"She does look quite pleased with herself, doesn't she?"

"You know, I owe you an apology." Matt reached out and took Georgia into his arms.

"That there are no pancakes for breakfast this morning?"

"No. Remember when I said that I just couldn't see you having a pig for a pet? I have to eat my words. Oddly enough, Spam really does seem to be the perfect pet for you." He kissed her temple. "And there's another thing I was wrong about. You really do belong here at Pumpkin Hill. As a matter of fact, I was so wrong about everything about you . . ."

"I was wondering when you'd 'fess up." She folded her arms across her chest. "It's about time."

"I figured I should do some penance . . ."

"Oooh! Do I get to choose?" Her eyes brightened at the prospect. "Anything I want?"

"I guess it's only fitting." Matt shrugged.

"Hmmm. I'll have to work on this one. It's important that I come up with just the right thing."

"I understand. Take your time."

"I have it." She snapped her fingers with glee. "Do you remember me telling you that my mother wrote a series of detective novels?"

"Sure. The guy's name was Harry or something."

"Harvey. Harvey Shellcroft."

"Right."

"Well, about six or so years ago, they were all made into TV movies."

"They were?"

"Yup. All twenty-three of them."

"With an all-star cast, one can only hope, the best director, producer . . ."

"Think of the worst B movie you've ever seen. Then cheese it up. Overwrite, overdirect . . . over-act . . ."

"No. You wouldn't . . . you couldn't be so cruel . . ."

"Your penance is to watch every one of those movies over and over again. Of course, I'll have to watch them with you, just to make sure that you don't cheat."

"Oh, of course. I can't be trusted when it comes to things like that."

"Maybe we'll have to watch one this afternoon."

"Well, that could prove a little embarrassing. You see, the architect will be here by one . . ." Matt reminded her.

"It's only nine."

"In that case, perhaps we should watch one now."

"I think that's a really good idea. Yes, that will surely go a long way in teaching me not to make snap judgments."

She pulled him toward the front hall, closing the kitchen door behind them to keep the animals from wandering around the house.

"I should tell you . . . that is, it just occurred to me that I don't happen to have any of those movies with me at this particular time."

Matt looked pensive. "We'll just have to do a practice run."

"Good idea," Georgia grinned. "Upstairs or down?"

"Oh, upstairs. Aunt Hope's old Eastlake sofa just wasn't built for what I have in mind . . ."

The architect was, thankfully, forty minutes late. Matt and Georgia were just coming down the steps when the dark blue station wagon arrived.

"I guess this means lunch will be a little late," Matt frowned.

"I have to drive into town anyway," Georgia told him. "I haven't been food shopping in a week."

She opened the kitchen door and Artie leaped through it and raced to the front door. Matt grabbed him by the collar on his way toward the front dining room and redirected the dog to the backyard. Spam, on the other hand, sat patiently by the back door.

"Oh, aren't you a good little girl?" Georgia laughed. "Are you trying to prove your manners are better than You-Know-Who's? And that you should be permitted to sleep in the house and he should sleep on the back porch? Well, maybe just in the kitchen. We'll see how well you do tonight. But don't get any ideas about the rest of the house. Strictly off limits to pigs."

Georgia gathered her handbag and her sunglasses, then carried Spam outside where she set her down on the grass. She waved to Matt, who was standing near the barn door with the architect, to let him know that she was leaving for Tanner's. She got into the Jeep and turned it around, pausing just for a moment to look at him. His back was to her, and he was pointing out something to the architect. Her heart swelled in her chest. She loved him so very much.

How, she wondered, did anyone manage to contain so much happiness, so much joy, as that which filled her at that moment?

I do believe that that's why music was invented in the first place, she thought as she turned the Jeep around and took off for town, as a celebration of the spirit. And so that we'd have something to dance to. Perhaps when she returned, she might have time to take a favorite Chopin piece up to the second floor of the barn, where she could set her joy to music.

Sunday brought an early morning shower, but by ten the sun had burned the moisture from the ground. Georgia had waited for this day. Matt was tense, she could tell, though he denied it, and she tried to set him at ease by telling him blond jokes.

"She was so blond, that where it said 'sign here,' she wrote *Gemini.*"

He had given her only the weakest of smiles.

"Did you hear the one about the blond who sent a fax with a stamp on it?"

A slight nod of the head.

"How 'bout the blond who spent twenty minutes staring at the orange juice carton because it said *concentrate?*"

A mere twitch of the corner of one side of his mouth.

Georgia gave up and settled back into her seat. Maybe he just needed to work through his apprehension by himself. Before they left the house, she had assured him that things wouldn't be as bad as he seemed to fear they might be, but he hadn't seemed convinced.

After that, the drive to Riverview was mostly a quiet one. Instead of the raucous music he generally played on the radio, he had slipped a tape into the tape player in the dashboard.

"Oh, I love this song," Georgia told him as Fleetwood Mac's "Landslide" began to play. "It's one of my favorites."

Matt merely nodded absently.

He parked the pickup in the visitors' lot, and sat with his hands across the steering wheel for a long moment before turning off the engine.

"Ready?" he asked, his voice raspy.

"Yes." Georgia nodded.

She reached for his hand as they walked up to the front door, and she gave it a squeeze. The squeeze she got in return was halfhearted.

"Mom's room is down here to the right, but she's usually in the dayroom around this time."

"Then let's just go there."

"Georgia, I should tell you that my mother . . . well, she may say things that don't make a lot of sense. She . . ."

"Matt, it's all right. You don't have to keep explaining."

"But I wanted you to understand." He ran his fingers through his hair in frustration, and paced in front of the dayroom door. "She didn't used to be like this. She used to be funny and smart and clever . . ."

She raised her fingers to his lips. "I know she was, Matt. I'm sorry I didn't know her then. But I can know her now."

"Next time you come, she won't even remember meeting you. She doesn't even remember me."

"Then we'll introduce ourselves." She stood on her tiptoes and took his face in her hands. "I'm not minimizing her condition, and I'm not trying to depreciate the extent of your loss. But we can't change what is. She's your mother, Matt. If we have to reintroduce ourselves every weekend for the next twenty years, then that's what we'll do. Let's just accept what is."

He nodded, and opened the door, holding it for her. They stepped inside the brightly lit room and he looked around.

"There she is. In the wheelchair. Near the windows . . ."

Matt grabbed a chair in each hand and led the way to the back of the room where wide expanses of glass overlooked a broad lawn and beyond, swiftly flowing water.

"Hello, Mrs. Bishop." Georgia took one of the chairs from Matt's hand and placed it in front of the wheel chair, and peered into the sweet face of the tiny white haired woman who sat there.

"Hello." Charity nodded pleasantly.

"My name is Georgia."

"That's a pretty name."

"Thank you." Georgia dropped her handbag on the floor. "Charity is a pretty name, too."

"I think I used to know someone named Charity, once." The old woman's face skewed into a frown.

"That's your name," Matt told her. "You are Charity."

"I am?" She looked puzzled for a long moment, then shook her head slightly as if to clear it and said, "Are you certain?"

"Yes. I'm certain." Matt positioned his chair next to hers and sat down.

"It seems like such a silly thing to forget . . ." Charity still appeared unconvinced.

They visited for almost an hour, Matt bringing his mother up to date on the family, avoiding, of course, the events of the past week, even though it was clear that she had no idea what, or whom, he was talking about. But he was never quite sure that maybe something—a word, a name—wouldn't spark her memory, so he always told her all the news from Bishop's Cove, all the news from O'Hearn.

"Mom, do you remember the book lady?" he asked as they prepared to leave.

"The book lady?" Charity thought for a moment. "Yes. The book lady."

"Georgia is the book lady's daughter." Matt told her.

"Oh. That's nice." Charity nodded agreeably.

"We're going to get married, Mom."

Charity seemed to ponder this. "You're going to marry the book lady? Will she still come and read to us?"

"No, Mom, I'm marrying the book lady's daughter. Georgia." He pointed to her.

"Will she still come to read to us?" Charity redirected her concern to Georgia.

"Yes, I'm certain that she will."

"Oh, that's good," Charity smiled. "I like it when the book lady comes to read."

"I'll tell her you said so." Georgia bent down and hugged the frail woman in the wheelchair. For one long moment, Charity's expression changed completely, the lines in her face seeming to ease and a faint twinkle lighting her eyes.

"Oh," she exclaimed, "a hug! I haven't had a hug in a very long time."

"Then you should have another one," Georgia hugged Charity again, suspecting that the old woman had had plenty of hugs, and saddened that she'd forgotten. "We'll be back next weekend. At least, Matt will be. I'm going to New York. To dance."

"I used to know how to dance." Charity's face took on a faraway look. "I used to dance with a very tall man. He had black hair, and wore Old Spice . . ."

She fell silent then, perhaps trying to recall nights when she had been young and beautiful and had danced with a very tall, dark-haired man.

Matt and Georgia walked in silence to the pickup, Matt opening both doors as soon as they reached it, letting out the worst of the hot air that had built up inside the cab.

"I love you very much," he said right before he closed the passenger side door.

"Well," Georgia told him when he got into the driver's seat, "I love you very much, too."

He started the engine and backed out of the parking space.

"Matt, are you really going to marry the book lady's daughter?" she asked.

He stepped on the brake, bringing the pickup to a stop. "Yes, I am. If she'll have me."

"Oh, she'll have you," Georgia unbuckled her seat belt and slid across the seat, "if you ask her properly."

"Georgia . . ."

"Book lady's daughter," she reminded him.

"Yes. Book lady's daughter. Will you marry me?"

"Will we live at Pumpkin Hill?"

"Yes."

"We'll need a new mattress. The old one is a killer."

"I take it that's a yes."

She nodded. "That's a yes."

"You'll never be sorry," he took her hands in his. "I promise you, Georgia. You'll never be sorry that you loved me. No matter what else happens over the years, I'll never give you cause to regret loving me."

Georgia tried to recall if she had ever heard words more beautiful. Deciding that she had not, and being unable to come up with what she considered to be an equally beautiful reply, she leaned forward to kiss him soundly on the mouth.

"Drive," she whispered softly. "Home to Pumpkin Hill. We have a life to plan . . ."

The following Sunday, Matt drove Georgia to Baltimore where she would take the train to New York for her first workshop as a prospective owner of a dance studio. She was excited by this new venture and chattered nonstop all the way, speculating on everything from the number of other dance instructors who might attend to the music they might dance to, what techniques she might learn, if she'd see anyone she had met over the years. Matt's head was spinning by the time they finally arrived at the train station, and the ringing didn't stop until she'd gotten on the train and the train had pulled out of the station.

Matt had decided to make a stop at the Aquarium, and it was while he was there that the idea came to him. The spark had been lit by a comment the architect had made, but Matt figured that being in Baltimore, where Georgia had danced for so many years, must have acted as a sort of catalyst. He bolted from the building and searched for the nearest phone book. He stood in the doorway of the phone booth, tapping his fingers on the thick book, trying to remember.

"'T' something," he muttered, turning to the listing of restaurants. "Thomas's . . . Trinity . . . Tuscany . . . yes! That's it! Tuscany!"

Matt dialed the number, then counted the rings until a young male answered.

"Is Lee Banyon there?" Matt asked.

"He's here, but he's busy."

"Ah, are there any tables free for lunch?"

"Just a minute, let me look . . . we'll have one in about ten minutes."

"Wonderful! I'd like to reserve it. The name is Bishop. Matt Bishop. And please ask Mr. Banyon if he'd have about ten minutes to speak with me. Tell him I need his help with something . . ."

The two weeks in New York had totally rejuvenated Georgia and had, if nothing else, convinced her once and for all that her decision to retire from professional dancing to open her own studio was exactly the right move for her. She met dance instructors from all over the country and learned as much from them over meals and social times as she had from the more formal workshops. She sat in on all the discussions where the business aspects had been covered, and made contact with several suppliers of dance equipment and costumes. She found a wholesaler who would sell her students ballet shoes and leotards at a discount, and would guarantee delivery in three days. All in all, by the time she boarded the train to Philadelphia, where Delia would meet her, she was exuberant and determined.

"Belize!" Georgia exclaimed when Delia told her where her mystery trip had taken her. "Oh, Mother, Gordon took you to Belize?"

Delia laughed as she eased the Mercedes into the exit lane coming out of Thirtieth Street Station and tried to recall the fastest way to I95. "He did indeed."

"Was it wonderful?" Georgia sighed.

"Totally," Delia nodded.

"Tell me what it was like. Every detail. Then I'll tell you my news . . ."

Delia glanced at her daughter's face. "Umm, maybe your news first . . ."

"Nope. I want to hear about every glorious minute of your wonderful two weeks with the wonderful Gordon Chandler first."

"Well, perhaps not every minute," Delia grinned. "But it was heaven. We went on a trip into the jungle . . ."

"And I'll bet you took notes every inch of the way."

"Not this time," Delia told her. "This time, I just simply enjoyed."

"Mother, I do believe this is a first for you. A trip where you simply enjoyed yourself."

"Oh, I did, darling. It was . . . heaven." Delia sighed, momentarily recalling a singularly perfect evening on a deserted stretch of exquisite beach.

"But now your news," Delia insisted, forcing herself back to the here and now.

"Matt asked me to marry him."

"Oh! And you said . . ."

"I said yes, of course. I'm crazy in love with him, Mom."

Delia looked in her rearview mirror before slowing the big sedan and stopping along the side of the road where she could hug her daughter. "Oh, Georgia . . . are you sure?"

"I'm sure," Georgia sniffed, her eyes puddling with tears. "I couldn't be surer."

"Tissues, sweetie," Delia pointed to the glove box, and Georgia opened it. "When will the big day be?"

"Actually, we're thinking about maybe having a double wedding with Zoey and Ben."

"Oh, a double wedding! How wonderful!" Delia dabbed at her eyes. She accepted the box of tissues Georgia handed to her, pulled a few out, then gave the box back. "What do Matt and Ben think of that?"

"They think it's a wonderful idea."

"Oh, both of my girls getting married on the same day!" Delia sighed. "Oh, it could be so romantic . . ."

"It will be, Mother."

"And you're happy, sweetie? You're really happy?"

"Totally. Truly."

"That's all I ask, Georgia. That's all I want, is for my children to be happy."

"And a little chocolate every now and again," Georgia said as she removed the gold foil box from the glove compartment.

"Well, of course. What is life without a truffle now and then?" Delia winked, put the car back into gear and pulled back onto the highway. "Open the box, if you would, and let's see what we have to celebrate with . . ."

Mother and daughter were still laughing and chatting when they reached the drive at Pumpkin Hill.

"Oh, Mom, is that Gordon there with Matt?" Georgia peered through the front window of the sedan.

"Yes. He thought he'd meet me here so that I wouldn't have to drive to the inn alone. We thought we'd stay with Laura for a few days and make sure that all is well with her."

Georgia frowned. "What are they doing at the chicken house?"

"Oh? Is that what that is?" Delia turned off the engine and removed the keys. "It's big for a chicken house, wouldn't you say?"

"I think Matt said that, at one time, they raised chickens commercially here." Georgia's feet couldn't carry her fast enough. She called to Matt, and he crossed the distance between them in three quick strides. He lifted her off the ground and swung her around, kissing her deeply before setting her onto her feet on the uneven ground.

"Hello, Gordon," she smiled. "I heard all about your trip. It sounded wonderful."

"It was wonderful. Best trip I ever took. Best vacation I ever had."

"So I heard."

"And I heard your news," Delia hugged Matt. "I couldn't be happier. Gordon, have you met my future son-in-law?"

"Yes," Gordon chuckled. "We were just discussing some of Matt's plans."

"Oh, you mean for the veterinary clinic?" Georgia asked.

"Among other things." Gordon nodded.

"What other things?" Georgia turned to Matt.

He scratched his chin, as if deciding whether or not to tell her.

"What other things?" she repeated.

"Well, you know that I had a long talk with the architect two weeks ago."

"Yes. He was going to send his contractor over."

"Oh, he did that. Actually, he's been back several times. We went over the barn six ways from Sunday, but neither of them feel it's a good building to retrofit into a commercial building."

"Why?"

"For one thing, it's too big to be cost effective, in terms of heat and air conditioning, plumbing. There's no insulation and it would cost an absolute fortune to do everything that would need to be done."

"Oh, Matt, I'm so sorry. I know how you counted on that . . ."

"It's okay. We came up with the perfect solution."

"The chicken house?"

"Nope. The smaller of the two barns." Matt pointed to his right. "Not only is it less space, so it will be less expensive to convert, but the construction is different, it already has running water, and the roof is newer. I don't know why I didn't think of it sooner. The architect has come up with plans that are just perfect. I can't wait to show you."

"That's wonderful! When can you start?"

"The loan has gone through, and the contractor has me on his schedule for the first week of July."

"Really? That soon? That's incredible! How long do they think it will take?"

"Maybe six weeks, if all goes well."

"You'll be able to hang out your shingle by the fall!"

"Before the fall. And I already have the shingle."

"You had your sign made up? Oh, show me!" Georgia's eyes were shining, reflecting her pleasure that his dream was, at long last, coming true. If her own dream had to wait a bit, that would be all right. Matt had waited a lifetime to start his own practice, to make his home here at Pumpkin Hill. She could wait a little longer for hers.

"Gordon, can you give me a hand here?" Matt lifted one end of the large wooden sign, and with Gordon's help, he stood it on end. "This will go right there at the foot of the drive, on the left side." He told her, watching her face as she read the deeply carved words, the grooves painted in gold on a dark green background.

"PUMPKIN HILL VETERINARY CLINIC—MATTHEW T. BISHOP, DVM." Georgia read aloud, smiling. She paused then, reading the rest of the script silently, then, it appeared that she read it again.

"BALLET IN THE BARN . . . AT PUMPKIN HILL. GEORGIA ENRIGHT, INSTRUCTOR," she whispered.

"Well, technically, it's not the barn, but somehow, Ballet in the Chicken House just doesn't seem to have the same ring." Matt deadpanned.

The expression on Georgia's face never changed. Her eyes were wide with surprise, her mouth moving, but no words came out.

"Now, this is, hands down, the best building on the property for what you will be doing. The contractor said it will be relatively easy to put in heat and air conditioning. He's going to use a heat pump, which will supply both," Matt continued, taking her arm and walking her around the side of the old building. "I asked Lee to stop out and take a look, and he talked to the architect and told them what you needed as far as the interior is concerned. It's not too late to make changes, if you want, but I think you'll like what we've come up with."

"You called Lee?"

"Yes. He was very gracious. He'll be out to see you next week, by the way. Said he was upset that he hadn't been able to warn you about the fire." Matt paused, then asked, "Does he think he's psychic or something?"

"He is." Georgia nodded.

"Well, he needs to talk to you about that. Anyway, he knew exactly where to get all the specialty things, like the floor."

"You bought me a floor?" She grabbed his arms. "Tell me."

"Well, it's being custom made by a company in Philadelphia . . ."

"Custom made?" She looked as if she was about to swoon. "Is it wooden? To fit over the concrete floor?"

"Yes," he nodded proudly.

"Slip resistant?" She had him by the collar, turning his head to hers. "Shock absorbent?"

"That's the one . . ."

"Delia, what do you say we head on back to the inn?" Gordon slipped his arm around her shoulders.

"Oh, but I want to see . . ." she started toward Georgia.

"Perhaps later," he said softly. "I think this one's on Matt . . ."

"Oh, you're right, of course." Delia nodded. "Let's just slip away. We'll call them in the morning. Matt and I need to talk. It seems to have been a very short six months."

"Six months?" Gordon frowned. "Six months since when?"

"Since Matt decided that perhaps we Enrights weren't so bad, after all." She tucked an arm around his waist and said, "I'll tell you all about it on our way back to the inn. Perhaps we'll get there in time to watch the sun set over the bay, just the two of us."

". . . two dressing rooms, a small office," Matt was saying as he led Georgia through the side door, "and a sliding wall—sort of like a big pocket door—so that you can have two separate studios if you find you need them. And skylights. I know how much you love light."

"This is incredible! It's wonderful! Oh, Matt . . ." She wandered, bright-eyed, around the room, envisioning the space as Matt described it. "It's just what I would have done. I can't believe you and Lee came up with all this. How soon . . . ?"

"The contractor will start to work on it as soon as the clinic is ready. I decided to do that first, because Doc Espey will be wanting to move the equipment out by the end of July. I figure your studio should be ready to open by mid to late September."

"Oh, Matt, it's so perfect. I can't wait to dance here." She gazed around the room again, as if unable to believe it. "It's the most wonderful gift in the world. The most thoughtful, loving gift . . ."

She went to him and put her arms around him, melting into him like a late spring snow.

"It's all so right, isn't it? You and me, and this place . . . it was all meant to be." She whispered.

"Somehow, it almost seems so," he agreed.

"Must have been the dandelion wishes," she told him, remembering the wish she had sent him that cold rainy morning just a few months ago.

"What was that?"

"Oh, maybe I'll tell you about it someday," she looped her arm through his. "Let's just say it's one of the secrets I learned from your Aunt Hope. Did I ever tell you, for example, what happens when you combine violets with lavender and leave them under someone's pillow?"

"Umm, I don't think so . . ."

"Oh, it's said to be a potent spell."

"Really? What does it do?"

"It's supposedly a powerful stimulant."

"A stimulant? You mean, like a love potion . . ."

"Actually, it's called a charm."

"I see. And have you been slipping your charms under my pillow?"

Georgia merely grinned and tugged Matt's arm, drawing him in the direction of the house. After all, there were some secrets she wasn't sure that Hope had intended her to share . . .

epilogue

The Bishop's Inn bustled with guests, the joy of the occasion and laughter. Delia paused in the doorway and beamed. Across the room, eager hands reached for the darling baby boy who had only so recently joined her growing family.

Robert Devlin Enright—Devlin, Nick and India had decided to call him—was as dark as his father, as beautiful as his mother, and a delight to all his loving aunts and uncles and cousins.

Could anything be sweeter than welcoming the next generation, Delia wondered.

A handsome, deeply tanned man with a rakish grin and a jaunty air entered the room through French doors, a stunning young woman on his arm.

Ah, that must be Rachel, his daughter. How interesting that she has chosen to follow in her father's footsteps . . .

His eyes scanned the crowd until he found Delia. He walked toward her, stopping to shake this one's hand or bestow a kiss on that one's pretty young cheek. Delia didn't mind. The pretty young cheeks belonged to her daughters, all of whom had come to adore Gordon, much as Delia herself had done.

And who could have guessed that life would hold such astonishing surprises?

As Gordon turned to introduce his daughter to August Devlin and her sea captain, Zoey and Georgia resumed their heated discussion. Plans, no doubt, for the wedding yet to come.

If those two manage to compromise enough to share a wedding day, I will eat my hat. The big one, with all the feathers on it.

While her daughters still insisted that a double wedding it would be, Delia had her doubts. The two had not managed to agree on a single thing. While Zoey envisioned a Christmas wedding with attendants in vivid red velvet, Georgia had her heart set on soft Victorian pastels. Zoey wanted a church draped in white roses and exotic white orchids, while Georgia dreamed of masses of cottage garden blooms. To further complicate matters, both wanted India and Laura in their weddings.

Separate weddings might go a long way to keeping peace in the family, Delia mused.

"Gramma, would you like a . . ." Ally took a close look at the tray of hors d'ouevres she was serving, trying to recall exactly what is was she was offering. ". . . a little fish thing?"

"Why, I'd love a little fish thing, sweetheart." Delia touched Ally's cheek fondly, then leaned slightly over the tray. "Now, are these little pink things salmon, do you suppose?"

"Yes. That's it," Ally nodded, then grinned. She had lost one of her top teeth the previous week and her gap-toothed smile tickled Delia's heart. "I guess *salmon* sounds better than *little fish thing . . .*"

"*Little fish thing* works fine for me, sweetie. Now, be a darling and see if your Uncle Nick would find a glass of champagne for me."

Ally took off to locate Nick, who was at that moment passing out cigars.

So much worth celebrating, Delia shook her head almost imperceptibly, all but overwhelmed at how much she had to be thankful for.

Jody appeared in the kitchen doorway and motioned for Corri Devlin to take yet another silver tray of goodies and offer them to their guests. Delia could not fail to notice that the eyes of one tall, strapping private investigator never left the pretty chef, who, for the first time that Delia could remember, had worn a dress. One that showed a little bit of curve, and a great deal of skin.

My, my, Delia grinned. *One might expect a private investigator to be slightly more discreet. You, my dear Jeremy, are very obviously and visibly falling flat on your face. Though Jody doesn't seem to be aware of it. You're a good man, Jeremy Noble, but you work far too hard. As does Jody, now that I think about it. I can't remember ever having been here at the inn when Jody wasn't busy in the kitchen. Well, perhaps you'll both slow down long enough to find each other.*

Laura, in a pale blue summer dress that draped easily around her body and flowed gently to the floor—what Corri had called a "floaty dress"—bent her head slightly to one side as August's Captain Pete related some story or other. The young woman laughed, and the sound of it soothed Delia's worried mother's heart. Laura had had such a fiercely bad time of it, these past few months, seeming intent upon doing penance for sins she had not committed. And there, off to the side, chatting with Ben, as if waiting patiently, stood Tucker Moreland, who had already begun the long process of helping Laura to put the past behind her. It would be Tucker who would help Laura take those first awkward steps toward the rest of her life, Tucker whose love would heal her and bring joy into her life.

And you, Matthew, Delia beamed as her future son-in-law cradled Devlin in his arms. *What a full circle you've come, my boy . . .*

"There's a rumor going around that you were looking for some champagne." Gordon appeared at her side and handed her a delicate fluted glass glowing with pale gold bubbly.

"Why, thank you, darling. Where is Rachel? I'm dying to meet her."

"She's talking sharks with Captain Pete. She'll be over in a minute."

"Silly of me, but I'm nervous about meeting her."

"Don't be. She'll adore you. She said she's waited years for her father to find the right woman, and she's delighted that finally, I have."

"Thank you, Gordon."

"For what?"

"For always knowing the right thing to say." Delia drew him to her with her eyes, those same clear sapphire blues she had passed on to her two oldest daughters. She nuzzled the side of his face and sighed, grateful for his presence in her life. She said,

"I was thinking it might be a good time to make a toast to officially welcome our precious Devlin."

"But first, I have one." He leaned closely and whispered for only her to hear, "To the remarkable woman who has shown me that it's never too late to find love. To the glorious surprise of having found her."

Delia smiled and touched the tip of her glass to his. "And to all those glorious surprises yet to come . . . for all of us."

Also by *New York Times* bestselling author

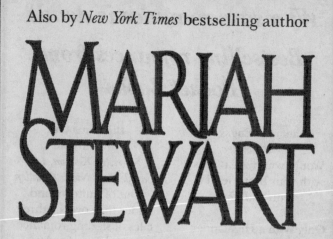

MARIAH STEWART

Voices Carry
Sometimes forgotten memories come
back with a vengeance...

Brown-Eyed Girl
She'll know the truth when she sees it.

Available wherever books are sold
or at www.simonsayslove.com

POCKET BOOKS
A Division of Simon & Schuster
A CBS COMPANY

13656

Who says romance is dead?

Bestselling romances from Pocket Books

Otherwise Engaged
Eileen Goudge
Would you trade places
with your best friend if
you could?

Only With a Highlander
Janet Chapman
Can fiery Winter
MacKeage resist the
passionate pursuit of a
timeless warrior?

Kill Me Twice
Roxanne St. Claire
She has a body to kill
for...and a bodyguard
to die for.

Holly
Jude Deveraux
On a starry winter night,
will her heart choose
privilege—or passion?

Big Guns Out of Uniform
*Sherrilyn Kenyon, Liz
Carlyle, and Nicole Camden*
Out of uniform and
under the covers...three
tales of sizzling romance
from three of today's
hottest writers.

Hot Whispers of an Irishman
Dorien Kelly
Can a hunt for magical
treasure uncover a love to
last a lifetime?

Carolina Isle
Jude Deveraux
When two cousins switch
identities, anything can
happen. Even love...

*A love like you've never known
is closer than you think...*

Bestselling Romances from Pocket Books

The Nosy Neighbor
Fern Michaels
Sometimes love is right
next door...

Run No More
Catherine Mulvany
How do you outrun your
past when your future is just
as deadly?

Never Look Back
Linda Lael Miller
When someone wants you
to pay for the past, you can
never look back...

The Dangerous Protector
Janet Chapman
The desires he ignites in
her make him the most
dangerous man in
the world...

Blaze
JoAnn Ross
They're out to stop a deadly
arsonist...and find that
passion burns even hotter
than revenge.

The Next Mrs. Blackthorne
Joan Johnston
Texas rancher Clay
Blackthorne is about to
wed his new wife. The only
question is...who will she be?

Born to be BAD
Sherrilyn Kenyon
Being bad has never felt
so right.

Have Glass Slippers,
Will Travel
Lisa Cach
Single twenty-something
seeks Prince Charming.
(Those without royal castles
need not apply.)

Love a good romance?

So do we...

Killer Curves
Roxanne St. Claire

He's fast. She's furious.
Together they're in for the ride
of their lives...

One Way Out
Michele Albert

Suspense crackles as two
unlikely lovers try to outrun
danger—and passion.

The Dangerous Protector
Janet Chapman

The desires he ignites in
women makes him the most
dangerous man in the world...

I Hunger for You
Susan Sizemore

In the war between vampires
and humanity, desire is the only
victor.

Close to You
Christina Dodd

He watches you. He follows
you. He longs to be...close to
you.

Shadow Haven
Emily LaForge

She followed her heart home—
and discovered a passion she
never dreamed of.

AVAILABLE WHEREVER BOOKS ARE SOLD.

www.simonsayslove.com

11903